BROKEN
ILLUSIONS

Also by Ellie James

Shattered Dreams

BROKEN ILLUSIONS

A Midnight Dragonfly Novel

ELLIE JAMES

St. Martin's Griffin
New York

This is a work of fiction. All of the characters, organizations, and events portrayed in this novel are either products of the author's imagination or are used fictitiously.

www.stmartins.com

ISBN 978-0-312-64703-2 (trade paperback)
ISBN 978-1-4668-0245-2 (e-book)

First Edition: May 2012

10 9 8 7 6 5 4 3 2 1

For Chuck, Ellie, and Jack.

Who says dreams can't come true?

Acknowledgments

No book is written in isolation. Above and beyond the actual fingers to the keyboard, there's the brainstorming and the research, the trial balloons, the time spent writing and the time spent imagining, the revising, the rethinking, the imagining all over again . . . And with that comes an amazing supporting cast for which I am forever grateful:

My wonderful agent, Roberta Brown, for your continued wisdom, belief, and energy.

My incredibly talented editor, Holly Blanck, for sharing my vision and my drive, and knowing when to say keep going, and when to say pull back.

My awesome friends Linda Castillo and Catherine Spangler, for the friendship, the support, and the ruthless red pens.

Faye, for all things New Orleans.

Amy H., Kim S., and my beautiful mother, for the early reads.

My Facebook friends, for patiently answering questions, and sharing my excitement.

And as always, my husband and children, for letting me play in Trinity's world, and not taking it personally when I forget to wash the clothes. Or fix dinner. Or about that school project, or what day of the week it is . . .

BROKEN
ILLUSIONS

Prologue

Everyone dreams. Some see color. Others experience only black and white. Some laugh, and some cry. Some run and hide, while others play and dance. Some return over and over again. Others never go back. Very few remember.

They are the lucky ones.

Sometimes my friends will talk about what they see and do there in the shadowy realm of their sleep. For them it's no big deal, a movie in their mind instead of a theater, a comedy or drama to be shared and compared. Sometimes it's funny, stupid stuff. Sometimes they go on amazing rampages. Sometimes they're naked or falling or flying. My best friend gets ravaged by a mysterious vampire at least once a week—or so she says.

For me, it's never like that. There are no smiles or laughter or yummy immortals, no silliness. No sex. No salvation.

I awaken in the predawn darkness, my heart racing, my body frozen, the echo of a silent scream burning my throat. Breathing hurts.

Remembering destroys.

I try anyway. I'm scared not to. They're messages—I know that now. From some place unseen, some person unknown. Sometimes they come while I'm awake, like when I enter a place where something bad has happened. Psychic residue has a way of hanging around. But usually, the messages come only when my guard is lowered. When my eyes are closed and my body sleeps.

When I awaken, they fade.

I don't need to look at a clock to know what time it is. The glowing numbers will show 5:21.

They always do.

Instead I lay tangled in the damp sheets, hot, sweaty, forcing myself to breathe. In, out. Slow, steady. I know the drill. I know the routine. A few minutes and I'll be able to move. A few minutes and a new day will begin.

But the remnants of the dream will linger as the hours pile up, not falling away until I close my eyes and the drowning begins anew.

ONE

"Do you believe in forever?"

Working to untangle two silver chains, I glanced toward the front of my aunt's French Quarter shop, where my friend Victoria stood with a baby-doll tee in her hands. Half an hour before she'd walked in from the rain without any warning, not even a text. She'd hardly said a word since, other than asking what she could do to help.

Stopping by was normal. Silence was not.

"Forever?" I asked, focusing on her and not who would be walking in any minute—or what we'd be doing after I turned off the lights and locked the door. "Where'd that come from?"

Robotically she placed the tee—bubblegum pink with the shop's name, FLEURISH!, emblazed in rhinestones—on top of the stack and looked up.

"What does it even mean?" she said, so totally a million miles away. "How can anything last *forever*?"

Brightly colored Mardi Gras merchandise crowded the display tables, beads and doubloons, parasols, even some crazy tutus that were actually selling. Upbeat music flirted from discreetly placed speakers—normally we went with Louis Armstrong or Harry Connick, Jr., but for the next few weeks my aunt insisted we flood the store with the traditional songs of the season.

The jazzy rhythms made standing still impossible.

But in that moment, I did just that.

Forever.

It was hardly a Saturday night, five weeks before Carnival, ten minutes before closing kind of thing.

But I also knew the twisty, timeless place where my mind immediately went was not where Victoria was coming from. She spun from one moment to the next, seeing and hearing, *feeling* that which was in front of her. It was the whole tip of the iceberg thing.

If she couldn't see it, it must not be there.

And I so knew what this was about. "You and Lucas had another fight, didn't you?"

With a distracted sigh, she picked up a strand of purple-and-gold beads someone had left by the T-shirts. "He thinks saying I love you makes everything okay," she said, twirling the necklace around her wrist. "And, once, maybe it did."

I glanced down at the tangled chains.

"I mean, for a long time, that was all I wanted to hear. When we first got together, all he had to do was look at me and I melted."

I knew that feeling well. It was exactly what would happen the second Chase walked in and the electric blue of his eyes locked onto me.

He'd said eight thirty, but with Victoria such a mess, it was best that he was late.

"I couldn't imagine a day I wouldn't feel the same way," she was saying. "Being with him was all I wanted."

I glanced at the clock. "And now?"

"IDK." She let the beads drop to the table. "So much has changed."

For all of us.

Most of the time life was like a river. It flowed from one day to the next, giving no real awareness of when the deep water ended, and the shallow began. There was no defining line, no before and after. It just flowed.

But sometimes there was a point. Sometimes there was an exact moment, and when you looked back, you saw it all, the moment, the place, and you knew, you knew how different things could have been if you'd made a different choice.

Four months had passed. Four months since the night a simple dare had turned into a nightmare we never saw coming.

Four months since one chapter ended, and another began. And Victoria was right—so much had changed. I think that's what surprised me the most, how one event could cast so many ripples. Even my aunt's life had turned. She would have opened Fleurish! anyway. That had been in the works. But Detective LaSalle had been a stranger then—and now the two were inseparable.

Yeah, that was awkward.

But for Victoria, it was the change itself that rocked her, the realization of how quickly life could turn.

"It's like now, whenever he says forever, I freeze up inside, like it's some kind of trap."

It didn't take a psychic to figure that out.

"Maybe that means he's not the one," I pointed out, as I'd done many times before.

"I think it's the word. *Forever.* Even things you want to last, don't." She shifted toward me, zinging me with the glitter in her eyes. "Think about it," she said. "Everything dies. *Everything.* Flowers, trees, animals. Love . . . people. I mean, really, from the second we're born, that's all we're doing. Dying."

I took a deep breath—a really, really deep breath. Victoria was many things, and she could definitely lose herself in drama, but that was a bit much, even for her.

Trying to lure her back from the edge, I let the hopelessly tangled necklaces slip from my fingers and snagged a purple-and-green rhinestone tiara.

"Aren't you just a ray of sunshine tonight," I teased, strolling over to plop it on her head. Stepping back, I gave her an overly bright smile. "Can't say I've thought about it like that."

"How can you not? I mean, you of all people, with your parents and your grandmother, Chase, and the thing with Jessica . . ."

My smile faded. Detective LaSalle said she was lucky, that the drifter who abducted her had taken others. Taken, and not given back. But after all these months, the thought of what she'd been through still twisted me up inside.

One decision. One cruel twist of fate. Sometimes that was all it took.

"How can you believe *anything* lasts?"

I glanced away, toward the antique mirror behind the jewelry case, looking long and hard at the new me. My hair was still long and dark and wavy, my skin still a hue of olive, and I still rarely touched dark eyeliner or goth lipstick. But like everything else, the changes were there, running deeper than the sparkly powders I'd grown to adore, staring back at me from eyes that looked as if they'd lived a lot more than sixteen years. In them a new awareness glowed.

How could I believe anything lasts? That was easy. How could I not? The things I saw, the coming attractions of events yet to happen, had to come from somewhere.

"Maybe not here," I said, rearranging bracelets and earrings. "But later—after."

"You mean like . . . *after we're dead*?"

I was no longer sure there *was* a before—or an after. There just . . . was.

"So what do you think happens?" she asked as I returned a pair of dangly fleur-de-lis earrings to their card. "Do you really think we go to Heaven and live happily ever after? Or that we come back and get reborn, get a do-over?"

I turned from the jewelry as the music shifted, and Big Chief started singing about smoking a peace pipe. (After a week of nonstop play, I knew the words by heart.)

The gleam in Victoria's eyes should have warned me.

"What if we could find out?" she asked, reaching for the camo messenger bag she'd dropped by the front display. She dipped her hand in, and for at least the fifth time over the past month, pulled out the Ouija board.

And over the music, the buzzing began.

"Victoria—" I started as the bell on the door jingled. I spun around—

The lazy grin stopped me. "Evenin', beautiful," the taller of the two guys drawled.

"Deuce," I said, smiling. He strolled in as he did a few times per week, his walk in rhythm to the music. His bandmate, Trey, made a beeline for Victoria—just like *he* always did.

"I thought ya'll were playing tonight," I said.

Looking every bit a sax player with his skinny black jeans and slim-fitting button-down with tribal tattoos, the two gold hoops in his ear, Deuce took me by the hand and twirled me under his arm.

"Not until eleven." Releasing me, he frowned. "What's wrong, Mile High? You lookin' way too serious."

I shook my head. The second they'd found out I grew up in Colorado, I became *Mile High*.

Chase had been less than thrilled.

"Just girl talk," I downplayed as Trey, basically a mirror image of his friend, repositioned the tiara I'd put on Victoria. His murmur was too quiet for me to hear.

"*Son.*" Next to the T-shirt display, Deuce started to dance—I was convinced that instead of blood, rhythm ran through his veins.

"It's Saturday night," he sang, even though that was Trey's role. Together, they called themselves the Blood Brothas and they gigged all over the Quarter. "Pretty girls should never be alone, so flip that sign and throw us guys a bone . . ."

I rolled my eyes.

"And come on down to Fat Cats, and let us show you a night that's—"

I cracked up. "You never give up, do you?"

"Not my style, buttercup."

I glanced at Trey and Victoria, who, despite still being rain-splattered, looked ridiculously awesome in her jeans and brown baby-doll tee, the way they stood a little too close, spoke a little too quietly, and knew exactly why she cringed when Lucas said forever.

"Come on," Deuce said. "What do you say?"

They were good—really good. Chase had even convinced his uncle to hire them for his Mardi Gras bash next weekend.

I glanced at the clock, then my phone on the counter. "Chase is on his way. We're hooking up with friends—"

"Bring them, too." Deuce glanced at Victoria. "Just quit breaking my bro's heart, angel face. You can't keep him waiting forever."

Her smile froze.

Forever.

Deuce shot me a questioning look. I shook my head, telling him not to ask. "We'll try," I promised. Nodding, he turned to the door, signaling for Trey to follow. "Lock up," he said, stepping into the cold February rain. "The crazies be out tonight."

I watched them go, crossing to twist the bolt as finally, finally my phone beeped.

"Omigod." Victoria laughed as I hurried to the counter. "Deuce so has a thing for you."

I grabbed the BlackBerry, saw Chase's name. "Are you kidding me?" I hated the way my heart started to pound. It was ridiculous. There was no reason to be upset.

Except he should have been walking through the door—not sending a text.

"It's all about you . . . *angel face*," I said, bringing up the message.

Hey, T. Lost track of time.

Telling myself everything was fine, I fingered a quick response.

No worries. We're just closing up.

A few seconds passed. A few more. Then it was a minute, and even before the words glowed up from my phone, I knew what was coming.

> Something's come up. Can't make it to the Quarter 2nite.
> U free tomorrow?

I stared at the words. I stared until they blurred, and then I stared some more.

Victoria crossed to stand behind me. "Trin?"

I didn't even try to hide the phone.

"Gee, I wonder what that something could be," she muttered.

But I didn't. I knew.

"She doesn't know when to give up, does she?"

Part of me wanted to hurl the phone against the huge, abstract fleur-de-lis my aunt had painted a few weeks before, even as the rest knew that wouldn't change a thing.

In the months since we'd found Chase's ex-girlfriend huddled in that abandoned hospital room, she'd yet to leave her parents' house, except for doctor appointments. Other than her family and best friend Amber, no one had even seen her. Except Chase.

He was the only one she wanted.

"She's been through hell," I said, fumbling out a quick response.

> No worries. I'm good tomorrow. CU then.

"I think it's an omen," Victoria gushed as his reply zipped in.

> I'll make it up 2 u. Promise.

"You know how sometimes everything just falls together?"

I returned the BlackBerry to the counter cluttered by collectible pins and buttons, jelly watches, and three different kinds of pralines.

"Like a sign," she said, retrieving the board. "He was supposed to be here, but now it's just you and me."

The hum came back, louder, stronger than before. It moved through me, vibrating—screaming. "Victoria—"

"Come on," she said, as she always did. "It'll be fun!"

How had I not seen where all the forever talk was leading?

"I can ask about Lucas and Trey, maybe Zach, about forever, and you can ask about Chase—"

"Dating advice from a Ouija board?" I said, trying not to laugh. "Isn't that what a Magic 8 Ball is for?"

Her smile reminded me of a kid on Christmas Eve—except she wasn't a kid, and trying to contact spirits was as un-Christmaslike as you could get.

"Why not?" she said. "I mean, even if it's really a subconscious thing, who's to say I can't find answers there? Isn't your subcon supposed to be smarter?" She pulled a small wooden triangle from the bag and, reverently, skimmed it along the golden hue of the board.

She didn't stop until she reached the word HELLO.

"I'll do all the talking. Just sit with me, okay? Julian says if I don't have at least one other person—"

"Julian?" Automatically I glanced toward the front door, where across the rain-slicked street, a silver sign glowed against the night: HORIZONS. People were in and out of the New Age shop from the time the doors opened until the minute they closed. Sometimes after.

Julian Delacroix was always there. Not only was he the owner, but he lived upstairs. The self-appointed metaphysical guru was many things—clever, smooth-talking, completely fascinating—but my aunt got edgy anytime she saw us talking.

"Since when are you hanging out with him?"

"Not hanging out," Victoria corrected. "Just asking questions."

"About the Ouija board?" His area of expertise seemed more sophisticated, but I guess it shouldn't have surprised me that a man with a shop slogan of "anything your heart desires," a man who reserved the entire second floor for *special customers,* would have an opinion about contacting spirits.

One of these days I was so going to find out why Aunt Sara didn't want me talking to him.

"I was looking for some new crystals," Victoria rushed on, "and was telling him about playing with the board. I mentioned being alone, and he got real serious, saying I should never, under any circumstance, try the board alone. That bad things would happen. He said if I'm serious, I should try it here at the shop since—"

"The lights flicker," I supplied before she could.

She nodded, her eyes seriously dark. "And the floors," she said. They creaked.

And the doors opened and closed, all by themselves.

"It's like a spirit city," she whispered.

Or maybe just a two-hundred-year-old building. It was one of those French Quarter things. The buildings had been around . . . *forever.*

But there was a big difference between my aunt's shop and the Garden District mansion where the rooms were always cold, piles of ashes and corn dotted the floor—and Jessica's life had come to a terrifying fork in the road.

"My point exactly," Victoria was saying. "Can you imagine all the people who died here? All the spirits that could still be around?"

I glanced away, toward the raindrops sliding down the front windows. Before signing papers, Aunt Sara had compiled a history on the narrow, three-story structure. Built by a sugar baron in the 1800s, the then-lavish mansion had been a part-time home for his socialite wife. Over the years the building had been turned into a boardinghouse, a restaurant, even serving a tenure as a brothel.

People had been born here—and yeah, they'd died—exactly like everywhere else in a city as old as New Orleans. People were born. People died. Everywhere, all the time. No big deal.

"You're doing it again," Victoria said.

I turned back to her. "Doing what?"

"What you always do when you start wondering what's possible— you're rubbing your mom's dragonfly."

I had no memory of lifting my hand.

"Please." Her voice was quieter than before. "I'd think you of all people would want to explore what else is out there."

I did. That was the problem. I . . . did.

But ever since last fall, every time I asked my aunt about my abilities, she got all quiet, and every time I talked to Chase about my dreams, I could feel him pull back. Maybe only for a second or two. Maybe only a fraction. It was almost as if he was afraid of what I would see next.

But it was obvious what had gone down with Jessica still lingered between us.

But Victoria . . . I'd told her everything, even things my gran had warned me to never speak of. I'd shared my dreams, my mistakes. She even knew about the guy who'd dragged me from the river and given me his breath, only to vanish a few hours later.

Dylan.

"Come on, Trin," Victoria said from behind me. "What can it hurt?"

Slowly I turned, my breath jamming in my throat just as it had that night we'd stepped into the darkness of the abandoned mansion. Open door number one, I remembered thinking; open door number two.

Life was about choices.

Months had gone by. Nothing else had happened. Nothing too freaky, anyway. Just dreams. Chase and I were—

I didn't know what we were. But we were more than we'd been before and when he smiled at me, when he touched me, my heart sang.

It was time to let go of the past. It was time to realize dreams could be just dreams, and games could be just games.

Victoria was right.

What could it hurt?

Ten minutes later, she scattered white granules around my aunt's worktable.

"What's that? Sugar?"

"Sea salt." One circle complete, she started a second. "Julian says it'll keep bad spirits away."

He would know. Secret powers and hidden ability were his thing—which in a city like New Orleans, made him a rock star.

"Go ahead and light the candle," she instructed.

Outside the rain slashed in unrelenting sheets. Everyone said this was normal, but for me, winter meant snow.

"He recommended sage," Victoria said as I extended my aunt's Zippo. "It's supposed to be cleansing."

Candle lit, I stepped back. With the windows closed and the space heater off, the flame flashed high, shooting little white sparks as it burned through the wax.

Then lightning speared in, and the room went dark.

TWO

Victoria looked up from a handful of crystals, the candlelight making the green of her eyes glow. "Wicked cool."

But the vibration humming through me was anything but. Not sure what was going on, I glanced around the small area that had once been a bedroom. Aunt Sara had a mini-fridge and microwave along the back, with stacks of boxes and crates lining the sides. We'd painted the main shop a pretty . . . *sage*.

Um, yeah. I tried not to read anything into that.

Here in the back room, a dark cranberry covered the walls, almost like—blood. Aunt Sara had seen no reason to repaint. She'd said it had *energy*.

Slipping on my hoodie, I joined Victoria at the table. She'd cleared the laptop and paper cutter, the tackle boxes filled with pliers and wire cutters, tweezers and clasps and other tools for making jewelry. Now, the Ouija board sat dead center.

She glanced up. Her hair hung like a pale curtain on either side of her face, making her look very much like the ethereal creature Deuce claimed her to be. *Angel.*

I sat across from her. Our knees touched. Julian said that was important. Then she reached for my hands—and the blast of heat blew me away.

"Whatever you do, don't let the pointer thingie off the board," she said. "And never, ever let it go to all four corners—or let go without saying good-bye."

"Angel of Protection," she then whispered, and with the words, everything else dropped away, "my guardian dear, to whom pure love commits me here."

My breath turned shallow.

"Ever this night, be at my side, to light and guard, to rule and guide."

A heaviness spread through me, much like the night I'd walked into that horrible room with the dirty mattresses arranged as an altar.

"Okay." As when she flirted with Trey, Victoria's smile was part nervous, part excited. "Here we go." Releasing my hand, she drew my right index finger to the pointer positioned over the word HELLO. Its triangular shape reminded me of a misshapen heart.

"You okay?"

I looked from our pale fingers to the glow of her eyes. "I'm good."

She moved first. Or at least I thought it was her. Beneath our fingers, the pointer started sliding in a methodic, clockwise circle.

Victoria closed her eyes and bowed her head.

I was supposed to do the same.

I didn't.

The pointer kept moving, one deliberate circle after another, each faster than the one before.

"Hear me now," she chanted. "I invite only those spirits who are for our highest good."

The pointer slowed.

"Any spirits who come through who are not, are to be absorbed into the light of protection."

Swallowing, I focused on the bright yellow flame of the lone sage candle.

"Harming none," she concluded.

The pointer stopped.

Darkness throbbed. The flame fought it, but my heart quickened anyway. Something told me to pull away. A voice deep inside, maybe. A . . . knowing. It *screamed* for me to pull away.

But I could no more have moved, than I could have understood the low voltage buzz beneath my skin. It was the same draw I'd felt that night with Jim Fourcade's son, in his small kitchen, when a dangerous curiosity had drowned out everything else. *Even Chase.*

I was so not proud of that.

"Is there anyone in the room with us?" Victoria asked.

The candle flickered, and the pointer shifted toward its first answer.

                            YES

My throat tightened. I'd been in the small back room almost daily since before Christmas. I'd been there when the sun had shone and long after it had set. I'd been there with my aunt and by myself. With friends, and with strangers. I'd never been scared. I'd never even been nervous.

But now . . .

"Thank you," Victoria whispered. "Are you . . . good?" she asked.

The triangle glided without hesitation, shifting in a slow circle before returning to the upper left.

                            YES

I glanced up at Victoria. Our eyes met.

"Are you sure you don't want to ask anything?" she said.

I shook my head as the pointer again started to slide.

                            YOU

Her eyes went really, really dark, but her smile was pure brightness. "I meant Trinity," she started to explain, but abruptly shifted
gears. "So, like . . . are you here for a reason?"

Nothing.

At first.

From the front of the shop, over the assault of the rain, the sound
of each second reverberated—until once again the pointer slid to the
right, hesitating before landing on two dark letters.

NO

"Then, like . . . are you here because . . . you lived here, or
something?"

The pointer shot left.

YES

Everything inside me stilled.

"Can you tell me your name?" Victoria asked through the stringy
blond hair hiding her face.

In my mind, I ran through the history Aunt Sara had compiled
while the pointer slid right, then left. Right, then left.

"Marie," Victoria whispered, shooting me a quick, questioning
glance.

I shook my head. The name meant nothing to me.

"Do you know why we're here?" she tried.

YES

"I like, need some help," she said, and the ridiculousness of it all
eased the tension from my shoulders. Here she sat in the cold shadows of my aunt's back room with a storm raging outside, chatting
away as if she were hanging with an old friend. "There's this guy I
really—"

The pointer shot to the top row of letters, stalling on the E.

"No, his name is . . ."

The triangle kept going, lower—to the V.

Then the I.

I yanked back, but Victoria's finger clamped down over mine, and through the silence came a broken rasp. "Victoria—"

The distorted heart veered back to the top row.

I jerked hard, freeing my hand and curling my fingers into a fist—but beneath Victoria's, the pointer kept moving, sliding to the L . . . en route to the E.

EVIE

She sagged. "I-I thought your name was Marie?"

The pointer didn't move.

"Is someone else with you? Are there two of you?"

I'd heard that was possible—once a portal was open, anyone could come through.

Thunder shook the room. Victoria's face went white.

There'd been no lightning.

"S-sorry," she stammered. "We just got . . . got scared. Please d-don't go! Marie! Evie! Whoever you are—"

Darkness pulsed, and the building groaned.

"Come back," she begged.

But the pointer didn't move.

The green of her eyes went black. Her knees started to shake. *"Omigod."* Her voice barely sounded human. "It's so cold in here . . ."

The room breathed, and the storm laughed.

I'd been warned. Aunt Sara had told me not to mess around. Julian had told Victoria not to release the pointer without saying good-bye. I just hadn't believed.

Drawn, I returned my finger to Victoria's and felt the cold stab clear to my bone.

"I'm sorry," I said, taking over the conversation as Victoria's eyes got glassy. "I didn't mean to insult you."

Along the stacks of crates and boxes, shadows dripped as the pointer started to vibrate.

I didn't think. I didn't plan. The words just formed, as if they'd been there all along. As if I'd known, as if I'd always known.

As if I'd done this before.

The current intensified, streaking from the pointer to my finger, pulsing up my arm, through my flesh. Penetrating.

"Are you still with us?" I asked.

Slowly, the pointer slid to the far right of the top row before zinging to the far left of the middle.

"MN?" The bloodred walls pushed closer. "What does that mean?"

Seemingly possessed, the triangle zipped back and forth, back and forth.

M N M N M N M

My breath stopped. I wasn't sure why. I tried harder—almost gagged on gardenia. "I d–don't understand. What's MN?"

"Not MN."

Through tangled blond hair, the green of Victoria's eyes glowed. "M–O," she corrected. "M–O–M."

Mom.

The word seeped through me, hot and cold and hard and soft, blending, merging. Destroying. *"No."*

The lights flickered.

Something unseen scraped.

I wanted to jerk back. I needed to jerk back, to yank my hands back and shove the table away from me, to bolt toward the shop, the door beyond. It wasn't even ten o'clock. Outside Royal Street was wet and crowded and alive. There were people, motion, activity. I would—

Nothing. I would do nothing, because my body would not let me. Just like in my dreams. My mind raced. *My mind begged.* But my body would not work.

"Whose mom?" Victoria asked.

A sheen fell over my eyes. Mist spilled in. Edges fell away.

The pointer sat dead still.

"Evie?" Victoria asked. "Marie? Are you still here?"

I stared. Somewhere inside, something fierce and urgent hacked against the cocoon of ice.

But like the pointer, there was only stillness.

"Marie . . . Evie . . ." Excitement shook Victoria's voice. "Are you mother and daughter? Did you die together—is that why you're both here?"

The screaming started, deep, deep inside.

But Victoria remained glass calm. "Or maybe you're looking for your mother—or your daughter. Is that what you mean?"

No.

No!

The golden flame froze against the darkness. The crystals glowed orange. But the pointer shifted, sliding to the bottom of the board. To the row of numbers.

22

Victoria's sharp breath shredded the silence. "What's twenty-two?"

Invisible chains wound tighter, binding me to the folding chair. Only my mind moved. Only my mind struggled.

The rest of me shut down, as the pointer kept spelling.

MOM

"Your mom was twenty-two?"

FIRE

Victoria's knee pressed mine. "Your mom died in a fire?" she asked.

The pointer spun out an answer.

Everything in me tensed.

NO

"Who then? Who died in a fire?"

Victoria didn't know. I'd never told her. It was one of the few things I kept to myself, the night fourteen years before, when flames ripped through a house and forever changed my life.

The pointer flew right, left. Right again. And there in the shifting shadows, I finally found my voice. *"No."*

"Wait a minute," Victoria whispered as her eyes widened. "Didn't *your* mom die in some kind of accident?"

I'd been told. I'd been given a few details. At first my grandmother had called it just that, an accident. But my aunt had told me the truth. There'd been a fire. I'd been two, asleep in my crib.

My mother had been . . . twenty-two.

Everything flashed, lightning that wouldn't stop, that blended together—and danced. *Smoke poured in. The heat. Coughing, I pulled myself up and grabbed the rails. "Mama! Mama-mama . . ."*

No one came.

Brightness, shimmering white and red and orange. And a hiss, a roar. Crackling, like the sparks from Mama's candles. But louder. Brighter.

I coughed.

"Mama-mama!"

I couldn't breathe. I couldn't see. Desperately, I grabbed my stuffed kitty and tried to do what I'd been told not to: climb out of my crib. I had to. I knew that. I had to get out. "Mama—"

The smoke thickened. The darkness deepened.

Flames licked—

"Trinity!"

I blinked, coughed, stared at the girl across the table from me. Pretty, blond—white as a ghost.

"W-what's going on?" Her voice sounded small and faraway, terrified.

"Mama . . ." Swaying, I blinked, staring at the odd wooden board on the table, the roman lettering. I blinked again, and the warped, heart-shaped pointer started to fly from letter to letter.

LOVE

"Omigod," Victoria breathed. "It is *your* mom."

Moisture flooded my eyes. Something far more awful gripped my heart.

"Stop!" The word tore from me. I didn't know why.

"What do you mean, *stop*? This is so cool! I mean—"

"No!" I tried to move. To understand. But all the pieces slipped and shifted, sliced. I was a little girl. I wasn't a little girl. I was in my crib—I was in my aunt's shop. I was two people at once, in two places. I was scared—I was euphoric. I wanted to run—

I could not move.

"It is, it is!" the girl said. No, not the girl. Victoria. Her name was Victoria. She was my friend. My *best* friend. I focused on her, on her tangled blond hair as if it were a lifeline, and tried to pull myself back into the moment.

The now.

Away from the fire.

"Her birthday!" Victoria gushed. "When is your daughter's birthday?"

Frozen, I watched the pointer glide across the board, up and down . . . back and forth.

APRIL 14

Lightning flashed. I was sure it did. It had to be lightning. Nothing else could be that bright.

That violent.

But no rumble of thunder followed.

"Where did she grow up?" Victoria asked, smiling like she'd discovered the most phenomenal trick in the world.

MTNS

Mountains.

Numbly, I stared at the pointer, my finger pressed against Victoria's, with its perfectly squared off, black-tipped nail. I was there. I was there! I could see myself, see everything. But from somewhere beyond my own body. Disjointed. Disconnected. Like I was floating . . . fading.

"This is so wild! Aren't you going to say anything?" Victoria asked. "Ask her something?"

I looked up, opened my mouth. Or at least I tried to. But nothing moved, and no sound came out.

"Don't be scared." Victoria's voice was soft now, gentle. "It's just your mom."

Just. My. Mom.

The flame glowed brighter, sending off brilliant white trails of smoke.

And the door to the front room slammed shut.

Victoria glanced over my shoulder. Her eyes went wide. And we both started to cough.

"I-I . . ." she stammered. "I . . . bet you're proud of your daughter, aren't you?"

The pointer moved. More slowly this time. Left, right.

D I

My blood ran cold before the pointer ever reached the third letter.

E

Victoria gasped. "D-die? I . . . I know you did, and that's so sad. But you're here now," she said, and I knew she was trying to keep her voice from shaking. "And your daughter could use your advice. There's this guy, Chase . . . but you know that, don't you? You know what's going on and if you could just help her—"

The pointer zipped without warning, racing to the top, left, right, left—

The door to the shop swung back open, and Victoria screamed.

THREE

The candle went out.

Darkness bled.

But the pointer kept gliding, glowing now, slow, steady, so deceptively innocent.

G R A

Light flashed through the room. Thunder shook the windows. I tried to move, knew I had to move, but something invisible held me motionless.

C E

"Grace," Victoria muttered. "What—"

From the shop, something crashed. And finally, finally, the invisible chains fell away. I jerked to my feet and twisted toward the door—

"Trinity, no!" Victoria shouted.

I wasn't about to stop.

Muted light filtered in from the street, illuminating the overturned necklace display and the T-shirts on the floor, the votives flickering against the darkness.

Everything spun, tilted. I ran for the door, freezing as I saw the silhouettes crouched low and blocking my path.

"Don't move," I hissed, inching toward my cell phone on the counter—and the Mace Detective LaSalle had provided as a precaution. "One step and—"

The shadow lunged. "Trinity—no! It's me—"

I caught the counter, braced myself. "Drew."

His eyes wide and dark, his clothes soaked, Chase's cousin stepped toward me, revealing his girlfriend crammed behind him.

Some things changed, but lots never did. Where Drew Bonaventure went, Amber Lane was sure to follow. Her black shirt and jeans were plastered to her skinny body, her long curls slicked back to reveal the heavy dark liner ringing her eyes, making her look very much like a starving raccoon.

"There she is," she said all saccharine sweet. "Everyone's favorite little voodoo queen."

"Yeah, well, at least I'm not afraid of a hamburger," I muttered as she slipped next to Drew, as if being next to him gave her relevance.

"Luc!" Victoria gasped, rushing toward a mannequin where her apparently on-again boyfriend slipped into view, as if she hadn't batted her eyes at Trey half an hour before. Sheet white, her hair a disaster, she dove into his arms. "Thank God you're here."

The storm flashed, and for a frayed second I was again staggering from that horrible house in the Garden District to find Jessica and Amber and the others incredibly pleased with their little prank.

That was probably the last time Jessica had laughed.

"Lookin' kinda pale," Amber said, then smiled in that razor-blade way of hers. "Oh wait, let me guess. It's a dark and stormy night and Trin-Trin had another bad dream?"

Drew shot her a look. "Amber—"

I kept my hand to the counter, made myself breathe.

But the shaking wouldn't stop.

"Trinity?" Drew asked, stepping toward me. "You okay?"

Something had happened. *Something had seriously happened in that back room.*

"You know I have Mace, right?" I detoured, not wanting them to know what was really going on. Not *them*. "Next time you decide to break in—"

"Dude, the door was open," Lucas said. "We walked right in."

Beyond him, hanging against the open door, the CLOSED sign still hung. I'd turned the lock. I knew I had.

"Are you crazy?" Victoria breathed, disentangling herself. "You scared us half to death—"

"Scared *you*?" Amber widened her eyes. "We're the ones who came in and found the place trashed, heard you scream . . ."

Victoria stepped back. Her mouth dropped open. "If it wasn't you—"

"Of course it was them," I said, not wanting her to finish. "Just like the truth-or-dare game last fall."

She spun toward me. Stringy hair slapped her face. "*Omigod,* it was the board! What if there was an evil spirit—"

I silenced her with my eyes, silenced her emphatically, but it was too late. Amber, grinning like she'd just been chosen as the next reality star, had heard all she needed to.

"Holy crap," she muttered. "You were having a séance."

"Don't be ridiculous—" But already she was racing for the back room.

I took off after her, cursing silently the second I found her squatting beside the worktable with the Ouija board in one hand, the triangular pointer in the other. "Now who's being ridiculous?"

I flipped on the light, and all the shadows fell away. "It's just a game," I said. "No big deal."

Victoria pushed up beside me, taking me by the arm. "How can you say that?" she whisper-talked. "You were there. It was crazy. You saw—"

I said it because I had to. I said it because I understood, even as I didn't.

Something *had* happened. But I had no idea what. And I wasn't about to start dissecting that fact in front of Amber.

"You said it yourself," I reminded her. "It's just a subconscious thing—"

Everything flashed. The image formed without warning, spearing in from nowhere and stabbing straight through me. I staggered, fell back—

Drew caught me. "Trin?"

Light cut in, like headlights through the darkness—and I saw him, saw him lying so horribly still. Blood covered his face. His hair was matted. His eyes were . . . closed.

"Chase." Somewhere deep inside started to shake. "Chase!"

Through the haze I could feel hands against my arms, fingers pressing against my hoodie. "Trinity."

Drew, I realized. I could hear him, knew that he was there, but through the rain-shrouded theater of my mind, I saw only Chase's unmoving body.

"Trinity!" It was Victoria now, the twist of her panic penetrating the haze. "Here, let me," she said, and then Drew's hands were gone and Victoria's were there, holding mine. They were warm, like sunshine.

"Come back," she whispered. "I don't know where you are, but you need to come back here, to Fleurish!"

Chase wasn't moving. He was wearing jeans. His T-shirt was the one I'd given him for Christmas, the gray Affliction with the tilted cross. It was plastered to his body.

"Tell me. Tell me where you are."

"Chase is hurt."

DIE

I couldn't breathe. "He . . . needs me."

The flood of light stole him, a bright, blinding flash, and he was gone.

I lunged forward, but arms held me back.

"Then why isn't he here?" Amber smirked.

"He's . . . in trouble."

The girl who'd framed me for vicious Internet posts gave me a *you are so pathetic* look. "Maybe in *your* dreams," she said. "But I can assure you Chase is safe and sound with Jessica—where he belongs." Her smile was unbelievably hateful. "Now, it's true they could be getting into trouble—"

"Omigod," Victoria cut in. "We didn't say good-bye." Her voice was barely a whisper. "We didn't close the portal! We let the spirits out—"

"No." I cut her off as fast as I could, but Drew backed away from me anyway, much like Chase once had when confronted with the choice to believe—or doubt.

Trying to stay calm, I grabbed my phone and stabbed out a text.

R U OK?

Victoria hovered. "Trinnie—what's going on?"

I stared at the blank screen, willing a response to appear. Just a word, that's all I needed. YES. Just one word.

Please . . .

"I saw him." Just like in the dream I'd had off and on the past few weeks. After nothing had happened, we'd written it off as harmless.

I had that kind, too.

"He was hurt," I said, "lying in the mud."

"Oh, God!" Victoria whisper-screamed. "The board. It said . . ."

DIE

Our eyes met. The unspoken word hovered between us. "No." But I could see it all over again, the pointer sliding at will, answering a question that had not been asked.

"We have to find him." I spun toward Drew, but he was already reaching for my hand.

"Are you *kidding* me?" Amber screeched. "She's a freak—"

But Drew and I were already running out the door. Julian was there. I had no idea why. But he was there on the sidewalk in the rain, and when I saw him, when my eyes met his, I knew that he understood.

I never thought to ask why.

"I need more, Trinity. Something specific."

Behind the wheel of his father's TrailBlazer, Drew swerved onto another narrow, rain-slicked road. The headlights cut in front of us. The windshield wipers slapped pointlessly. "You know how many roads like this there are out here?"

I did. A lot. We'd been at it for almost an hour, starting at Jessica's house. Her father said Chase had left around ten—but no one had heard from him since. He wasn't answering his phone, wasn't returning texts.

For the fifteenth time, I hit send. *"Answer me."*

The screen remained blank.

"Omigod, where are you?"

Sheets of rain destroyed visibility. Trees crowded in from both sides, partially concealing the swelling canal to the right.

"Trinity, maybe you should call your aunt," Drew said. "Maybe her boyfriend can—"

"Not yet." That would take too long. "A little farther, okay?"

"Look, try my uncle then and make sure Chase isn't home asleep or—"

We saw the fuzz of lights at the same time, a dim beam slanting toward a canal. Then the restored Camaro.

Wrapped around a tree.

"Shit." Drew slammed on the brakes, sending the big SUV into a slide. We fishtailed left, right—

Somehow Drew regained control.

I had the door open before we even stopped, and started to run. Rain pelted me. "Chase!"

Drew sprinted past me, reaching the mangled car first and yanking at the driver's side door.

"Is he—" The cracked, blood-smeared windshield stopped me. "Oh, my God." Grabbing Drew's arm, I squeezed between him and the car and saw the collapsed airbag—and the empty front seat. "Where is he . . . I don't . . ."

We both twisted around. "Chase!"

I ran, staggering through the garish beam of the headlights. Drew took off in the opposite direction.

"We're here!" My feet slipped against the muddy incline. "Where are you?"

"Cuz!" Drew yelled behind me.

Nearly blinded by the rain, I shoved the hair from my face and pushed forward, never saw the fallen tree. I went down hard, landing on my hands and knees. The impact sang through me, but I quickly scrambled to my feet. Then lightning glittered, and everything else stopped.

FOUR

He lay by the edge of the canal, one leg in the water, the other twisted at an unnatural angle. He was on his back, his head turned to the side—just like I'd seen in my mind.

I lunged, but my foot slid away from me, and I went down again. "Chase!" I didn't try to get up. I crawled. He was right there. Right . . . there!

And then I was pulling myself through the mud, reaching for him, sliding my hands from his chest to his neck.

"Oh, God," I whispered into the laughter of the rain. "Come on, come on, come on!"

His flesh was wet, cold, but beneath my fingertips came the most amazing flutter.

"Fuck!" Drew shot beside me and dropped to his knees. "Is he—"

"Call nine-one-one!" I shouted, and started to cry. My hands found Chase's face, his jaw, his cheekbones, finally easing back matted bangs to reveal the source of the blood.

He must have been conscious after the crash. He'd gotten out of the car, was trying to go for help.

"We're here," I whispered, and through my tears, my mouth found his.

"Trin." His voice was low, strained, but strong and beautiful and the most phenomenal gift ever.

"Sh-h-h." Against the side of his face, my hand shook. "Don't talk."

"I'm . . . sorry . . ."

The rain still fell. The wind still blew. But I felt none of that, felt nothing but the band squeezing my heart. Easing back, I found his eyes open and filled with something I didn't come close to understanding.

"No reason to be," I murmured in between soft, gentle kisses.

The coppery tinge drove home how close I'd come to losing him.

"Paramedics are on their way," Drew said, easing Chase away from the canal. "Your mom and dad, too."

"Thank you, God." I shot Chase's cousin a quick smile of gratitude. "And you, too."

Soaked, covered in mud, Drew looked from his cousin to me, the oddest glow in his green eyes.

Closing mine, I dropped my head to Chase's chest and tried not to drown in the steady thrum of his heart. Vaguely I was aware of his arm closing around me, his hand tangling in my hair.

"That's some seriously cool shit," I heard Drew mutter as sirens carried on the wind. "You knew," he said. "You eff'in—"

The sky flashed again, and the puddle beyond Chase glowed. I hung there, sprawled against him, as everything inside me tightened.

". . . like totally awesome," I heard Drew saying, but then he stopped. "Trinity? What the shit?"

Chase's hands found my arms and squeezed, but I couldn't feel it— couldn't feel anything. "What's wrong?"

I blinked against the rain, but the Mardi Gras mask remained partially submerged in the puddle.

"No, no, no, no . . ." Then I was crawling, blindly pulling away from Chase and dragging myself through the mud toward the puddle, reaching out and stabbing my hand—

"Trinity!" Drew caught my arm. "What—"

"The mask! Oh, God—the mask." It was only a few feet away—exactly like all those months before. "He was here!"

Arms closed around me. Chase. Strong. Pulling me against his body. "Baby—"

Sirens screamed from all around us. Headlights cut in.

"No!" I squirmed against Chase, had to touch. To feel. To find the mask before—

Drew plunged his hands into the slop—

And the glow went dark.

"Leaves," he said, rocking back and opening his palms so that I could see. "Just leaves."

I sagged against Chase, staring at the evidence in his cousin's hands. I could tell him to try again, keep looking. I could beg him.

But I knew what he would find, what they always found when the unseen masqueraded as the seen.

Absolutely nothing.

He was okay.

That's what I kept telling myself. Chase was okay. Paramedics brought all car-accident victims who'd lost consciousness to the ER. He'd been awake, talking. The CAT scan was precautionary.

But as seconds dragged into minutes, minutes into over an hour since Drew and I had rushed into the chaos of the emergency room, rational thought faded, and like a freshly kicked anthill, my imagination took over. *Something was wrong. They'd found a brain bleed. He'd lapsed into a coma, was being raced to surgery. The Ouija board.*

Hugging myself, I started to rock.

"His dad said half an hour," I reminded Victoria, who'd arrived with Lucas and Amber right after we did. Chase's parents had gotten there a few minutes before.

Almost the entire football team had gathered, some inside, some hanging outside.

Word spread *really* fast.

"But it's been twice that." I kept staring at the door on the other side of the registration desk. His dad had come out once, all grim-faced and stony-eyed, telling us Chase was being taken for a scan and would receive immediate treatment, and promising to let us know as soon as he knew anything.

People had come and gone since then. A lot of them. Patients had been called back. Family members had followed.

But for every *one* called back, Saturday night craziness brought three more to the waiting room.

Victoria glanced at her iPhone, then at me. "An hour fifteen. I'm sure he'll be out soon."

I hugged myself tighter, didn't understand why they kept the place so cold. It was the middle of winter and half the people around me were coughing or sneezing.

"Maybe you should ask them for a blanket," Victoria suggested.

I stared at the TV mounted across the room, at an episode of *Friends* I'd seen at least twenty times, but heard only babies crying. I'd counted three.

"Should I add anything else?"

Robotically, I turned to see Victoria holding her phone out to me. "What?"

"A prayer request," she said. "I put that Chase was in an accident and is in the ER, and that everyone should pray."

From the small screen, the words blurred. I blinked, tried to bring them into focus. "No . . . no, that's good."

Immediately she thumbed the blue share button.

I stood. I had to move. Across the room Drew stood with his parents, his father a slightly younger replica of Chase's father. Amber, completely dry with her wavy hair perfect, sat in a chair next to him, glued to her phone. I could see her fingers flying. Lucas, thank God, had gone outside—

"Trinity!"

I'd been trying not to panic. I'd been trying to be calm, rational. But the second I heard my aunt's voice, I turned and launched myself into her arms.

"Ah, *cher*," she murmured, hugging me against her, hugging me so, so tight. "We were at a movie, I had my phone on mute—I just saw your message." She pulled back, her worried eyes finding mine. "How's Chase?"

"IDK," I said on a rush, blinking back the sudden flood of tears. "They took him back forever ago and we haven't heard anything—"

My words stopped the second I saw the man striding in from the parking lot, all casually dressed in faded jeans and some kind of fitted button-down. But the look on his face, the sharp lines and assessing eyes, was all cop.

I didn't even notice the fleece blanket in Detective Aaron La-Salle's hands until my aunt took it from him and wrapped it around me.

"You're so cold," she said, stroking the stringy tangles from my face. "You can't stay in these clothes—"

"I'm not going anywhere."

"Of course not. I can give Aaron the keys, let him run get you something to change into."

Not caring whether I was wet or dry or cold or hot, I was about to shake off the offer, until I saw the way Detective LaSalle was studying me. And then everything just kind of flashed, and I knew that he knew. Somehow, someway, despite the fact I hadn't said a word about it in my texts to my aunt, Detective LaSalle knew that I was the one who'd found Chase.

"That'd be great," I said, but he was already stepping closer—and backing me straight toward the corner.

I knew exactly what was coming. If I had a bad dream, he wanted details. If I had a weird thought, he wanted to talk about it for hours. He was so set on staying one step ahead of any and everything bad, I could barely breathe without him playing twenty questions.

Despite the fact my aunt had invited him to go with her to a friend's wedding in Mexico in a few days, I couldn't forget who he was, or how he'd come into my life.

I was all about exploring my abilities, but I had no desire to be Detective LaSalle's own personal oracle. Or guinea pig.

"*Trinity.*" His voice was concerned. "The accident report says you found him."

"Aaron—" my aunt said as I glanced toward the door from the waiting room. "Do you have to do this now?"

"Only a few questions," he murmured, and out of the corner of my eye, I saw him lift a hand to her arm. "While everything's still fresh."

Her unhappy sigh made me clench my jaw.

"Trinity," he said, so, so gentle, but I knew—*I knew* inside he was stoked. "Can you tell me how that came to be? How did you know about the accident? Where to look—"

I twisted back toward him. "*We didn't.* He was late, not answering my texts, so we just started driving—"

"The roads he would have taken?"

"Yes."

"Are you sure you didn't . . . *see anything*?"

It was a point-blank question. I didn't want to point-blank lie— but I didn't want to tell the truth, either. That would lead to so many more questions, and really, in the end, what did it matter? We'd found Chase. The accident was over and done with.

"I was *worried*," I said. "My imagination was going—"

That *gotcha* look flashed in his eyes. "Your *imagination*."

I bit down on my lip, said nothing else.

But Aunt Sara did. "That's enough," she said, and even after all these months, I still didn't understand how she could wrap steel in sugar. "The hows and whys aren't important right now."

Detective LaSalle's eyes lingered on hers, but finally he relented, excusing himself to make a few calls.

"*It's taking too long,*" I said, after I was sure he was gone. "Chase's dad should have been out by now—"

"Don't go there," Aunt Sara said, rubbing her hands up and down my arms. "Don't get ahead of yourself."

I looked toward the darkness beyond the windows, where Lucas and about ten other guys stood in small groups, most of them focused on their phones.

"Ah, *cher*," my aunt murmured in that soft way of hers, the one that made me feel warm and connected. She worried about me. I knew that. She kept wanting me to see someone, and talk. "You remind me so much of your mom."

Everything slowed. I felt myself turn toward her, felt the rhythm of my heart change—*deepen*. My parents had been gone a long time. I didn't even remember them—but wanted so very, very much to know. To know . . . *everything*.

"How?" I asked.

My aunt's eyes were brown, and when she got emotional, they swirled like melted chocolate. "She didn't like to talk about what she saw, either."

So not where I'd thought this was going. "But she read tarot cards in the Quarter," I said, confused. "She worked with the cops. If she didn't like to talk about what she saw—"

"Those were her outlets. They were safe—they weren't personal. But with your dad . . ." She let out a slow breath. "She never talked to him about her dreams."

I pulled the black-and-gold blanket tighter. "Why not?"

She reached for me, skimming her thumb beneath my right eye. "Protection, I think. She didn't want him to live with what she saw."

Protection. It sounded like such an awesome word. You protect people you love. You try to make sure something bad never happens. It's why my grandmother had taken me from New Orleans when I was two years old.

But sometimes protection backfired. Sometimes it left you without defenses of your own.

"She knew, didn't she?" I whispered. "She knew he was going to die with her, but didn't want to freak him out."

Against my face, Aunt Sara's hand stilled. "I don't know," she said quietly. "Your mom couldn't always tell what she was seeing. She said a lot of times they were just random little snapshots, out of time or place, context."

I looked away, back toward the window—and saw Chase all over again, lying without moving.

Just like I had in the dream.

Through the reflection, the door leading from the waiting room swung open, and his father appeared.

FIVE

The noise, the babies crying and the loud sitcom, all the people on their phones, the man who'd been moaning for over an hour, blurred into a low drone. The room lengthened. And the blinding white of the fluorescent lights showed every line carved into Richard Bonaventure's face.

He was a handsome man. A surgeon, he was also a serious man. But I'd gotten to know him over the past few months—it was pretty hard to play Just Dance and *not* get to know someone better. I knew how easily he smiled and laughed. I knew his dry sense of humor.

But in that moment it was the doctor I ran toward, the one who'd gotten a call from his freaked-out nephew on a rainy cold night. I'd heard Drew. I'd heard the way his voice shook . . .

And now I saw the echo of that reflected in Richard Bonaventure's tired eyes.

"Ricky—" Drew's father said as we all reached him at the same time. "How is he?"

My heart slammed so hard I could barely hear. "Dr. Bonaventure—"

He looked from his brother to me. "It's good news," he said, smiling, and my eyes filled. "A few scrapes and contusions, a pretty wicked headache—but the CT scan is clean. He said his ankle hurt so we took an X-ray, but that was clean, too. Just a minor sprain."

Drew and his dad hugged. Victoria reached for her phone. Aunt Sara came up behind me and put her hands to my shoulders. But I didn't move, couldn't move, just stood there with silent tears running from my eyes.

"Can I see him?" I asked.

Dr. Bonaventure's eyes crinkled. "I have strict instructions not to show my face again without you."

The smile started deep, spread fast.

"Come on." Putting a hand to my back, he steered me through the doors, past the nurses' station, down a hall lined with patient bays—to one halfway down on the right. He reached for the curtain and pulled, and it was all I could do not to launch myself into the cubicle.

Chase sat on the edge of the narrow bed, with wires running to his chest and oxygen at his nose, the flimsy white-and-blue hospital gown no match for the width of his shoulders. His hair hung into his eyes, cuts crisscrossed his cheekbone, and the corner of his mouth was swollen, but he was there and he was okay—more than okay, perfect.

Everything else slipped away, slipped totally away, leaving only the overwhelming need to dive into his arms.

"Chase—"

He started toward me, but his mother held him back. "Not yet," she said with a hand on his arm.

Susan Bonaventure was a lot harder to read than her husband.

"You're okay," I said, and then I was stepping into him and closing my arms around him, burying my face against his neck.

I so did not care about the antiseptic smell.

"You're okay," I whispered. "You're really okay."

I squeezed my eyes shut, wishing I could drown in that moment, in the absolute perfection of feeling him hold me.

"Of course I am." He eased back, lifting a hand to my face. "Hey," he said, swiping at the tears that had once again started to fall. "Don't cry."

Everything was watery, glistening. "I was so scared," I whispered. "When I saw you lying there—"

"Sh-h-h. Over and done with."

I closed my eyes. Maybe it was minutes before Dr. Bonaventure told me Chase was being discharged. Maybe it was longer. I really didn't know, couldn't stop thinking about how close I'd come to losing him.

If Drew and I hadn't found him . . .

If we hadn't gone looking . . .

If I'd ignored the vision, misinterpreted it, written it off as a remnant from the strange dream I'd been having . . .

A premonition, I realized. A warning. I knew that now. And hours later, long after kissing Chase good-bye and returning to the condo, I slipped between my sheets and reached for the dragonfly dangling against my chest, and whispered into the darkness. *"Thank you."*

I run. Around me, yellow bleeds into peach, then orange, purple. Light fades, and the sky glows.

"Where are you?" I scream.

The wind laughs, and the skeletal trees slip closer.

I spin around. Or maybe that's the ground. I don't know. I just know everything is turning, tilting.

"Please! Answer me!" But night falls quickly, and shadows steal light. Still I run, while around me, the whole world twists like an out-of-control carnival ride. "I'm here!"

The sky cracks, and the concrete buckles. And then I see him, see him lying so horribly still . . .

"No!" But already I'm falling.

Already I'm drowning.

"Trinity!"

Blindly, I reach toward the different voice, grab for the forgotten safety of his hand, but find tall grass instead. I pull, try to hang on.

"Trinity!"

But the water rises, and my body slips.

"No—no!"

Alone in the darkness, I still, listen.

"Omigod, you're crazy!"

The voice . . . I know that voice, have heard it before. But I can't place it.

"No—stay away—you'll never get—!"

Silver flashes, sharp, glistening, and her frantic pleas dissolve into screams.

I came awake on a violent slam of my heart, jerking as my eyes flew open, my throat burned, and Delphi watched me through wide, worried eyes. Robotically I lifted a hand to her pointy face and rubbed between her ears, feeling more than hearing her purr.

As always, simply touching her made the band around my chest loosen.

It was still so hard to reconcile her with the terrified and emaciated cat that appeared on my doorstep the week after we found Jessica. I'd brought her upstairs and fed her, but it had taken weeks for her to venture from beneath my bed. Even then there'd been something about the unblinking look in the green of her eyes, something wise and . . . knowing.

Her name came to me in a dream.

Now she watched me, just as she did every time I pulled myself from a dream. The first time I'd seen Chase in the grass, she'd sat crouched beside me as I'd lain in the predawn darkness, squeezing the phone and listening to his sleep-roughened voice promise me he was fine. I'd begged him to be careful—but just as my mother had been unable to stop the fire, how did you protect against something as random as lying in the grass? Chase walked his black Labs every morning. He ran track. He was outside all the time.

The dreams, the premonitions, didn't come with dates and times and places. Maybe that's why I'd finally agreed to play with the Ouija board last night, some psychic nudge that it was time. It made sense. I couldn't help but think the board was another channel, another way for my subconscious to communicate—*or warn.*

More than a little awed, I slipped from bed—and headed for the kitchen.

"You gonna eat that, T, or stare at it all afternoon?"

I looked up from the brownie I'd reached for when Chase had first dragged the game board from the box and placed it between us. Now everything was set—the pieces in their starting positions, the cards stacked facedown in three piles, the murder weapons carefully arranged.

Half the brownies I'd brought over were gone.

The second I'd finished baking them, I'd gotten dressed and headed over, arriving late morning. With the sweep of bangs falling against his forehead and his dark Saints T-shirt stretched tight enough to reveal how much time he spent in the weight room, Chase now sat sprawled on the sofa where we'd shared our first kiss—and so many others since then—as if this was any other Sunday, and last night had been any other night.

But no matter how hard I tried, I couldn't stop staring at the bluish-black swelling around his eyes—and his totally busted lip.

"You saw me, didn't you?" he guessed. "That's how you found me by the canal." Something in his eyes changed, the blue going darker. "You're seeing it now."

My heart just kinda stopped. His parents had hovered for over an hour, until announcing a few minutes ago they were going to the store. We were finally alone, with the exception of his younger brother Austin upstairs, playing Street Fighter with some friends.

This was the first time Chase had looked at me—really, really looked at me. And I didn't understand. He was the one who'd been in the accident. He was the one who'd spent hours in the ER, whose father wouldn't let him leave the house for twenty-four hours.

But he looked at me like I was the one hurting, and he didn't know how to make it stop.

"It was like a flash," I told him. "You were lying in the grass, just like in the dream." And finally it broke, that cheerful, everything's-fine wall I'd slapped around all I didn't want to feel, the fear and the shock, the horror, the possibility that I was too late. That I'd lost him.

Forever.

"And I was so scared," I admitted. "I thought you were gone—"

He reached for me, dragging me across the game board to straddle his lap. "Let it go," he said, sliding the hair from my face. "I'm here. I'm okay. It's over."

"But it keeps playing. Every time I close my eyes I see you all over again and it's so real—"

"Then don't close your eyes." He put a finger to my mouth. "You can't torture yourself like that, living in a future that isn't going to happen."

I looked at him, and wanted so badly to believe. He always did that, made me want to follow him to a world where the sun always shone and the only dreams that came true were those involving winning football games, going to college, and living happily ever after.

But then, I knew his life had been far from perfect.

He urged me closer, anchoring me against him with arms around my middle. "Think about the future that *will* happen. Think about our trip this summer—about Pensacola."

The warmth was immediate, radiating like sunshine from his body into mine. I sunk into it, running my hand along the barbed wire tattoo braceleting his arm, and held on so, so tight.

"Sugar white beaches," he murmured against the side of my neck. "Turquoise water."

I closed my eyes, wanted to see. Tried to see . . .

He kissed his way up to my earlobe. "That's where I go when I need something good."

I'd never been. I'd never been to the beach, never seen a dolphin play, never felt a wave crash over me. And I wanted it, wanted it so, so badly.

Pulling back, I lifted my hands to his face, skimming my thumb gently along his busted lip. "When do you go there?" I wasn't sure where the question came from—or why it scraped on the way out. "When do you need something good?"

His eyes flashed, for just a heartbeat, before he glanced away, back toward the plate of brownies.

And I knew. I knew when he went there, when he needed something good. It was when he thought about last fall. When he went back to the house on Prytania, to Big Charity . . .

He said he didn't. He said he didn't go back, didn't remember, didn't even think about it.

But I knew that he did. We all did.

"Last night," he said, returning his eyes to mine. "That's where I went while in that tube having the CT scan."

It hurt to swallow.

"Can you see it, too?" he asked. "Can you see this summer?"

I tried. I wanted to. I'd pulled up pictures on Web sites.

"Trinity—"

"It's strange," I said, sliding my hand from his face to his hair. "I could never have imagined this a year ago." The emotion was still there, the emotion I'd chained away before. But it was different now, the edges not quite as sharp, but still capable of slicing. I leaned into him and feathered my mouth against his, something inside me twisting at the faint, coppery residue of blood.

"Being here, with you, like this. It's like I'm living a—"

Dream.

The word stuck in my throat.

"Fantasy," I said instead. I had everything I'd ever wanted. "But when I start to look too far forward . . ." I closed my eyes. Because when I did, when I tried to go to this summer, to the beach, to the moonlit nights he talked about, everything inside me went blank.

"Trinity—"

I opened my eyes and drank him in, the blue, blue of his eyes and the dimple, even the scrapes along his cheekbone. "I want that," I said, with a force that surprised me. "I want Pensacola. And I want Mardi Gras, and I want—"

My heart to quit twisting.

I looked away, toward the game board, where the wrench waited in the ballroom and the candlestick in the hall, the knife—

"Trinity?"

Something inside me stilled. I blinked, blinked again, turned back to Chase, and smiled.

"And right now," I said, sliding back from the warmth of his body. "I want right now—because you are so going down."

A low gleam came into his eyes. "You think so?"

I resumed my place on the other side of the board. "I know so."

While his brother shouted at the game upstairs, Chase readied ours, picking up a pile of cards and fanning them facedown. "Pick one—but don't turn it over."

I did as he instructed, sliding the card into the little brown envelope marked CONFIDENTIAL.

Two stacks later, one for location, one for murder weapon, and our crime was set. He said he and his mom had played all morning, with Chase claiming to have schooled her three times out of five. Given her occupation (an attorney who once worked in the D.A.'s office), I suppose it made sense that Clue was her game of choice.

"I'm Miss Scarlet," I said, fingering the red piece—

"I saw you last night, too."

I looked up, the way his bangs fell against the raw glow in his eyes making something inside me go all raw and glowy, too.

"You were on a streetcar," he said, his voice so, so quiet.

That should have warned me.

"And you were wearing this tight catsuit—"

I laughed out loud. "That's called a concussion, Bonaventure."

"—and there was this crowd around you, but you were looking at me, with your hands wrapped around a pole, dancing—"

The total and complete shift from serious to . . . whatever this was, blew me away. "So now you're getting your jollies on a trolley?"

"Hey!" He play frowned. "You can't blame a guy for dreaming—"

"So that's what you want me to do, dance my way up St. Charles—"

"Not with an audience."

I shifted, bringing up a knee and wrapping my arms around it. "So what else do I do—*in your dreams?*"

The darkening of his eyes was so subtle, I almost missed it. Around us nothing changed—not the video game blasting from upstairs or the dogs barking outside, the game waiting between us.

But I knew. "It's bad, isn't it?"

He turned and reached for another brownie.

"Chase, *please*. Tell me."

His hand stilled against the plate. He held himself that way for a long moment, his bicep straining against the barbed wire tattoo.

Sometimes it looked like it was going to bust.

Not touching the brownies, he pulled back. "Everyone has bad dreams, T. That's just part of it."

"Then why won't you tell me?"

"Because I don't want you to go back."

And from one breath to the next, I knew what he saw when he closed his eyes.

SIX

"The morgue," I murmured.

His eyes burned, just like the night we'd stepped into a darkness so deep every emotion I'd ever felt had wrapped around me, and squeezed.

"You see me in the morgue."

His shoulders tensed. "With that guy and the knife at your throat, and I'm looking at your eyes—"

I looked down—and saw the knife. It lay on the game board, small and plastic and totally benign, but I felt it anyway, felt it all over again, the cold fissure hovering just out of sight.

If I reached for it, tried to destroy it, I knew there would be nothing there.

"Like you said," I murmured, picking up my own brownie, the one I'd held for over fifteen minutes without bringing it to my mouth. Lifting it, I took a small gooey bite. "Over and done with."

"I kill him," he said. "This time *I* do it. It's all slow motion, I lift the—"

"Chase Bonaventure," I said, not letting him finish—not *wanting* him to finish. Not wanting to spend one second longer in that dark horrible place. "In the morgue—with the gun."

The slow press of his lips told me he knew exactly what I was doing. "I thought you didn't know how to play."

"Oh, I know how to play." With another decadent bite, I slid the red game piece—and saw the Ouija board all over again.

Blinking, I placed Miss Scarlet between the Lounge and the Hall. "It's just been a while."

His slow smile was pure Chase, the one that I'd known for six months, the one from my first day at Enduring Grace. "Don't say I didn't warn you."

Never looking away, I polished off the brownie. "Bring it."

"Best three out of five wins."

Chase snagged the cards I'd extended and slapped them into separate piles—one for suspects, one for locations, one for weapons. "You're brutal."

He so hated losing. "Like a lamb to slaughter," I purred with devastating innocence. With me taking the first two games, his back was against the wall. "Must be rusty luck."

His cough was garbled.

"I'd forgotten how fun this is," I said, twirling Miss Scarlet's piece in my hand. "You sure you want to be Colonel Mustard again?"

He shot me a glance. "I'm always Colonel Mustard."

I plucked the last brownie. "Suit yourself."

Eyes narrow, he watched me pop it in my mouth.

"You want me to pick the crime cards?" I offered.

He fanned out the suspect stack and slipped one from the middle. "Like you did the first two times?" He moved on to the pile of locations. "I'm not sure that was the best idea I ever had."

Biting back a smile, I watched him draw a weapon, then place all three in the CONFIDENTIAL envelope.

He was convinced that by simply touching the cards, my psychic abilities were able to determine what they were.

Savoring the blast of chocolate, I watched him shuffle and deal the cards, then slide one stack toward me. I picked it up and sorted by category, using my score sheet to prepare my strategy.

Trapped inside during long Colorado winters, Gran and I had spent hours with a board game between us.

This time I had five room cards, which meant Chase only had three. That gave me a lot of leverage.

His parents had gotten home from the grocery store before our second game. Already I could smell the sausage and chicken jambalaya they were fixing for dinner.

Rolling the die, I chose the Billiard Room as my first destination.

"I think it happened here," I bluffed, even though I held that card in my hand, which meant it couldn't be in the CONFIDENTIAL envelope. "I did it," I said, referring to Miss Scarlet as I reached for the suspected weapon. "With the revolver."

I held that card, too.

Chase looked up from his cards. "You're playing me again, aren't you?" The blue of his eyes practically burned a hole through me. "You're sitting there all innocent . . . but I'm betting you have two of those cards in your hand."

I kept my expression blank, casually shrugging my shoulders. "Would I do that?"

He grumbled under his breath—but did not produce any of the cards I'd asked about, which told *me* Miss Scarlet was the culprit.

He, however, had no way to deduce that.

Rolling the die, he veered into the Library, studying his cards before looking up.

"It happened here." Deliberately he shifted a weapon into the scene. "With the rope—by your hand."

Inside I laughed as I was forced to admit I had none of those cards—which meant he, too, had identified me as the killer.

The cat-and-mouse game went on from room to room, scenario to scenario. By the time I landed in the Kitchen, I was pretty sure I had it figured out: Miss Scarlet. In the Kitchen. With the—

My fingers slipped against the knife, and everything flashed.

"No—stay away—you'll never get—"
Silver glints, sharp, glistening—
I snatched my hand back.

"Trinity?"

The walls of the spacious room pushed in on me as I lifted my eyes—and the game board crashed to the floor.

"What?" Chase was across the sofa before my heart could beat. "What happened?"

It all came back, the images from the night before, the scene I'd witnessed play out several times before. "Last night—the dream—the end was *different*."

I'd been so wrapped up in the realization that I'd foreseen Chase's accident, the variation hadn't registered.

"It was like the channel changed, and you weren't there anymore. It was so dark, and I could hear someone screaming."

"Who?"

"I don't know—a girl." The voice had been . . . familiar.

"What else?"

I stared at the game piece on the carpet. "A knife."

"Have you ever seen that before?"

Confused, trying to piece it all together, I tried to go back, to replay it all over again, second by second.

"Did *you* see anything last night?" I asked. "Was there anyone else there? Another car?"

"No."

"What about earlier—with Jessica?"

"Trinity—"

"What were you even doing?" I asked, my voice stretched so thin I hardly recognized it. I'd been trying to play it cool, but the questions shot out of me. "Why were you even on that road?"

He looked toward the pool beyond the windows. I couldn't see his eyes, only the tight line of his jaw.

"Chase—"

"Hang on," he said, and before I could stop him, he rolled from the sofa and vanished upstairs.

I sat there a long moment, trying to understand. He'd looked . . . upset, distant—the way he always looked when Jessica came up.

Frowning, I reached for another brownie, but remembered they were all gone. Instead I picked up my BlackBerry. I'd put it on silent, not wanting to get distracted by anything while I was with Chase.

Now three texts waited.

Listening for him, I pulled up the first, from my aunt. She wanted to know how Chase was—and to let me know Detective LaSalle wanted to talk to me.

I had no doubt about what.

From upstairs, I could hear Chase harassing his brother as I pulled up the second message, from Deuce.

> Your aunt told me what happened—wicked. Told you
> the crazies were out. Glad you're okay. Let me know
> if you need anything.

I smiled. He was a good guy.

The laughter from upstairs continuing, I clicked on Victoria's name.

> How's Chase?

The text was from an hour before. I quickly replied.

> Perfect!

Not more than thirty seconds passed before her reply arrived—Victoria could be counted on to answer fast.

> OMG! You'll never believe what I read on the 'net last night!

My breath slowed as another text zipped in.

> Julian was right. We seriously screwed up not telling the board
> good-bye. There was this girl who got scared and shoved

the board off the table. When she woke up the next morning
her back was covered in scratches . . .

Against the screen, the words glowed. I felt the shaking start,
even as I made my fingers slide along the keys.

That's not why Chase had an accident.

But as I hit send, something cold slipped through me. I glanced
toward the staircase, realizing I hadn't told him about what had happened in the shop. It hadn't seemed cool to pile that on him the
second I arrived.

I hadn't realized we'd lose over an hour playing Clue.
When I looked back at the screen, her reply waited.

I think we need to close it B4 anything worse happens.

My breath slowed as I jammed out six words.

Nothing else is going to happen.

Victoria wasn't known for her seriousness, but in that moment, I
could tell she absolutely was.

Is that really a chance you want to take?

Maybe my premonition of the accident had no logical explana-
tion, but the rest did.

I know it's freaky, but storms make the power go out.
Drafts blow out candles. We were moving the pointer . . .

"Who are you texting?"
I looked up, hadn't heard him coming. "Hey . . ."
"Who's that?"

My heart slammed hard. "Victoria."

Shoving something into his jeans pocket, Chase crossed the room. "What's she up to?"

I tilted the phone toward me, didn't want him to see what we were talking about before I told him about the Ouija board. "Just stuff."

He dropped down next to me, squinting at the BlackBerry.

It was instinct that made me clear the screen—that was all. But the second his hand caught mine, I realized my mistake.

"Why'd you do that?" he asked.

The suspicion in his voice killed me. I stared at his fingers against mine, at the phone caught between our hands, and realized that in clearing the texts, I'd sent his imagination down a dark path. I could see it in the hot burn of his eyes.

"Do you have any idea what that does to me?" he asked, his voice so raw it hurt. Abruptly he pulled back and stood. "When you hide things? When I ask you questions and you don't answer?"

The way he looked at me, with doubt turning the blue of his eyes black, it was like drowning in a room full of oxygen. My breath just stopped.

"Probably the same thing it does to me when you go straight to the worst-case scenario," I whispered.

"You *cleared* the screen, T. You didn't want me to see something. Maybe it *was* Victoria—or maybe someone else. How do I know? Maybe it was that cop's son—"

"No." I moved fast, jumping to my feet and going to him, putting my hands to his arms. "It wasn't him."

I knew better than to say Dylan's name. Despite the fact I hadn't seen him since the night at Big Charity, Chase had a hard time letting go of the fact I'd been wearing another guy's shirt.

"This is me, Chase," I said, looking up at him and, unlike with the game, doing my best to let everything I felt show in my eyes. "You *know* me."

A muscle in the side of his face twitched.

"Here." I lifted my BlackBerry to his hands. "You can see—"

He refused to take it.

I sucked in a sharp breath, let it out slowly. This was not how I'd planned to tell him about the Ouija board.

"Chase." I waited for him to look at me before continuing. It took a second, but as his parents' voices drifted from the kitchen, his eyes returned to mine.

"Have you ever done something at the spur of the moment?" I hated how rock still he stood. "Something that spiraled out of control—"

He had. We both knew that. No matter how far we moved from the afternoon he'd walked away from me, its shadow never fully went away.

"Tell me." His voice was stripped bare. "Tell me what you did."

"It's not what you think," I rushed to tell him. "Last night at the shop Victoria had a Ouija board—"

Through those long bangs, awareness flashed in his eyes.

"And we started messing around, and all this weird stuff started happening—"

"What kind of weird stuff?"

I tried to soften it. "It was during the storm, and it got real cold and the candle went out, and the board kept saying bizarre things—"

The change was abrupt. There among the play of afternoon shadows, Chase went from looking like he was about to get his heart yanked out, to looking like someone facing an unseen enemy. "What did it say?"

I didn't know why telling him was so hard. I'd told him much, much worse. "Just stuff," I muttered, but knew that was never going to cut it. "That someone was going to die—"

He moved fast, taking me by the shoulders. "Who?"

"I don't know."

"Me?"

"No!"

On a harsh breath he released me and looked toward the fireplace, shoving his hands through his hair. "That's what Victoria was texting about."

"Yes."

"Why didn't you tell me?"

"I was going to—*today*. But I didn't want to hit you with that the second I got here, and then we were having fun—I wasn't even thinking about it."

Something changed in his eyes, softened, all that devastating doubt fading into a blue so heartbreaking my breath caught. Jessica's lies had done a real number on his ability to trust.

"You can't do that," he said, stepping closer to take my face in his hands. "You can't hide things—"

"I wasn't hiding—"

He shifted, pulling back one hand but leaving the other against my cheek. "I should have been there," he said. "None of this would have happened—there wouldn't have been an accident, no reason for you to have a vision or a bad dream."

He made it sound so simple: one plus one equals two. And it was true there were always choices. How could you not wonder? Could things have been different with a different choice, or did all roads, ultimately, lead to the same destiny? If he'd been with me at the shop, would the accident still have happened? Maybe at a later time? With a different outcome?

Or maybe, everything had happened exactly the way it was supposed to. The dreams and the Ouija board, the flash, had all worked together to make sure I found Chase before the canal claimed him.

"Now close your eyes," he said.

It was such an odd request. But I could no more have denied him than I could have stopped the sun slipping low against the horizon.

With complete and absolute trust, I closed my eyes, and thought about Pensacola. We'd be together, away from school and New Orleans and . . . Jessica. We'd be away from bad memories and making new ones. I'd see the surf for the first time, and like so many other amazing firsts, it would be with him.

Water formed, darker than I expected, surging up toward the shore and breaking—

I winced, tensing as he lifted my arm to wrap something around my wrist.

"You can look now."

I did. Actually, I stared. A long, thin strip of leather coiled around my wrist, with a delicate silver chain laced through it, a few charms—a cross and a fleur-de-lis and a dragonfly—and words etched into the leather: HONEST, STRONG, SMART, CURIOUS, FEARLESS, IMPULSIVE.

I looked up at him. I'd never seen a wrap bracelet like it. It was almost as if it had been custom-made—

"Your aunt helped me," he said. "I was going to give it to you last night."

Everything just kind of froze. "You *made* this?"

He made a funny face. "Do you like it?"

Blown away, I stepped into him and pushed up on my toes. "I *love* it," I whispered, wrapping my arms around him and holding on tight, wishing the moment could last . . . forever.

I'm not sure what made me look down. But the second I saw the flash of silver on the carpet next to my foot, everything inside me tightened.

"No—stay away—you'll never get—"

The breath of cold swirled deeper. Squeezing my eyes against it, I focused on the warmth of Chase's body.

But when finally I looked down again, just like the black feather mask the night before, the knife was gone.

By the time I got back to the condo, it was after seven and I knew I would be up late studying for my chem test.

Jazz drifted from my aunt's iPod speakers. I saw her first, standing behind a chair at the table. She had her back to me, her hair pulled into a loose knot and her arms lifted.

Detective LaSalle sat in the chair with his head bowed and his shirtsleeves rolled up, making a guttural sound as she worked his shoulders.

If I could have, I would have slipped back out. But she shifted toward me as the door opened, her eyes meeting mine. "Trinity— you're home."

I tossed my keys onto the table where I always kept them. "Don't mind me," I said, heading toward the hall. "I've got a big test—"

Detective LaSalle twisted toward me, and something inside me jumped. He always had that *cop on the hunt* look in his eyes, hard, assessing, even when he and my aunt were kicked back watching a movie. The guy never relaxed. I was used to that.

But as he pulled back from my aunt's hands, for a weird second, he was a stranger all over again, at the condo for the first time, full of questions about how I knew Jessica—and why I thought they should search the mansion in the Garden District.

"What's wrong?" I asked, looking back and forth between them. "What'd you want to talk to me about?"

Aunt Sara didn't have much makeup on, just a light shadow at her eyes, making her look a lot younger than thirty-three. She had on her favorite jeans and a SAVE THE GULF tee. Wire-wrapped turquoise dripped from her ears—another creation she'd been playing with.

Since opening the shop, she was constantly sketching or experimenting, working up designs and possibilities. It was bizarre to come in and find her and Detective Tell-Me-Your-Secrets beading a necklace or stirring essential oils.

"Aaron needs to talk to you," she said, stepping back.

Standing, he retrieved a thin manila folder from the table. "Want you to take a look at a few pictures."

I stayed where I was. "Why?"

His eyes met mine, and his mouth twisted.

"Trinity." My aunt's voice was oddly quiet.

Detective LaSalle shoved a hand through a thick wave of hair, a gesture of frustration I almost never saw from him. "Got a call about a missing girl." His voice was flat. "No one has seen her for over twenty-four hours."

This was New Orleans. People vanished all the time. Sometimes they said good-bye or scribbled a note, sometimes they just went to the restroom and never came back. Sometimes those left behind noticed immediately, and sometimes days went by. Sometimes longer.

"And?" I asked.

He looked up from his iPhone—I couldn't tell if he'd received a text, or had been reviewing one. "Her coworkers said she's been jumpy, looking over her shoulder."

I shifted my weight from one foot to the other. "And you think I might be able to help?"

The strangest look passed between him and my aunt. She stepped toward me, twisting my grandmother's wedding ring on her right ring finger.

"It's more than that, Trin," she said, but didn't need to finish. The buzz started all over again, lower, deeper, and with it I stepped toward the table.

"He thinks you know her."

SEVEN

The eyes. They stared up at me, wide and dark, *knowing*. Next to the photo lay a torn scrap of paper—with my name written all over it, big and small, in print and in cursive, black and blue and pink. Neat.

In red.

"We found that in her apartment," LaSalle said as I braced my hands against the table, and tried to breathe.

"Grace," I whispered, and the room started to spin. *GRACE,* I'd spelled out with the Ouija Board.

DIE

"You know her," Aunt Sara murmured.

I looked up. My aunt was crazy pale. I was pretty sure I was, too. "She's a palm reader," I said. "The one I told you about last fall."

"Have you talked to her since then?"

"No."

She looked up from the scrap of paper. "Then why would she write your name?"

I seriously needed to sit down. "I don't know." Only that a whole bunch of mismatched pieces were falling together into a very bad picture.

"Have you . . . *seen* anything?" Aunt Sara asked.

Slowly, I shook my head, even as the dream from the night before played at the edges of my mind.

"When was the last time you saw her?" Detective LaSalle asked.

I made myself look at him, even as I knew what I was going to see: that sharp, locked-in look that reminded me of a starved dog catching that first whiff of blood.

Four months. I'd last seen Grace the night LaSalle's partner had hauled me down to the station, and Chase had walked away. When I'd run from the guy with the mask, and opened my eyes to find myself in the arms of a stranger.

"Last year," I murmured, reaching for Delphi as she jumped onto the table. "Do . . . do you have any leads?"

"Nothing yet," he said. "No signs of forced entry at her apartment. No screams, no nine-one-one calls. No blood. Her purse was on the sofa, wallet still there. By all accounts, she walked home Friday night, and vanished."

And the very next night, after spelling out her name with the Ouija board, the sound of a girl screaming had sliced into the dream I'd been having for weeks.

But I couldn't bring myself to say that, not to Detective LaSalle— not yet. Because really, I had nothing more than that. Maybe it was all some kind of psychic SOS—or maybe a random vibe I'd picked up on.

Until I knew for sure, I didn't need him breathing down my neck.

Delphi followed me into my room.

Detective LaSalle wanted me to go to Grace's apartment. He wanted me to stand where Grace had and smell the air she'd smelled, to close my eyes and see if I picked up on anything. He wanted me to concentrate on her name before I went to sleep. He'd even given me a picture to slip beneath my pillow. Seeding dreams, he called it.

I'd tried to tell him it didn't work like that, that the dreams found me and not the other way around, but he'd insisted.

Studying was a waste of time. Every time I looked at the periodic table, I saw the letters of the Ouija board. I wanted to chalk the weirdness up to coincidence, but the frightening possibilities slipped through me, exactly like when I'd keyed in on Jessica. *What if. What if the Ouija board had spelled out Grace's name as a warning—or a cry for help. What if she was reaching out to me—*

Absently my hand settled against Delphi's face, and she began to purr.

With Jessica, I'd seen full-blown snapshots. I'd seen the room where she'd been held, and I'd seen *her*. I'd seen her dirty clothing and the terror on her face. I'd even . . . *felt* her.

With Grace, all I had was her name and a sliver of cold somewhere inside.

Mind racing, I dragged my laptop next to Delphi and did another search on Ouija boards. The stories were everywhere, Web sites and message boards dedicated to Ouija board horror stories. So-called experts warned that they were not a game—and that you should never remove your hands from the pointer without saying good-bye.

Pulling the quilt close, I switched to Facebook and found over seventy-five recent posts on Chase's page.

Lucas and Amber's names jumped out at me, back and forth, the most recent from two minutes before.

Lucas Albright: Dude, what good is a psycho girlfriend if she doesn't warn you?

Amber Lane: Warn? That's not what Trin-Trin does. She never says anything until after the fact. Then she plays hero.

Lucas Albright: True dat.

Amber Lane: Did you see that room in her aunt's shop? Did you feel how cold it was?

Lucas Albright: If the rain had gotten inside, it would have turned to ice.

Amber Lane: Just like her.

Lucas Albright: Drew said she led him straight to Chase. How eff'd up is that?

Amber Lane: Is Victoria ok? If I were you, I wouldn't let her near Chase's little voodoo queen.

Lucas Albright: Tryin'. Think maybe she's got some kind of spell or curse on her.

Amber Lane: Prolly. What'd she say about the séance?

Lucas Albright: Nuthin. But she gets this messed-up look in her eyes like she's scared as shit and holding out on me.

It was all right there on Chase's page, for the whole world to see. Or at least all of his friends—and his parents.

Sighing, I slid the laptop aside, texted Victoria about what Lucas and Amber were saying, then flipped off the lamp. And slid the picture of Grace under my pillow.

Sleep came surprisingly fast. One minute I was petting Delphi and in the next my eyes shot open. Adrenaline raced. Disoriented, I tried to move, but a visceral knowing wouldn't let me.

I wasn't alone.

Around me the room breathed, and the shadows slipped closer.

Delphi tensed. Moonlight showed her crouched low, her ears flat and her eyes huge and dark, fixed. Her little body didn't even move with breath.

She felt it, too.

I made myself breathe, let it out slowly as I looked deeper into the darkness.

And then the alarm went off.

The moment broke. It was odd, because tangibly, nothing changed. Delphi and I still didn't move. The collision between night and day still bathed the room in shadows. And the heater still rattled—

The heater. That's when it hit me, the only difference besides the scream of the alarm. The heater blew. It had been blowing all along.

But the room had been cold.

Now sweat bathed my body, and my breath came on a hot rush.

Delphi rose and crept to the edge of the bed. Watching her, I allowed myself to move, sliding my hand under my pillow to retrieve the picture of Grace.

"What's going on?" I whispered as if she could hear me. "What are you trying to tell me?"

I barely made it to school on time.

Only a few minutes before homeroom, I yanked open my locker—and saw the Ouija board. It dominated the small space, not the same one from Saturday, but darker, with letters of red. All except the three that had been smudged away—D, E, and I.

DIE

I moved to close the door, but before I could, Amber slid in, smiling like she did when she took the field to cheer. "What's the matter, Trin-Trin? Lookin' a little pale."

And she was looking ridiculously pleased with herself. "So original, Amber," I muttered.

"I mean, I sure hope some evil spirit isn't keeping you awake at night. I've heard sometimes that happens—"

I smiled right back. "Funny thing about evil spirits, sweetie. Once they're free, you never know what's going to happen."

Lined in thick black, her eyes widened. "Are you threatening me?"

I was kinda surprised she leapt from point A to point B so quickly. Normally, subtlety flew right by her.

"I'll let you figure that out," I said as first bell rang and the hall started to empty.

"Oh, I've got it figured out," she said, swooping in and retrieving the board. "And soon everyone else will, too."

It was all I could do not to roll my eyes.

"First Jessie gets hurt, then Chase. Why, you're worse than a black cat."

"Then maybe you shouldn't be standing here," I said. "I mean, you never know what might happen."

"You think you're so untouchable just because you've got Chase whipped and your aunt is doing a cop. But I see you for who you are. Ever since you showed up, bad things have been happening—"

"Knock it off, Amber."

Chase had such an awesome knack for timing—it's probably why he was killer on the football field. He came up behind me and slid his arm around my waist, easing me against him.

"Chase." Amber's eyes got all narrow. "You sure you should be here today? I mean after Saturday night—"

"Yeah, I saw all your concern on Facebook."

Amazing how quick I could go from ready to smack someone to melting inside.

"Look," she said, sweeping a long coffee-colored ringlet from her face. "You can delete any post you want, but that doesn't change the truth. I was there Saturday night. I *saw* what happened. You didn't."

"And we all know how reliable you are," he muttered.

"Remember that night at the house on Prytania?" she rolled on.

"When we went into that room with those mattresses? Remember how still Trinity got? How cold? That's how she looked Saturday, almost . . . dead."

Chase's hold on me tightened. "Give it up, Amber. It was just an eff'in game."

"A game?" she shrieked, and now her eyes glittered. "If that's really what you think, then maybe you need to play with her next time, instead of poor Vic. You can pretend to be the dead dad while your girlfriend pretends to be her dead mother—"

The moment just kind of stopped, at least for me. Chase and Amber were still going at it, but my heart screamed so hard I could feel it pound in every pulse point of my body.

She couldn't know. She couldn't. Victoria had *promised* . . .

"You're messed up, you know that?" Chase said as the second bell rang. The disgust in his voice would have made me feel good, if I hadn't realized what was coming. "Trinity doesn't go around making up crap like you do."

Her mouth twisted. "For your sake, sha, you better hope she does." With her flare for drama, she swirled around and waltzed off, vanishing around the corner, leaving only me and Chase beside my locker. When he stood motionless like that, with his feet shoulder width apart, it drove home how much bigger than me he was. Usually that made me feel safe.

At that moment, I felt anything but. Because the second I glanced up at him, I knew Amber's words had done more damage than he'd let her see.

His eyes met mine. "Your mom?" he said, and even if I hadn't noticed anything else, the lack of emotion in his voice would have told me something wasn't right. The more upset Chase was, the less emotion he showed. "What's she talking about, T?"

There was no point pretending a little bomb hadn't just exploded. I'd told him about the Ouija board, but I hadn't told him exactly how weird things had gotten.

"I thought it was my subconscious," I said quietly.

He didn't move, other than the rise and fall of his shoulders. *"But you don't think that anymore?"*

Yesterday I'd told myself what happened with the Ouija board had been about Chase's accident, another psychic warning, just via a different channel.

I no longer had that luxury.

"Detective LaSalle was at the condo when I got home last night," I said.

I saw him brace. "And?"

Stepping into him, I lifted a hand to his chest. In that moment, I really, really needed to touch him.

"What happened with Jessica?" I whispered, searching his eyes. "I think it's happening again."

Omigod, Im SO freaking sorry!!!

It wasn't until after bombing the chem test that I saw Victoria's text. Stepping into the hall, I scrolled through the other messages that had piled up during first period.

The rumor mill spun fast.

I didn't tell him, I promise!

Him, of course, was Lucas.

He was asking me all these questions, trying to figure out what happened. He wanted to know who came through. I told him no one. But he kept on and finally he guessed it was your mom. I told him to be real, but he wouldn't stop and got it in his head that's what happened. I am SO SORRY. Amber is such a bitch.

Maybe I should have been mad at Victoria, but I knew her. She wasn't a good liar. When Lucas tossed out the possibility of my mom coming through, her eyes had probably gotten real big, or she'd stammered or looked away, something that made Lucas realize he'd hit pay dirt.

Aware of the way everyone was looking at me, I texted her back and told her not to worry about it.

Then I bit the inside of my mouth and clicked on Chase's name.

I want to know everything.

There'd been no time for details before class, only a quick overview. And he'd left homeroom as soon as he'd turned in his test. We wouldn't have a chance to talk until lunch.

OK. No secrets—promise.

After sending that, I stared at Detective LaSalle's name. I hated the jolt I got every time it flashed across my phone. I tried to think of him as simply my aunt's boyfriend, but since he didn't think of me as simply his girlfriend's niece, I had a hard time.

Realizing I was about to be late to history, I made myself pull up his message.

Sara says you didn't dream last night. Try not to worry.
Maybe something will click at the apartment.
I'll be waiting when school gets out.

The dragonfly stopped me cold.

Standing inside Grace's apartment, I stared at the shimmering sun-catcher for a long time. A ceiling fan whirred nearby, making the iridescent green glass flutter against the window. Through wide wings, sunlight fractured into a distorted rainbow.

My thoughts raced. Pieces of the puzzle slipped closer, sharper now. But I couldn't make them fit.

"Trinity?" Detective LaSalle asked. "You okay? Are you getting something?"

I made myself turn from the hauntingly simple dragonfly, the one so very, very much like the figurine of blown-glass in my bedroom. "Not yet."

He stood by the door, dressed as he always was in pressed khakis, a light blue shirt, and sport coat. Dark sunglasses hid his eyes and, I knew, the fatigue that came from lack of sleep. He'd been at our place until after one.

"Take your time," he said. Despite the sunglasses, I knew he watched.

Grace's apartment was little more than a single room with a fridge, stove, and sink to one side, a bathroom that looked more like a closet, and an Oriental screen standing in the middle, pretending to be a wall. A hollow door led out to the musty hall. Toward the back, beyond the futon that served as a bed, a lone window overlooked a courtyard.

I'm not sure why that fascinated me so much, the secret gardens of the French Quarter, these thriving little oases tucked away from the rest of the world. But I loved that about the city, that you could be walking down the most crowded, foul-smelling street, looking at sad, run-down buildings, while just beyond the brick and concrete, something beautiful thrived.

Illusions, I thought, turning from the window. Everyone created them. Even places.

I still hadn't talked to Chase. I'd looked for him at lunch, but Drew said something about Chase getting treatment on his ankle in the weight room. I'd texted him, told him I would be at Fleurish! later if he wanted to talk.

He'd said ok.

I really wished I hadn't glossed over things the night before. I just hadn't wanted to worry him. Unfortunately, with Chase, there was no such thing as a harmless secret.

I turned, running my hand along a pink-and-black striped blanket draped over the futon. It was neatly folded and placed, no sign of a struggle or anything out of the ordinary. At the front of the room, milk crates served as a table, much like they had at Dylan's—

I stopped the memory before it could go any further. The last thing I needed was to return to his apartment, or the moments I'd spent there.

"It looks like she just walked away," I murmured, taking in a half-eaten banana, now gross and brown on a small white plate.

"But never came back," LaSalle said.

The thought unnerved me. To get up one morning and start breakfast, run out for a second—

I twisted toward the love seat, where a large, peace-sign tote sat next to an open paperback: *Gazing into the Eternal.*

"Can I touch it?"

"It's been dusted."

Carefully I reached for the book, and a thin dark object fluttered to the ground. Kneeling, I reached for it, felt my breath catch the second I recognized the feathers.

I didn't want to touch it. I didn't want to feel anything.

But I had to.

Refusing to let my hand shake, I reached for the Mardi Gras mask—and saw the picture on the floor, half concealed by a pair of well-worn leather sandals.

I reached for it and turned it over, and the last hope I'd had of everything being a simple coincidence quietly fell away.

EIGHT

Three young women, their images little more than bleached-out shadows, stood with their arms around each other, laughing. Two of them were blond—my mother was the only brunette.

"See something?" LaSalle asked.

Quickly I slipped the photo and mask into the book. "Nah, just stuff." I'm not sure why I lied. It was just instinct.

Secrets, I realized. They were as much a part of me as they were of this town, and of Grace. She had a picture of my mother. And not only had she known my name, she'd scribbled it before she disappeared.

I wanted to know why.

After putting the book down, I turned to the sun streaming through the dragonfly and felt the unmistakable pull of fate and destiny and all those things my grandmother taught me not to believe in all over again.

"Nothing happened here," I said, not sure where the words came from, but confident they were true. Whatever happened to Grace had happened somewhere else.

"Are you sure?"

"Yes." I surveyed the room again, lingering beyond the back

window, where ivy thrived in the dead of winter. "I can breathe. When I close my eyes, nothing flashes."

As if to demonstrate, I did just that.

And saw the black boots.

Abruptly I opened my eyes and twisted around, looked against every wall, beneath the futon, every spot visible on the floor, even at Detective LaSalle's expensive-looking loafers.

"Trinity?" he said as I blinked hard. "What is it?"

"I don't know. I just . . ." There were no boots. "It's nothing."

He reached for his phone and tapped the screen. "Why don't you touch some of her clothes," he suggested. "That used to help your mother."

While he texted, I went down on my knees and ran my hands along T-shirts and jeans in hot-pink crates. In another I found gypsy-style maxi dresses. The fourth held underwear. I didn't touch those.

After checking to make sure Detective LaSalle was still focused on his phone, I wandered back to the front of the apartment and ran my hand along the love seat, careful to keep my back to him.

He never saw me swipe the picture of my mother, and slip it into my back pocket.

Fleurish! was a mess.

Detective LaSalle and I walked in a few minutes before five and found Aunt Sara hurriedly folding T-shirts, while keeping an eye on a group of older women clustered around the jewelry, and two more smelling candles.

We joined her. It took twenty minutes, but by the time the chatty lady from Phoenix left with the turquoise and vintage cross necklace gift wrapped, Detective LaSalle had straightened the front display, and I'd told my aunt about coming up empty at Grace's apartment.

I wasn't ready to talk about the picture.

"I'm bummed I couldn't help," I said. "I was hoping something would pop." Like it had at the house on Prytania.

With her hair pulled into a loose ponytail at the base of her neck,

Aunt Sara looked up from wrapping pink ribbon back around the spool. "You tried. That's all you can do."

"But it's not enough." Sparks shot from a votive near the end of its wick. "It's like this vague scavenger hunt, with clues coming to me that I don't understand or can't remember—"

LaSalle looked up from his phone. "What clues?"

"That's the problem," I said. "I don't know. Sometimes I get this feeling that there's something there, something I'm supposed to understand. Like this morning—I was convinced I wasn't alone, that someone was there, watching me."

My aunt dropped the spool to the counter as the memory of Delphi's ears flat back, her eyes locked onto something unseen, crawled through me.

"But I couldn't move," I murmured. "Couldn't see. It was like I was awake but dreaming at the same time, but I couldn't make myself go either direction, couldn't focus." And I could feel it again, standing right there by the candle display, the paralysis, the way my chest had burned.

"It's like some kind of clue was *right there,*" I said. "And if I just could have gone back, back into the dream, I could have seen . . ."

As if in slow motion, LaSalle slid his phone into his pocket and stepped toward me. "What if," he said, his voice really, really weird, "I can take you?"

Something crazy and fast zipped through me. "Take me—"

"No—" my aunt said, hurrying over. "We talked about this. *No.*"

He was tall and she wasn't, so even though she stood right up in his space, all he had to do was look past her to make eye contact with me. *"Aaron."*

Something odd flashed in his eyes. "Sara—"

"I said no."

I'd never heard them raise their voices at each other. I wasn't even sure they'd had anything as basic as a disagreement.

"No to what?" I asked, stepping toward them. I could tell that it was big.

But it was like I wasn't even there. While my heart was about to pound out of my chest, they stood locked in a silent battle of wills.

"Um, hello?" I tried again. "One of you needs to talk."

Detective LaSalle looked away first, toward me. "Your dreams," he said gently. "What if I can take you back into your dreams?"

I felt my mouth drop open. "That's possible?"

"With hypnosis, yes," he said as my aunt glared at him.

I made myself swallow—but so didn't understand, not what he was talking about—not why she was so edgy. "Hypnosis?"

He stepped closer, reaching for her hand.

She yanked it back.

"It's called dream regression therapy," he said. "It's still experimental."

"Which is why she's not doing it." Aunt Sara breathed. "It's too dangerous."

But a new door swung open inside me, revealing a world of possibility I'd never imagined. But I'd hoped. I'd . . . obsessed. What if I *could* get back into my dreams? What if I could explore what I saw, see *more*? That would have made a huge difference with finding Jessie.

"What's dangerous about it? How soon can we start?"

"As soon as you want," Detective LaSalle said as if my aunt was the one no longer present. And I could tell that really pissed her off.

Aunt Sara was many things, but willing to be taken lightly was not one of them.

"There's no proof that it's dangerous," he said, answering my first question second. "I would be right there with you—"

Aunt Sara grabbed his wrist. "You don't know that. Julian said it's all hypothetical."

Julian?

Fascinated, I glanced out the window, to the sign glowing across the street.

"He doesn't know what will happen," Aunt Sara said, as something inside me hummed.

"It's not natural. It's not *normal*. You put her under and lower her into a dream—what if she finds something she doesn't know how to handle? What if she can't wake up?"

Shadows fell from the narrow building, darkness gaping from the second-story window.

"She could go into the wrong dream," Aunt Sara kept on. "Unlock something that can't be put back—"

"Wait a minute." I shifted my attention back to her. "Let's start over—you can actually put me back into my dreams?"

"Not me," LaSalle said. "Julian."

Aunt Sara brought her hands together, as if in prayer. "Trinity." Her voice was beyond strained. "Please. This isn't a good idea."

"But Julian has a ton of clients." And he was right across the street. "If he can help—"

"Dreams are supposed to be natural," she said as the bell on the door jingled and several men in business suits stepped inside.

"Especially *your* dreams." She lowered her voice. "And your mother's. They come to you when they're supposed to. It's not something you can force."

Scared, I realized. My aunt was scared.

"You can't start fooling around with stuff you don't understand."

God, she would have freaked if she knew about the Ouija board.

I looked at her, and felt my heart twist. From day one, she'd been supportive, taking me into her home, her life. Listening when I talked and answering questions no one else would. She'd been my constant, the one person I could rely on when everything else blew up in my face.

Seeing her like this, pale, rattled, unnerved me.

"You mean I'm supposed to *understand* this?" I asked with a quick little smile. And then she smiled, kind of, and as I reached for her hand and squeezed, the awful tension of the moment released.

"It's almost six," Detective LaSalle said, and he offered up a smile of his own, the slow, lazy kind that guys used when trying to wiggle out of trouble. "Am I in the doghouse, or can we still go to eat?"

Customers kept streaming in.

Normally Mondays were dead, but with Mardi Gras a few weeks away, every time I turned around, the door was opening. Aunt Sara had warned me that was going to happen, but I'd thought she meant on the weekends.

"I think I need an eight," a sweet schoolteacher from Wisconsin said. While a few of her friends tried on necklaces, she sat on a velvet ottoman, trying on a pair of fleur-de-lis rain boots. We'd only had them for a week, but with funky colors and a cute two-inch heel, they were flying out the door.

"Be right back." Turning, I widened my eyes at Chase before heading to the back room. We'd been trying to talk for half an hour, but never got more than a few minutes before someone else came in.

With each interruption, he got quieter.

He said nothing as he went back to folding the *FLEUREVER* T-shirts for the second time since he arrived. I didn't get why people couldn't leave things the way they found them.

"Here you go," I said a few minutes later, returning with a big box.

The woman shoved aside the size 7s and reached for the 8s. "Thank you." Sliding her feet in, she stood and headed toward her friends, more dancing than walking. "Char! What do you think? Aren't these great?"

With a necklace around her neck and one dangling from each hand, the taller woman turned. "Oh . . . those are so *cute!*"

That's the way it had been all evening.

By the time I handed them their bags—with two pairs of boots and five necklaces—the Mardi Gras CD had run through three more songs, and Chase had finished the T-shirts.

"Maybe we should lock the door," I said with a quick glance toward the front of the shop.

Through the glass, from across the street, the sign for HORIZONS glowed—and something inside me pulled.

Chase didn't answer.

Turning toward the register, I found him not three feet away, standing real still. He looked all casual in his jeans and tight, retro Aerosmith shirt, but I knew he was anything but. And I knew exactly what he was staring at.

The door to the back room.

Crossing to him, I lifted my hands to his shoulders, but dropped them without touching. The bruise, partially hidden by the sweep of bangs, still discolored his temple. If possible, the scrapes along his cheekbone looked worse. "You okay?"

"I wish you'd told me all this last night."

"I know." I should have. But a lifetime of being warned not to share my secrets—or my fears—made it hard to open up. It was that old habits thing. Even bad ones could be hard to break.

"I just didn't think the gory details mattered." Big mistake.

"What matters is you telling me, versus Amber telling me."

And it was a big difference, I got that.

Stepping into him, I lifted my hands to his chest. "She can't stand that we're together."

"Then don't give her ammo."

I smiled, trying to lighten the moment. "I don't know, the kind that blows up in her face doesn't sound like such a bad idea."

His lips quirked—just enough to tug at a scab and cause a trickle of blood.

I lifted my hand to wipe it away, but he turned before I could, stepping toward the door. This time he pushed it open and walked through.

With a quick glance toward the front windows, I made sure no one was about to come in, and followed.

The warmth stopped me. Saturday night it had almost been cold enough to see my breath.

"Your mom," he said, skimming a hand along the worktable. It was cluttered again, full of Mardi Gras beads ready to be tagged and put out front.

"You think she was trying to warn you?"

I looked away, toward the walls that had looked to bleed. Now, with the bright light overhead, they looked cheerful and red.

"I don't know." That was the problem. I had an ability—a gift. But no one could tell me exactly where it came from (other than my mother's side of the family), and how it worked. "I can't say she wasn't, but I can't say she was, either. Maybe it was my subconscious or some kind of psychic SOS."

Chase turned to look at me.

"But," I made myself continue, "I keep thinking no matter where the message came from, maybe the Ouija board is like another channel for information to come through." It was hard to put it into words, but to me, it was starting to make sense.

"With Jessica," I said, my hand automatically lifting to the leather bracelet around my wrist. "I *saw* her." Two nights before she went missing.

"But with Grace, it's just her name and maybe her voice. I haven't actually *seen* anything." Just the darkness and the cold—

Another wave swept through me, so fast I winced.

Chase lunged toward me. "Trinity—"

"No, I'm okay," I said, but he reached for me anyway.

I looked up at him, and hated what I had to ask. But I had so many questions—and knew only one person who could answer them.

"Does she ever talk about it?" I asked quietly. "Jessica?"

The change in him was subtle, like a door slowly closing, but the result was impossible to miss. "Not much."

I made myself continue. "In the hospital, she told me she could feel me, when she was alone in that room. Do you think you could get her to talk to me? To tell me what it was she felt—"

The way his mouth tightened made the bleeding start all over again. "T . . . you know she's not comfortable around people yet."

This time I didn't wipe the trickle away. "Except you."

"Trinity—"

"No, it's okay." I stepped back. "I understand." And I did. "She feels safe with you. I get that." Chase was that kind of person. "She knows you won't hurt her."

I hated the way the words scraped.

He twisted, back toward the worktable. "The Ouija board," he murmured, and my heart sank. I *needed* to talk to Jessica. She was the only one who'd been on the other side of my dreams, and was still alive to talk about it.

"Did it say anything you *didn't* already know?" he asked.

Biting down on my lip, I let it go—for now—and ran back through those freaky minutes. "Just a few names. When Victoria asked who we were talking to, it spelled out Marie—and Evie."

"They don't mean anything to you?"

I shook my head as the bell on the front door jingled. "Nothing," I said, turning to head back into the shop.

Chase didn't follow.

It took about five minutes, but finally the two businessmen chose blinged-out FLEURISH! t-shirts as souvenirs for their little girls, paid, and left.

Standing behind the counter as jazzy parade music drifted from the speakers, I stared through the front windows, to the glowing sign across the street.

HORIZONS.

All I had to do was walk inside, and step back into my dreams.

"What if she knew?" I murmured as Chase came up beside me. It was the only possibility that made sense. "What if Grace realized something bad was going to happen and left my name for the cops to find, like a safety net?" The implications rocked me. "What if before anything even happened, she planned to reach out to me for help?"

Chase pulled me back against him. "You're cold."

And he was so, so warm.

Twisting around, I grinned. "Think you can change that?"

His smile was slow, lazy. Pushing up on my toes, I angled my face to his, and then his arms were around me and mine were around him, and what started out soft and gentle quickly escalated.

I never heard the bell jingle—but I did hear someone clear their throat.

Jerking back, I twisted toward the front, where my aunt and Detective LaSalle stood looking discreetly at the T-shirts Chase had refolded.

"Aunt Sara," I said, hurrying from behind the counter. "I'm sorry, I just—"

She looked up, and grinned. "Forgot to lock the door?"

I laughed. "Not exactly what I was going to say."

"All my fault," Chase said, coming up beside me.

"No apologies necessary." She slid a glance at the antique clock on the counter. "Why don't you get on home, *cher*? I'll close up."

"I can stay—"

"No need."

All the while, Detective LaSalle stood quietly, watching.

After grabbing my purse and telling Aunt Sara I'd sold the last pair of size eight rain boots, Chase and I headed to the door. I had one foot outside when he swung back toward my aunt. "Hey, Sara?"

She'd just stepped out of the back room with a handful of beads. "Yeah?"

Against mine, his hand tightened—that should have warned me. "Is there anyone in Trinity's family named Marie?"

Half in, half out, I froze.

"Are you kidding?" she said, draping the beads along a series of fleur-de-lis jewelry trees. "The better question is who's *not* named Marie." She looked up. "Why?"

He shot me a quick look before no-big-dealing her question with a shrug.

"Just one of those Internet things," he said, "about common names. Trinity said there were no Maries in her family, and I bet that there were."

Music drifted in from Bourbon, while from the river, a cool breeze blew. I was barely aware of either.

Nor could I believe how fast Chase had come up with that lame excuse.

Nor could I get past my aunt's answer.

"So who's named Marie?" he asked.

Aunt Sara let the last strands of beads pool against the counter. "It was her mother's middle name," she said, truly like it was no big deal. "And her mother's, and her mother's before her. I never understand how Trinity ended up with Rose."

Chase practically dragged me outside, not stopping until we were two buildings down the street. Then he turned me toward him, and the light in his eyes almost blinded.

"Still think it was just your subconscious?"

1:57.

The green of the clock glowed against the darkness of my room. For over two hours I'd been watching the numbers creep deeper into the night. I tried to sleep. I wanted to sleep. That was my best chance of connecting with Grace.

But sleep would not come.

Delphi sat beside me, her green eyes narrow, staring without blinking. Back when she'd first come to live with me, I'd tried to ease her onto her side in that classic, C-curl cat shape. But Delphi was not a lay-on-her-side kind of cat. She was a croucher. She always had all four paws on the ground, ready to take off.

Gradually, as weeks turned into months, I'd quit trying to turn her into the lazy cat Victoria had, and accepted her for who she was. I had no idea of what she'd been through. Or, for that matter, how she'd come to be on my doorstep.

Now, if I concentrated, I would have sworn I could hear the soft, faint rumble of a purr.

I loved it when she purred.

2:01.

Aunt Sara and Detective LaSalle had come in after ten. From my room, I'd heard them talking about their upcoming trip to Mexico.

With the Grace case active and me involved, he was no longer sure he should leave. Aunt Sara didn't have a choice. She was in the wedding.

2:03.

Frowning, I checked Facebook, but nothing had changed in the fifteen minutes since I'd last looked. Chase must have fallen asleep. His last text had been around midnight. Victoria had dropped out an hour before that. Her parents had a strict no-phone-after-eleven rule.

2:06.

The heater blew. I could hear it rattling. But the wind blew against my window, and my room wouldn't warm.

2:07.

My mother's middle name was Marie. So was her mother's, and her mother's . . .

2:08.

Grace had a picture of my mother . . .

2:09.

Closing my eyes, I ran through all the pieces—they were starting to fit.

I turned over and dragged the covers with me. With the soft cotton blanket in my hands, I concentrated on breath. In, out. Slow. Steady. I refused to look at the clock.

"Trinity."

My heart slammed.

"Omigod! You're here!"

The voice was quiet—desperate. I spun toward it, but found a long, empty street. Buildings lined each side, old and faded, out of time and place.

"You shouldn't have come," she whispered. "He's too dangerous."

I'd only talked with her once before. Months had passed. But I recognized the voice, and the fear trembling through it. I tried to run toward her, but my body wouldn't move. "Grace?"

"You have to go—there's not much time!"

"Where are you?" I scanned the street. A big, pale green urn lay on its

side, broken, with dirt spilling against cracked concrete. Weeds had replaced whatever had once grown within. "Tell me where you are!"

Wind swept down the street. Dust swirled.

"Grace?" I called. "Please!"

I fought to move, twisted free on a violent rush and started to run. "Where?" I shouted. "Where are you?"

"Sh-h-h! He'll hear you."

My feet splashed down in a puddle. Mud and water streaked up against the bare skin of my legs. "Who? Who'll hear me?"

"He hears everything . . ."

The voice echoed around me, no point of origin or end. I stopped and twisted, looked from building to building.

Once they'd been beautiful. Once they'd . . . invited. Now they stood forgotten, faded, with broken windows and darkness gaping from within. Paint peeled, and doors hung open.

"Be careful!" The voice was little more than a terrified whisper. "He's coming!" she cried, and this time I lunged toward the closest structure, one of weathered green with a series of missing French doors and empty balconies and window boxes above.

I darted inside—and stopped cold.

NINE

Through the darkness a brilliant green dragonfly glowed.

"Grace?"

With silence from all directions, I made myself cross toward the sun-catcher. "Grace, please," I whispered. "Talk to me."

Something warm whispered against me. I turned toward it, saw the crate several feet away. Green.

Glowing.

I started toward it.

Sudden footsteps stopped me. They were strong, purposeful.

I ran, feeling my way through the darkness and darting behind the first obstruction I found.

The room breathed. Or maybe that was me. Or maybe—

The dragonfly glowed brighter, fracturing invisible sunlight—and the boots came into view.

Black.

Just like—

I jerked awake, surging up in bed with the embers of a silent scream searing my throat. Blinking, I lifted a hand to my neck and felt my pulse racing, my skin like ice.

The clock read 5:21.

"Omigod," I whispered as Delphi nudged against me. She was so very, very warm. "Grace."

I'd been there. Wherever Grace was, I'd been there. I'd heard her. She'd been begging me to leave . . .

I'd been close. I'd been so, so close.

And there in the cold, predawn darkness, I knew what I had to do.

"T, when are you going to tell me where we are?"

"Sh-h-h." With a tight smile I glanced from Chase to the driver's license in my hand, lifted it to the thin space between the door and the frame, and slid.

"What are you doing?" he whisper-asked. I don't know what it is about silence that makes you lower your voice, but I was grateful that he did. "You can't just break in—"

But I could. After a quick jiggle the flimsy lock gave way, and when I put my gloved hand to the knob and twisted, the door fell open.

"Come on," I mouthed, slipping into darkness so pure that, for a chilling heartbeat, I was back in the basement of the condemned hospital.

Chase pushed in behind me and quickly but quietly closed the cheap wooden door—his hands were gloved, too. I'd insisted on that. But I'd told him little else.

If I had, he might have said no.

And if he'd said no, I didn't like plan B.

More than twelve hours had passed since I'd texted him, asking if he could meet me after dinner. The clock had read 5:47. I'd still been in bed—he'd been asleep. Before homeroom, he'd pulled me aside, wanting answers.

Blind trust wasn't his thing, but that's what I needed him to give me.

"Trinity—" he said now. "Where are we?"

I slid my hand into my messenger bag, retrieved a small flashlight, and clicked it on. "Grace's apartment."

He moved fast, taking me by the shoulders and twisting me toward him. "Are you crazy?"

Something inside me tensed. "I'd rather think of it as *inspired*," I said, going up on my toes and pressing my mouth to his.

He didn't kiss me back.

"Crazy isn't my favorite word," I added, brushing the bangs from his eyes.

The lines of his face stayed tight, reminding me of the way he'd looked when I first told him about my dreams: part intrigue, part disbelief, but mostly concern. "You know what I mean."

"I do." Slipping from him, I eased deeper into the coldness of Grace's small apartment. Either there was no heat, or it had been turned off. "But I had to come back," I said. "I dreamed something last night."

"About her?"

I ran my flashlight along a series of crates, most full of magazines and books. *"I found her."*

"Then what are we doing here?"

The second my light hit the green, I stepped toward the crate and went down on my knees. "This," I said, dragging it toward me. "I . . . saw this in my dreams."

There had to be a reason.

Chase crowded in behind me, pressing against my back. "What is it?"

I shivered. That made no sense. "Looks like pictures." Tilting the crate, I let everything spill around my knees. "And letters." I shifted through the assortment of envelopes, all from some town called Belle Terre, all addressed to Grace Fontenot.

Until that moment, I'd never known her last name.

Chase reached around me, his gloved hand picking up a torn scrap of newspaper.

I felt him still.

"What is it?" I asked, shifting my light to the paper.

The sight of my parents' names was like a quick punch to the gut.

"Omigod," I whispered, taking in words that threw me back to the night I'd finally learned how they died. Words like *fire* and *arson* and . . . *too late.* But this was worse. This was more.

This was their obituary.

In Grace's apartment.

The shaking started, deep, deep inside. Chase pulled me closer, holding me as I slid my arms inside his jacket and held on.

"She must have known her," I murmured. "Grace must have known my mom, or at least heard of her."

Chase held me tighter.

"She must have realized—"

The knock killed my words. We jumped, Chase shooting to his feet and positioning himself between me and the door.

"No," I whispered, disentangling myself. "It's okay." He tried to stop me, but I twisted, hurrying to open the door before she could knock again. "Victoria."

Long, silky blond hair fell against her face, making her eyes seem bigger—darker. "What is this place?" she whispered, as if she, too, knew better than breaking the silence. The whole building was like a mausoleum. If I hadn't known better, I would have sworn it was abandoned.

But someone lived below, and someone lived above. Detective LaSalle had told me that.

Jerkily, I took her by the wrist and tugged her inside, quietly closing the door.

"Did you bring it?" I asked, my breath suddenly shallow. "Do you have the board?"

Victoria sat statue still. Behind her, a coarse trail of sea salt circled the three crates serving as a makeshift table. Along the edges, amid crystals she'd gotten from Julian, six sage votives flickered.

In the center, the Ouija board waited.

"You really want to do this?" Chase asked. We stood by the window overlooking the secluded courtyard. Every time I tried to pull away, his arms tightened around me.

"I have to," I said. "Saturday, I didn't understand what was happening. I didn't know what the board was tapping into." And really, where the answers came from still didn't matter. Only that they came. "Now that I know about Grace, there are questions I need to ask—"

The shadows made the blue of his eyes glitter. "Let me, then. Tell me what to ask, and I'll do it. You can watch—"

"It doesn't work like that." My chest tightened. My throat burned. It was so tempting to bury my face against his neck and hold on, pretend this wasn't happening. But in those fragile moments when I'd first awoken from the dream, I'd known I had to try again. Grace had done her best to reach out to me.

I had to reach back. And the glow of the dragonfly told me it had to be here, where her energy would be strongest. "It has to be me."

"How do you know that? We're in her apartment. The board is the same. Victoria is the same. We can ask for Marie—"

I pushed up and fingered the sweep of bangs hiding the fading bruise. "You're not me." It all came down to that. I was the connection. I was the link. Maybe Marie would come again, or maybe Evie. Maybe my mom.

Maybe no one.

But I had to try. I was the one being called.

"It'll be okay," I said with a soft kiss against the corner of his mouth. This time we would be together. This time there would be no bizarre accidents. "I promise."

He so didn't buy that. But he let me go, holding my hand as I stepped over the line of salt and sat in a folding chair beside Victoria.

He took the chair on my other side, but never released my hand.

"We all have to touch," she reminded.

Inching closer, we used our knees to create an unbroken circle.

Her eyes met mine. In them I found none of the excitement from Saturday night, only a dark, steady awareness.

"Whatever you do, don't let go this time," she whispered. "And remember, we have to say good-bye. Okay?"

I looked from her to Chase, then at the dark lettering of the board. "Promise."

"Okay," she whispered. "Here we go."

The walls pushed closer.

"Angel of Protection," she began in the same singsong voice from a few nights before, "my guardian dear, to whom pure love commits me here."

Saturday I'd had no idea what to expect, or what to ask. Now questions blasted me.

"Ever this night," she chanted, "be at my side, to light and guard, to rule and guide."

Chase squeezed my hand. I concentrated on the warmth of his, the strength of his fingers. But tingles of cold streaked up my arm.

Robotically he turned to look at me. His eyes were narrow, aware, the dull glow telling me he knew the train was coming, coming really fast, and we were straight in its path.

"Look," Victoria said, half laughing—half not. "I can always leave if you two—"

"No." I swung from Chase to the golden hue of the board. "I'm ready." To prove it, I moved my right index finger to the pointer.

Pressing her lips together, Victoria placed her finger next to mine. But Chase did not move.

I glanced at him, saw his shoulders wider than usual, every muscle in his body tense, even his neck. His face was like stone, his jaw and mouth tight, the blue of his eyes nearly black, and once again we were back in that morgue, locked in silent communion.

"I kill him," he'd said Sunday. *"This time* I *do it."*

Blinking, I reached out in the only ways I could, squeezing his hand and pressing my knee firmer against his.

"Just don't let go," I whispered. "No matter what happens, don't let go."

His dimple reappeared. "Not gonna happen," he murmured, and then his finger joined mine and Victoria's.

"Hear me now," she said, exactly as she had before. "I invite only those spirits who are for our highest good."

And like before, the pointer started to slide in a slow, clockwise circle.

Chase stiffened.

Victoria closed her eyes and bowed her head.

This time I did the same. And before she could finish, I took over the chant. "Any spirits who come through who are not for my highest good are to be absorbed into the light of protection."

I would have sworn I started to float.

The pointer circled slower, its movement hypnotic.

"Harming none," I whispered as Chase squeezed my hand and I inhaled, drawing the scent of sage deep within me.

And through the silence, the hum began, more of a vibration than a sound.

The triangle stopped. I jerked, felt myself start to pull away. But Chase held on, tightly enough for both of us.

And I had to see him. In that moment, for some reason, I needed to see him as badly as I needed to breathe. I opened my eyes and found him staring, not at me but at the pointer.

If I hadn't felt his pulse through his skin, I would have had no idea that he breathed.

"Chase—" I'm not sure why my voice broke.

His eyes remained fixed, but his throat worked, and when he spoke, his voice was not one that I recognized. "Is there someone here?" he asked.

Two of the votives flickered, and again the pointer glided, this time to the upper left.

YES

Victoria's finger stiffened. "Thank you," she whispered, just as she had before.

My heart started to pound really, really hard. "Marie—" I started, but Victoria's eyes flew open so fast I stopped. *"W-what?"* I asked her.

Blond hair hung limply around her face. "We're not supposed to supply names." She visibly swallowed before shifting her attention back to the board. "Are you . . . good?"

My breath just kind of stopped. I'd forgotten to ask the most important question of all.

Amid the shifting light of the candles, the pointer streaked to the opposite side of the board.

NO

"Then get the hell out—" Chase started, but the pointer kept swirling, moving in a clockwise circle until it returned to its point of origin.

YES

Chase's eyes met mine, and my breath released.

"Is this what it did before?" he asked.

Nodding, I focused on the white glow of a single candle. "Will you . . . will you tell us your name?"

I stared as the pointer shifted in a methodical circle.

YES

Victoria nudged me.

Chase sat motionless.

"W-what is it?" I asked.

Beneath our fingers, the pointer flowed eagerly to the middle row, a letter on the left, then directly above. Back to the middle, this time to the right. Once again, directly above. Then back to the left.

MARIE

Saturday the name had meant nothing.

Now it meant everything.

"Holy crap," Chase muttered, and in my mind, I screamed for him to be quiet. But those words would not come. Only words for the board, the spirit. *"M-mom?"*

Time slowed, crawled. The darkness throbbed. The word yes was so close, up a row and slightly to the left.

The pointer slid down, glided right.

S

My whole world just stopped.

The pointer kept sliding, marginally to the right, hesitating before zipping up a row and zinging left, then dropping to the last row of letters and gliding to the second to last.

"Stay?" I whispered as one of the candles crackled. "I am," I promised on a violent twist of my heart. "I promise! I'm not going anywhere this time. I know you're trying to tell me about Grace—"

The pointer zipped in a quick zigzag, up then down, up then down.

"Away," Chase murmured, and my breath jammed.

STAY AWAY

Victoria gasped as Chase shot forward, crowding the board like it was a football he was about to destroy. "From what?" he asked. "A place? A person—*Grace?*"

The pointer moved fast, zinging from the right to the left to the middle.

TRAP

His grip on my hand tightened, punished. "What kind of—"

"No." The word came out amazingly firm. "It has to be me," I reminded, my eyes locked on his. We were touching in every way we could, our fingers, our knees, our hands locked together. But it wasn't enough. "Please. You have to let—"

The slow, steady glide of the pointer, without the prompt of a question, killed my words.

TEN

My finger tensed, as if I could stop what was coming, but the triangle swirled faster, one letter after another.

"Love," Victoria muttered as the letters kept piling up. "Won't."

The votives flickered. My heart slammed hard. I could feel it throb beneath my eyes and at the corner of my mouth as the triangle hovered over the last letter.

Victoria tensed. *"Die."*

LOVE WONT DIE

Something tickled the back of my neck, but my body was no longer my own. I couldn't move, could barely feel. It was all so hazy and far away, disconnected.

"W-what do you m-mean?" The words didn't want to form. "Whose love—"

Chase jerked. "Trinity—"

I ignored the warning in his voice—and his death grip on my hand—even as the cold wouldn't stop bleeding, until there shouldn't have been anywhere else to go.

And yet the chill kept spreading. "Grace's? Mine?"

The crystals glowed.

"T, don't—"

But the movement of the pointer, first left to D, then back to the E, killed *his* words, too.

The triangle kept moving, slowly, methodically.

D E S T

Everything blurred, wouldn't stop blurring, the letters and the crates, Chase and Victoria and the room . . . It zipped in and out of focus as I forced myself to swallow. Forced myself to breathe. Both burned.

I N Y

"Destiny," Victoria murmured as the triangle stopped on the last letter.

The shaking started deep inside me, slowly at first, faster. Jerking. And the pointer shot up to the middle row, up again to the letters above.

M I

My whole body spasmed.

"What the eff—" Chase muttered as the letters kept coming.

N E

"Mine." The strangest sensation swept through me, a vague, relentless current of disjointed energy. "I-I don't un-n-nder-tand—"

Vaguely I was aware of Victoria's scream—and Chase twisting toward me. But the room started to dissolve. Like raindrops, sliding down glass. But none of that mattered. None of it felt real, only like . . . a dream.

"W-w-w . . ." My tongue thickened against my mouth. "Wh-at are y-you taw-king . . . abwout?"

Behind me something crashed, and the room started to strobe. I could see my hand shaking, even as the triangle jolted from letter to letter.

TOO LATE

Chase was lunging toward me then, his voice so very, very far away. And he let go. He let go of my hand, and grabbed me by the arm. "Trinity, stop!"

Around me everything crackled.

"Omigod!" Victoria screamed, but I couldn't see her anymore. Couldn't see anything. Only the beautiful warm glow of the board, and the rapidly moving pointer.

DREAMS

"Y-yes." The vibrations made the word echo. "Y-yes—"

Faster, faster, never slowing, never stopping.

NEVER LET

"Go," Victoria murmured.

NEVER LET GO

"I w-w-w-o-o-o . . ." Won't. The word was there, in my mind. My heart. I could think it. I won't. I won't let go.

But I couldn't give it voice. Couldn't give anything voice. Wasn't sure I still had one. Everything was pulsing, twitching—

"Oh, God!"

On some distorted level screaming registered. But it wasn't real. It wasn't happening. There was only the triangle veering along the roman letters.

"Chase—omigod, what's happening to her?"

"Trinity!" He was holding on tighter now, tugging, trying to wrap me up . . . "Say good-bye—say good-bye *now*!"

The shadows slipped closer, swallowing—consuming. I tried to fight them, to fight the disjointedness of my own body. But the cold paralyzed me—and a new word formed.

FOREVER

Everything stopped. The buzz fell silent. The candles went dark. Only breath remained—slow, hypnotic. Mine. Chase's. Victoria's.

And the room's, cold—vacant.

"Don't go," I whispered, and this time the words came clearly. With a strange tingling in my hands and feet, my face, I stared at the pale finger remaining against the pointer, and realized it was my own.

"Come back," I whispered. "Mom—"

It took a second to realize Chase had his hands on my face, and every ounce of blood had drained from Victoria's.

"Holy fucking crap," she whispered.

I blinked against the heaviness.

"Trinity." Chase's voice. Quiet. Strong. "Look at me."

Through the haze I did, sifting through shadows that weren't there to find him crouched beside me, his eyes like steel on mine.

"What do you see?" he asked, his voice so phenomenally steady.

I don't know why my eyes flooded. "You," I whispered, moistening my lips. "I see you."

His throat worked. "Say good-bye."

I blinked, lifted my free hand to join the one he had against my face. "I'm not ready . . ."

"You have to," he said again, this time harder, more forceful. "To that stupid board—"

Slowly I turned to the golden glow of what so many people believed was nothing more than harmless fun, and the small pointer resting over the letter R.

FOREVER

"Do you believe in forever?" Victoria had asked me only a few days before.

Now I stared.

"Close the portal," Chase said. His voice was unbearably gentle. "Close it before—"

He didn't finish. He didn't need to. Sometimes words were necessary, and sometimes they weren't. Sometimes there simply were none.

I stared at the board, the vibration now a deceptive hum, the last dying breath of a current. "I-I can't."

"You don't have a choice," he said, and then his finger was there again, side by side with mine. And together we guided the triangular pointer. Victoria joined us as we crossed the U.

Together, we brought the triangle to rest over the word at the lower right corner.

GOODBYE

I sagged like a collapsing balloon, felt the air rush out of me as Chase dragged me into his arms. "Jesus—don't ever do that again."

I sank against him. He was so solid, and so warm, but through the cotton of his T-shirt, I could hear his heart pounding a sprinter's race.

"That didn't happen Saturday," Victoria whispered from somewhere behind me. "I swear to God, Chase, if she'd been doing that I never would have agreed to this."

I pulled back. "What?" I twisted toward Victoria. "What didn't happen?"

Her hair was stringy, tangled, as far from perfect as I'd ever seen. Her eyes were dark voids. "The twitching," she said, looking at me like she was afraid. Of me.

For me.

"Your eyes and mouth—your hands. Your voice wasn't yours. You couldn't talk—"

The fog pressed closer. Only a few minutes had passed, but much like a dream that you awaken from only to realize you no longer remember, I couldn't find the pieces. Only the sensations. "It was like something else was controlling—"

Forceful footsteps killed the rest of my words.

"Shit!" Chase shot to his feet, pulling me with him. Victoria grabbed the Ouija board.

In the hallway, the footsteps stopped outside the door.

Chase tugged me toward the futon. "We've got to get out of here!"

"There's only the one door," I said with more breath than voice. "The windows—"

The doorknob jiggled.

"Omigod!" Victoria whisper-shrieked. "It's too late."

I lunged toward the Oriental screen separating the front of the apartment from the back. Chase and Victoria dove in after me, the three of us yanking the flimsy structure as close to the wall as we could.

And the door fell open.

ELEVEN

A narrow glow cut through Grace's small apartment. Standing as still as death, I could feel the rise and fall of Chase's chest behind me, see Victoria huddled at our feet.

The door closed. Footsteps moved deeper into the small room, light sweeping in a broad arc. And in that one horrible second, I realized our mistake.

The screen was little more than a flimsy silk curtain.

Daylight made it opaque. Night turned the silver into a pale shadow. But with that same darkness, a beam of light would shine straight through, silhouetting whatever was concealed behind.

The footsteps fell quiet.

My chest tightened. Chase's breath stopped. And the silence started to throb.

I wanted to see. Someone was there. Someone had come into Grace's apartment, had not turned on the light—

Across the room, one of the crates scraped.

Chase slid a finger to my mouth, pulling me closer.

The light swung our direction. We hung there, frozen as it passed along the wall behind us, slow, seeking . . .

The room breathed.

We didn't.

The beam slid along the top of the futon once more, then jerked back to the front and fell to the floor.

I moved fast, tugging Chase's hand as I sank to the floor next to Victoria. He slid next to me, his body crouched like Delphi.

Relief made me dizzy. If the flashlight swung back toward us, the futon would conceal our outlines.

Seconds crawled into minutes. Shuffling interrupted silence. I tried to keep my breath slow, measured, but every beat of my heart jackhammered more violently than the one before.

And I couldn't do it any longer, couldn't sit frozen while a few feet away, someone pawed through Grace's things. There was no time to text LaSalle. By the time he arrived . . .

Mime-like, I shifted toward the edge of the futon. Chase tried to stop me, but I kept stretching. He yanked. I resisted.

And through the small crack between silk and wall, the front window came into view, and the brilliant green of the dragonfly glowed.

I froze.

Chase froze.

Silence thickened into a muted heartbeat. I knew there would be warmth, even before I sucked in the breath.

Grace.

The dragonfly shone brighter, fracturing moonlight into a thousand shards of green, revealing the tall figure in the long black trench coat—and the boots.

Everything flashed. I blinked hard, tried to clear the paralyzing web from my mind and bring myself laser sharp into the moment—and away from the dream.

The boots remained.

Chase tugged at me, tried to draw me back.

The scent of fresh sage almost made me gag. I couldn't move. Even when the trench coat swirled toward us, one heavy black boot coming down with breathless quiet beside the purple love seat. Then the other.

Silver flashed—and I saw the knife.

Chase's hold on me tightened.

Moonlight glinted off the blade—exactly as I'd seen Sunday, when we'd been playing Clue. I stared at it, at the gloved hand curved around the handle, and for a crazy moment, I felt the slice all the way to my bone.

Soundlessly, Chase slipped a hand to my heart, and spread his fingers wide.

The trench coat swished toward the back of the room. Chase braced. I could feel his body lock up, ready to spring forward.

But he had no weapon.

The blade of the knife angled higher . . .

Now it was me holding on, me holding back. I dug my fingers into Chase's arm as the figure shifted, and the ski mask came into view.

The intruder moved fast, boots pounding against the wood floor. The long coat swung around his legs as he crossed—

At the last minute he turned, and with something secured under his arm, yanked open the door and vanished.

I sagged. Chase dragged me back, careful to keep me behind the screen.

His shirt was hot—damp, his heart pounding like he'd been running as fast as he could. "Sh-h-h," he half said, half breathed.

I clung to him, and in the silence, the darkness, started to count.

At five hundred and twenty-nine, he pushed to his feet and reached for me. "He's gone."

Victoria's sob said it all. She scrambled up and brought her hands to her face, sliding sticky hair back from both sides. "Omigod—omigod, *omigod* . . ."

But I just kneeled there, staring.

"Trinity?" Chase came back down. "Come on—we gotta go."

Trancelike, I looked up at him. I was still trying to understand. "Those boots," I murmured. "I know those boots."

His eyes went a little wild. "What do you mean you know those boots?"

"I've seen them before." Twice. "Yesterday, when I was here with LaSalle."

"He was wearing them?"

"No," I said. "No." Then I made myself stand and slipped the flashlight from my pocket. Clicking it on, I directed it toward the crates with Grace's clothes. "I was standing there, and I saw them by the sofa." For just a flash. A second. Then they were gone.

"Maybe they're her boyfriend's or something." The sheen in Victoria's eyes told me the shock was starting to fade.

"No," I said. "They weren't there."

"But I thought you said—"

"It was a premonition," Chase murmured, stepping back.

My heart kinda stopped. And I hated the quick little fissure that went through me. I had no idea what the Ouija board was trying to tell me—or exactly where the warnings were coming from, but lines were starting to turn the dots into a picture.

Or a maze.

A trap, just like the Ouija board had spelled.

Being afraid wasn't going to help.

"I saw them last night, too," I said, rubbing my hands along my arms. "In a dream."

Chase's jaw tightened.

I moved past him, toward the front of the room, where beside the love seat a crate lay on its side, the one I'd come to find, the one from my dream—the one that had glowed. Around it, scattered on the floor, lay a lifetime of pictures and letters.

"WTF?" Chase muttered, joining me. "What was he looking for?"

That was the ultimate question.

"What if he's not done?" Victoria gasped from behind us. "I mean, what if he got spooked but comes back—"

Chase took me by the hand and yanked me toward the door. "Come on. She's right."

I didn't want to go. Someone was trying to tell me something, to warn me. The pieces were all there: the boots and the crate, the Ouija board, the word *trap*.

Forever.

Chase practically dragged me into the hall. We locked up, hurried toward the stairs.

We were halfway down when we saw the man waiting at the bottom.

The thick, shoulder-length dreads threw me.

"Well, well," he drawled, and with the voice came recognition. The cornrows were gone, but the diamond stud in his ear was the same. So was the *you are so busted* glitter in his unmistakably sultry eyes.

He could blend in anywhere, I remembered thinking once. Be anyone.

Even his smile deceived. "What a surprise."

Aunt Sara stood by the big window overlooking the glimmer of the city, her boot-cut jeans and charcoal shirt casual, her posture anything but. Her shoulders were stiff, her arms locked around her chest. Dark hair fell softly against her face, framing how firmly pressed her mouth was.

I'd never seen her pulled so deeply inside herself.

She hadn't said a single word. Not since Detective DeMarcus Jackson showed up with me and Chase and Victoria. (By some miracle we'd convinced him to take us to my aunt's, instead of the station.)

Detective LaSalle was already here. I could only imagine what he'd told my aunt. Jackson, his partner, had made it sound really bad. Sitting in the back of his SUV, I'd heard him, the words he used: kids broke in, messing around, caught them red-handed, look guilty as hell, claim someone else was there.

Now LaSalle kept shaking his head, as if he was my father, and I'd totally let him down.

"Why didn't you call me?" he asked. I'd had no choice but to tell him about the ghost town dream—and the Ouija board. "I would have taken you back to Grace's. You didn't need to break the law."

I winced. On the sofa next to me, Chase squeezed my hand.

"I didn't think about it like that." It had seemed harmless, like following clues on a scavenger hunt. "I wasn't even sure the dream meant anything. That's why I went to her apartment, to see if I could put the pieces together. I didn't think anything bad would happen—"

"You didn't think period." With his hands steepled together, he kept tapping them against his mouth. "If you had, you would have realized putting the pieces together is my job, not yours. What if this other person discovered you were there? What if he saw you or came after you—tried to silence you?"

"I would have stopped him," Chase said.

"But that's just it," I said, pulling away. I stood, while on the other side of me, Victoria sat quietly. She'd begged the cops not to call her parents—

Of course, they had.

Mr. and Mrs. Crochet were on their way.

"Don't you see? I was *supposed* to be there. If I hadn't been—or if we'd been there all official with you and the lights on—that guy would never have come in, and we still wouldn't know anything."

"And what do you think we know now?" Detective Jackson asked. Like last fall, he stood off to the side, watching. Just watching. That was what he did. "What have you learned that we didn't know before?"

"Boots," I said. "I saw boots."

"Boots?" he repeated.

I nodded, my gaze slipping to his expensive-looking loafers. Combined with his silky purple shirt and pressed black pants, I was pretty sure the call he'd received from Grace's downstairs neighbor, reporting footsteps above, had interrupted something a lot more enjoyable.

"Cowboylike," I said. "Black, a little scuffed."

"You have any idea how many black cowboy boots there are in this city?"

I sighed. "It's a start."

"Why didn't you mention the Ouija board?" Detective LaSalle took over, as I'd known he would, sooner or later.

Across the room, if it was even possible, Aunt Sara went even more statuelike. There was something in her eyes, though, a dark, vacant glow that told me she was acutely aware of what was being said.

"Like maybe Sunday night?" LaSalle said. "When I first asked you about Grace?"

I stared at my aunt, really wished she'd look back. *"I'm sorry,"* I whispered. This was not the outcome I'd envisioned. "I didn't know what was going on. I'd thought it was just some freaky game," I said. "That my subconscious made the pointer move."

Aunt Sara closed her eyes.

"And now?" LaSalle's voice was suddenly gentle.

I looked back at Chase. This time he'd been there. He'd seen. The residue lingered in the way he looked at me, the way he'd held my hand on the way back to the condo, but never quite looked me in the eye.

"I think," I said very slowly, "there's more to it."

Detectives LaSalle and Jackson exchanged a quick, unreadable look.

"Let's go back to the beginning," LaSalle said, picking up a small notebook. "To Saturday night. I want to know everything."

Realizing I no longer had a choice, I looked to the bar, where a small, framed picture sat, of me and my aunt taken the day Fleurish! opened, and told them everything. I even showed them the picture I'd found of my mother.

"I think she must have known her," I said, handing the faded photograph to Detective Jackson. "Maybe our moms were friends or something. Maybe they both worked in the Quarter." It made sense. Psychic abilities often ran in families.

Detective Jackson looked up from the image. It was wild how different the dreads made him look. They were thick and gnarled, hanging past his shoulders and gathered into a low ponytail, making him look more like a hot musician than a cop.

"Maybe Grace and I were even friends." I rushed to fill the silence, except the second I said the words, I knew how silly they were. I'd been two the last time I lived in New Orleans. "Or maybe last fall

she realized who I was. Maybe she knew about my mother and assumed I could see things, too. I think that's why she scribbled my
name." As a clue. "She's reaching out to me."

"Sounds like you've got this all figured out," Detective Jackson
drawled.

When Jessica had gone missing, he'd been the skeptic. He'd
doubted me far longer than Detective LaSalle had.

Obviously he still did. "I'm *trying*."

We wound down from there. Victoria's father arrived, exchanging
a few quick words with Jackson before putting a hand to Victoria's
back and steering her to the door. She glanced back before leaving,
and the quick stab of guilt made me blurt out, "I'm sorry!"

Detective Jackson left a few minutes later, leaving me alone with
Chase and Aunt Sara, and LaSalle. The four of us had been alone in
the condo so many times before. We'd had dinner and played poker,
even strung necklaces. It had always been lighthearted, even if I
sometimes caught LaSalle watching me, as if he knew, *just knew,* I
was hiding something. That was the cop in him, the job he was
trained to do. I didn't like it, but I tried to understand.

He walked across the room now, to where my aunt still stood.
Somewhere along the line she'd turned to stare at the night.

"Hey." He put a hand to the curve of her shoulder. "You okay?"
She stiffened.

And I knew what I had to do. On a deep breath I started toward
her. "Aunt Sara—"

She twisted toward me. "I can't talk to you right now." Then
before I could even process what was happening, she was across the
room and grabbing her purse.

"Sara—" Detective LaSalle called, but she turned the dead bolt,
opened the door, and walked out.

The clock slipped past ten. I kept glancing from it to the door, but
while the second hand ticked from number to number, the knob
never turned.

"You know she's coming back," Chase said, turning me to face him. We still sat on the sofa. He'd flipped on the TV, but neither of us were paying attention. "Give her time."

I knew that. She had to come back. She lived here.

But I had no idea what would happen when she did. "I've never seen her all closed up like that, like she didn't even want to look at me."

"She's scared," he said, feathering his finger along my cheekbone. "She knows what could have happened tonight."

I looked up. "Nothing happened—"

"Don't." Just one word, that's all it was, but the force behind it, the naked emotion, obliterated whatever I'd been about to say.

"I was there," he said. "I saw what went down."

The blue, blue of his eyes quickened through me—maybe that's why I tried to pull away.

But his hold tightened. "It was like that old house all over again," he said. "But worse. Amber nailed it yesterday—you didn't even look alive."

"Chase—"

"You didn't *feel* alive, either," he said. "You were like ice."

I tried to remember. I tried to go back to those bizarre moments when the pointer had spelled out word after word, and I'd started to twitch.

"It was like it wasn't you anymore," he said. "Almost like someone else—" The glow in his eyes went dark. *"Someone else,"* he repeated, his voice eerily quiet. "Someone else was there."

Everything inside me stilled. "What? What are you talking about?"

"The board," he said, and I could tell he was living it again, every second, every breath. "Right after it spelled out *love won't die*—everything changed."

I looked away, found Delphi watching me through those unblinking eyes of hers. And I wanted to ask her *What?* What did she know?

Because I knew that she did.

"The temperature dropped," Chase said. "And the triangle started jerking instead of gliding—"

I twisted back toward him. "Too late," I whispered.

The pointer had spelled out *too late*.

God, what had we done?

He pulled me back to him. I held on, held on tight, tried to concentrate on the rhythm of his heart. But it wasn't steady. It was frenetic—just like the pointer had been when it spelled out *never let go*.

"You have to stop," he said, easing back so that his eyes burned into mine. His hands found my face, sliding the hair back, exposing me in every way imaginable. "You've done enough. You don't even know Grace. Let the cops—"

"Did you talk to Jessica?" The question shot out of me. One second I'd been thinking about Grace, and the dream, and the Ouija board, and in the next I saw Jessica alone in that small dark room, hunched on the floor, rocking.

She was the missing piece. She was the only one who could tell me what, exactly, it meant to be on the other side of my dreams.

His long bangs were falling into his eyes, but Chase made no move to push them back. "She texted me this afternoon."

She texted him every afternoon. And every evening, every night . . .

"Did you ask her?" I said, sliding my hand to squeeze his. "Did you ask if she'd talk to me?"

TWELVE

Chase pulled back.

"*Trinity,*" he said, and before he said anything else, I knew what was coming. "I don't think that's a good idea."

"Chase, *please.*" I kept my eyes on his, using them to communicate how important this was. "I know you're trying to protect her, but I have to know. I have to know if she consciously reached out to me. I have to know if she could feel me——"

"No, you don't." He stood so fast I never saw him move. One second he was there with me, the next he was gone. "You can't ask her to go back like that, to live it again."

I just stared at him. My throat burned. My heart hurt. "What if it's the only way for me to go forward?" I asked quietly. And then I did what I should have done all those months before, when he'd pulled away, and instead of going after him, I'd let him go.

I stood, and went to him. "What if it's the only way for *us* to go forward?"

His eyes flashed. The line of his jaw went really tight. Those were the only warnings I got. He pulled me to him, crushing me against him and tangling his hands in my hair, his mouth slanting against mine in a mindless rush that made my knees wobble.

It was a long moment before he pulled back to frame my face with his hands. I concentrated on that, the warmth of his palms, the strength of his fingers. Then the blue of his eyes found mine, and I couldn't breathe.

"Trust me." His thumb skimmed my bottom lip. "What happens with us has nothing to do with what happens with her."

But the screaming inside wouldn't stop. "Chase—"

"You have to step back," he said. "Before it's too late."

"What if I can't?"

He tensed.

I curled my fingers into the soft cotton of his shirt. "Don't you think I'm scared, too?" I hated how hard the words were to say. "I *know* what you saw," I said. "I know how freaky it was."

My grandmother had warned me people wouldn't understand, that they'd be afraid. That they'd walk away.

But I was coming to realize that holding everything in could be just as devastating as putting it out there, and trusting.

"And I'm so scared," I said, "that when you look at me, you won't see my hair or my eyes, you won't see *me*. That you'll see *that*—"

His eyes went dark as he pulled me against him and tilted my mouth to his. There was nothing slow or gentle about the kiss, nothing tender or tentative. It was all fire and urgency, a volatility I'd never felt from him. I kissed him back, wishing we could be like that forever—

Forever.

The word jarred me, took me back to Victoria's words from Saturday night.

"Flowers die. Trees die. People die. Love dies . . ."

I pushed that aside, refused to dwell on what came before, or what came after. Aunt Sara was right.

The moment you were in was all that mattered.

I run. Tangled vines swirl along the ground like snakes, trying to stop me. But I won't let them, can't let them. Can't let anything stop me.

"Come back!" I shout, but the figure ahead vanishes behind a tree.

Sprinting, I hurdle a fallen trunk, my foot twisting on something unseen. I stagger, falling forward as moonlight glints off the silver blade . . .

I came awake hard, fighting to breathe as the green of Delphi's eyes glowed. I tried to remember. I tried to go back, needed to see . . .

Grace had been there. At first. And the fading buildings. They'd been there, lining both sides of the empty street. The toppled planters.

But there'd been more.

Swallowing, I closed my eyes and concentrated. Running. I'd been running—

The breath lodged in my throat.

Not running—I'd been chasing. There'd been someone ahead of me—*they'd* been running. I'd been in pursuit.

I opened my eyes, looked at my hand.

I could feel it there, could feel it still, the knife, the overwhelming surge of adrenaline. The hot kiss of . . . *anticipation.*

Sickly, I became aware of other things, like Delphi's unblinking eyes, her ears flat back, my jeans still on my body.

And memory started to return.

We'd been on the sofa. Chase had been holding me. I'd felt . . . safe. I must have fallen asleep.

Shifting, I swung toward the grandfather clock—but found the small digital on my nightstand. The green numbers glowed 5:21.

I had no memory of Chase leaving.

"So your aunt didn't say anything?" Victoria asked as we got out of her car and made our way toward the angel at the entrance to Enduring Grace, with her arms outstretched in welcome.

Or surrender.

"She was asleep." After showering and getting dressed, I'd quietly opened the door to Aunt Sara's room and found her still in bed.

I had no idea when she'd come home.

"Maybe she's going to let it blow over—"

Victoria's words broke off so abruptly I twisted toward her, only to find her peeking around one of the gigantic oaks. "What are you doing?"

She flashed me a nervous smile. "Making sure I don't see Lucas."

Rolling my eyes, I turned back to the fountain—and felt my heart thud hard against my chest. Chase stood there, with the white shirt stretched across his chest and the dark blue of his pants making his thighs look more muscular.

"We had it out last night," Victoria said. "After I got home. He was pissed that I'd gone somewhere with you and Chase without telling him—can you believe that?"

Actually, I could.

"I don't see him," I said as Chase started toward me.

"He actually *forbid* me from hanging out with you again."

I swung back toward her. "Forbid?"

Her eyeliner was darker than usual, her eye shadow even smokier. "Forbid," she repeated.

And all I could think was . . . please. Please let this be it for them. "What'd you say?"

Her shoulders went gymnast-square. "I told him forever just ended," she huffed out, then, as Chase came up beside me, she slipped from behind the tree and took off toward the buildings. "Wish me luck."

"Luck!" I said, because she was totally going to need it.

"Hey."

My heart gave a familiar little kick. "Hey."

He didn't step toward me. "You . . . okay?"

I watched him, didn't understand how closed up he looked. "I'm good."

"Good." Then his eyes found mine, and even before he spoke, everything else fell away. "I talked to Jessica."

The sprawling house sat back from the street, all stucco and red roof tiles, a series of strategically placed courtyards as inviting as they were secretive. With its dark wood trim and arched windows, the series of balconies protected by wrought iron, the place could have been lifted straight from Spain.

I'm not sure why that surprised me.

At the heavy door, Jessica's younger sister answered. Four months had passed since I'd last seen her. That morning, in the hospital waiting room, Bethany had been pale and robotic, shell-shocked.

Now, with long, side-swept bangs and hair that skimmed her shoulders, she glowed as she looked up at Chase.

That, at least, hadn't changed.

"Hey," she said.

His eyes crinkled. He drew her in for a quick brotherly hug, much as I'd seen him do the fall before, when Bethany had still attended Enduring Grace. While Jessica recovered, the Morgenthals had hired a private tutor so Bethany didn't have to face daily questions and whispers.

"It's good to see you," I said as they pulled apart.

She glanced at me, and I could see the veil of caution slide back over her. "Trinity."

We'd never been friends, but there'd been nothing bad there, either. I'd always felt kind of sorry for her, and I'd always thought she was a little embarrassed by her sister's stunts.

Bethany, as Victoria had once said, was the anti-Jessica.

"She's upstairs," she said, widening the door so we could step inside.

The house, with its strong Spanish influence, was beautiful. Arched doorways branched off in three directions, revealing a series of rooms with gold walls and slate floors and bold dark furniture. Pillar candles and votives and ornate picture frames covered almost every surface.

"She's quiet today," Bethany said as I turned to find her sweeping the hair from her face as she exchanged a worried look with Chase. And while there was no way Jessica could have heard her—the music from what sounded like a cartoon was way too loud—Bethany more whispered than talked. "She was really up this morning, but for the past hour she's hardly said a word."

He glanced up the stairs. "You sure she's up to this?"

Bethany lifted a shoulder, let it drop. "IDK."

I'm not sure what I'd been expecting, but the swirl of anticipation reminded me of the only time I'd stepped on a roller coaster.

I was so, so close. What Jessica had to say could change *everything*.

Realizing both Bethany and Chase were now barefoot, I toed off my Skechers (I was still in my school uniform) and joined them beside a tile-top table with a huge crystal vase of white lilies.

"I really appreciate this," I said, mostly to Bethany. "I promise I won't push her."

"I think it'll be okay." She sounded a lot older than fourteen. Then she turned and started upstairs.

For a moment I hesitated. I'd thought about Jessica a lot since last fall. The night we'd found her something inside me had shifted, and I'm not sure it had ever shifted back. Jessica and I had never been friends. But the second her eyes had lifted to mine, I'd known the Jessica from before, the one who'd vowed to make my life hell, no longer existed.

"You coming?" Chase asked.

"Yeah." I took the three steps separating us, and together we climbed toward the swelling soundtrack I suddenly recognized from Disney's *101 Dalmatians*.

But he did not reach for my hand, and I did not reach for his.

At first I didn't see her. I was too caught up in what was straight in front of me: the built-in shelves crowded with trophies and medals, the artfully placed shadow boxes containing everything from baby shoes to cheerleading outfits. There was a whole collection of them, from teeny tiny to one I recognized from Enduring Grace.

Then I turned toward the back of the room, and forgot to breathe.

The curved sofa was gorgeous, like one you'd find in some funky Beverly Hills mansion belonging to a party-girl heiress. It was posh and dark purple, with tons of fringed throw pillows. She sat dead center, staring straight ahead at the wall-mounted plasma TV. A massively furry white dog stretched out on the other side, using her lap as a pillow.

The dog's eyes warned me not to take another step.

Once I'd thought we looked like twins separated at birth. But now her hair was way darker than I remembered, way darker than mine. And it was wavier, too. Not curly, not frizzy, just thick and wavy falling beyond her shoulders, her side part creating a curved sweep that hid the right side of her face.

Her eyes were dark but somehow soft, riveted on the Dalmatian puppies on the TV behind me. I saw no eyeliner.

Her mouth was a pale shade of pink—but I saw no trace of lipstick or gloss.

I saw no earrings, no necklaces or rings.

I saw no skin, either. Other than her face and hands, everything was covered. She had her legs curled under her, a wool blanket between her and the dog. A faded blue-and-black flannel shirt covered everything else, its sleeves far too long for her arms, its buttons secured all the way to the top.

I'd never seen Jessica secure anything to the top.

The ceiling fan stood motionless. The heater blew. Neither Chase nor I had even worn jackets.

Bethany moved first. She broke from us and crossed to the sofa, plopping down on the other side of the dog and smiling at the TV. "I love this part," she said, burying her hand in white fur.

Jessica didn't move.

Throat tight, I made myself swallow as Chase started toward her. "Hey, stranger," he said, and even though he'd told me, even though I knew he was one of the few people she would talk to, *even though I understood,* talking about it was one thing. Seeing it was another.

At the sofa, he eased down on the other side of her, close, but not touching. "Is it okay if I pet Sebastian?"

Her eyes slanted to his, then lowered to the dog in her lap.

"Of course it's okay," Bethany said, watching carefully. "He loves when you're here."

I tried not to squirm.

Chase moved casually, lifting a hand to ruffle the dog's shaggy face.

Even from across the room, I heard the happy canine sigh—and felt something inside me twist.

"What a good boy," Chase muttered, and I couldn't help but wonder how many times he'd said those same words.

I looked to the wall behind the sofa, where white picture frames hung in an arrangement clearly designed to appear random. There must have been fifty of them, some 4×6, a lot of 5×7s, even a few 8×10s. Some were casual and non-posed, Jessica cheering and Bethany dancing, both girls playing with a miniature version of Sebastian. Others were obviously orchestrated, such as the ones of the girls on podiums with medals hanging around their necks—and the ones of Jessica in gorgeous dresses with perfect hair and perfect makeup, and Chase looking amazing, at too many dances to count.

It was the first time I'd seen pictures of him without the sweep of bangs falling against his forehead.

Quickly I glanced back to the two of them sitting side by side on the sofa. Somewhere along the line the gap between their thighs had vanished.

I'm not sure what made him look up. But he did, giving me a tight smile before turning back to Jessica. "I've got Trinity with me," he said, his voice so very, oddly gentle. "Remember we talked about that?"

I'd never heard him sound like that, as if he were talking to a young child.

Her eyes shifted to mine, and my heart twisted. I knew what she'd been through. I knew what she was *still* going through. She'd been abducted, blindfolded, kept in the dark. She'd been left alone, locked in a filthy room, subjected to hour after hour of silence. She'd been given water and bread and chocolate.

I knew because I'd been there.

Now, she still couldn't sleep with her lights off, just as she couldn't stand the sight or scent of fudge or brownies or anything with cocoa. She hadn't left the house in four months, not even for Christmas mass.

Even her shrink came to her. He was the same one Aunt Sara wanted me to see.

"Hey," I said awkwardly. We'd spoken only once since her ordeal, in the hospital after she'd been rescued. She'd asked for me. She'd reached out and taken my hand, told me thank you.

Then she'd blown my mind.

"You were there," she'd whispered. *"I don't know how . . . but I could . . . feel you."*

At the time, shaken by all that had gone down, I hadn't thought to question further.

Now those unspoken questions drove me.

Making myself move, I crossed to the sofa. Briefly I thought about sitting on the other side of Chase, but he was already between me and Jessica in so many other ways.

The fringed ottoman seemed a better choice. "Thank you for letting me come over."

Lowering her eyes, she stared at Chase's hand against the top of Sebastian's deliriously happy face. Great Pyrenees, I realized. He was a Great Pyrenees, and he was gorgeous. And though I couldn't be sure, I would have bet he weighed more than Jessica. He was definitely bigger.

I had no idea how to start.

"Trinity has a few questions for you," Chase said, taking over. "About last fall."

Jessica closed her eyes.

"Does this have to do with the Ouija board?" Bethany asked as, behind us, the stolen puppies barked. "Amber was telling me—"

"Amber needs to shut up," Chase bit out as I swung toward Jessica's sister.

"Are you dreaming again?" Her eyes, so like her sister's, widened. "Is that why you're here?"

I frowned.

"Omigod," she breathed. "About Jess—"

"No." I shook my head. "No." Realizing I had no choice but to dive in, I looked back to Jessica. Eyes unblinking, she stared at the TV, where the Dalmatian parents raced through the streets of London.

Chase let out a tense breath. I looked at him sitting there, still in his white polo shirt and navy pants, and my heart hurt. He was right there. He was so close. All I had to do was reach out, and I could slide the bangs from his forehead—bangs he'd not had when he and Jessica first started to date. I could reach for his hand, and hold on.

And I wanted to. I wanted to touch him.

But I knew how totally uncool that would be.

"Jessica," I made myself say. "When you were in the hospital, you told me you could feel me." I waited for some kind of response or acknowledgment. Chase shifted toward her. Bethany pressed her lips together.

Jessica did nothing.

"I could feel you, too," I said. "Sometimes when I was asleep, and sometimes when I was awake."

I didn't want to go back, either.

"It was like you were talking to me, begging me to help."

Puppy-rescue music swelled, but Jessica's face, stunningly beautiful without all the makeup from before, remained expressionless.

"And I need to know," I said. "I need to know if you really were trying to reach me."

I saw her stiffen and knew that she'd heard me.

"Dr. Linus says she's blocked most of that," Bethany said. "That it was too much, so her mind just erased it."

My throat tightened. No. It couldn't be gone. I couldn't come this close . . .

"There's another girl in trouble," I blurted out. "I've been dreaming of her—"

Chase's eyes met mine.

"But I don't know," I rushed on, hating the way my voice thinned on the words. "I don't know if she's really trying to tell me something—or if I'm just imagining things."

Jessica looked down, started to rock.

Bethany and Chase exchanged a quick, loaded look. "I think we should go, T," he said. "She's not ready for this."

I'll never know what made me reach out. I probably shouldn't have. I knew that the second I moved. But frustration and disappointment blew through me, and before I could stop myself, I was leaning forward, crossing the gulf, ignoring the stop sign in Chase's eyes, and reaching for Jessica's hand. I took it, held it, and everything else just froze.

The bracelet slipped low on her wrist, a few strands of tightly wrapped leather, three words visible: FAITH, BELIEVE, TOGETHER.

My hand fell away, sliding to the leather at my own wrist as her eyes lifted to mine. They were dark, bottomless, and in them I saw everything, and nothing at all.

"I'm sorry," I said, jerking back and standing, backing away from the sofa, the wall of pictures. *Them.* "I should never have come here." Turning, I hurried to the stairs.

Five words stopped me cold.

"I thought it was you."

THIRTEEN

It took a second to realize the hesitant voice belonged to Jessica.

Trying to breathe, I turned back to find her leaning forward and watching me.

"When I got the note," she said, and her voice was stronger now, edged by the same desperation that glistened in her eyes, "daring me to go back to the house on Prytania."

Everything slowed.

"I thought you were trying to get revenge," she said, sitting a little straighter.

Chase and Bethany still flanked her, but the room shrank to just her, and me, and how it all began.

We'd both had choices. We'd both had the ability to steer events in a different direction. The second we arrived at the abandoned mansion, I'd realized Jessica and Amber were up to something, and I'd known it wasn't going to be good. I could have walked away. I could have aborted *everything*.

The horrible chain of events that unfolded afterward would have stopped before it ever started.

Or would it have?

That question had no answer, because I'd been too wrapped up in the game of chicken—and so had she. She'd seen me as a threat, and she'd wanted to teach me a lesson I wouldn't forget.

I hadn't.

Neither had she.

"That's the only reason I went," she said as the sound of all that crazed dog barking fell quieter, filtering around me as if it came from someplace far, far away. "To prove I wasn't scared of you."

My throat tightened. The backs of my eyes burned. She sat there, she sat there on that sofa, a shell of who she'd once been, but stronger somehow. I didn't get that.

"I never saw him," she said. "I was in the room with the mattresses and the door closed. I ran to it and found it locked, and even though I kept telling myself it was all some stupid joke, I got scared and begged you to come back."

Now it was my turn to close my eyes.

"I don't know how much time went by," she said. "But it was so dark."

I made myself look. Jessica had lived it. The least I could do was keep my eyes open.

"I was sitting in the corner when the door opened—and he came in."

He, of course, was the drug addict who'd been preying on girls in the Quarter. Later, after Jessica was safe and he was dead, Detectives LaSalle and Jackson had found all sorts of mementos, even photographs, in the guy's run-down house in New Orleans East.

"I'm sorry," I said, stepping forward. Because I was. So very, very sorry. Nobody deserved what Jessica had been through.

"And still I kept thinking of you," she whispered as I froze and Chase's eyes went dark. "Over and over, I just kept thinking, *Trinity, please. Trinity, please don't let this happen. Please come get me.*"

It was hard to find my voice. "Why?"

"I don't know." She tilted her face so that the sweep of hair fell away, and a scar came into view. "At first I thought he had you, too, that you were somewhere close. Then I realized that wasn't right— but I still felt like you were close."

I drew my hands to my face, surprised to find my skin like ice. She'd felt me, and I'd felt her.

"Then later," she said, "after he took me to that awful place, I couldn't feel you anymore."

A strange sound broke from my throat.

"So I started trying to find you," she said. "I don't know why. It doesn't make sense. But in my mind, I kept calling for you—*praying* to you."

Me. Not the cops. Not her parents. Not . . . God. *"Why?"*

Her eyes, glittering now, met mine. *"I don't know,"* she said, shaking her head. "It was like I just . . . knew. I knew I needed you."

The room tilted.

Abruptly she stood, the big white dog bolting to his feet beside her. Nothing prepared me for her to walk away from Chase and cross to me, to take my hands from my face and close them in the surprising warmth of hers.

"That other girl," she whispered, her eyes dark and desperate. "If you hear her, if you're dreaming of her—then she needs you, too."

Jessica's words stayed with me long after we said good-bye.

Chase drove me home. Normally he cranked Lynyrd Skynyrd or Aerosmith, but as we pulled away from Jessica's, he switched to Arcade Fire. Neither of us spoke. I don't think we knew what to say.

I'd hoped. I'd hoped she'd be able to fill in some gaps. I'd been so curious to know if my dreams were one-way streets, or two-way. If what I saw, what I heard, was only in my head, something I created, or if it came from somewhere else.

According to Jessica, it came from somewhere else.

Lifting a hand to the dragonfly at my chest, I closed my fingers around the smooth edges and glanced at Chase. He had one hand draped over the wheel, his eyes straight ahead.

I had no idea where he was, and for some reason I didn't understand, didn't want to ask, either.

By the time we reached the Warehouse District and he walked me upstairs, all I wanted was to be alone.

My chest tightened as we stepped inside, until I saw the lights were off and realized Aunt Sara was still at the shop. A quick glance at the grandfather clock showed I still had a few hours before she would be home after closing.

I had no idea what to say to *her,* either.

Dropping my backpack, I turned back as Chase flipped on a light. The second I saw him, the way he was looking at me, I knew something was about to happen. He stepped toward me, coming so close he could have touched me. But he didn't. Instead he watched me as if he was afraid if he blinked, I wouldn't be there anymore. It was crazy how his eyes could literally hold me.

The moment stretched. My mouth went dry. I wasn't sure why. I knew I needed to say something, but the seriousness in his eyes scattered my thoughts. "Chase—" I tried, but he didn't let me finish.

"You saw the bracelet."

I looked away, tried to step back, but he moved faster, reaching out to stop me with a hand to each shoulder. "Don't—it's not what you think."

I made myself look up at him, not sure why it hurt so badly. He and Jessica had been friends forever. She'd been through hell. There was absolutely nothing wrong with him extending a gesture of friendship, especially after what she'd been through.

But . . . *the bracelet.*

"It doesn't matter," I said, trying to smile.

He stepped closer, getting rid of that last little bit of space between us. "Yes, it does."

I swallowed.

"I didn't make it," he said, and the dizzy thrumming of my heart slowed. "I saw it at a store, and she was having a really hard time, and I thought maybe it might help her."

I stilled.

"And then I started thinking about you," he said, and now his voice was quieter. "What words would be right for you."

Mechanically, I glanced down at the band of leather coiled around my wrist.

"Honest," he murmured, lowering his hand to the bracelet. "Strong. Fearless." Slowly his thumb rubbed. "Impulsive."

I looked up. My throat was still tight, but for very different reasons.

"But there were no bracelets like that," he said when our eyes met, "because you're you, and no one else is."

I'm not sure why I wanted to cry. *"So you made it,"* I whispered.

"For you."

Sometimes, like in that moment, the blue of his eyes totally stopped me. There was so much there, not only the honesty of the moment, but the remnants of all that had gone down since we'd met—and long, long before I'd walked into his life. We moved forward, that was true. But the past wasn't like a whiteboard that could be erased. Whatever happened, *happened*. And like invisible baggage, it moved forward with us.

The smile started somewhere inside me—I could literally feel the warmth of it slide through me.

"Thank you," I whispered, as Delphi joined us, weaving between our legs. "Thank you for being *you*."

The blue of his eyes deepened. He looked at me for a long moment before glancing down, to my chest. At the same moment he lifted a hand to my mother's dragonfly, and skimmed his thumb along the crystal in the center.

From one breath to the next, I knew something had changed.

"What?" I asked.

He kept rubbing the crystal.

"What?"

He closed the dragonfly in his hand and lifted his eyes to mine. "She was fearless, too."

Delphi kept weaving, rubbing her pointy face against my legs, but the low buzz only I heard warned me not to move.

"T, I saw you at Jessica's."

And there in the silence, all that talk about leather bands and special words disintegrated into something very different.

"And I saw you last night with that stupid board—it was like you were someone else."

I braced myself, but already it was too late.

"And I know why," he kept on. "Because you want to be like her." His hand opened, and the yellow-green crystal glowed. "And it scares me."

The words were so quiet I almost didn't hear them. I stood there, so completely and totally blown away I had no idea what to say. We'd talked about my mother—we'd talked about both my parents. The fact that neither of us had known those who gave us life was one of the many things that drew us together. But I'd never seen him look like this, and I'd never felt the threadbare wall slowly sliding between us.

"Chase, nothing's going to happen to me—"

"You don't know that," he said, letting the dragonfly fall back to my chest. "You *can't* know that."

The buzz turned to more of a drone. I stepped back, had to step back. Blinked. Tried to understand how things could shift so dramatically from one breath to the next, without even a hint of a warning.

"No one knows what I see," I said, trying to make him understand.

His eyes darkened. "That doesn't mean they don't see you."

I blinked.

"Whoever has Grace—what if they're watching? What if they saw you at her apartment with LaSalle? What if they keep watching, if they find out who you are, about how you found Jessica?"

I took a quick step back.

"It's not a big leap to figure out what you're doing," he said. "What you *can* do."

We still stood in the entryway, but the walls pushed in on me, forming a tight little box. Delphi was still there, at my feet. I could feel her, but couldn't look away from Chase. "No one's watching me."

But with the words the band around my chest pulled tighter, and the cold returned, the visceral awareness that someone *was* watching.

"What if they try to stop you?"

No. My mouth formed the word, but no sound came out.

He reached for me, his hand closing around the bracelet at my wrist, his thumb sliding to cover one word: FEARLESS. "Silence you just like your mother—"

I didn't let him finish. *I couldn't.* I went up on my toes and lifted my hands to the sides of his face, bringing my mouth to his. The kiss was supposed to be soft, reassuring, but suddenly I couldn't get close enough.

Wasn't sure I ever could.

"Trust me," I murmured as a guttural sound ripped from somewhere inside him. "Please just trust me."

The blue stone glowed like an ocean lit from within.

Long after Chase left, I sat on my bed with Delphi in my lap and my mother's larimar stone in my palm.

Sometimes called the Atlantis stone, the rare, recently discovered gemstone had been my mother's favorite. It comes only from one location, in a mountainous area of the Dominican Republic near the Caribbean Sea.

My mom had mined this one herself.

I held it, much as she would have, and felt the warmth stream through me. My grandmother had talked about my father, but not my mother. For so long she'd been a big blank in my life. Being here, with her dragonfly at my chest and her larimar in my hand, made me feel like I'd finally gotten her back.

Once Gran read a book about what would happen if you could have someone you loved back for just one more day. What would you say? What would you do?

For me, there were so, so many questions.

"Would you tell me to step back?" I whispered above the gentle rumble of Delphi's purr. "Or that it's my destiny to step forward?"

I was still holding the stone when Aunt Sara got home around ten. Normally if I didn't come out to say hi, she'd come to my room. But her footsteps never came down the hall.

This was the longest we'd gone without talking since I'd come to live with her.

Knowing I should get up and go tell her how sorry I was about the Ouija board, I sunk down in my bed and closed my fingers around the larimar. Delphi rearranged herself, curling up on top of the covers next to me.

I wasn't aware of closing my eyes.

"*Sweet, sweet girl . . .*" The voice was soft, quiet, drifting in from somewhere unseen. "*You break my heart.*"

I became aware of the darkness then, the web pushing down on me, holding me.

"*I would take it all away if I could.*"

I tried to break free, knew I had to wake up. I could feel her, feel her *right* there, the hand at the side of my face, so soft, sliding back a strand of hair, the soft press of her mouth to my forehead.

"*Sleep well, cher.*"

I kept fighting long after the silence started to throb. I needed to go across the hall and tell her—

The feel of her arms closing around me gave me strength. She hadn't gone. She was still there, holding me close to her body—crying.

Reaching, straining, I finally made my eyes open—

—and saw my mother.

FOURTEEN

She was beautiful.

She leaned over me, long, dark hair streaming against me. I could feel it—feel her.

"Mama?"

The sky was so red, only a few gray clouds streaking like shadows across the horizon as a cool breeze blew, and somewhere in the distance, a bird cried.

I squeezed my eyes shut, opened them a heartbeat later, and this time the sky was gone. I was in a room, I realized, a small sterile room with white walls and fluorescent light.

But she was still there, her head bowed as if in prayer.

Slowly she looked up, and I saw her eyes—my eyes. They were wide and dark, drenched with pain and wisdom, an awareness that cut through me. Her lashes were wet. Tears ran down her face.

"Mama . . . why are you crying?"

Her hand found my face, and cradled. "I never wanted to leave you."

My throat closed up. "I know that."

"But I couldn't stop it," she said, and then she was reaching for me, pulling me close. "I had no choice."

I closed my eyes and held on, held on so very, very tightly. She smelled of *vanilla and gardenia, and together like that, body to body, I could feel her heart beating with mine.*

"Mama," I said, pulling back—but the bright brilliant blue of the sky blinded me.

"You're so beautiful," she said, once again touching the side of my face.

I squinted at the sharp pinpricks of light stinging my eyes, and found her standing in front of me, smiling. A warm breeze sent hair whipping into both of our faces.

Neither of us brushed it back.

"I'm so proud of you," she said, and then the tears were there again, glistening like raw diamonds. "You've got such a great future ahead of you."

Happiness swelled from deep within me. I smiled and stepped into her, hugged her tight.

When we pulled back, I noticed the gown fluttering around my legs— and the cap in my hand.

"He's waiting," she said, and from one breath to the next, my eyes met hers, and awareness flowed.

I wanted to turn. I wanted to run. I wanted to run without stopping, not until I reached him and his arms locked around me. Until I held on, held on as tightly as I could—forever.

Instead I hesitated. "I don't deserve him," I whispered.

Her hands found my face again, her touch devastatingly soft. "Yes, you do."

"I hurt him—"

"He loves you," she said in that voice of hers, the soft, gentle one that touched me in so many fragile places. "He's always loved you."

I wanted to believe her. I wanted so very much to believe her.

Taking a deep breath, I lifted my hands to hers and squeezed, then turned and—

The first light of dawn whispered through the window. *"No."* Squeezing my eyes shut, I tried to go back. "Not yet," I whispered. *"Please."* I wasn't ready. I didn't want it to end.

I hadn't felt his arms.

"I want to go back," I said into the silence as Delphi rubbed her face to mine. *"Please, please, please let me go back."* I could still feel it, all of it, the warmth and the happiness, the awareness that forever was real, and it was beautiful.

But I didn't know how to go back.

Slowly I opened my eyes to find Delphi watching me, the embers of something amazing burning through me—and the smooth blue larimar glowing like a forgotten sea in the palm of my hand.

"I've been wondering when you would ask," Julian Delacroix said that afternoon, after I filled him in on everything that had happened since Saturday night, including the Ouija board, and my dreams.

"Then, why didn't you say anything?" I'd spent my first few classes debating whether I should go see him—and the last few counting down the minutes until I could. "If you knew I had questions . . ."

"You weren't ready."

"And now?"

Dressed in black as he always was, he leaned against an antique armoire filled with glittering geodes in all colors and sizes. Between us, votives flickered, and crystals glowed. "The questions you're asking suggest that you are."

I glanced at Victoria, who'd insisted on coming with me to Horizons the second I told her what I was doing. Chase was supposed to be here, too.

But wasn't.

"It's a mystery as old as time," Julian said as Victoria nudged me and widened her eyes. "Where do we go when we sleep? What happens? What does it mean?"

Inside me everything quickened. "That's what I need to know."

"Dreams are as natural as breathing," he said, picking up a long amethyst and lifting it toward a black light. "But not everyone remembers. Fewer understand."

With dark, shoulder-length hair pulled behind his neck and wide cheekbones, deep-set eyes, he looked like he belonged in some big-budget Hollywood action flick, where by day he did something benign like . . . run a New Age shop, and by night he mowed down terrorists. There was an energy to him, a perpetual awareness as if he knew my every secret just by looking at me.

"We live most of our lives in a trancelike state," he said, replacing the crystal among the others and moving toward a display of essential oils. "Most people never fully experience the reality of each moment. We dwell on what is already done and worry about what may never happen. It's rare that we take in all that's present at any given moment."

That was something I was working on.

"Think of it as static," he said. "A bad cell signal. As long as there's interference, you're not going to see."

"So, like, when we wake up from a dream," Victoria said, "but don't remember anything, it's like a dropped call?"

Julian smiled—this time it was indulgent. "In a way."

Her eyes sparkled. "Cool."

Dreams as cell signals. I'd never thought of it like that. "So how do I keep the calls from dropping? How do I call back?"

Julian removed a cork from a vial of dark glass and lifted it to his face. "You try harder," he said. "You realize that your body is just a vessel, or shell. A vehicle. You are what's inside." Eyes on mine, he stepped toward me. "And when you go to sleep, you leave the shell behind."

"What does that have to do with cell phones?" Victoria asked.

Julian crossed to us, offering the vial.

I took it and inhaled, inhaled again, would have sworn I'd smelled the scent before. "Cinnamon," I murmured.

"And lemongrass," he said. "With a little bay leaf."

Victoria leaned in for a whiff, and frowned. "Ewww."

"So where do we go?" I asked, lifting the vial to my face again, "if we leave our bodies behind?"

"Not if," Julian said. "When."

Victoria wandered off, toward a display of Mardi Gras–themed voodoo dolls. The vendor had come in to Fleurish!, too, but Aunt Sara had refused to even look at them.

"It's called the astral plane," Julian said, and the strangest gleam came into his eyes. "It's a different dimension, a higher dimension where physical bodies aren't necessary. It's where we go every night when we sleep—and when we die."

I felt myself go very, very still.

"It's where our dreams come from," he said. "And, I think, your visions."

A lifetime of images flickered through me, dreams and visions, of my dog Sunshine and my grandmother, my parents in a field of waving green, Jessica and the dirty room, of darkness and water, the sensation of falling, drowning. Of strong arms closing around me and dragging me back, of screaming and shouting . . .

"While we dream," he explained, "messages are sent from our psyche in the astral, here, to our physical body."

Answers. All I'd had to do was walk across the street.

"You and your friend Grace. You can't speak here, in this dimension. You're separated. But in the astral, if you're there at the same time, communication is possible."

"That's wild," I whispered.

"And yet," he said very, very quietly, "you know what I say is true, because you have experienced it."

I closed my eyes, and breathed again of lemongrass and cinnamon.

I had. I'd experienced what he described so many times, and not just with Grace, either.

"Wherever your friend is," he said, "she knows how to find you. How to reach you. She knows it's her only chance."

I opened my eyes, and felt something fast and sharp rush through me. "So you think it's possible that's she's trying to communicate with me—through the Ouija board, and my dreams?"

"Grace, or someone else."

"Like my mother?" I asked. "I . . . dreamed of her last night— that she was at my high school graduation, hugging me."

His eyes narrowed. "Have you been thinking about her?"

That was easy. "All the time."

"Then maybe she's trying to tell you that even if you can't see her, she's still with you," he said. "Or maybe it was just a dream."

But from his voice, the look in his eyes, I could tell he didn't think so.

"Jessica said she could feel Trinity," Victoria said. With hair falling like pale silk against her face, she jabbed a needle between the legs of a voodoo doll—and grinned. *"Take that,"* she murmured. Then: "She said she felt like you were there, right, Trinity? That she . . . *prayed* to you?"

Even now, twenty-four hours later, the word bothered me. No one should be praying to me.

"She was receiving messages from the astral," Julian said, looking out the window, toward my aunt's shop. "She could have encountered you there, and fixated on you—or maybe some spiritual being was projecting to her."

"Like a movie?" Victoria asked.

Julian turned back toward us. "It happens every night. But most people are too distracted by the illusions of their own lives, their dramas, to hear or see what's being shared. If you can't get rid of the interference, you can't hear."

"Wicked," she muttered.

"What intrigues me are the buildings." He moved to flip the sign on the door to CLOSED. "Long hallways with doors is a classic subconscious structure, but it's not as common in dreams." He turned back toward me. "That's where we need to start."

My heart kicked.

"And the dragonfly," he murmured more to himself. "It could be a symbol, or maybe an image placed by someone for you to see, to communicate something."

"Like the boots?" Victoria asked.

Julian smiled at her before shifting his attention to me. "Or maybe you were actually seeing the night in Grace's apartment. Events happen in the astral before they reach us here."

It was a lot to process. "So . . . if I see things there, before they happen here, there's time to change them, right? Like I did with Chase?"

Now it was Julian who stilled. "How do you know you changed something? How do you know you weren't always supposed to get there just in time?"

I opened my mouth, clamped it back shut.

"So tell me," he said, watching me very closely. "Do you want to try?"

My breath caught. *"Try?"*

"To return to your dreams," he said. "To look around and see what else there is?"

The hum started low but spread fast, vibrating out through my arms and legs. Yes. Yes! "But Aunt Sara said—"

"You're safe with me," Julian said. "Far safer than if you start experimenting without me."

Slowly I looked from him to the window, where across the street, the FLEURISH! sign glowed. Aunt Sara had taken the afternoon off, to pack for her trip.

"I don't know, Trin," Victoria said, and when I turned to her, she looked more than a little spooked. "After what happened with the Ouija board, maybe you should, like, sleep on it or something."

I shook my head. "No, but . . . can we wait for Chase?"

Julian frowned. "I have another appointment in an hour. We can try again tomorrow—"

"No, no." Too much could happen between now and then. "I want to try."

"Good." With one last look at Fleurish!, Julian turned toward the back of his shop, motioning for us to come, too. We followed him through a series of doors with multiple locks, to a narrow staircase.

The second floor.

FIFTEEN

I'd always wondered.

There'd been so many stories about flashing lights and screams in the middle of the night, limousines pulling up after midnight, even an account of someone running from Horizons wearing only a white gown.

But none of that, not the rumors or my imagination, prepared me for what was behind the closed door at the end of the narrow hall.

Everywhere I looked, white glowed. White walls, white floors, white ceiling. A white shade pulled over the window, bracketed by white curtains. White candles with white light. White crystals. White robes hanging from white hooks.

And in the middle of the room, centered beneath a low-hanging white light, a white cot.

"Make yourself comfortable," Julian said to me and Victoria as he crossed to a tall armoire. White, of course. His black pants and shirt created a stark contrast. "That's key."

Breathe. That's all I could think about. Breathe in, breathe out. Slow, steady.

But I was so ready to get started.

"What we're going to do is very simple," he said, rolling a

gleaming silver cart from inside the cabinet with no shelves. On it, silver instruments glimmered. "You'll close your eyes and drift off, leaving your body behind."

Victoria grabbed my hand—her skin was like ice. "Trinity—"

"How, exactly, does that work?" I asked.

He pulled a small white box from somewhere unseen and set it next to a gauge. "A lot like hypnosis."

"That doesn't sound so bad," I whispered to Victoria, but, secretly, my heart raced.

"Well . . . like, what if she gets lost or something?" Victoria asked. "What if she can't get back into her body?"

Julian's smile was oddly gentle. "It doesn't work like that, Victoria. Trinity won't get lost."

Still holding my hand, she made a funny face. "But . . . could anyone else get into her body while she's gone?"

"No," Julian said. "That's not likely."

I jumped on that. "Not likely? What does *that* mean?"

"Theoretically, it is possible. But nothing you need to worry about. It's very rare."

Victoria didn't look so sure. "What about bad dreams?" she surprised me by asking. "Could she slip into one of those instead of the ghost town?"

"She'll go where she needs to go." Julian's voice was matter-of-fact. "Bad dreams are typically nothing more than manifestations of stress or fear, anger . . . violence even. We live in a world where we are so bombarded by negative energy, we come to crave the adrenaline rush, even in our dreams. Just think of how popular fairground rides are—"

"I've dreamed of a roller coaster," I whispered, and he smiled. It had been huge and wooden, hulking sinisterly against a bloodred sky.

"Then maybe you will again today—if that's where the message is."

I stared at the cart, the cords and monitors and syringes lined in neat little rows.

"Are you ready?"

Slowly I looked up, and nodded.

"Excellent," he said, gliding the cart to me. Then he extended his hand. "Follow me."

I put my palm to his, and felt the warmth seep deep, deep within me. He urged me to follow him toward the cot, and I did.

But we walked right past it.

"I'm afraid you'll need to wait here," he said when Victoria started to follow.

I twisted toward her, and saw how big her eyes were—and how dark. "It's okay," I said. "Really."

And then Julian was lifting his hand to the side of the armoire, and the huge piece of furniture glided to the left, revealing a secret room on the other side. Still white, but smaller. More intimate.

Here music drifted, soft, transcendent. And here the scent of vanilla and lavender flirted with the trickle of a tabletop fountain.

"Make yourself comfortable," he instructed, gesturing toward a heavily cushioned sofa.

Somewhere in the back of my mind the bizarreness of it all registered, but I could no more have turned back than I could live without breathing.

"Drink this," he said as I approached, handing me a cup of what looked like tea, and for a fraction of a second, I was back in Dylan's—

Bed.

I pushed aside that thought the second it formed. I knew better than going back to that night, even the mere memory. Finally, after all these months, what had gone down between us no longer seemed real.

"It's chamomile," Julian said before I could ask. "It'll help you relax."

I sunk against the sofa, wrapping my hands against the warm mug. Then, slowly, I sipped just as Dylan had—

Not Dylan, I corrected, tugging my thoughts back to the moment. Julian. I sipped as *Julian* instructed.

"Try to relax." He was across the room now, at a switch I'd not noticed before, dimming the overhead light until only the glimmer of the candles remained.

"What's going to happen?" I asked.

"I'm going to ask you some questions, guide you to the place you told me about."

"Then I'm going to look around—and explore?"

Just the thought had my heart beating really fast.

"Exactly." Back by the sofa, he kneeled to secure a white cuff around my upper arm. "Just remember that in the astral, the laws that govern here no longer apply. You can fly or walk through walls, objects."

Like I'd done before.

"As a precaution, I'll be monitoring your vitals while you're gone."

Gone? Vitals?

"If anything veers out of normal ranges I'll bring you back."

I blinked at him. Already my eyes felt heavy, my tongue thick. "Why . . . What do you mean? It's only a dream, right?"

His expression tightened—I had no idea if it was a smile, or a frown. "There's no such thing as only a dream, Trinity. What we experience there is as real as what's happening right now."

The room shifted. It was slight, subtle, like a flash of vertigo, over the second I realized it had happened.

"If your mind experiences fear, your body experiences fear," he murmured soothingly. "If you run, your heart rate accelerates."

I tried to hold my eyes open.

"Don't be afraid." He took my hand and squeezed. "I'm here and I'm not going anywhere."

Chase, I thought again, but the thought dissolved as quickly as it formed.

"Relax," Julian said, and really, my body couldn't have done anything but.

"It's completely natural," he went on in that same singsong cadence Victoria used with the Ouija board. "Think of it as going home."

The room started to fade. "Going . . . *home?*"

"Home," he murmured. "Where we all began. It is this world we come into with birth, the physical world. And it is this world we eventually leave, with death—" he said as I tried to quiet the hum interfering with words. "And every night before then, behind closed eyes.

"It makes you wonder, doesn't it?" he asked. "What is real—and what's imagined? The place where we come from, where we return? Or is it the here, the now?"

My eyes fluttered.

"Which is permanent?" he went on, softer. "And which is only a field trip?

"Now count for me," he murmured. "Backward from ten."

The rhythm of my body slowed. "Ten." The word was mostly a breath. "Nine. Eight." With each number I hesitated, waiting for something to happen. "Seven. Six . . ." And with each successive step backward, disappointment rubbed a little harder.

"Five." I opened my eyes to ask him why it wasn't working—but found a street before me, and the faded pastel buildings.

I spun around, found I could move easily now. There was no more heaviness. No more restraint.

"Tell me what you see."

Julian's voice. It was Julian's voice I heard, even though I no longer saw him—or felt his hand on mine.

"It's not raining." That was the first thing I noticed. "The sky is blue, with big white clouds." Floating . . . drifting. "And the sun, it's so bright . . ."

"Good, very good. Tell me what else you see."

Weeds sprang up from cracks. "It's empty." Except for the broken urns lying on their sides. "Like a ghost town."

"The same as before? With buildings on both sides? Doors closed?"

"Yes."

"Then go find her, Trinity. Find Grace."

"I don't know how—"

"Yes, you do."

Swallowing, I looked away from the sky—and gasped.

Julian's voice sharpened. "What is it?"

"The dragonfly." Its pale green wings fluttered against the washed-out color of the street.

"Trinity."

I stilled. *"Grace?"*

"Do you see her?" Julian asked.

I shook off his question. *"Grace? Are you here?"*

"You shouldn't have come back."

My heart slammed hard. "Where are you? Tell me where you are!"

"He knows," she said. "You have to be careful—he knows everything."

"Who?"

"He's watching. He's always watching."

"Who?" I asked again. "Just tell me—"

"Hurry," she said. "You have to get out of here—"

Spinning, I see two big, tattered flags flapping violently in the wind. Turning back, the dragonfly is gone. "Grace!"

The breeze swirls harder, churning up an onslaught of dust—and the sky turns gray.

"No, wait!" I shout. "Come back!"

"Trinity." Julian's voice was solid, an anchor. "What's happening?"

"She wants me to leave," I told him, talking to him in one dimension while I searched another. "She says he knows I'm here."

"Who?"

"I don't know."

"Then tell me what you see."

"The buildings," I said. "Old and made of wood." From another era, Victorian maybe. Gingerbread. With porches and shutters. "They look . . . sad." Tired.

"Look inside."

Instinct takes over. I pass structure after structure. One looks like an old general store, another like a saloon, then a bank.

"Talk to me," Julian instructed.

"No!" Grace shouts.

I stop, don't understand the sudden thickness in my throat.

"Trinity."

I don't know what makes me turn. But the second I see the strange tear, a rip almost, right through the fabric of space itself, I start to move.

"Trinity—what's happening?"

The tear isn't sharp or jagged like paper, but soft and smooth—perfect. Beyond, the most amazing light glows.

"Tell me what you're doing," Julian instructed.

Drawn, I lifted a hand to touch a seam that was not there. "I see an opening," I told him. "I'm stepping through—"

"No! Don't—"

On some dimension the urgency in his voice registers, but I don't care, can't care, can't focus on anything but the beautiful pink glow.

"Trinity—"

Behind me something whooshes. I try to spin around, but my body moves differently, not jerking, but sluggish, trancelike.

The buildings are gone. All of them, just . . . gone.

In their place stands a beautiful old white house, except it isn't old anymore, like it should be. It's huge and new and . . . perfect.

"Trinity—answer me!"

Something warm feathers against me. Lifting my face to it, I close my eyes—and see my mother. She's smiling, standing arm in arm with another woman, much older.

The firstborn daughter, of the firstborn daughter, of the firstborn daughter.

My aunt's words sweep in from the past, the future, reminding me I'm all that remains. My mother and her mother, her mother before her, are gone. I am the only one left. The legacy they bestowed upon me, the gift they shared, either lives with me, or it dies.

"Trinity, you have to listen to me. I need you to turn around—and come back."

I open my eyes, and smile. "No."

"Trinity—"

"I have to go inside." Already I'm crossing the soft green grass, toward the columns supporting a wraparound porch.

At the door I take the knob, twist, and step inside.

SIXTEEN

A soft light glows from across the room. A lamp, I realize.

A dragonfly.

Vaguely curious as to where my shoes are, I cross the warm wood of the floor. At the tall dresser I reach for the delicate glass, and stagger from the shock. It jolts through me like an electrical current, buckling my knees and sending me to the floor. "No—"

I absorb the blow with my body, while, cradled in my hands, the blown glass survives.

"Trinity! Tell me what's happening. Where are you?"

I look up, toward where, beyond the window, darkness gapes.

"A room," *I say, taking it all in, the narrow bed against the wall, the bookcase and the rocking chair.* "A child's."

"Is Grace there?"

"No."

"What do you see?"

"Stuffed animals," *I say, pushing to my feet. I turn, don't understand the slow swirl of longing.* "Books and blocks and a blanket, a little phone with a cord."

"Are there any other doors?"

"No," *I say, twisting.* "Just the one I came through—" *My breath catches.*

"What is it?"

"It's closed." I left it open.

Pushing the hair from my eyes, I try to inhale, but cough instead. "It's hot." And from one heartbeat to the next, the air thickens, turns acrid . . .

"Trinity?"

My eyes sting. My throat burns. Swallowing, I gag instead.

"Trinity—"

I reach for the urgent voice, know I have to reach for it. Reach for him. But through the numbing quiet comes a hiss, and the rest of his words crumble.

"Come back!" Coughing, I spin in a circle. "I can't . . . breathe . . ."

The hiss morphs into a crackle, and darkness billows from beneath the door in thick heavy waves. My body no longer wants to move.

Sobs mix with screams. Dazed, I drop to my knees and grab the blanket, drag it to my face. They'll come. They have to. They're here, in the other room. They'll hear. They'll know. They'll come.

She promised she would always keep me safe.

"Trinity!"

The shout fractures the haze, and with a surge of terror, I make myself crawl toward it.

"Trinity! The window! Go to the window!"

"Daddy," I whimper. Or maybe I only pray. Or cry. I don't know, I can't be sure. I only know that I have to get away from the hissing. The floor beneath my hands and knees is hot, like the glowing coal I picked up from a campfire while my daddy shouted for me to stop. I can't drop it, though, like I dropped the coal. And I can't run crying for my mommy. I can only crawl across the floor. In my mind, I can see her, though. In my heart, I beg. "Mama-mama!"

She promised.

"Trinity! Open the window!"

Behind me something crashes, and light explodes. Except it's not the light, because the dragonfly's gone and the color is too bright, too suffocating, and as I twist back, orange flames lick closer.

"Trinnie—now!"

My body sags. I try to breathe, but my throat closes. With my last breath I reach for the edge of the window, and push.

Darkness consumes me. The air is cool and fresh, and I drink of it as *deeply as I can. Blinking, it takes several tries to bring the field into focus, the waving grass dotted by daisies, the soft blue sky and gentle drift of fluffy clouds, and that's when I realize night has gone, leaving rays of yellow to slip from a veneer of white.*

"Trinity! You need to answer me—now!"

Startled, I reach for the voice, know I need to grab onto it, hold it. "Where are you?"

"Where are you?" *he asks, but I don't understand, don't understand how I can hear and not see.*

"In a field," *I say anyway.*

"Are you alone?"

The chains from moments before fall away, and with the breeze I twirl— and see the boy. "No."

"Who's there?"

He runs closer, shaggy dark hair falling against his eyes. His clothes are old, faded cutoffs and a white T-shirt, and in his hands he's holding a garden hose.

"Better run!" *he says, and then I am, I'm twisting from him and running, laughing as I feel him getting closer.*

"Trinity. It's time to come back."

I trip, stumbling. But still I run, through the tall grass and flowers, because still, he follows.

"A promise is a promise," *he calls, and then I'm at the door, the one that had not been there before. And I'm opening it and rushing inside, and the day again falls away.*

Silence whispers. I stand there so very, very still, waiting for my eyes to adjust.

"Trinity? Talk to me."

"I'm here," *I whisper, and then someone else is, too, watching me from across the room. I can't see him, but I know.*

I always know.

"You," *I breathe. Not detail, the darkness won't give me that. But I don't need light or my eyes to see. He's there like he always is, tall, unmoving.*

"Turn around—now. It's time to come back."

But I don't know why I would turn around, not when he's in front of me.

And then he's moving and so am I, and I can feel him even before his arms close around me.

"I'm here," he murmurs as his hands fist in my hair. "I'm always here."

I know that. Even when he's gone, he's there, in my mind. My dreams. "I've missed you," I try to say, but the words are more breath than voice.

He doesn't need them. Because he knows. "I always find you," he says, and even though I can't see, I can feel the softness of his lips against my face. "Always."

"Always," I echo, and then I'm lifting my mouth to his, dying a little with the first kiss, the first shared breath. It's slow and soft, achingly tender.

I can't get close enough. Touch him. It's all I want to do. Touch and feel, hold on, never let go.

"You don't need to be afraid anymore," he promises as I sink into him, loving the remembered feel. It's been so long.

"I'm not." I draw back to drink him in. His eyes. I need to see his eyes, the silver gleam that's always there, the one that burns through me even when he's—

Gone.

My fingers dig into him. "Don't go." I'm not sure why I want to cry. "Please don't go again."

"I'll find you." His voice is lower than before, hoarse. "I always find you."

My eyes fill. And my breath stops.

"Trinity! Jesus Christ—"

"No!" I cry out for him, reach for him. But my hands slip through air. "Come back!" But something strong is dragging me away. "No!"

"Trinity!"

I lunge for him, fighting the arms imprisoning me.

"Breathe, damn it!"

But I couldn't. My body wouldn't let me. My heart didn't want to. Because he was gone, and I—

"You son of a bitch!" someone screamed as I clawed at whatever I could find. "What the hell have you done to her?"

The moment crystallized around me. For a frozen second I hung there, suspended in that mindless place where the world spun around me, but dots didn't connect and lines wouldn't form. Nothing touched. Nothing hurt.

"Easy now." The voice was familiar. "Just take it slow and easy."

Around me the static slowed, the jumble of black and white gradually fusing into shape and form. "No," I whispered as the warmth faded. "No, no . . . not here." But the cold, sterile room kept right on forming.

"Don't rush," came the robotic voice, the one I was supposed to obey, even as I wanted to turn and run back. "Just breathe nice and slow."

With one strong, final blink, I found him crouched beside me, his eyes narrow, the lines of his forehead furrowed. "Julian."

"You're safe now," he murmured, as the pressure of two fingers against the pulse point at my throat slowly registered. "Give yourself a second to adjust."

I blinked harder, tried to understand, to remember. "My dreams," I whispered as the pieces kept shifting, jagged fragments that sliced every time I tried to hold on. "She was—" I grabbed his forearm. "Grace!" She'd warned me to stay away.

Be careful! He sees everything . . .

"Did it work?" I managed through the dryness of my throat. God, I was so thirsty. "Did I find her?"

Julian's expression gentled. "Yes, you talked to her."

"But—"

"The tear led somewhere else."

I sagged back, started to cough. "Cold," I whispered, but then someone else was there, pushing past Julian to the edge of the sofa, reaching for me . . .

"You're here—" I started, but then I lifted my eyes to the blue of his, and the cold bled deeper. *"Chase."*

He breathed my name. "I'm here," he said, pulling me into his arms and holding me, as somewhere inside, I started to cry.

I buried my face against his neck, wanting it all to go away, the confusion and the scrape of loss, wanting only to be back . . .

I didn't know. I didn't know where I wanted to be, only how I wanted to feel. It hovered at the back of my mind, without form or context, just warmth.

Pulling back, I didn't understand the glitter in Chase's eyes. It was scared and worried and . . . so, so sad. He held me, but it was as if that whisper-thin veil again hovered between us.

"Were you dreaming?" he asked.

I looked away, couldn't stop shaking. "I . . . don't know. It's fuzzy." Images drifted, but none of them connected. "It was like the channel kept changing. I heard her, but . . ."

He lifted a hand to the side of my face, returning my eyes to his. "What happened?"

Moments, I realized. Our lives are defined by them. Some bring happiness. Others destroy. For months I'd wondered how I could simply forget about something as fundamental as the night my parents died. Aunt Sara had tried to console me by saying I'd only been two years old.

But I'd known. In my heart, my soul, I'd always known I *should* remember. That night—that moment. The one that etched a stark line in my life, dividing it into before, and after.

"*I remembered.*" The words were threadbare, but I didn't care. I didn't care about the sting at my eyes, either. Only the fact that I hadn't forgotten. "It was there all along."

Against my back, Chase's hands tightened. "What? *What* did you remember?"

"The fire. I was there—"

"*No.*"

The shaken voice stopped me.

"How could you?" my aunt exploded, and then I was moving, twisting around as she closed in on Julian. "I told you to leave her alone! I told you not to mess around—"

"Aunt Sara!" I shot to my feet and reached for her, putting myself between her and a dead-still Julian. "It was *me*," I said. "*I* came to him for help."

"You're a child," she seethed. "He's a grown man."

"I'm not a child—"

"He knows this isn't a game. He knows what can happen. But he did it anyway—"

"Sara." Just her name, that was all Julian Delacroix said. But so much more passed between them, a dare and a challenge, a warning. Something else.

"I'm okay," I rushed to tell her, manufacturing a smile as proof, even as, inside, I shook. It was all fading, second by second, images that had been real and stark and . . . familiar, terrifying, amazing, retreating so that only impressions remained.

But I didn't want my aunt to know how shaken I was.

How confused. "See? Nothing happened."

She stood there so rigid, her body totally closed in on itself. "You don't know that."

"I do," I said. "I'm good—it was just like dreaming."

Her attention shifted behind me. "I swear to God, Julian, if you ever look at my niece again—"

"Stop it!" The edges of my vision blurred. Shaking, I reached for her, tugging her away from our audience toward the opening to the outer room, where Victoria stood with a hand to her mouth.

With a quick shake of my head, she slipped into the hall.

My aunt was one of the most easygoing people I'd ever met. Sure, she had her moments. Cajun ran through her blood. But she was more the steel magnolia type, who could cut you to your knees with a smile while serving lemonade.

Rarely had I seen her lose control.

I'd *never* seen her come unglued.

"Please," I said, and if my voice cracked on the word, that was okay. "Don't be mad. I was just trying to—"

"What? You were just trying to *what,* Trinity?"

Not *cher,* like she usually called me. But my name.

She almost never said my name. "Help. I was trying to help."

"By doing something I explicitly told you not to."

"I'm not a child," I said again, as rationally as I could. I knew she loved me. I knew she worried. We'd been down this road before. But . . . "I'm almost seventeen. You have to trust me. You have to let me fix—"

Her hands came up fast, taking me by the shoulders. "There's nothing to fix."

I knew the way she gripped me was supposed to silence me, but I couldn't stop. She just didn't get it. "But my dreams—"

Her eyes flashed. "*Could get you killed.*

"My God." The words were a whisper—the kind with sharp, stinging edges. "You just don't get it, do you? How am I supposed to get on that plane tomorrow morning when you keep pulling stunts like this? How am I supposed to trust—"

"Aunt Sara, stop." A lifetime of being told what I could and couldn't do boiled through me. "I was just—"

"Disobeying me."

I'd been trying. I'd been trying to hold on, understand. But in that moment, it all snapped. "Well maybe that's because I don't need you to do that," I said through the hurt and frustration. "I don't need you to decide what I can and can't do. It's not like you're my mother—"

The second the words left my mouth, I wanted to yank them back.

She winced, stepping back as if I'd struck her. "No," she murmured. "I'm not."

She turned and walked from the room.

The Quarter didn't care about drizzle or wind or falling temperatures. The Quarter didn't care about time, or consequence. Or inevitability. It was where you went to get lost, and not be found.

I took one street after another, Chase beside me. Not once did he reach for my hand. It was as if he didn't want to let me go, but didn't want to touch me, either.

I had no idea what I wanted.

Hours had passed. I wasn't sure how many. I only knew that the second I'd seen the stricken look on my aunt's face, the second I'd realized how badly I'd hurt her, I'd run after her.

But it had been one second too many.

I'd turned right. She must have turned left. I'd quickly circled back, but not quickly enough. It only took a few steps in the wrong direction to make turning back impossible. Time moved forward. There was no such thing as a perfect do-over.

Maybe I should have gone home. She would be there, if not now then later. Neither of us could hide forever. Sooner or later we would have to talk. But I wasn't ready. I didn't know how to take it back.

"You can't walk forever."

Wrapping my arms around my waist, I glanced toward the Square, where Grace had sat behind her table. The rain was barely more than a mist, but enough to send the artists for shelter. Only a handful of spiritual advisers sat hunched under black umbrellas.

"You're not going to find her here," Chase said.

"*I know.*" But that didn't stop me. Across Decatur, I headed for the river. I don't know why that was important, but as I closed in on the railroad tracks, I realized where I'd been headed all along.

I'd always known someday I had to go back.

There along the brick walkway running the length of the levee, I finally stopped, keeping my arms wrapped around my ribs. Breathe. It was all I wanted. To be in the moment and not look to either side, not worry about what the next breath might hold—or what ghosts might be closing in from the past.

Or the future.

"It just keeps flowing," I said, staring at the water. Day or night, hot or cold, still or chaotic, the muddy current ambled on. Sometimes it was lazy, methodical, the barges moving in slow motion. Other times, eddies sucked at whatever they could find.

I looked downriver, toward the lights of the Crescent Connection, twinkling against a blanket of ebony. It was all so crazy innocent. "No matter what, it just keeps flowing."

Chase reached for me. "You're tired," he said with the oddest undercurrent to his voice. "Let me take you home."

Beneath the bridge, a barge inched closer. "I'm not sure I have one," I said, and before I could draw another breath, Chase lifted a hand to my face and nudged me toward him.

I'm not sure why I wouldn't let myself move.

"Yes, you do," he said. "Your aunt loves you. You know that."

Love. It was such a complicated word. At first it's basic. You love your parents, your siblings, your friends, and they love you. End of story, no strings attached. Then your world gets bigger and your dreams take you in new directions, and when you close your eyes you fantasize about a different kind of love, the huge, all-encompassing kind, what it's going to feel like when that one perfect guy sweeps in and changes *everything*. Make it better—happier.

But as you get older fantasy blurs with reality, and all those pretty dreams shift into something as seductive as it is dangerous. A dare, a game, a risk.

Then before you realize what's happening, the fantasy morphs into something you might not be ready for, more like a lock than the magic key you once dreamed of.

And you realize there's no such thing as easy.

"Love isn't supposed to have conditions," I said, staring at the dull haze of moonlight from behind the clouds. "Or rules. It's not supposed to *hurt*."

Chase stiffened. I felt it, even through the feather-light touch of his fingers.

Love was something we didn't talk about.

"How can it not hurt?" he asked quietly. "When someone else has that much control over you?"

SEVENTEEN

Control.

Maybe it was inevitable. When you care about someone, when your heart gets involved, everything tangles. You want to make them happy, even if that means sacrificing what you want or need, what you believe.

But sometimes you wake up one day and realize that in trying to make someone else happy, trying to give them what *they* want, *they* need, to make sure *their* boat never rocks, your boat no longer exists.

Victoria and Lucas proved that.

"Then something's wrong," I said. "Love isn't supposed to be about control—there has to be give and take, compromise. *Trust.*"

His hand fell away.

There were so many nights when I lay in my bed with Delphi at my side and the phone to my ear, listening to his voice, as if he were right there beside me. I could close my eyes and, there in that hazy place, we were together.

But other nights when we sat side by side, I would have sworn he was a million miles away.

"It's about acceptance," I said. "Appreciating someone for who they are, about *wanting* them for who they are. Not who you want them to be."

Around us the sounds of the night deepened, the slurp of the river and the hum of crickets and toads, jazz from the Quarter. But Chase stared toward the lights of the riverboat *Natchez*.

Sometimes silence spoke more than all the words in the world.

Closing my eyes, I sucked in a breath, felt it feather against a longing I didn't understand. It was like trying to work a puzzle you couldn't see, but knowing—*knowing*—that somewhere out there, a piece waited, and it was perfect.

"All my life people have made decisions for me," I said into the darkness. "My parents, my grandmother, now my aunt." And some-times . . . Chase. "They've decided what I do and don't need to know, where I should and shouldn't be, who I should and shouldn't see . . ."

I felt him move, felt him shift toward me. And when his hand found mine, I waited for warmth to slow dance through me.

Cold slipped deeper.

"And I'm so tired of it," I whispered. "So tired of everyone think-ing love gives them permission to keep me in this tight little box and play God—"

"Not God," he said as I opened my eyes. "Just someone who knows how special you are—how different. That when you close your eyes, you go somewhere else." Curled around mine, his hand tightened. "Who's scared one time you won't come back."

"But it's time for *me* to make those decisions," I countered. "I want to *fly*—to spread my wings and see where they take me."

"And if you fall?"

I felt my eyes go wide, and realized we were no longer talking about my relationship with my aunt. "Then I get back up and try again."

The drizzle kept falling, like an ethereal wall slipping between us. "Once when I was a little girl, I was playing in a wooded area at dusk, and I saw the most beautiful—"

Dragonfly.

I'd seen a dragonfly in the mountains.

Shaken, I lifted a hand to my pendant, and felt a door somewhere inside me slip open, and the memory slide through.

Gossamer fine wings of iridescent green fluttered against a bright pink flower. "Look how pretty!!"

"It's a dragonfly," he said, edging closer.

"I've never seen one before!"

"You shouldn't be seeing one now."

Excited, I scrambled for my insect collecting kit.

"No, you can't—" he said, but already I was closing the net around the beautiful wings and ushering my prize into one of the jars where I kept roly-polies and moths and ants.

"Wait 'til I show Gran!" I said, running toward the house.

Dylan caught me by the arm. "You have to let him go—he can't live in a jar."

But I'd just grinned and run off.

"What?" Chase said now, tilting my face to his. "What did you see?"

Against my palm, the yellow crystal glowed. "A dragonfly," I murmured. "I wanted to keep it in my room."

His shoulders rose, fell.

"But I killed him instead," I said, the words, the memory itself, shredding on the way out.

"You had no way of knowing—"

But I had.

Wrapping my arms around my middle, I turned and looked out over the mist-shrouded river.

Dylan had warned me.

God, where did that memory come from?

Chase drew me back against him, his arms tight around my waist as he looked out over me. I could feel the rise and fall of his chest, the warmth of his breath.

"Trinity—" Maybe it was his voice, the tension stretched through it, or maybe the way I felt his body tighten, like he was in the starting blocks before a track meet, but slowly I turned, and slowly I saw his eyes, glassy, drenched with the same confusion I'd seen a few hours before at Horizons.

"You stopped breathing."

He stood right there, his legs against mine, his hands on my hips, but the words came at me from some faraway, distant place, and even as I heard them, they didn't fully register. *"W-what?"*

"That's why your aunt freaked—she thought you were gone."

So much hit me at once, slinging in from all directions—the memory of Julian's fingers against my throat, of Chase reaching for me, holding me. Of my aunt, how shaken she'd been, her eyes huge and devoid, the way she'd talked to me—

—and those last few moments before I'd been pulled away, when he'd promised he would always find me. My eyes had filled, and my breath had—

Stopped.

"No." It didn't make sense. I'd been . . . somewhere else. I'd been in my mind. How could what I felt have bled over . . . *"That's not possible."*

But it was, I realized with a quick twist of panic. Julian had warned me: what I felt in the astral was as real as the cold mist stinging my face—and the darkness hollowing out Chase's eyes. If I ran, my heart rate would accelerate. And if I stopped breathing—

"Oh, my God." I dove into his arms and held on, needing to feel his arms around me.

He was real. He. Was. Real.

Not the dream.

"I'm sorry," I whispered against his neck. "I didn't mean for that to happen . . ."

"Sh-h-h." He wrapped me tighter, burying his face against my hair and splaying his hands against my back, as if he was scared to let go. And I didn't want him to. I wanted to stay like that forever, captured in our own little bubble where the rest of the world couldn't touch, didn't matter.

But even as the fantasy formed, reality circled closer. "It's over now," I whispered.

But it wasn't. It wasn't over. Grace was still missing and the dreams were still coming, and with them, discoveries and memories and possibilities I had no idea what to do with. I'd seen the past and maybe the future, and in doing so—

I'd let down my aunt.

Everything shifted, all the newly discovered pieces—from my dream regression, the aftermath settling into a picture I'd never seen before. Never even imagined.

But Aunt Sara had been there. She'd lived it all. Not only had she lost her brother and sister-in-law, she'd lost her mother. And me. Sure, Aunt Sara had visited, but even as a child I'd sensed the strain in her relationship with Gran.

"All I've thought about is me," I whispered, shivering as Chase eased back to skim a finger along the dampness beneath my eyes.

"I have to tell her I'm sorry," I said, pulling back and turning away, hurrying toward the street.

"Where did you go?"

On the other side of the railroad tracks, I stopped and turned, didn't understand why he still stood there, why he hadn't moved, wasn't coming with me.

Why he looked like he was standing on the edge of a nightmare, and didn't know how to turn away—or turn back.

"With Julian," he clarified as I brought my hand to my heart. "Where did you go after the fire?"

The night slowed. And I think I knew, I think even as I took that first step toward him, the one that was already too late, I knew.

He'd been there. He'd seen—*heard*.

"I waited for you," I said against the burn of breath in my chest. And I hated that, I hated that I felt like I'd done something so, so wrong, when all I'd done was close my eyes.

"I wanted you to be there." I needed him to know that.

"I wanted to be," he said. "Then I could have stopped—"

I lifted my eyes to his, and before I even said anything, he realized he'd just taken Aunt Sara's side.

"No," I said quietly. "Stopping isn't the answer."

And I could have drowned in it all, in that exact moment, the
way he stood there in the cold drizzle, with the river etched behind
him and his wet hair falling against eyes that . . . burned.

"Why did you scream for Dylan?"

Everything fell away. It was all still there, the levee and the stars
and the music from the Quarter. I knew that. But I couldn't find any
of it, couldn't *feel* any of that, only the way Chase looked at me, as if
he had no idea who I was, had never had any idea who I was—and
the shattering realization that I did not need to close my eyes for the
nightmare to return.

"Fourcade's son." Chase's voice was flat, empty, mechanical. "You
said his name."

I looked away, down to the slabs of granite where, a few months
before, I'd lost more than just my balance. I knew it was wrong, but
the memory was there, as strong as the arms that had dragged me
from the river.

I'd done everything I could to whitewash what had happened, not
just that night, but other nights, when I'd closed my eyes and found
someone else in my dreams. Found them *both* in my dreams. Sometimes we all ran. Sometimes only I ran. Sometimes Chase reached for
me—and other times he walked away.

Sometimes Dylan shouted my name—and sometimes he slipped
into the shadows.

That's where I tried to keep him. I'd refused to see his face. I'd
refused to give him a name. But after the dream regression, I could
no longer deny. I knew who'd been with me in the darkness,
who'd crushed me in his arms and promised he'd always find me.
Who I'd reached for.

"You screamed," Chase said hoarsely. "You were . . . *terrified*."

Inside, I started to shake. And even with my eyes wide open,
the images—*the memories*—kept right on crystallizing. I *had* been
terrified . . . so very, very terrified.

But not because Dylan had hurt me. At least not physically.

Slowly, I made myself look back at Chase—and the doubt I found there, the doubt that glowed despite everything—almost killed me.

"Were you dreaming?" he asked, and his voice was so, so quiet, the kind of quiet that came from holding on tight—from knowing that if you let go, even for a fraction of a minute, your whole world might blow up on you. "Or remembering?"

The cold of the night clawed closer, and finally I understood the way he'd looked at me in Julian's little white room, the hollow of fear—and hurt.

"I'm sorry," I said, but my voice broke on the words, and my breath turned to a sob. Normally what I saw behind closed eyes were movies that had yet to happen, coming attractions hovering in the ether.

But the fire and the field, the dark room . . . They'd felt sharper and more defined, like . . .

Memories.

"I don't understand any of this, Chase. I don't know why I see what I see. I can't control it. It's just there."

The skin across his face stretched tight. "It has to come from somewhere."

No, no, no, was all I could think. "Chase, *please,*" I said, stepping toward him, needing to touch him, to hold on and make him believe—

He took a quick step back.

I winced. "This isn't what I want," I said through a hot rush of tears. "All I'm trying to do is help Grace. I have no idea why Dylan was—"

He turned and walked away. Just like that. Chase. Turned and walked away.

Again.

I stood there shivering and trying to breathe, to understand how things could twist so horribly from one breath to the next. How he could just—walk away.

But I knew. Even as the question formed, I knew the answer.

"Chase!" I shouted, doing what I hadn't done last fall, when we'd both been blinded by hurt and confusion.

Fear was a powerful weapon. It drove us, contaminated us, made us destructive. We became so consumed by the need to protect, we never realized that too often, the knife we were lifting was to our own heart.

"Don't walk away from me," I shouted, my heart slamming as he stopped abruptly, as he stood there on the other side of the tracks, not looking back, but not walking away, either.

I caught up to him and lifted my hand, held it there, hovering a breath from his shoulder.

"I don't know how to do this," I said with the same quiet he'd exerted only a few minutes before. Except I wasn't as good at it as he was, and emotion leaked through. "This is me, Chase. Me. Trinity. And I'm standing right here, thinking about Pensacola, and the beach, being with you, running into the turquoise water you've told me about . . .

"And I don't know how to make this better," I whispered. "I don't know how to fight your imagination—"

He never let me finish. His mouth came down on mine, absorbing my words. For a second I just stood there, trying to process, completely unprepared for the desperateness of his kiss, the way he gathered me close and consumed me, as if somehow he could make all the bad go away, make it better. He'd never kissed me like that, sad and lost and seeking, scared . . . And even as something inside me quietly ached, I reached for him, wanted to give him what he wanted. *Needed* to give him. Needed him to give me . . .

Hurting, confused . . . *scared,* I gave myself to the moment, to him. The kiss deepened, as if we were both trying to get something from each other, something important—a promise, an apology. If we could only get close enough, somehow everything would be better. We could connect—forget. Just . . . be.

He pulled back without warning, just a whisper away, enough for his eyes to find mine.

"When I heard you say Dylan's name," he breathed, "all I could think about was . . ." Through the damp sweep of his hair, his eyes flashed. "I wanted to hurt him."

Like Chase had been hurt.

"I was crazy," he said, still holding my hips pressed against him, but somehow pulling away. "I wanted to hurt him for being in your dreams, when I wasn't."

My heart plummeted as his grip tightened.

"I never stopped to think about what he was doing there, only that it was him and not me."

I reached for him, had to reach for him, my hand sweeping the hair from his forehead. "But it's *you* I'm touching," I promised. "You're who's real."

The look in Chase's eyes didn't change. He didn't even acknowledge that I'd spoken. He was trapped in that other place, by something only he saw.

"And then you stopped breathing."

I was pretty sure I did all over again.

"And everything crashed down and I realized—" His words died hard and fast, his eyes narrowing on something behind me.

I swung around and saw him, the figure at the edge of the Jax Brewery parking lot, standing in the shadows. Watching.

I moved without thinking, tried not to run. Because I knew. I could tell by the way he stood so obscenely still.

"Omigod, what are you doing here?" I asked, rushing up to him. "How did you find me?"

Detective LaSalle's mouth twisted at the silly question. "I'm a cop, Trinity. It's what I do."

"What's wrong?" A thousand possibilities crashed down on me. "Is it my aunt? Is she okay—"

"No," he said flatly. "She's not." His eyes shifted to the levee behind me, along the perimeter of the parking lot, back to me. "She's out of her mind, is what she is."

Chase reached for my hand. "But she's not hurt?"

The lines of Detective LaSalle's face tightened. "Depends upon how you define hurt."

She was unpacking.

I found her in her bedroom, standing at her big poster bed with her suitcase open on the mattress. I could see her coral bikini and flip-flops tucked next to the shorts and Saints T-shirt she slept in. But her black stilettos lay on the floor—and the amazing lavender dress we'd spent weeks shopping for was scrunched in her hands.

For a few moments I watched her, waiting for her to turn or cross to her closet, to do something other than stand statue still. But she didn't move, and neither did I.

Dave Matthews blasted from down the hall, but I would have sworn I heard my aunt breathing. She was still dressed for the day—in dark skinny jeans and a drapey brown shirt with a studded cross on the front—but I had no memory of the outfit from earlier at Julian's. I had no memory of anything but the stricken look in her eyes.

Candles flickered. Five of them, small gardenia votives from the huge dresser. Through the triple mirror, I could see the sweep of her long bangs, but not her eyes.

I really wanted to see her eyes.

"I thought you were gone."

The quiet words barely registered above the music. I hadn't realized she knew I was there.

I could have pretended. I could have pretended she was talking about me not being home yet. But so much stood unsaid between us, not just about earlier and Tuesday night at Grace's, but from always. From *forever*.

We'd been together six months. We'd shared the condo and meals, the terror of Jessica's disappearance. I'd shared my dreams. She'd shared stories about my parents. But we'd never gone deeper. Everything had hovered at the surface, warm, pleasant, but never plunging too deep. Never prodding too close to truths we pretended didn't exist.

Until this afternoon.

Until I'd done something she'd explicitly told me not to, and in doing so, had ripped the "everything's fine" veneer from between us.

"I know," I whispered, stepping into the shadows that kept circling. "Chase told me."

She tensed. It was hard to imagine considering how still she stood, but I could tell. "You were so pale. Even your lips. You were so pale, and still, and all I could think was that it was happening all over again."

The raw honesty surprised me. And with it the last bit of uncertainty fell away. I moved without thinking, knowing that I'd done this to her. I'd thrown her back into a nightmare that I'd only begun to remember, but she'd never been able to forget.

"No." Easing up behind her, I lifted a hand to her forearm. It made no sense how scared I was to touch her. This was my aunt. We touched every day. But much like our conversations, much like our sharing, only on the surface.

"It's not happening again." The words were as tight as my fingers against her arm. "I'm okay."

She shifted toward me, her eyes meeting mine. "But you weren't, *cher,*" she said. "You weren't."

Not for the first time, I realized there are two levels to the spoken word: the level on the surface, and the level beneath—darker, guarded, laced with vulnerability.

"I can still see you," she said, but her razor-thin voice told me she was no longer there with me in the candlelit room. "I was home for the weekend. It was after midnight. I was in bed and heard the phone ring . . ." Eyes dark, she never looked up from the suitcase. "I found Mama sitting on the side of her bed, staring."

Much, I imagined, like my aunt was doing.

"The phone was on the floor."

My throat tightened.

"I picked it up," she said. "Detective Fourcade was still there."

How had I never asked her about this? How had I never wondered?

"I . . . I got her dressed," she went on in that same threadbare voice, the one in which the past still lived. "And we drove down there. And Mom just . . . stared the whole way. It was like she wasn't even alive."

I wanted to look away. I wanted to look toward the glow of the candles or the vintage crosses on the wall by her bed.

But Aunt Sara had not been given the luxury of looking away, and I knew I couldn't, either.

"I'm sorry," I said instead, and though the words were nowhere near enough, I needed to say them.

I'm pretty sure she didn't hear me. "And then there you were," she said. "All small and dirty, your hair sweaty and tangled, soot on your face and nightgown, all wrapped up in Jim Fourcade's arms. Sleeping."

The breath of warmth came from somewhere unseen.

"I'll never forget that moment," she said, although it was obvious she wished she could. "He looked up with those crazy silver eyes, and they were hollow and horrified. But he was holding you like you were made of the most exquisite glass, and he was afraid if he breathed too hard, you would crumble."

It was the way his son had held me years later.

I closed my eyes and could see it in my mind, but had no idea if it was memory, or simply the image she painted. But I could see that look in Jim Fourcade's eyes—ravaged, wild—the way he'd looked last fall when he'd emerged from his garage to find me standing on his property.

"Mary Mother of God," he'd said. *"You're the girl."*

At the time, I'd felt my defenses snap into place.

Now I just wanted to hug him. And her. My aunt.

"I took you," she said, twisting toward me, and I saw her, which meant either I'd opened my eyes—or had never closed them to begin with.

"I took you and held you and rocked you . . ." Through long side-swept bangs, her normally vibrant eyes were so beyond the point of seeing. "And I bathed you, dressed you. Sang to you . . ."

I felt my hand rise, felt my fingers press against my lips. Felt the hot salty sting against my eyes.

We weren't strangers. We weren't two people merely bound by blood and relatives and circumstance. At least, we hadn't been. Once, there'd been so much more.

I didn't remember.

But she did.

What must that have been like, was all I could think. What must that have been like to have me suddenly show up in her life and treat her like she was a stranger?

"At the funeral," she was saying, and then it was her eyes that were filling, the tears she never shed that were sliding down her cheeks. "You never said a word. Not for the three days before, or the two after."

I swallowed.

"You were so sweet and soft, and you'd just cling to me, your little arms curled around my neck. And then you'd pull back and peek at me with those big lost eyes of yours, *begging* . . ."

Without words. The feeling came rushing back, words and emotion trapped behind a dam in my heart, and I knew, I knew if I were to look at the triple mirror, I would have seen the devastation all over again.

But I couldn't look away from my aunt.

"And then you were gone," she said quietly. "Just . . . gone."

EIGHTEEN

Illusions are funny things.

We all have them. They materialize from that deepest place inside of us, decorative fantasies we slap on the world around us to make it the way we want it to be: better, happier. Safer.

And yet rarely are we aware. We skate along oblivious to the deceptions that shape us—*deceptions we ourselves create*—until that one moment when the edges of reality break through, and the illusion crumbles. Only then, as the remains slice through our fingers, do we realize we'd been clinging to a lie.

And wish we could get it back.

But there's no going back, not after you know. The truth is like the sun. It doesn't matter if your eyes are open or closed. Once the clouds are gone, light shines.

And if you're not prepared, you get burned.

I'd arrived in New Orleans with little more than my grandmother's Buick to my name. Prior to that I'd lived in jeans and T-shirts and hiking shoes. I'd worn lip balm, not lip gloss, had never thought about mascara or straightening irons. I'd had no use for jewelry—or a cell phone.

And then Aunt Sara whisked me away in her sleek shiny Lexus, drove me through streets crowded with buildings old and new, to the Warehouse District, where a centuries-old factory had been revitalized, and she lived. From the moment she'd swept open the door to her condo, my life had changed—and the illusion had taken off.

My father's younger sister was beautiful and glamorous, with expensive clothes and eclectic taste, perfect hair and makeup, awesome jewelry she designed herself, with friends and creativity and confidence.

That's what had drawn me, fed me. Her confidence. She took everything in stride. She smiled, shrugged, moved on. Even when I'd confided in her about my dreams—*and they'd started to come true*—she'd kept everything together and walked me from one day to the next, as if this was just the way things were, and everything was okay.

And I'd started to believe.

But now, standing in the ashes of a past that had never fully gone away, the illusion—created by her, by me, I no longer knew—fell away, and there she was, not the hip artist who ran a shop in the French Quarter, but my father's little sister, the nineteen-year-old who'd lost everything.

Because of dreams—and secrets.

Had she known? I found myself wondering, as what little color there was drained from her face, leaving the candle-cast shadows to dance against flesh the hue of death.

Had she known that I dreamed, too?

The firstborn daughter, of the firstborn daughter, of the firstborn daughter.

And with the memory, I had my answer. Yes. She'd known. Aunt Sara had known that I dreamed. She'd known that I saw, that I knew.

And she'd taken me in anyway. Even though the blood that ran through my veins was the same blood that had destroyed everyone she loved.

She stood there now, with the lavender dress wadded in her hands, looking at me through eyes that had seen too much.

"What do you mean, gone?" I asked.

"The moon was so bright," she said, as if giving testimony. "Even though it was the dead of night, it was like the lights were on. And I ran. From room to room, screaming. For you—for Mom. All I could think was someone had been there, had come for you—and I'd slept through it."

My breath caught.

"The note was on the kitchen table," she said, her eyes no longer flooded, but unnaturally dry. *" 'I've taken her,' "* she said, and without being told I knew she was repeating what she'd read that night.

So many questions ran through me. But in the end, only one mattered. "Why?"

Her smile looked like it hurt. "He was her favorite," she said, and without asking, I knew she was talking about my dad. "I always knew that. He was her best and her brightest, so very much like Dad. When she lost him . . ."

I moved without hesitation, crossing the space between us and putting my arms around her. Six months before I'd been the one in need. She'd been my anchor.

Funny how quickly roles could change. "No. She loved you, too. She talked about you all the time—"

"I lost everything," she murmured. "The fire took my brother, and then she took you."

I pulled back. "Not . . . *forever.*" It was amazing how that word kept slipping in. "I'm here."

"She changed the locks," she kept on as if I hadn't said a word. "Two weeks after she left, I came home from college and found the house boarded up."

I couldn't imagine.

"Her attorney told me my mother didn't want me inside ever again."

The house that still waited all these years later, beautiful on the outside. Empty inside.

"Four years went by," she said. *"Four years.* And then one day Jim Fourcade shows up and tells me to pack a bag."

I felt myself go very, very still. This was my life. And it was being told to me like a story.

"And they brought me to her."

"They?"

"Him and his son," she said, and something inside me shifted.

Not strangers, I thought again. None of them. They'd all been there. They'd been part of my life. Even Dylan. *"You were the one sent away,"* he'd said. *"You were the one scrubbed of your memories—not me."*

That memory scraped through me, and for a fragile heartbeat I was back in that small dark room, crushed in his arms.

I always find you.

I blinked, blinked again, realized my aunt was still talking, and the image—*memory?*—went away, just like Dylan had done. A few hours. That's all it had been. A few hazy hours, and a whole lot of . . . illusion.

Why, then, did he still come to me when I closed my eyes? And why, *why* had he found me in the darkness, and promised he would always be there?

"It took three days," Aunt Sara was saying as I made myself stop, *stop it all.* Stop remembering. Stop wondering.

"We didn't travel a single major highway. It was like . . ."

After all this time, confusion still darkened her eyes.

"He was afraid," she said.

"That someone was following you?"

Her gaze met mine, and finally, I think, she saw me. But not as I was in that moment, not at sixteen. But at six. "You didn't recognize me."

The air slipped from the room. "Aunt Sara . . ."

"You were playing," she said. "You were out back with Sunshine, and you were playing, and I walked out and called for you, and you looked at me—"

Like a stranger.

The same way I'd treated her when I came to New Orleans.

"I'm sorry," I whispered.

Finally she moved, the dress for the wedding drifting to the ground as she brought her hands to my face, and cradled. "My sweet, sweet girl. You were there with those big beautiful eyes and pigtails, six years old, and I started to cry."

My eyes filled.

"But then you ran off with little Jim and Mom came to stand beside me. She didn't touch—she wasn't that kind of person. But I can still hear her, still see the bright blue Colorado sky. *'She doesn't remember,'* she said. *'She's safe.'* " And finally the pain in my aunt's eyes fell away, leaving a shimmer of warmth—and a tight smile. "And I knew she was right. I could see it. You were happy and safe and alive, and that was all that mattered."

"Until today." Finally I realized the full extent of what I'd done. Actions had consequences. But sometimes we didn't know until it was too late. "When I quit breathing."

"Yes."

"I'm sorry," I whispered again, wishing I could take away the hurt. "I didn't know. I didn't mean to be so selfish."

The strangest look came into her eyes. "Selfish?"

"All I thought about was me," I admitted, hating the truth. "My life and my drama, my pain. I never once—"

"Stop that."

Maybe it was the sharp tone, or maybe the way she pulled back, magically gathering herself into the illusion from before, the one of my hip aunt, poised and graceful despite the tangled hair falling into her face.

"Let me tell you what selfish is," she said. "Selfish is holding on too tight, because you're scared to let go, even though you know you have to."

"Aunt Sara—"

"Selfish is keeping someone else in the dark because that's where you want them—"

I swallowed hard.

"You're so like her," she murmured. "So like them both."

My mind raced to keep up. "Who? My mother?"

"And mine," she said. "I used to fault her. After she left, after she took you, all I could think was what a coward she was running like that, hiding up in the mountains. But now . . ." She let out a sharp breath. "It wasn't about her," she said. "It was never about her. It was about you, making sure you were safe, no matter what. She walked away from everything she loved . . ."

Including her own daughter.

". . . to make sure you lived."

My heart thudded hard. Guilt bled.

"My mom, your mom . . . they never could see eye to eye, but at the core they were exactly the same, always doing the right thing, no matter how hard it was. Putting other people's needs first, making sure they did everything in their power to help, to protect." A heavy beat of silence passed before Aunt Sara tilted my chin so my eyes met hers. "Just like you."

My eyes filled all over again.

"Not selfish," she said, softer now. "Not even close."

I didn't know what to say.

"I'm the selfish one," she said. "I'm the one so paralyzed by the thought of losing you again that I'm willing to let an innocent girl die."

Illusions, I thought again. We all had them. Sometimes they protected—and sometimes they destroyed.

"Not selfish," I murmured, echoing her words. "Not even close."

"When I see you, I see your mom all over again, and I'm so scared your big heart is going to lead you onto a ledge you won't be able to pull back from."

Like the ledge my mother had walked out on, stalked step for step by a psychopath.

"That's not going to happen," I promised.

"If we hadn't gotten there . . ." Her words trailed off, and I knew that for that fraction of a second, she was reliving what happened in Julian's room. "I can still see how pale you were, how still . . ." Her hands found my shoulders. Her fingers dug into flesh. "What happened, Trinity? Why did you stop breathing?"

I wanted to tell her. I wanted to tell her everything I hadn't been able to tell Chase.

But I didn't know how. "It was nothing," I said, slipping from her grip to retrieve the dress from the floor. Automatically I started to fold it.

She stopped me. "Julian says something went wrong. That instead of finding Grace, you slipped into the past."

My throat burned.

"He says the memories are still there, locked away where no one can find them, where they can't hurt."

The walls, I realized. It was the walls that were crumbling. *Illusions.*

"Was it the fire?" she asked. "Is that why you stopped breathing?"

The gentleness in her eyes reminded me of the way a mother looks at a newborn. *"No."*

"Then what?"

The collapse just kind of happened. One second I was standing there amazed by how quickly roles had again shifted, then the next my eyes were filling and she was hugging me tight, promising everything would be okay.

It wasn't until I let go, that I realized how tightly I'd been holding on.

"I don't know," I said. "I don't know what I saw. I don't know what happened. But it felt so real, like I was really there."

Her hands slid along my back, slow, soothing. "Julian says you were."

My eyes tried to close but I wouldn't let them, didn't want to see—or feel. "There was a field," I said. "And a boy, running."

"And you? What were you doing?"

"I followed him."

"Do you know why?"

Through the shadows, the mirror revealed the damp glow in my eyes. "Because I wanted to."

She seemed to absorb that. "And where did you go?"

I gripped her arms and stared up into her eyes. "I kissed him."

Her shoulders fell on a shallow exhale.

"And he kissed me," I said, and even though my eyes were wide open, I could feel it all over again, the frenzy and the need—the urgency.

"Just like he did in his apartment," I whispered.

Her gaze sharpened. "Whose apartment, *cher*?"

"Dylan's." I waited for the shock to blast into her eyes. "I kissed Dylan."

The moment stilled, blurred, but condemnation did not come. Only a soft smile. *"Oh, sweetie."*

"I don't know why I stopped breathing." Only that Chase had heard me cry out for another guy, and I had no way to get past that. "It's like I was being yanked away before I was ready."

She lifted a hand to smooth a tangle from my face—and everything inside me stilled.

"Aunt Sara," I breathed, taking her hand as she tried to yank away. I wouldn't let her though, couldn't breathe as I stared at the gouges along her wrist.

"I did this to you." And with the words the memories slashed back, the arms pulling me, the way I'd thrashed and clawed. *"Omigod . . ."*

Her eyes were so, so gentle. "It's okay. You were frightened, confused—"

"It's not okay! I hurt you—"

She caught me by the upper arms. "You're here now. That's what matters."

I looked away, at the suitcase on the bed. "Please don't cancel your trip because of me. Naomi's one of your best friends."

"Aaron's commanding officer asked him to stay, follow up on a few leads."

My heart sunk—I knew she'd been looking forward to getting away with Detective LaSalle. "Then he'll be all over me like glue," I pointed out. "My own personal guard."

And with those words came the memory from last fall.

"So . . . what? He appointed you my bodyguard?"

The burnished silver of Dylan's eyes had glowed. *"I wish it was just your body."*

I didn't know why I couldn't forget.

"I can stay at Victoria's," I said. "She's going to Chase's uncle's party Saturday night, too."

Aunt Sara took the dress and let it drop open, carefully refolded it before placing it in her suitcase.

And the weight on my chest lifted.

"Promise me you'll stay away, Trinity." Reaching for her awesome black stilettos, she looked up to blast me with the seriousness in her eyes. "From Grace's apartment, Horizons, Ouija boards—the past. The future." Her hand curled around the shoe. "Can you do that? Can you stay right here in this moment, where it's real?"

She might as well have asked me to stop breathing. "I've never been very good at that."

"But it's all we really have, *cher*. The past is over, and the future doesn't exist. You can't keep torturing yourself by reliving events that are over and done with, or forcing yourself to touch and feel things that haven't happened—that might never happen."

Just like Julian said—and again I couldn't help but wonder about their relationship.

"You make yourself experience fear and grief," she added quietly. "You mourn people you don't remember, or who haven't even died."

Chase. Automatically, my hand slid to the bracelet circling my wrist, my finger skimming the word FEARLESS.

"You long for someone you barely know."

Dylan.

"But what if I *can* change it?" I said, looking up. The possibility haunted. "What if I can change what I see—if I can *stop* it?"

"It doesn't work like that."

"But last fall, if I'd warned Jessica—"

"She would have thought you were crazy." The words were firm but gentle, and as much as I hated it, 100 percent true. "It's not your script to write. All you can do is live the best way you can."

It sounded fatalistic. Why would I be given the ability to see, if I couldn't do anything about it?

"I'm trying," I said. *"I'm trying."*

"I know you are."

I'd walked into the room raw and fragile, but as always, Aunt Sara found a way to settle the ground beneath me.

"I was wrong," I said, lifting my eyes to hers. My throat was tight, but I refused to let the words hide there. "At Julian's. When I said those horrible things to you, that you weren't my mother . . ."

Humidity-ruined hair fell against her face. Smudged mascara stained like bruises beneath her eyes. Her lips were dry, her cheeks pale. But the soft gentle way she looked at me gave her a haunting beauty.

"If I could handpick anyone," I said, and yeah, my voice shook. "If I could handpick anyone to be my mother, it would be you."

Her eyes turned glassy. "I love you, too," she whispered, taking my hands and squeezing them. "You're the most important thing in the world to me, you know that, don't you? The thought of losing you—"

I didn't let her finish. "You're not going to."

I helped her finish packing, told her good night, and closed her door behind me. After making coffee, I curled up on my bed with Delphi and fired up my laptop, talked to Chase a few minutes, checked Facebook, and texted with Victoria until her dad took away her phone.

I didn't want to sleep. Because I didn't want to dream. But there on the sofa, my eyes drifted shut, and through the shadows, I returned to his arms.

"You don't need to be afraid anymore."

And, for that moment, I wasn't.

I opened my eyes to the fire-washed glow of the sky. Hues of red faded into streaks of orange and peach, the faintest flush of yellow visible above the shadows consuming the horizon. Through a swirl of crimson a hawk soared with wings spread wide, a field mouse dangling from its claws.

Cringing, I started to turn away, but the giant ice cream cone stopped me. It rose up from the corner of a blue building, its white tip swirling above the wave of the roofline.

And then I realized I still dreamed.

"Wait!" I try to twist around. "Where'd you go—"

But my body won't move, and he does not answer.

My heart starts to race. Something is wrong. I should be able to move in the astral. I should be able to walk through walls and fly—that's what Julian said.

But I can do nothing but stand and stare as a missile streaks in toward the building. From it red drips, and my breath cuts into my throat.

"No." I try to scream, but my voice is no longer there.

The missile collides with the building, and the words ICE CREAM SHOP *appear.*

A brush, I realize, watching red paint glide against the softest of baby blues.

Lifting a hand to my mouth, I pull away, realize that I can. I can't turn or twist, but I can move farther back—and widen my view.

The girl sits at an angle, her eyes focused on the canvas in front of her. I can't tell their color, only the intense concentration as she meticulously wields her brushes. There's no makeup on her face—her hair, long and sleek, more burnished red than brown, is pulled into a tight ponytail. Her clothes are simple—an old yellow T-shirt and a pair of torn, faded blue jeans.

I watch her, not understanding. "Who are you?" I whisper.

She pulls back, her chin at an angle, as if . . . listening.

NINETEEN

Yes!

"*Behind you,*" *I say.* "*Turn around—*"

Slowly, she does, and the whitewashed blue of her eyes rips the breath from me.

Afraid, I realize. She's terrified.

"*It's okay,*" *I rush to say.* "*I'm not going to hurt you.*" *But already she's standing and grabbing the canvas, running for the back of the . . . restaurant?*

Tables draped in white cloths sprawl in all directions.

"*Come back!*" *But already she's gone.*

Confused, I step back, step back again, and for the first time see the sheet of glass that had been there all along, a see-through wall between us.

Slowly I lift my eyes, and see the elegant lettering in the darkest of purples: GASTON'S PLACE.

And everything goes dark.

"No!" I shouted, but already my eyes were opening and my room was coming into focus, the gauzy sheers blowing against my window, Delphi crouched beside me, her ears flat, the glow of the computer from across the bed.

Different, was all I could think. There'd been something different about the dream, as if I was a voyeur rather than a participant. Usually I lived what I saw. I touched and felt and ran. Held on and let go, whispered and screamed.

This time I'd been able to do nothing but watch.

"While we dream, messages are sent from our psyche in the astral, to our physical body."

Julian's words made me sit up straighter. A message, I realized. Someone had been sending me a message. Someone wanted me to know . . . something. But who? And what?

And most of all, *why*?

There was nothing to go on, nothing concrete—just a picture of a hawk flying over an ice cream shop, a girl painting, and—

Gaston's Place.

Scrambling, I grabbed my laptop and fired up Google, my fingers flying as I keyed in the restaurant name.

And froze as I stared at the results:

Gaston's Place
Belle Terre's Best
Belle Terre, Louisiana

Detective LaSalle stood at the counter with a cup of coffee in his hands, watching me. And I would have sworn he knew. I would have sworn he knew just by looking at me that I'd had another dream.

"Hey," I said, slinging my backpack over my shoulder as Aunt Sara stepped from her bedroom.

In a pair of tight black pants with a long, square-necked sweater in the brown of chocolate, she looked awesome. "Sleep well?" she asked.

I smiled. "Great."

"Good." She pulled me in for a half hug as we made our way toward her suitcases. "Remember what we talked about last night," she said as Detective LaSalle came toward us. "And call Aaron if anything happens."

Biting the inside of my lip, I nodded.

"Anything," she emphasized.

"I will." But not because of a dream—at least, not yet.

"You'll be at Victoria's, right?" he asked.

I nodded.

He studied me a long second before turning to reach for her suitcase.

Aunt Sara hugged me, holding on a few seconds longer than usual. "I'll be home Sunday morning."

I nodded again. "And I'll be fine."

We left together, Detective LaSalle and my aunt getting into his car, while I slid into my grandmother's Buick for school.

I was halfway there when I made an abrupt U-turn.

I couldn't do it. I couldn't sit in class all day, smile and try to pay attention, not while the dream played over and over in my mind. Something kept nagging at me, nudging. I was missing something.

I needed to figure out what.

Suspended high above a glowing white statue of the Virgin Mary, the dream catcher twisted in the breeze.

At the bottom of the porch, I stood for a long moment, watching, much as I had last fall. Uniform feathers crawled along beaded strands of red and black, toward the intricate web in the center. Like fish swimming toward bait, I remembered thinking back then—and couldn't help but think again.

The bike was gone. I'd noticed that the second I emerged from the tunnel of trees to see the brick house waiting in the clearing. Only a pickup sat in the gravel drive, an older one, and instinctively I knew I was safe.

I didn't want to think about what I would have done if the motorcycle had been parked beside the truck.

I was still standing there when the screen door creaked. "Trinity?"

I twisted toward the wraparound porch, and saw him. He emerged from the house he'd rebuilt after the storm, with his long silver hair pulled into a ponytail, concern sharp in his eyes—and a dish towel in his hands.

Last time, it had been a grease rag.

"Hey." My smile just kind of happened—unlike his son, Jim Fourcade had that affect on me. Maybe it was because he'd been friends with my mother, or maybe his quiet, steady strength, but the second I saw him, warmth streamed through me.

"God, it's good to see you," he said, meeting me halfway and wrapping me in a tight bear hug. "It's been too long."

Four months. It had been four months since I'd seen him—or his son.

I'd thought about calling or dropping by, but I'd never known what to say—or who I would run into.

That was probably the biggest reason I'd stayed away. Because of Chase, I'd told myself. The Fourcades made Chase uncomfortable.

But as I hugged Dylan's father, the low hum vibrating through me had nothing to do with Chase.

"I know," I said, pulling back to smile up at him. "It's been crazy."

"Would you like to come inside—" he started, but stopped, his all-seeing eyes narrowing. "It's happening again, isn't it?"

I don't know why that surprised me. He was, after all, the cop who'd worked alongside my mother. He knew how our abilities worked. He'd been the one she turned to.

And really, why else would I be on his porch on a Friday morning, when I should have been at school?

Pressing my lips together, I nodded.

His frown cut deep, deep into his face. "I was afraid of that," he said on a rough breath. "Are you okay?"

The wind kept whipping hair into my face. I pushed it back, but no sooner than I lowered my hand, the strands were slapping again. "Yeah."

His eyes remained sharp, focused. With a hand to my shoulder he led me across the wooden planks to a white porch swing, and together we sat while I told him everything that had happened since Saturday night.

"But what I don't understand," I said as wind chimes tinkled, "is how did she know? If what Julian says is true and sometimes what I see is put there as a message . . . how do I know? How did my mom know when what she saw meant something versus when it was just a dream?"

He looked away, off toward the tall cypress trees in the distance, where dogs barked but could not be seen.

"I mean, usually what I see is familiar—places I've been or people I know." I'd never dreamed of something as random as a stranger in a restaurant. "But the girl last night—"

He swung back toward me. "You said she was painting? A bird with a mouse?"

I nodded.

His eyes went very far away. "Sometimes your mother would dream in symbols like that," he murmured as a sleek gray tabby cat wandered around the corner—and stretched out in a swath of sunlight. "And it would drive her crazy trying to understand."

"And did she? Was she usually able to link them to the case she was working on?"

"Sometimes." He rubbed a hand against the stubble along his jaw. "She would tear herself to shreds trying."

I looked away, toward the dream catcher twisting in the wind.

"But sometimes," he said quietly, "when you want something bad enough, your mind tries to give it to you, even when there's nothing there."

I swung back toward him. "W-what?"

The silver of his eyes was darker than I'd ever seen it. "Sometimes your mother would dream of you," he said gruffly. "You were only a little girl, but she'd see you beautiful and grown up, like you are now."

Somehow, I swallowed.

"Once she saw you riding a bike," he said, "and once she saw you graduating."

Everything stilled. I would have sworn it. The breeze stopped, and the dream catcher froze. "Graduating?" I whispered.

"From high school." His smile was sad. "It ripped me up to see her cry like that."

"In the dream?" I whispered. "She was crying in the dream?"

"When she told me," he said. "I didn't ask about the dream."

My throat was so tight it hurt to breathe. "I . . . I had that dream two nights ago."

Nothing prepared me for the way he swung toward me—or how sharp his eyes got. "You *what*?"

"I had that dream," I said again, as slowly the dream catcher again began to dance. "That I was wearing a gown with a cap in my hand. That it was my graduation—and she was there."

His eyes closed, and his wide shoulders, the ones I'd cried on, slept on as a little girl, dropped.

"And it was so real," I whispered, seeing it again. Feeling it. Living it. "Do you think she gave me that?" I asked. "Do you think she projected that image for me to see?"

His jaw tightened as he opened his eyes. "Like I said, sweetheart. When you want something badly enough, your mind tries to give it to you."

"You don't need to be afraid anymore . . ."

Something inside me shifted. I tried to focus on the song of the birds and the echo of the wind chimes—but saw only the small, shadowy room, and a raw, burnished gleam.

"But how do I know the difference?" The question gnawed at me. If I needed to forget, I wanted to. But if I was supposed to remember, to act, I didn't want to screw up and pretend nothing happened. "Between what's real and what's not? I mean, with Mom, it's obvious. But what about the girl painting? How do I know?"

Jim Fourcade took my hands and squeezed. "You take it one day at a time. That's all you can do."

"But that restaurant *exists*," I said. "And the girl—what if . . . she's the next victim?" The thought haunted me. "What if, like Jessica, I visualized this girl *before* something happens to her?"

"Let me make a few calls," he said. "See if anyone at this Gaston's Place matches your description. Would that make you feel better?"

"You would do that?" I asked.

"For you, cricket," he said, with warmth glimmering in eyes that had seen way too much. "Anything."

Cricket? "Thank you," I said.

He smiled, but the gleam, as raw and penetrating as his son's, had me glancing back toward the feathers along the beaded lines of the dream catcher—the exact same pattern inked on Dylan's arm.

"It's a fine piece of work," he said.

It was more than that. "I always wanted one," I said, remembering the Native American craft store Gran and I had once visited. An old woman had sat weaving while her grandson slept in a basket beside her. After a few minutes she'd lifted her eyes to mine, and smiled.

The night air is filled with dreams, she'd told me. Good dreams are pure and find their way among the feathers to the sleeper.

Bad dreams were trapped, held there in the web, until the light of day destroys them.

"I could get you one like it," Detective Fourcade offered. "I'm sure the artist would be happy to make you one."

From the moment I'd arrived, I'd felt the current, subtle, raw, moving through me like low-wattage electricity. But in that moment, the hum started to pulse. "The artist?"

"My boy," Jim Fourcade said. "Dylan."

TWENTY

The morning sun caught on the stream of delicate feathers, each meticulously placed . . .

"*Dylan made this?*"

"My *shi'cheii* taught him."

I told myself to look away, look away fast—forever. But couldn't. "Your what?"

"My mother's father—Dylan's great-grandfather."

Now I did turn, slowly, the wind whipping long strands of hair into my face.

"The Navajo is strong in him," Jim Fourcade said with the quiet pride of a father. "Far stronger than it is in me."

I just stared. I didn't know why, but I couldn't stop. "Navajo?"

His smile almost looked apologetic. "My mother was Native American, my father Cajun. I'm the result."

So much hit me at once, as many questions as answers. "That salve," I murmured, seeing it all over again, the tube Dylan had brought to his father, the gooey substance he'd spread over my palms—the gouges that had been gone within hours. "That was . . . *Navajo*, wasn't it?"

The light in his eyes glowed, as if lit from some transcendent place inside him. "It was Navajo that healed you, yes."

My breath caught.

"For years Dylan spent summers with my *shi'cheii*—they taught each other much."

I'm not sure what made me stand and cross the porch, reach for the slowly spinning piece of pale driftwood—or why I suddenly felt a breath of warmth whisper through me.

"That's why I asked Dylan to keep an eye on you last fall," his father said. "Because the blood in him is strong, and I knew he would keep you safe."

The feathers were soft against my fingers, delicate, far more delicate than I would have guessed.

I jerked my hand back. "I-I have to go." To get away from there, away from the mysticism of the dream catcher and the warm voice of the father, the stories of the son who'd given me his breath—then walked away without saying good-bye.

The son who sometimes came to me in my dreams.

"Yes," Jim Fourcade said, standing and crossing to me. "I'm sure you do."

I looked at him, at a strand of silver that had worked free of his ponytail and scraggled against the hollow of his cheek, and would have sworn he'd aged a few years in the few minutes we'd spoken.

My own hair kept blowing into my face—I made no move to push it away.

"I'll make those calls this morning," he said, lifting a hand to curve around my shoulder. "I'll let you know what I find out."

I drove slowly. I turned the radio off. I kept my BlackBerry on my thigh. Realistically, I knew it was too soon to hear back from Jim Fourcade—it wasn't even nine thirty. Most people were just getting to work.

But I couldn't shake the feeling something big was about to go down. Because of the dream, I knew. There was something in the dream—a message or a clue, something about the girl or the restaurant. Belle Terre wasn't far—

It hit me without warning, what should have hit me all along. Belle Terre.

Enduring Grace loomed ahead, but the tree-shrouded entrance barely registered. From one breath to the next I was back in Grace's apartment, kneeling in front of the crate from my dream, lifting envelopes addressed to Grace—all with a return address of . . .

Belle Terre.

Everything blurred for one wobbly heartbeat, and then I was turning, turning fast, not into the parking lot, but toward the Interstate.

Jim Fourcade could make calls. And maybe someone would recognize his description of the girl—maybe they wouldn't. Maybe she existed, maybe she didn't. But I'd been shown her—or the restaurant or the town—for a reason.

And I needed to know why—if it was a clue, a warning, or, if as Jim Fourcade suggested, my mind was trying to give me what I wanted by filling in the blanks.

I didn't stop to think. I didn't stop to consider or plan. I didn't stop . . . period. No way could I go to school and pretend to pay attention, not while the image kept playing in my mind. Not until I saw for myself.

"I wish you were there," I said, zipping along the narrow state highway. But it was the middle of second period—there was no way Chase could have answered.

After last night, I really needed to hear his voice.

"I wish you were *here*," I said more quietly. "We might have our first real break about Grace. I'm headed to check it out now. Not sure when I'll be back, but I'll call you as soon as I know something."

Throat tight, I squeezed the phone tighter. "I-I'm sorry about last night."

I didn't know what else to say.

Ending the call, I tossed my BlackBerry onto the seat beside me and concentrated on the substandard road. Trees, some living, some dead, some trapped in that fragile place in between, crowded in from both sides. Only a few streaks of sunshine leaked through to the blacktop. There was no shoulder, the lines of yellow and white majorly faded. There was nothing behind me, and nothing in front of me.

It was like driving off the end of the earth.

The GPS said I had twenty miles and thirty minutes to go. Eyeing the remains of my mocha, I knew I shouldn't drink anymore until *after* I found a bathroom. So I cranked Lady Gaga and accelerated as the world around me blurred, until just beyond a drawbridge, cypress trees gave way to a clearing, and a gravel drive led to RAYMOND'S END OF THE ROAD.

The name fit. The run-down building sat back from the road, with precisely one gas pump out front. It didn't even take a credit card. Next to it, two old ladies who looked ready for church—or a funeral—stood with the hose stretched toward their shiny white Cadillac.

Three pickups, two beaten up, one new, occupied the spaces closest to the door. Parking to the side, I grabbed my phone and slipped from the car, shivering. I'd slipped on my hoodie, but this close to the Gulf, a cool dampness permeated everything.

Inside, heat blasted, and grease mingled with cigarette smoke.

"Mornin'," the ancient man behind the counter greeted.

I glanced at him and smiled, when all I really wanted was to hold my breath and run to the bathroom. "Hi."

His face was long and lean, scruffy. "Bathroom's dat way." He pointed beyond the display of fried everything, toward a doorway between two coolers.

"Thank you!" I turned as a gorgeous gold car with dark windows pulled into the parking lot.

As far as bathrooms went, the small room wasn't bad. Finishing up, I used a paper towel to open the door, then braced myself for the onslaught of grease and smoke.

The guy looked like a football player. That was my first thought as I grabbed a Red Bull and headed for the counter. My second was maybe he really was, because his clothes were obviously expensive. He stood at an angle, revealing a thick gold chain around his neck and a big gold nugget ring on his right hand, an equally big diamond in his ear. His light brown hair was military short.

"With *boudin*," he was saying as the older man heaped food into a Styrofoam container. "And some cracklins." Then he glanced at me. "Raymond makes the best cracklins."

I edged past him. "I'll remember that."

"Traveling alone?"

It was an innocent enough question. The farther south you drove, the friendlier people got. In New Orleans, you could know a complete stranger's life story before you could finish a soda. But something cold and slimy crawled over me.

"Meeting someone." I sidestepped with a quick glance at the man called Raymond.

He closed up the Styrofoam. "You ready, darlin'?"

I felt my smile tighten. "Yes."

"You're not from around here, are you?" he asked, ringing up my drink.

"Of course she's not," the guy with biceps bigger than my thighs said. "I'd remember someone this pretty."

"I'm sorry, I have to go," I said, grabbing my change and my drink and hurrying outside.

At my car, I fumbled with my keys and unlocked the door, started to slide inside—and saw the feathers.

I stood unnaturally still, staring first at the grease-stained concrete where a black mask lay in a puddle, then lifting my eyes to make sure no one waited inside the car.

I tried to breathe. I tried to think. Be rational. It was February. Mardi Gras was a few weeks away. Masks were everywhere.

But even as I tried to grab onto the logic, the buzz turned to a roar, and a hard slam of my heart destroyed the paralysis. I ripped myself away as the front door opened, and a shadow fell across the pavement.

I didn't look. I slid into my car and yanked the door shut, locked it, turned the key, and gunned into reverse. It wasn't until I swung onto the narrow road that I checked the rearview mirror, and saw the gold car sliding out behind me.

The road curved. I took it fast, never slowed. My hands clenched the wheel. My foot jammed the gas.

"Chill, Trin," I whispered, reminding myself the road only led two directions—north, and south. The fact the guy at the counter was behind me meant nothing other than that he was also traveling south. No big deal, end of story.

But then I glanced at the mirror and saw that he'd zoomed up on my tail.

"No," I told myself. No. I was imagining things, being paranoid, letting seeds of the fear everyone else tried to plant take root.

But the headlights zipped closer, and blind instinct took over.

The road was narrow, the faded line down the middle solid and yellow. There was no shoulder, just a blur of gravel dropping to a canal. I chanced a look at my GPS. Nine miles. That's all that was left. Then I would be in Belle Terre. There'd be people, a sheriff. I could pull into a gas station or a bank, safely reach for my phone. I could—

The road curved sharply to the right.

I went with it, accelerating when I should have braked—and the gold car veered into the oncoming lane.

Relief rushed through me. He was in a hurry, that was all. He was going to pass—

The impact of metal slamming into metal shocked me. Shaken, I twisted toward the car, clenching the wheel to keep control of mine, but darkly tinted windows prevented me from making eye contact. He came at me again, harder, faster, his big car steadily eating up my lane. Adrenaline rushing, I floored the gas pedal—and the side of the road dropped away.

Someone screamed. It had to have been me. But everything happened horrifyingly slow, distorted, as if I was a witness rather than participant.

The canal rushed up. My car veered down. At the moment of impact the airbag exploded against my face.

And everything went black.

TWENTY-ONE

"Get out!"

My eyes opened and I surged forward, felt everything start to spin. Dizzy, I hung there, trying to understand—*remember.*

"The door—open the fuckin' door!"

I swung toward the garbled voice, but something strong and sharp cut into my chest, holding me against—

The seat belt, I realized, and on a vicious rush, the fog cleared—and memory came. The cold water of the canal was spilling into the car, rising up like a bathtub filling.

"Try the window!" someone shouted.

Frantically I reached for the button—and saw the guy from the gold car, his face distorted against the glass. "Hurry!" he shouted.

I reeled back into the rising water—and everything inside me started to scream.

The car shifted, tilting as it slipped deeper into the canal.

Crew-cut guy yanked at the handle. "Unlock it!"

And then it would open, and he would reach for me.

"You're gonna fuckin' drown!"

My throat closed up. Breath wouldn't come. My body started to shake.

There was only one way out—

The car shifted again.

Cold . . . I was so cold.

I didn't have a choice, I realized. I didn't have a choice. If I wanted out, I had to go to him—

"What the hell are you waiting for?" he shouted, his mouth pressed to the glass.

The canal kept rising.

Oh, God, I thought. Oh, God, oh, God, oh, God . . . It was happening, happening again, the watery grave I'd dreamed of so many times—just like I'd lived last fall when I'd fallen into the river. Then Dylan had come in after me—

But Dylan was gone, and Chase was in New Orleans, and no one knew I was here, and the water—

I lunged across the seat and yanked at the switch, grateful my grandmother's Buick was so old the locks were manual and not automatic.

"Fuck!" gold car guy shouted as he tore open the door and grabbed for me.

Every instinct I had screamed for me to pull back, pull away, fight—

But the water was so cold—and there was no other way out.

He shot in, one hand fumbling with the seat belt while the other closed around my arm and dragged me from the car.

The second the breeze hit me, I yanked back, twisting—

"You stupid little bitch—" he bit out, hauling me against him.

I kicked and hit, screamed.

He waded from the canal, his big arms locked around me so tightly I couldn't breathe.

The second we hit land, he threw me to the muddy bank. "That's a hell of a way to thank me for saving your fuckin' life," he muttered.

"Who are you?" I scrambled back. "Why are you—"

Silver flashed—and the words died in my throat.

"Time to say nite-nite, sweet thing."

I tried to find my feet, but he was on me with the syringe before

I could stand, straddling me and driving me back to the mud. "This'll only hurt for a second."

"No—oh, my God!" I shouted as my hands came up. I wrenched beneath him, tried to drive my knee.

He pressed harder.

Somewhere in the distance tires screeched.

"Help!" I shouted—or maybe I cried. I didn't know. "God, please—"

"Get your goddamn hands off her!"

He reared back and his eyes got wide—

My heart slammed. My throat burned. "Help!"

But already he was dragging me, running. I thrashed—but the needle stabbed into my arm. I screamed, twisted. "No—"

The heaviness came fast, a curtain falling, consuming—and my body stopped responding. I tried to call out, but words wouldn't form, and voice wouldn't come. And then I couldn't see—

"Kill you—"

Couldn't hear.

And then there was nothing but the bleed of yellow into peach, then *orange, purple. Light faded, and the sky glowed.*

"Come back!" I shout. "Please—where'd you go?"

The wind laughs, and the trees slip closer.

I spin around—or maybe that's the ground. I didn't know—didn't understand, just knew everything was turning, tilting.

"Please! Answer me!" But darkness falls, and shadows steal detail. Still I run, while around me the world burns. "I'm here!"

The sky cracks, and the concrete buckles. And then I see him lying without moving . . .

"No!" But already I'm falling.

Drowning.

"Trinity—no!"

Blindly, I reach out, grabbing for the safety of his hand, but find tall grass instead. I pull, try to hang on.

"Trinity!"

But the water rises, and my body slips.

"No—no!"

I struggle toward the voice, and against the shadows, the faded buildings glow.

"Turn around!" someone whisper-shouts. "Now! Go back. Quick!"

"Grace?" My voice is raw.

"Tell me where you are!"

"He knows you're here! It's all a game—"

The street narrows. The buildings start to crumble. "Grace—" I cry, running toward the only door that remains. I reach for it, yank—

Something hard tackles me from behind. I go down, the impact singing through my legs as they buckle. "Game over, sweetheart."

Disoriented, I blink against the shadows. "What game?"

"I win." His voice is so quiet, so dead, it's obscene. "I always win."

"No!" I try to scramble to my feet, but he grabs my arm and yanks, dragging me across the grass.

"Be nice, and I'll let you say good-bye."

Frantically I twist, jabbing two fingers into his windpipe.

He staggers—and I run.

"Trinity—"

The shimmering tear appears from nowhere. I lunge for it and vault through, collapsing the second—

He catches me, holds me. "I'm here—I've got you."

Run! I have to run. I know that. I have to get away. But his words drift through me like the softest of feathers, and the part of me that's been afraid, running, wants to hold on. But I'm so tired, and as my breath slows, I can no longer remember why I'm supposed to be afraid.

Warmth blankets me. I sink into it, letting it surround me, fill me. For a long time I allow myself to simply exist there, blissful, safe, wishing I could feel this way . . . forever.

Gradually other sensations register, something brushing the side of my face, a voice so phenomenally quiet it can only have come from the deepest place within me, that place where no one can touch.

"Don't fight—just rest for me."

But I don't want to rest, not until I've seen.

Streaks of sunlight sting my eyes, but I see him, see him cradling me, one hand against my face, the other holding one of my own.

"Hey." It is the same voice, the same drugging voice that called me back when I was lost—and caught me when I fell. "Welcome back."

I blink against the blur, trying to bring everything into focus. Clouds drift, and trees stand guard. "Where am I?"

"With me," he murmurs, running a hand along my hair. "You don't need to be afraid anymore."

"I don't understand—"

"Sh-h-h." He pulls me closer. "Rest."

Silver. I stare up into it, burnished, mesmerizing, and feel something inside me stir. And with it, reality nudges against illusion.

"None of this is real," I realize against the slow bleed somewhere inside me. I know what is about to happen—what always happens when the hazy dots of consciousness reconnect, and the dream falls away. "You're not here."

A ghost of a smile plays with his mouth. "Then where am I?"

"You're . . . gone."

His thumb strokes along my palm so, so gently. "Then how are you talking to me?"

"The way I always do." This time it is me who smiles. Me who remembers. "Hold me first," I whisper. "Please just . . . hold me." And with the words, my eyes drift shut, and I once again drift through the sanctuary of my dreams.

They say history cannot be rewritten.

The past is the past, what's done is done. We can only live within the existing constructs of our life, and move forward.

But that's not true. Facts *are* rewritten, every single day. We all do it. With time, the edges of memory fade, and fiction creeps in. Colors dim, love fades, devastation dulls. We all do it, softening, adjusting details to make them easier to live with. It's how we survive.

Even my gran. She took the earliest years of my life and white-washed them, sanitizing the murder of my parents into a random accident and glossing over my abilities, doing everything she could to scrub away my birthright.

I did it, too. When I was a little girl, sometimes I would go to bed early, lay there beneath a quilt but surrounded by daylight, squeezing my eyes shut, waiting, just waiting, for that magic moment when consciousness fell away, and my parents came back.

There broken pieces fused, and we were together again, long after they'd been taken from me. There my mother would hold me and promise everything would be okay, and my father would smile. There, we were a family. Nothing could touch us.

There, we were safe.

Maybe we move forward, but the sum of our experiences stays with us, and makes us who we are. We can return over and over again. We can relive every moment, make them last longer, turn out better. If only behind closed eyes.

I drifted there now, in the asylum of my pretend past. And while a vague sense of unease pulled at me, I wasn't ready to leave. I wanted to linger, to wrap myself in the illusion that everything was okay.

His hand was warm, soft. I could feel his fingers along my face, the way they stroked, hesitating before sliding lower, his thumb against my bottom lip. Gentle. Tentative. I wanted to stay like that, to make the moment last, and then last some more.

But curiosity nudged me to open my eyes.

He wasn't wearing a shirt. That was the first thing I noticed. His chest was bare save for a sprinkle of dark hair. And even though my whole body ached, I wanted to lift a hand and touch.

He sat on the edge of a small bed, next to where I lay. That was the second thing that registered. Shadows fell against his face, making his cheekbones look sharper than I remembered. His mouth was full, his nose strong. But it was his eyes that made my breath catch, the steady glow that made so many promises.

A dream, I realized. I'd once again awoken inside a dream. *"You're still here."*

His eyes find mine, and warmth gleams. "Where else would I be?"

Where he always is when I wake up. "Gone."

"I told you I wasn't going anywhere."

Memories drift, hazy, frayed, but not close enough to touch. "No." *There's no fear here, no caution or reason, no reservation.* "That's not what you said."

Against my face, his fingers still. "Then tell me what I did say."

Sometimes memory sharpens, and sometimes it distorts. But sometimes it crystallizes, and sometimes it sustains. "That you'd always find me," *I murmur, reaching for his hand.*

He takes over, sliding his fingers among mine.

For the first time I look around. "But you lied," *I say.* "You left." *Without saying good-bye. One second he'd been there, in the morgue, holding a gun on the psychopath with a knife to my throat—and then he'd just been . . . gone.*

"And you didn't come back."

"I'm here now."

Reality edges closer, cuts deeper. "No." *Beyond the curtains, light slips into the small room. The haze will fade then, and he'll leave.* "If you were real . . ." *I squeeze my eyes shut and concentrate on slowing my breath, holding on.*

I'm not ready for the dream to end.

"If I was real, what?"

I struggle for words, can find none.

"I'd be right here," he promises. "Right where I am."

I want to believe him. I want to grab onto his vow and hold it. But the ledge is narrow, the fall endless. I'll wake up then, and—

"No." Reality slips closer. "You're going to leave again—just like you always do."

Beside me he shifts, bringing his face to mine. "Not always."

So close. All I have to do is lift a hand, and touch. "Stop it," *I whisper.* "Please."

"Stop what?"

"Torturing me."

"Is that what you think I'm doing?"

I've never stayed in the dream this long. Sometimes we talk, but these words are different.

"This isn't right," I say. I can't stay. I know that. I have to go back.

"Good-bye," I make myself say. That's a first. Always before, he's the one who leaves. This time it has to be me.

But shadows still fall. Light still leaks around faded brocade curtains. Crimson, I realize. Dark and thick, with gold roses. I still lie in a small bed—and he still sits next to me.

"No . . ." I whisper. The word burns.

His chest is still bare, endless, impossibly defined. Along his bicep the intricate pattern of the dream catcher—

My breath stops. Or maybe that's my heart. I'm not sure.

"Welcome back." His smile is slow, lazy.

I make myself blink again, make myself swallow—can't stop staring at the lines of the dream catcher inked against his bicep. "Omigod . . ."

"Easy." He reaches for me. "You've been out—"

I wrench away, yanking the covers with me. "No." The room is small, sparsely furnished. The heavy curtains are drawn. The bedside clock reads 1:37.

"No, no, no . . ." Not real. It's not real, not any of it. He isn't there—I'm not there. Not really. "This isn't how it happens. I'm still asleep. This is all just—"

"A dream?" His eyes are so very, very dark. "Afraid not, little girl."

I freeze, but the months fall away, and for a fractured moment I'm back in the kitchen of that small French Quarter apartment, backed against the cabinets. I hadn't been thinking clearly. I hadn't been thinking at all.

"Careful, little girl," he'd said. "You don't want to start a game without knowing who you're playing with."

"Stop it," I say now, scrambling back. "Please just . . . stop."

"I wish it was that easy," he says quietly. "But not everything can be stopped once it's started."

My throat closes up on me. I try to swallow, to breathe—then I see my clothes, damp and draped over the back of a chair across the room.

And the last of my denial shattered.

"Oh, God," I whispered, looking up at him, at the angles of his face and the hair slicked back to reveal the burning silver of his eyes, so narrow and concentrated, as if, like me, he didn't trust himself to blink, much less look away. *"It's really you."*

TWENTY-TWO

Four months had passed. Four months since three snarling rottweilers had raced toward me, and with one quiet word, he'd stopped them.

Alletez.

Four months since I'd turned to see him standing in the shadow of his father's patio, since he'd kneeled before me and gently applied the amber, sulfur-smelling salve to my palms, and within hours, they'd healed.

Four months since he'd gone into the river after me, giving me first his breath, then his shirt. Since he'd spun around when I screamed, silently lifting his gun. I'd had no doubt he would kill the man pressing the knife to my throat.

Four months since he walked away.

I'd never seen him again.

Except that wasn't true, either. That was just what I remembered. The rest, the images that came to me behind closed eyes, belonged to some alternate time and place.

"Give yourself a few minutes," he said, leaning closer. "You've been out awhile."

Fragments of memory hovered, but none of them fit. Everything was fuzzy and jumbled—hazy.

I'm not sure why I lifted my hand, but all I could think was touch—I had to touch.

His skin was like fire. I laid my palm there, against the inked feathers along his bicep, and felt the warmth seep through the fog.

"I don't understand," I murmured. "How is this not a dream—I was driving—"

It hit me hard, and it hit me fast. I surged forward, my throat tightening all over again. The car—the canal—the water pouring in—someone had dragged me out. "Oh, my God, it was you—"

I tried to scramble back, but Dylan caught me, taking me by the arms with a gentle strength that stopped me. It was only then that I realized how badly I was shaking.

"*Trinity.*" His voice was druggingly steady. "Don't even go there," he said, his eyes holding mine. "You know that's not true."

I did. I knew that. Dylan would never hurt—

"But I don't understand . . ." Beyond the width of his shoulders, the walls of the small hotel room pressed in on me. "The guy in the gold car. He—"

"—can't hurt you anymore." Gently, Dylan eased me back against the bed and pulled the sheet to my shoulders.

Nothing made sense. "He had a syringe—"

"It was a sedative. You've been out awhile."

Memory flashed—and my arm throbbed. Robotically I looked down, lifting my hand to touch the small red welt. "But . . ." I had no idea where the dream ended and reality took over. "You . . . you were there? I didn't see—"

But I *had* heard . . .

"Get your goddamn hands off her!"

The voice had been furious—lethal. I stared at him now, watched his face twist with something I didn't understand.

This was the second time, I realized numbly, the second time I'd gone under, and he'd pulled me back.

The second time I'd opened my eyes to the silver of his.

"How did you know?" The words scraped. "How are you always here when everything falls apart?"

The corner of his mouth, with the faintest residue of dried blood, lifted. "Good timing, I guess."

"And bodyguarding," I murmured.

The smile, if it had even been one, faded. "It'd be easier if it was only about your body."

I looked away, across the room, where a gun that looked like the one he'd held in the basement of Big Charity lay on the dresser.

"My father was worried. He didn't have a good feeling when you left."

"He . . . he said he was going to make some calls," I remembered. "He told you to follow me?"

"When you never showed at Enduring Grace, it didn't take much to realize you were headed for Belle Terre."

A whole new picture began to form. "You were *looking* for me?"

The silver went really dark. "I got to the End of the Road about ten minutes after you," he said roughly. "Raymond remembered you—and the guy with the gold car."

My throat tightened. If he'd been a few minutes later—

"The bastard already had you out of the water when I got there," he said, and finally the light in Dylan's eyes dimmed and he looked away, down toward the edge of the mattress—but I was pretty sure he was not seeing the floral bedspread.

"I ran. I shouted your name—"

"I heard you." My voice was as raw as my throat. "But I thought it was a dream . . ."

His shoulders tensed, drawing my attention to a scar across the left side. "Is that why you asked me to stop torturing you?"

Looking away, I stared at my clothes draped over the back of the chair. But I knew it didn't matter. I could look away, walk away. *Run away.* But this was one memory I could not rewrite. Dylan had been there. He'd heard my incoherent ramblings.

I'd been so sure it was a dream, the way the sun had been slanted through the trees, falling around us. The way he'd cradled me. I'd felt so safe . . .

"Hold me," I'd whispered. *"Please just hold me."*

And he had.

"Tell me what I did," he said now, and without thinking I looked back up, and felt my blood thicken.

"I was confused," I sidestepped. "Mixing up my dreams—"

His eyes did exactly as I'd asked—held me. "And I was there?" he asked. "In your dreams?"

Wrong, was all I could think. This was so wrong, being here with him, feeling what I felt . . .

I glanced away, noticing a paper bag on the dresser, plastic bottles sitting next to his gun. "I'm thirsty . . ."

A garbled sound ripped from his throat. "I bet you are." Standing, he retrieved one of the bottles. He was taller than Chase, but leaner, his shoulders wide but not bulky. "It's not much but—"

"Where are we?" The question just hit me—I had no idea how I hadn't asked before.

"Belle Terre."

I felt my eyes widen. I was there . . . the place from my dreams. Scrambling, I fisted the covers around me and swung my legs over the edge of the bed—

The room wobbled. "Easy," he said, catching me as my knees buckled, guiding me to a cheap wing chair.

Sitting, I lifted a hand to the throb at my temple. "It hurts," I whispered as he went down on a knee beside me.

"Probably the airbag," he said. "It's normal for things to be fuzzy."

I looked at him, knew it was wrong to hold on. "Everything keeps spinning . . ."

"That's shock." He edged closer, his eyes concentrated on my face.

I tried to look away, to breathe, but something wouldn't let me move. I had no precedent for this, no fallback for waking up in a hotel room with a guy I hardly knew—and the realization that somewhere along the line my clothes had been removed.

I tried to remember. I wanted to. Maybe I'd taken them off by myself. Maybe he'd held up a blanket or closed his eyes.

I wasn't about to ask—especially when his eyes darkened, and his voice quieted. "I need to touch you."

Something inside me quickened. "Touch me?"

"Your head," he murmured, lifting a hand toward my face. "Is that okay?"

My mouth was so dry I could barely swallow. *"Yes."*

Gently, with a deliberation I remembered from before, he skimmed a finger beside my eye. "Am I hurting you?"

I hadn't realized I was holding my breath, until it whispered from me. "No."

"Good." The pad of his finger made a slow, soft circle. "What about this?"

I closed my eyes.

"The bleeding stopped," he said, and then his hand was gone, and with it the steady current of warmth. "Open your eyes for me."

Wordlessly, I did.

I looked away as he leaned in, concentrated on the dream catcher against his bicep. It was the same, the exact same as the one that hung outside his father's house—the one he had designed. *To trap bad dreams.*

"Pupils look good," he said, and pulled back. "Nothing's changed."

But that wasn't true. Everything had changed.

"You could have taken me back," I said, not understanding why my voice was so hoarse. "You could have taken me back to New Orleans."

"No." He handed me the water bottle he'd retrieved a few minutes before. "I couldn't have."

The words did cruel, cruel things to my equilibrium.

I unscrewed the cap and took a much-needed drink. *"Why not?"* I needed to know. "Why couldn't you take me back to New Orleans?"

Still kneeling in front of me, he rocked back, and his eyes found mine. "Because that's not where you wanted to be."

He made it sound so simple. "What about the guy in the gold car—you don't think he'll come after me again?"

Now his eyes gleamed, the silver lit from the fire inside him. "Not stopping you doesn't mean I won't stop him."

Words. They were just words, that was all. Words from a veritable stranger.

But they drifted around me, drifted through me, and in that moment, they were more than enough.

"You ready?" he asked.

I looked from the water to his outstretched hand, to the sunlight leaking through the curtains.

"To see?"

I reached for him, holding on as my feet found the ground and I stood. This time I didn't sway.

Dylan opened the curtains to a mostly empty parking lot bordering a wooded area. "My father said you dreamed of this place."

"Last night." Along the street, seriously old-looking buildings stretched in both directions. But they weren't the falling down kind of old, but the restored kind—the cool kind, like brightly colored . . . *gingerbread houses.*

"And so you come to see for yourself," he said, "even though my father said he would check it out for you."

The sky was an incredible shade of blue, dotted by endless fluffy white clouds. "There's more," I said, lifting a hand to the glass. "This town . . . I'm supposed to be here." Had I been seeing this street all along? "It's linked to the girl who's missing."

"Are you ready to find out?"

I twisted around so fast the room spun all over again.

He caught me, steadied me.

"Is this what a concussion feels like?" I asked.

"You don't have a concussion." He dragged the chair toward me. "Here. Sit."

"How do you know?"

"Because I do," he said, helping me onto the cushion. "What's your name?"

I eased in a breath, eased it back out. "Trinity Monsour."

He lifted his hand. "How many fingers am I holding up?"

I looked at them, cringing at the reddish, skinned-up knuckles. "Three."

He reached inside the paper bag and pulled out a black T-shirt, yanked it over his head—

—and the dream catcher went away.

But his eyes never left mine. "What's my name?"

I'm not sure why I hesitated—maybe because I always did when his name touched my throat. *"Dylan."*

His smile was slow, lazy. "See? No concussion."

"Where . . . where's my phone?" I had to call . . .

Chase.

Dylan glanced toward the bathroom counter. "Drying out." He gestured toward the dresser, where a BlackBerry almost identical to mine sat. "You can put your SIM card in mine."

Other realities were starting to register. I would have to tell Aunt Sara. LaSalle would want to know why I'd gone to Fourcade instead of him. "My grandmother's car—"

"I had it towed," Dylan said, nudging the brown bag toward me. "You need to get dressed."

Because I wasn't . . .

Refusing to dwell on that fact, I looked inside the bag—and saw the neatly folded jeans and T-shirt. But before I could lift them, Dylan was shoving his gun into his waistband and crossing to pull open the door. "Let me know when you're ready."

Behind him, the heavy metal clanged shut—and my eyes filled. Minutes. Sometimes that was all that separated a good outcome from a bad—life from death. If Dylan hadn't been following me, if he'd arrived a minute or two later . . .

The possibilities chilled.

Still woozy, I made my way to the bathroom, found my SIM card on a towel, then brought it back and slipped it into Dylan's phone.

Two messages waited, one from Victoria, asking where I was and if I was okay, and the second, from Chase.

Got your message.
Hope this ends it.
CMWYC.

My eyes flooded, and for a fractured heartbeat it was last night again . . .

Not wanting to go back, I picked up the bag, dumped out the clothes, and saw the book. It landed facedown, the leather of its back cover blank. I flipped it over without thinking, my eye snagging on a bag of M&Ms on top of the blue jeans. Then I saw the small lock on the book. And the dragonfly. With iridescent wings outstretched, it soared across the cover, fluttering above one single word: DREAMS.

His hair was longer.

It was such a ridiculous thing to think about considering everything else going on, but as we settled into a booth along the front window of Gaston's Place, I found myself wondering why hair that had been military short was now almost long enough for a ponytail.

Something had happened. Something had changed. In the four months since I'd last seen Jim Fourcade's son, it didn't look like he'd had his hair cut even once.

Chase went once a month like clockwork.

Chase.

Thinking about him made my heart hurt. He was so not going to be happy when I told him what happened—or who'd chased off the guy from the gold car.

Dylan's BlackBerry sat on the white cloth covering the table between us. Trying to figure out what I was going to tell Chase, I reminded myself it didn't matter why Dylan had let his hair grow but shaved his goatee. It didn't matter that he looked leaner, that the silver of his eyes looked even more burnished. It didn't matter that I was pretty sure the ink at the back of his neck was new—or that he'd

specifically chosen a seat that allowed us both to see the whole restaurant, but kept his back to the wall.

"Is there someone you need to call?" he asked.

I looked up. "No . . . not yet." It was still early. School hadn't
let out. And I didn't know anything more than I had a few hours
before—except that someone had gone to extreme measures to keep
me from coming to Belle Terre.

"My card's still inside?" I asked as the door opened and two older
men came in. So far, we'd seen a handful of customers, the hostess, and
three waitresses. None of them looked like the girl from my dream.

"Unless you took it out."

One of the men turned toward me.

Instinctively I pulled back.

The hostess nudged him, and, frowning, he followed her to a
back table.

"No texts have come through?" I asked.

Dylan slid the phone toward me. "See for yourself."

I glanced at the dark screen, then back at him. "Not scared I'll
find out all your secrets?"

"Not from my phone, no."

My smile just kind of happened. It was fast and spontaneous,
completely unexpected. "Then where are they?"

The corner of his mouth lifted. "Somewhere safe," he said as the
waitress, Aurora, slid two glasses of ice water between us. With that
razor-sharp sweep of hair cutting against his cheekbone, he glanced
up at her through heavy-lidded eyes, and gave her a devastating smile.

And I knew he was finally going to ask her about the girl I'd seen
in my dream.

"*Perfect.*" He lifted his glass for a long, deliberate sip. "Looks like
it's my lucky day after all."

With soft blond curls bouncing around her face, she flashed a
self-conscious smile and turned away—but not before her eyelashes
fluttered.

Words failed me. I sat there and looked at him, watching him as
he watched *her* flutter away.

"Omigod, are you *serious*?" I asked, not even wanting to touch my water. "What are you waiting for?"

Eyes still all smoldery, he shifted his attention back to me. "It's too soon."

"Too soon? It's been twenty minutes—"

"Trinity." He shifted, watching. "I know what I'm doing."

A man in all white stepped from the kitchen, looking from table to table.

"Then maybe you should tell me," I suggested as the chef-looking guy slipped back through the doors.

"It's called waiting until the time is right."

I looked away, toward the window where the big block letters announced the name of the restaurant—exactly as they had in my dream.

"Some things can't be rushed," he said as I kept looking away, beyond, toward the moss swaying from the parade of oaks sloping toward the bayou across the street.

When he spoke again, his voice so quiet I almost didn't hear it above the light jazz of the restaurant. *"Especially when they matter."*

TWENTY-THREE

I didn't want to look, because I didn't want to see. But I could no more have continued to stare at the trees than I could have ignored the band tightening around my chest.

He sat across from me, sprawled against the red plastic of the booth, the dark hair falling against his face, cutting in a straight line along his cheek.

"And this matters," he said in that same smoke-and-honey voice, the one as soft as the feathers of his dream catcher. And for a fleeting second I had to wonder . . . *what dreams did he catch?*

But there was nothing soft about Dylan Fourcade—or the way he saw without looking. It radiated from every line of his body, the preternatural awareness, the . . . knowing.

"The Navajo is strong in him," his father had said. *"Far stronger than it is in me."*

I hated the quick blade that cut through me—the quick denial. Dylan and I had been friends as children. The ties of our parents bound us. He was here because his father had sent him. That was all that *mattered*—not the fog that drifted through me every time his eyes grew heavy and he touched without lifting a hand.

I looked away. Near the kitchen, two waitresses quickly turned and vanished behind swinging doors.

"That book," I said, changing the subject and pretending I wasn't aware of the way people kept staring, *as if there was something very wrong about me being there.* "The one with the dragonfly—what is it?"

I felt him shift, heard him let out a slow breath. "It was your mother's. I thought you should have it."

Everything around me, the sights and the sounds, the possibilities, fell away, leaving only the two of us—and the leather-bound book I'd left in the hotel. *"My mother's?"*

His shoulders rose again, fell again. "I found it in a box my dad packed away after the storm."

My heart kicked hard, bringing a new kind of possibility. "What is it, a journal?"

He started to answer, but Aurora appeared with our po-boys.

"Can I get you anything?" Her eyes sparkled as she looked at him, and only him. She, unlike everyone else, wouldn't even look at me. "Some mayo or ketchup—Tabasco?"

His smile could have melted polar ice caps. "Not right now."

With another flutter of her eyelashes, she flushed and took the path to the kitchen like a runway.

It was all I could do not to jump across the table and shake him. "Dylan—"

"It's locked," he said as the man at the back of the restaurant, the one who'd been staring at me, lifted his phone as if to text—or take a picture. "It wasn't my place to open it."

Locked—protected. Something of my mother's . . .

I looked away as the man aimed his phone at us. "Everyone's staring at me."

Dylan popped a fry into his mouth. "I know."

"Don't you wonder why?"

He went to work on his sandwich. "That's the beauty of taking your time," he said, between bites. "You never know what might happen."

I looked from him to the fried shrimp spilling from my sandwich.

"I don't understand any of this," I said. "My dreams are mine—no one knows what I see. Who would try to run me off the road? Why?" My stomach churned, but I made myself take a bite. It was my first of the day. "Why does everyone look like they're scared of me?"

Dylan reached for another fry. "Maybe they are."

I barely tasted the shrimp. "But—"

"Hey, Aurora?" he said as the waitress left an older woman sitting by herself—and staring at me. "Got a sec?"

The curly blonde fluffed over. "Can I get you something?"

Dylan kept his movements all casual, lazy almost. "Just wonderin' if you can help me out with something."

Her smile widened. "If I can."

He slid his arm along the back of the booth. "My friend's looking for someone," he said. "The girl who paints here—"

Aurora's smile froze.

"She's about fifteen," Dylan added, but already Aurora was shaking her head. "Brown hair in a ponytail—"

"You must have the wrong place," she rushed.

He made a playful expression. "No, no, I don't think so. We saw her—"

"No, you didn't," she said, twisting away.

Dylan's hand snaked out, stopping her.

Her eyes went wide and dark.

The man in white stepped from the kitchen.

"We just need to talk to her." It was the quiet voice—the persuasive one. "We have reason to think she could be in danger. Maybe you could ask—"

"You're in the wrong place," she said again, really, really fast.

And then she was gone.

She didn't come back, either. Only the man did, the owner, and only to give us our check.

———

By the time we walked into the bookstore over an hour later, it was obvious the people of Belle Terre didn't want to talk.

Which totally meant they knew something.

Everywhere we went, people stared, but no one claimed to have any idea who we were talking about. In the hardware store, Dylan asked about a guy instead, the one from the gold car.

But the owner had been as closed-mouthed as everyone else.

Frustrated, I savored the scent of espresso as my eyes adjusted to the dim lighting inside Isobel's Curiosities. Books crowded the shelves. Purple velour couches sat scattered throughout. A few were occupied, but most sat empty. Funky stools sat in front of the coffee bar, where crystals lay in small piles among magazines and books.

"Can I get you something?" a girl asked, emerging from a door behind the counter.

The second she saw me, she stopped in her tracks, and something inside me snapped. "What is it—why does everyone keep—"

Dylan didn't let me finish. "Water for me," he said, sliding an arm around me. "An iced mocha for my friend."

I stood without moving, tried not to feel, not the warmth of his body—or the way his hand curved around my shoulder.

"Java chip," he added, guiding me to the cluttered bar.

The girl, with her long blond hair hanging straight and her eyes blue like the sky, nodded and hurried away.

Easing onto one of the stools, I absently reached for a small pyramid of pink quartz. Its edges were smooth—

Silver flashed, and my heart started to race.

I hung there, frozen, my arm outstretched, the leather of the bracelet Chase had given me coiled around my wrist, staring, staring without seeing, but feeling . . . feeling something unseen lock around me, and the hot kiss of adrenaline streak into my blood.

"Trinity?"

My hand started to shake, and my breath started to chop.

Dylan crowded close. "What? Tell me what's happening."

I looked at him, blinked, blinked again, and the tight, unseen grip released. "I . . . I don't know."

"You're white as a ghost."

"I . . ." Didn't know how to explain. "It was like I saw something, and then someone grabbed me."

"Do you still feel it?"

I shook my head, sending tangled hair against my face as the girl returned with our drinks.

Dylan watched her, but didn't say a word as she set them in front of us.

She didn't say a word, either.

"Has this happened before?" he asked after she left.

I nodded. "A few times this week."

He glanced toward the door, back at me. "We need to get you home," he said, frowning. "There's nothing here—"

"Not yet." It wasn't time. That was all I could think. It wasn't time.

Stalling, I dragged the frappuccino close and brought the straw to my mouth, took a long, shivery sip—and saw the deck of tarot cards.

And I knew why I wasn't ready to leave.

Stillness fell around me as I reached for the cards in colors of black and purple, dark teal and cranberry. And the second I touched, a low current streaked through me.

I closed my fingers and my eyes, but when I inhaled, I no longer smelled espresso. Only . . . sage.

"My mother used to read these," I said, opening my eyes to look at Dylan. He sat very still, watching. "But you know that, don't you?"

His hand closed around his glass of water. "You've never touched them before, have you?"

I separated the deck into three small stacks and placed them face-down on the bar. "No." I had no idea why. I could have. Any evening I could have walked to Jackson Square and sat at a table, touched the cards, had a reading.

I could have gone to see *Grace*.

The current became more of a vibration. Robotically, I returned the cards to one stack, then fanned them out. The same pattern adorned the back of each, a swirl of teal with glowing stars and moons, vibrant flowers—and two jokers.

"Do you remember her?" My voice was soft—the question like a stone on my heart.

"Yes."

Because he'd been there.

"What about me?" I asked, watching my index finger skim the cards. "Do you remember me?"

"Yes."

The moment locked, held. For so many years my past had been a black hole, a gaping void without memory, or image. Without feeling.

But since coming to New Orleans, light had begun to flicker in the darkness. And from the moment I'd opened my eyes to find myself in Dylan's arms on the bank of the river, sensation had stirred.

I didn't understand how I could want something and deny it at the same time.

But he'd been there. He was part of it, part of the matrix. He knew things I didn't. He remembered. I could see it in the glitter of his eyes, just as I could see something had happened since we'd last been together. It was written all over him in soft dull colors, more than shadows but not solid enough to touch.

Swallowing, I realized I'd quit caressing the cards, instead my finger rested on one, and one alone.

An odd calm settling through me, I slid it from the deck. "My aunt says you came to see me in Colorado," I whispered, but didn't look—not at Dylan, and not at the card.

This time, he moved. His hand found mine, a single, blunt-tipped finger sliding onto the card I'd isolated.

But he did not touch me. "Once."

I'm not sure why I stared, why I couldn't look away from the card, our fingers, the way his nail was trimmed neat, the pinkish flesh beneath, the strong half moon against his cuticle.

"Did we . . ." My throat tried to hold onto the question, but something inside me, something stronger, refused to keep living in the dark. "Did you ever chase me with a hose?"

I felt more than heard his breath, felt more than heard the rush. "It made you laugh."

I closed my eyes. And saw . . . saw it all over again, the tall waving grass and the bright blue sky, the spray of water . . .

It hurt to swallow. It hurt to remember. Because if that was real, and the fire was real, then the rest of what I'd seen while on Julian's couch had to be . . .

But that was impossible. Dylan and I had only been children.

There'd been nothing childlike about what had gone down there in the shadows.

"Aren't you going to look?"

Dylan's question was so quiet the fluted New Age music almost stole it.

I could have said no. That's what I should have said. No. I wasn't going to look. I'd already seen too much.

But I opened my eyes, and saw that somewhere along the line, I'd flipped over the card.

The image stared up at me, intricate and dark and beautiful, two pale purple towers glowing beneath a crescent moon, a sparkling river with a snarling dog on each side, and there beneath the surface, a crawfish.

"The moon card," Dylan said, skimming his finger along the curve of the water.

Something wild and fantastical fluttered through me. "What does it mean?"

"That you face a great choice," came a voice from behind me, strong, sure, as hypnotic as the slow glide of the pointer along the Ouija board. "And the time has come to make it."

TWENTY-FOUR

I swung around.

She stood in the shadows, her hair white and long and flowing, her eyes ethereal, her skin ageless. She wore a long lavender robe and several strands of beads around her neck, gemstones with pendants of ancient coins and goddesses.

"W-who are you?" I asked.

She lifted her hands together in front of her, as if in prayer. And from each bony finger, a different stone glowed. "I am Madame Isobel."

Which meant it was her shop—her cards. "What kind of choice?" I asked.

"You have traveled far," she said in that same rich, monochromatic voice. "The darkness has been great. But now the moon rises, and a watery path emerges."

Water . . .

Dylan's hand slid to cover mine.

"And you feel disoriented, as if walking in your sleep. And you no longer know what is dream-state, and what is real.

"Now you must pass under the moon, between two towers ancient and mythical, and suddenly when you look, it is another land you see."

Say something. I knew I had to say something. Ask something. But words would not come—and the woman did not stop.

"Here are the mysteries you seek, the ones that have driven you, defined you. You now stand in that water," Madame Isobel said, sliding in to tap a finger against the center of the card. "On one shore safety awaits—on the other, the primal land of illusion and madness."

Wordlessly, I lifted my free hand to the pendant at my chest, and curled my fingers around the steady warmth of my mother's dragonfly.

"The choice is yours, child." Her eyes, so dark and timeless, met mine, and the vibration within me strengthened. "You can succumb to the visions and trickery, the hidden enemies—or you can reach for the boat, and pull yourself through."

I just stared. She spoke in riddles, but it was like she could see straight inside me—like she knew. *Everything.*

"You must not be afraid," she said, and then she was taking my hand from Dylan—and I let her have it, let her close it in the surprisingly warm strength of hers. "You are strong, and you will survive wherever the roller coaster tries to take you."

My throat was so dry I couldn't swallow. "You know why I'm in Belle Terre, don't you?"

A strange sheen moved into her eyes. "Do *you*?"

I glanced at Dylan, at the hair cutting against his jaw, and again felt the slow, steady swell.

"Fear creates illusions," Madame Isobel said, turning my hand over in hers. "And terror creates traps. Both prevent us from becoming who we are meant to be."

So much hit me at once, questions and answers and possibilities— and recognition. This stranger, this woman I had no memory of meeting, knew the most secret places inside me, my journey and my struggle. My . . . choice.

"Have we met?" She was, after all, a psychic. "My mother used to—"

My words trailed off as she turned my hand and skimmed a finger along the padded section beside my thumb.

Her eyes grew distant. "Yes," she murmured. "I believe we have."

I looked at Dylan. My throat burned. Something inside me started to unravel. But the second I saw the way he stood there, so quiet and unmoving, but totally, completely aware, the tight band released, and my breath came.

"This is not the first time you have walked this path," Madame Isobel said, and now her voice was sad.

"W-what do you mean?"

She dragged her finger along a series of lines in the fleshy part of my palm, some thin and small, others deep and long. I'd never noticed them before.

"There were many others," she said, glancing from my palm to Dylan.

I would have sworn I heard her breath catch as she looked back down, this time just below my pinkie—and squeezed her eyes shut.

"What?" I asked. "What do you see?"

She remained motionless, her head bowed, as flutes and harps trickled into the vacuum.

Then she looked up. "The answers you seek," she murmured, "cannot be found here."

I lifted my hand higher, urging her to keep looking.

But, twisting a ring of black onyx, she stepped back and took a deep breath. "But there *was* a man who did not belong," she said, point-blank. "Yesterday."

Dylan spoke before I could. "What did he look like?"

"A wrestler," Madame Isobel said. "Wide shoulders and big arms—hair short like a soldier. A thick gold chain and ring."

The chill was immediate. *"Omigod."* He'd been there, the guy from the gold car, the day before. "What about the girl?"

I had no doubt Madame Isobel knew who I was talking about.

"Sometimes," she said in that same oracle-like voice she'd used when describing the moon card, "you must accept no answer as *the* answer."

"No—" I stepped toward her, but she tensed, and Dylan reached for me. "She was here." Frustration pushed me. "I know she was. Why won't anyone tell me? She could be in trouble—"

Madame Isobel put her hands to my shoulders. "You do not need to worry about anyone here."

And with that, she turned and flowed out the front door.

I lunged after her, darting into the bright afternoon sunshine.

But Madame Isobel was neither left nor right. She was gone.

Afternoon bleached the sky, transforming vibrant blue into a whitish gray. So close, was all I could think. I was so close to . . . something.

Standing in the old white gazebo across from the bookstore, I stared at the intricate pattern of lines running through my palm. My lifeline was long but broken, I knew that. But the rest, like so much else, was a mystery.

What had Madame Isobel seen?

Closing my fingers into a tight fist, I looked across the short brown grass of the park to the playground, where a little girl swung from monkey bars while a woman tossed a baseball with a young boy.

Every time I sought answers, new questions came. I'd been right to come here. I knew that much. I also knew Madame Isobel spoke the truth: the fact no one would answer my questions was, in and of itself, an answer.

The new question was *why*?

The girl, with dark hair falling against her shoulders, glanced my way as she swung from the bars. I smiled—but she turned and hurried away.

With the wind whipping around me, I looked back at Dylan standing at the front of the gazebo, alert, watching—watching *everything*.

Everything but me.

And that place inside me, where I'd shut away the craziness of the night four months before, the total *wrongness* of it, nudged against the walls I'd slapped around it—walls I'd *had* to slap around it when Chase had pulled me back into his arms and told me how sorry he was for doubting me—and Dylan had walked away.

I'd told myself it didn't matter. Dylan and I may have played together as children, but we were strangers now. Whatever recklessness had driven me to kiss him had burned out as quickly as it had flared. None of it meant anything—*he* didn't mean anything. The fact that he hadn't said good-bye—that he'd stayed away as if nothing had happened—didn't mean anything.

But now, out of the blue, here he was, beside me again, resuming his role as my protector and leaving little doubt that he would hurt someone, if he had to. Hurt someone badly.

And all the lingering questions from before, the unwanted emotion, tangled through me all over again.

"I don't understand," I said before I could stop myself. "Why are you here—why did you follow me?"

He looked beyond me, beyond the monkey bars, toward the cypress trees sinking into the bayou. "I already told you—"

"No, you told me about your father," I said, swiping the hair from my face. "But he's not here. You are."

And Jim Fourcade didn't look at me like it hurt, didn't touch without lifting a hand.

And he didn't speak in riddles.

And his voice didn't swirl like a drug—or a dream.

"And I want to know why. Why you and not him? Why didn't you tell him no?"

With the wind falling quiet, Dylan turned from that spot across the water to look at me, making me wonder what he was trying to see. And then his eyes took on that dark gleam, the one that revealed the fire inside. "Because he didn't ask."

Behind me, the little girl shrieked. "W-what?"

"I didn't say no," he said with that same crazy stillness. "Because he didn't ask."

"Then—"

"I'm here because this is where I need to be," he added with a quick glance toward the playground.

Need.

He looked back, and the corner of his mouth lifted. "But you would have."

"Would have what?"

"Said no." There was no emotion in his voice, just a simple statement of fact. "If my dad or your aunt had told you I was going to keep an eye on you . . ." Stepping toward me, he lifted his hand, the movement so slow I could have stepped back before his fingers found my hair and slid it from my eyes.

But I didn't.

"You would have said no."

I wanted to deny what he was saying—there was no logical reason for me to reject protection.

"It's written all over you," he said, and somehow I hadn't realized he was still touching me, his hand to my face, his thumb gliding along my cheekbone. "Like a closed door."

I took a quick step back, realizing too late that in moving, I was validating his words. "I'm not the one who closed it."

He'd done that. He'd done that the night at Big Charity.

"But you're not opening it, either."

I turned toward the little girl, but the memory found me anyway, the one from Julian's couch, of the darkness and the closed door, what had happened when I pulled it open and stepped inside.

The body follows the mind, I'd once read. The body has no sensor of its own, no way to discern reality from memory or fantasy. What the mind conjures, the body feels. What the mind sees, the body experiences. That's why Aunt Sara didn't want me exploring my dreams—or stepping into my visions. She didn't want me to feel the terror or the grief, the pain.

But this wasn't pain. The sensation curling through me, the residue from that room, wasn't grief or terror, either. But it did hurt.

The door between us had closed last fall, and it had to stay that way.

"I can't," I said as the girl ran around the curved red slide—and stopped in her tracks. "I can't open it again."

Because if I did, I wouldn't be able to breathe.

"What are you so scared of—"

I pulled away from him, watching the little girl sneak a quick look at the woman and boy, then start toward the gazebo.

I crossed to her, smiling as she stopped and stared up at me. "Hi."

Her eyes got really big.

Sliding the hair from my face, I went down on a knee. "You're really good on those monkey bars."

But it was like she didn't even hear me. "I didn't think you were real . . ."

My heart kicked up a notch. "Real?" I asked with a funny face. "Why wouldn't I be?"

"Because they said you weren't."

To her, it was clearly some big exciting secret. "Who?" I said. "Who said I wasn't?"

"*Everyone!* My mom, Mr. Philippe, Brittany . . ."

I felt Dylan come up behind me. "Who's Mr. Philippe?"

"Aurelia!" The woman swung around, jerking a hand to her forehead.

"The gallery man," she said, waving.

"What gallery?"

"The one down the street," she said as the woman—her mother?—started toward her. "I always thought you looked so scared—but you're really pretty."

"Aurelia!" The older version of her raced up behind her. "I told you—"

"Mom—look! It's the girl from the pictures . . ."

Her mother froze.

"She's real!" the little girl gushed, but already her mom was springing back to life and taking her by the arm.

"No, it's okay—"

The mother looked stricken. "Don't mind her," she said. *"She doesn't know what she's talking about."*

Aurelia tried to protest, but her mother dragged her away.

Everything flashed. *"Omigod."* But then I was the one pulling away, hurrying away, down the street in the direction the girl had pointed—the little girl who hadn't been coached, who didn't know to be afraid or protect—toward the gallery she'd mentioned.

"Trinity—"

At the crosswalk, I hurried to the other side, stopping outside an old wood-frame church. Hoping someone could tell me where to find the gallery, I took the steps and reached for the heavy front door—and saw the sign: PHILIPPE'S PLACE.

I'd found the gallery without even trying. And yet instead of reaching for the handle, I lifted my hand and pressed my palm against the dark wood.

I felt him even though he said nothing, felt him come up behind me. But as usual, he stopped in that fraction of a breath before his body found mine.

And I just stood there, suspended between a past I didn't understand and a future that kept shifting.

"I saw her," I told him. "In my dream, I saw the girl painting." And I couldn't help but wonder, if I hadn't spoken, if I'd simply stood and watched, what would have come next? Would she have added me to the scene of the hawk and the ice cream shop? Would I have looked . . . *not real,* as the little girl said?

"That's why everyone's been staring at me," I knew. "That's why I'm here, why I *had* to come here—why I was drawn here."

"All you have to do is open the door."

A literal door, hard and solid and closed, separating me from the answer I craved.

"I don't understand," I murmured. "How can a complete stranger paint pictures of me?"

Dylan stepped closer. "The same way you saw her, and Grace."

I twisted so fast I had no time to prepare for how little space separated us. He caught me, his hands to my arms, his fingers curving. Around us, the breeze blew, cool, I knew, it had to be cool.

But as the hair whipped against my face, I felt only warmth, and when I looked up, I found a certainty far beyond eighteen years.

"And Jessica," I murmured. Against logic or reason, I'd seen them all.

And they'd seen me.

"But sometimes things just are," he said, and even had he not touched me, I would have felt him. And I wasn't sure why, wasn't sure why he wouldn't let go, when it was obvious I had nowhere to go.

"That's why I'm here," I said, lifting my hand to the dragonfly at my chest. "To find out what *is*."

"Then open the door."

Four words. That's all they were. Simple, straightforward, obvious. I had only to open the door and walk inside.

"What if she was mistaken?" I said, vaguely aware of a blur of motion to my right. "What if there's no link between me and the portrait?"

"You're stalling."

Turning, I lifted a hand to swat the mosquito, and saw the dragonfly hovering at the door.

"If you want to see what comes next," Dylan said, as somewhere beyond, a bird screamed, "you have to open doors."

I stared at the gossamer-thin wings of the dragonfly—strong enough to carry, but fragile enough to be destroyed by the slightest pressure—and no longer knew which door Dylan was talking about. The one to the gallery—or the one within me.

Lifting my hand to the heavy gothic door, I reached for the handle. But I didn't turn it, not until Dylan put his hand to mine. Then, together, we pressed the lever and stepped inside.

TWENTY-FIVE

The chapel, with its white steeple and gothic windows, had to be at least a hundred years old. And while the people of Belle Terre no longer worshipped within, the shadowy vestibule still radiated church. Maybe it was the dark wood floors and walls, the ornate candelabras. The stillness, the quiet.

"There's no one here," I said, looking around.

Behind me the door closed, and Dylan crossed to a desk and picked up a black business card. Retrieving his phone, he glanced down and frowned. "It's after five."

On a Friday night. I hadn't even considered that.

"You have a missed call."

Something inside me twisted. I hurried over to him, taking the phone from his hands—and finding Chase's name.

There was no message.

Uneasy, I shot him a quick text before crossing to the door to the inner sanctuary.

> Can't talk now.
> I'll call you soon.

If Chase had heard my voice, he would have known something was very wrong.

Sliding the phone into my pocket, I reached for the handle—

"You can't go in there, darlin'."

I spun around to find an older man with military short white hair emerging from a dark corridor. Overhead a sign read RESTROOMS.

"Are you Philippe?"

His smile was warm, friendly. "Not in this lifetime," he drawled as I noticed the utilitarian nature of his blue work shirt and the broom against the wall, the rag in his hand. "Maybe I'll be gettin' luckier in the next."

"Do you know where I can find him? I need to talk to him."

The older man's smile faded, as his eyes narrowed. Thoughtfully, he lifted a hand to rub his whiskers. "You from around here? You look awfully—" His eyes flared, then got really, really dark. "You're her."

My heart kicked. "You've seen me before?" Robotically, he crossed the lobby.

I followed. Because I knew. I knew where he was going, and I knew why the hum had started inside me, why it grew louder.

Why the dragonfly had hovered outside.

The frame was museum quality, lavish and intricate in antiqued shades of bronze and ebony. It hung on the wall, safely away from the sun, in a place of perpetual shadows. Trapped inside of it, beneath a sheet of glass, a soft green dragonfly fluttered against a blur of camellias, and with eyes the color of night and skin the color of death, I screamed.

The lobby fell away, taking with it the remains of the day and the echo of the silence, leaving only a vacuum without a molecule of oxygen.

Through the haze I was aware of Dylan moving toward me, the feel of his hand against my back.

"*Sweet Christ.*" The janitor's voice was garbled, distant, as if water filled the void. "I thought you were dead."

I tried to turn to him, but my body wouldn't move. Breathing hurt. But then Dylan was doing what I couldn't, stepping toward the old man who stood like a bystander at a grisly crime scene.

"Why would you think that?"

"I-I . . ." The man stepped back, shaking his head. "Look at her," he breathed, glancing beyond Dylan to the vividly hued painting that could not have borne a stronger resemblance to me, had I posed. "Does she look alive?"

It was impossible to tell which she he meant.

Inside the shaking started, the fissures of cold springing up in an unwanted free-for-all. *This* is what I'd wanted. *This* is why I'd come. For answers.

But I'd never expected to find myself in the throes of death.

"Who is she?" Dylan asked.

"I . . . I can't really say."

"Can't—or won't?"

"Can't. Never asked," the janitor said. "Most of the time I try not to even look at her."

But I couldn't stop. Her features had a swirling, dreamlike quality, as if thick glass separated her from the world beyond, trapping her, holding her back. Her dark brown eyes were wide, drenched with devastation—and acceptance.

And they were mine.

"What about the artist?" That was Dylan. There was no way words could have squeezed through my throat. "What can you tell me about who did this? It was a girl, right?"

Did. This. Not paint. Not create.

Did. This.

"Nothing," the janitor muttered. "I'm afraid you'll have to come back in the morning . . ."

Spending the night in Belle Terre was not part of the plan. Spending the night in a small hotel room with Jim Fourcade's son was so much worse.

He sat by the door, in the dainty buttery yellow chair that looked like it belonged in a child's portrait—not as a seat for a guy in faded jeans and a charcoal T-shirt, working a switchblade against the lock on my mother's book.

I could have had him take me home. I could have come back in the morning. Except my car sat dead in the parking lot. And even if I'd found a ride—from Chase or Victoria, Detective LaSalle—there was the small complication of Fleurish!

I was scheduled to open at ten tomorrow morning.

It was way simpler and more efficient to spend the night and head home in time for work.

Curled around the BlackBerry, my fingers throbbed. I looked up, toward the remains of the bloodred sunset. Standing at the window, I'd watched every second of the transition, but had no memory of when night had taken over.

But I knew when the phone rang. The sudden interruption kicked through me, and even before I saw his name, I knew.

Acutely aware of the way Dylan glanced up, I turned toward the VACANCY sign flashing against the darkness.

"Hey," I answered quietly.

"Where are you?"

The bluntness of the question caught me off guard. "*Chase.* I-I'm still in Belle Terre. I was going to call you in a few minutes—"

"Maybe you should call Detective LaSalle."

I froze.

"He's looking for you."

Oh, God.

"Which is weird, since I thought he was *with* you," Chase said.

And everything started to spin. *"W-what?"*

"All day." His voice was quieter now, relentless, much like it had been last night on the levee, when he'd told me he wanted to hurt Dylan for being in my dream. "I thought you were with Detective LaSalle."

My mind raced. I tried to remember. What had I said, what exactly had I said in my voice mail?

"No." I'd never said LaSalle. I was sure of that. "I didn't . . ." Want to feel like a rat in a cage, didn't want him to watch and study, see into dreams that might have had nothing to do with Grace. "I didn't want to drag him into this until I knew for sure."

A garbled sound broke through the phone. "Drag him in? T, he's a cop. That's his job."

"I know that." I wanted to be home. I wanted to be at Chase's house and looking into his eyes, touching him. I wanted him to touch me back.

I wanted all this to be over.

"I wasn't sure about what I was seeing," I told him, "and didn't want to make anything official. I just wanted to look—to see if what I saw in the dream is even real."

"And is it?"

"Yes."

"Then why are you still there?"

It was a simple question—it deserved a simple answer. But there wasn't one. Not a simple one. "There's someone else I need to talk to."

He didn't say anything, but I could hear him, hear him breathing— and my heart squeezed.

"Chase," I whispered. "Say something."

Several seconds passed. Several long seconds during which the heater blew, its breath blowing the curtain—but the warmth didn't come close to touching me.

"T," he finally said. His voice was softer now, and it was all I could do to swallow. "This isn't a game."

I knew that. The stakes were way higher.

"I wish it was," I said, staring at the leather band wrapped around my wrist. "I wish I *could* put everything back in a box and stash it in a closet." Like we'd done last Sunday, before . . .

Before so much.

It was hard to believe how badly everything had blown up in less than a week.

"But it's my life," I said, hating it, hating it all, the dreams that wouldn't stop and the distance that kept spreading. "And I can't walk away."

I'd just never imagined what I might be walking toward. It had all seemed so harmless. Sure I'd known the danger, but I'd never really thought that it would touch me. *Touch us.*

I'd never realized what I discovered could change everything.

"Think about Pensacola," I said to him, as he'd said to me a few days before. That's what I was trying to do, to project beyond this moment, to what lay ahead.

But for me, the image still wouldn't form. "Think about the water and the beach—"

"You shouldn't be there alone."

His voice was softer, more tender, and with it I glanced at the window, where through the reflection I saw Dylan sprawled in that silly little chair, with the knife in one hand, the gun in his lap.

"Come down then." That would solve everything. "It's not too late. Get in your car and—"

"T—"

I squeezed the phone. *"Please."*

"I can't."

Through the reflection, Dylan's eyes lifted to mine, and the hot burn of awareness seared through me. "Why not?"

The second I heard his rough breath, I knew. "You're with Jessica."

"She had a rough day," he said—and my eyes filled.

My day hadn't been very good, either.

"Trinity?"

I sucked in a slow, deep breath, refusing to let myself cry. "You have to trust me," I said, and even though I tried to stop it, emotion leaked through. "I'm safe—I'll be home in the morning. We'll go to your uncle's party. Nothing's changed."

There wasn't much to say after that, other than good-bye. But long after the line went dead, I held onto the phone, *Dylan's phone,* and looked out at the night.

"Do you want to go back?"

The words were so quiet I almost didn't hear them. I made myself swallow, didn't want to look—

He still held the book with the dragonfly cover in his hands, his
legs sprawled, his lean, runner's body no match for the little chair.

"No," I said.

"I'll take you—"

"No."

His eyes narrowed, and I saw it, the Navajo in him, could see it
so clearly now that I knew, the silky dark hair and olive skin, the
sharp cheekbones and hawkish eyes, the . . . awareness.

Maybe that's why he was so good at touching without lifting a
hand, seeing without looking.

He shifted, the sweep of hair falling against his face. "You left
out a lot."

The coil inside me, the one that kept squeezing and squeezing,
squeezed even harder. "He doesn't want me here. He wanted me to
step back—"

"And you? What do you want?"

Around my wrist, I could feel leather cutting into flesh, but I
didn't look down. "Pretending something isn't happening doesn't
mean it's not."

Something in Dylan eyes shifted. "But you know why he wants
you to step back, don't you?"

I closed my eyes.

"You scare him," he said, and when I looked again, I saw the
switchblade was closed. "You scare a lot of people."

"But not you," I said—and then I saw the book open against his
jeans.

He looked up. Our eyes met. "Ready?"

TWENTY-SIX

Everyone dreams. Some see color. Others experience only black and white. Some laugh, and some cry. Some run and hide, while others play and dance. Some return over and over again. Others never go back. Very few remember.

I looked up from the yellowed pages, where time had reduced black ink to gray. The handwriting was beautiful, like calligraphy. Not even time could take that away.

"You okay?"

Pressing my lips together, I glanced toward the dainty chair where he rolled a water bottle between his hands. He'd gone outside after handing me the journal, muttering something about checking the perimeter, but I think we'd both recognized the lie. And for it, I'd been grateful.

"It's all here," I said. In her own handwriting, her own words. "Everything she felt, feared."

His hands stilled, but he said nothing, just as he said nothing when he'd come back inside and found me cross-legged on the bed, reading.

I hadn't trusted myself to look up. Even now, I wasn't sure why.

"It's like she knew," I said. "It's like she was documenting every-thing. *For me.*"

His eyes softened. "Maybe she was."

The hot swell of emotion I'd been fighting leaked through, flooding my heart and my eyes and everywhere in between. "That would mean . . ." The punch of realization was quick, brutal.

"Aunt Sara said my mother knew she would never see me grow up," I said as tears turned everything watery. "But I thought what-ever she'd seen, whatever she'd known, came after she married my dad. After I was born. But . . ." I breathed against another surge of emotion. "What if it was before? What if she always knew?"

Dylan put down the water. "Your mom loved you," he said. "All she wanted was for you to be okay."

I blinked him into focus, the penetrating eyes and sharp cheek-bones, the sweep of hair along his jaw that made me want to reach out. Funny what time could do. Sometimes it made feelings, memories, fade, and sometimes it made them grow.

Abruptly I looked back down, to the journal in my lap.

I awaken in the predawn darkness, my heart racing, my body frozen, the echo of a silent scream burning my throat. Breathing hurts.

   Remembering destroys.

   I try anyway. I'm scared not to. They're messages—I know that now. From some place unseen, some person unknown.

Just one day. That's all I wanted. To look into her eyes and ask the questions that haunted me, to find out how she'd lived with the coming attractions of so many lives, including her own. I knew some of the preparations she'd made, but they were physical, tactical. My questions ran deeper. If only there was a way—

The second the possibility formed, the answer came. "Do you believe in the astral plane?"

Dylan answered without words, glancing away from me, toward the flashing VACANCY sign beyond the window.

"You do, don't you?" And with the realization came new possibilities. Julian said the body was a shell, the physical world only temporary. He said we could leave the body and go to the astral, meet there . . .

Something inside me started to race. I'd thought myself alone when I'd closed my eyes and let go. I'd gone looking for Grace, that was true. But I'd found someone else.

The light was shining brighter now. If Dylan had been there . . .

He knew. He knew *everything*.

Once, I would have executed a sharp U-turn and backtracked as fast as I could. But there was nowhere to go, not when everywhere I turned, the truth waited.

"I tried to go," I said and he swung toward me so fast I scooted back, forgetting about the wall until I rammed into it.

"Why would you do that?"

For the first time, his voice faltered. I just wasn't sure what leaked through—surprise, or fear?

"Julian thought—"

"Julian?"

I eased the hair from my face, my fingers hesitating at the fading tenderness along my temple. "He said if I could find Grace there, I could find her in the real world."

Dylan looked as if I'd punched him. "Did it work?"

"No."

"Did you find . . . *anyone*?"

You.

"Me," I said instead. "I found me as a little girl, the fire . . ."

He closed his eyes.

Maybe I should have looked away, given him the privacy that naked, unguarded moments deserved. But for a heartbeat I couldn't look away from the way his shoulders strained against his T-shirt and his legs, hip-width apart, stood braced. And even without the glow of silver, I saw the restraint.

I made myself look down, back to my mother's journal. Because I hadn't meant to do it, to open that door, the one that protected that place inside me, the one that wanted so badly to understand. I hadn't even meant to touch it.

But the second even the crack appeared, emotion surged.

I lay tangled in the damp sheets, hot, sweaty, forcing myself to breathe. In, out. Slow, steady. I know the drill. I know the routine. Just a few minutes and I'll be able to move. Just a few minutes and a new day will begin.

"Some doors shouldn't be opened."

I looked up. "That's not what you said before. You said opening them was the only way to see what was inside—"

"The past is different. We close doors for a reason."

"What reason?"

The lines of his face tightened. "To prote—"

"Don't." I was off the bed in a heartbeat, halfway to him before everything started to spin.

TWENTY-SEVEN

He caught me as I glared up at him. "Don't say *protect*."

"It's not a bad word, Trinity."

I looked away, and the room tilted again.

"Careful." Easing me back to him, he lifted a hand to slide the hair from my face. "Just breathe for me."

But I couldn't. I couldn't breathe for him, not without making everything misfire. Because somewhere along the line, the wall I'd hammered up between us, the wall that *had* to be there, the wall that made sure that what happened behind closed eyes never bled into what was real, crumbled.

And I could no longer be sure, I realized. I could no longer be sure where the wall belonged, or even *if* it belonged. If there were really separate worlds, or just . . . *separate sides*.

"What's happening?" I whispered. *To me?*

He helped me back to the bed. "You're exhausted."

Dark spots clouded my vision. I sat with my hands braced against the mattress, more than ready for the roller coaster to slow—*stop.* "Maybe I should see a doctor."

"You don't need a doctor."

The rational part of me suggested it might be a good idea to get a second opinion. But something in Dylan's voice, his touch, said that wasn't necessary. "Is that the Navajo in you talking?"

He stilled.

"Your dad told me."

His eyes narrowed, his fingers whispering across the tenderness at my forehead. "It's not your body I'm worried about."

Everything slowed, my breath, my heart, even the rush of air from the heater. It all thickened, swirling through me as if someone had slipped me another sedative.

"You wouldn't do that, would you?" I asked, using my voice to continue a conversation in my mind.

His thumb skimmed a slow circle against my temple. "Quit fighting."

It was so tempting to just . . . *let go.*

"Or maybe you would," I said, not yet ready, not ready to sink into the pillows and close my eyes. I'd done that before. I'd let go. "It's not like I really know anything about you."

His fingers stilled. "What do you want to know?"

Everything, I realized. Because in truth, I knew little more than who his father was, that he had a knack for showing up when I needed him most, that as children we'd run through a field—and that the Navajo ran strong in his blood. "How old are you?"

"Eighteen."

"Did you graduate?"

"G.E.D."

"College?"

"Not right now."

The room grew fuzzier, the lamplight taking on a mercurial glow, and with it, I felt myself sinking toward the pillow. "What do you mean . . . not now?"

"I had to drop out."

There was something in his voice, something dull and sad. "Why?"

His eyes met mine. "Because I had to."

"That's not an answer," I muttered as, despite how hard I fought, I felt myself start to drift.

"Because someone needed me," he whispered, and then it didn't matter how hard I tried to hold on.

I let go.

His chest rose and fell with each rhythmic breath.

He made no sound. His eyes were closed. His long legs were crossed at the ankles. Curled around the gun, his hand was slack. And yet I still couldn't tell if he slept.

It was such a simple thing. Close your eyes, go to sleep. Rest. But even with his eyes closed, Dylan Fourcade was alert, as if nothing, not even lightning from a clear sky, could catch him off guard.

Except when I'd mentioned the dream regression.

He'd tucked me in. He'd closed the curtains and turned off the lamps, pulling the bathroom door partially closed to allow only a sliver of light to leak through. But he'd left his shoes on.

And yet I was the one who'd been running.

My heart still raced. I'd come awake with a surge of adrenaline, paralyzed for several choppy breaths, until I'd opened my eyes to find Dylan. For a long time I'd just laid there and watched him, trying to link my breath to his. Slow, steady. In. Out.

Giving up, I slipped from bed and eased toward the door. I couldn't stay there one second longer, not with the heater rattling and Dylan breathing.

The second the cool night air hit me, I took a deep breath. By the time I lifted the bottle of water from the vending machine, my movements weren't as jerky. And when I drank almost the whole thing in one long sip, only then did I realize how completely I'd resisted feeling anything, even thirst.

Out of habit, I checked the BlackBerry, not thinking about what I might find until the notifications registered.

Eight messages waited—seven text, one voice—from three senders.

My heart started to race. I'd forgotten. I'd been so blindsided by everything that had happened, I'd forgotten to check in with my aunt. Victoria and I texted every night.

And *Chase.*

With the VACANCY sign flashing, I stared at his name. All my life I'd dreamed about finding someone who cared about me, what it would feel like, be like. How he'd look at me and hold me, make me feel stronger than before, prettier. *Better.*

I'd never imagined how complicated it could be.

But I'd been a little girl then, alone in the mountains with only my grandmother, and my dreams.

Now, almost seventeen, I'd learned there was a difference between dreams, reality, and fantasy.

It would have been easy to slip the phone back into my pocket. But that wouldn't make the messages go away. And it wouldn't make reality any less difficult.

My aunt was having a great time, but I could tell she was a little worried. She'd left me one garbled voice mail, followed by three texts.

U've been quiet. Hope all is ok. Text me when u can.
Naomi rocked the wedding. Prettiest. Ever. Guess u r asleep.
Text me in the AM. I'm hitting Tulum around noon.

Blinking against the sting at my eyes, I thought about calling, but knowing the time, I texted.

Sorry! Fell asleep! Glad the wedding was great. Miss you!

Then I tackled the mess that was my best friend:

Whazzup? Where r u? Amber sez Chase is with Jessica again.
How does that not kill you? And u say Lucas needs to get a grip.
But seriously. Where r u? Why won't u answer?
Want to tell you about Trey. R u ok?

That was one message, and to it I fired back a quick response.

All's good. Got hung up. B back in the AM. Sorry!

I leaned back against the cool, concrete wall.

Chase had texted me three times, all between 11:11 and 11:22.

Sorry about b4

I'm thinking of Pensacola.

CMWYC

Not sure what else to do, I turned and started to walk.

The town slept. There wasn't a single car on Main Street, just the parade of streetlamps ending where the old chapel sat, and the woods took over. Maybe that's where I was headed all along, back to the gallery. Or maybe it was a whim. But the second I saw the glow of white against the night sky, I knew there was no turning back.

At the steps leading to the old door, I hesitated. The wind had fallen quiet, darkness spilled from all directions, and yet the hum grew louder as I spun around—and saw the dragonfly.

It couldn't have been the same one from that afternoon. I knew that. And yet familiarity gripped me, and when its gossamer wings carried it toward the back of the building, I knew I was supposed to follow.

Thick grass cushioned my feet—bare, I realized for the first time. Dylan had slept in his shoes, and yet I was the one who'd slipped into the night. But I hardly felt the cool dampness against my feet, not when I saw the dragonfly veer toward the building, and vanish.

I froze, stared, was vaguely aware of pinching myself to see if I dreamed.

The pain registered, but I also knew it didn't necessarily mean anything. Sometimes I felt nothing in my dreams. But increasingly, I felt everything.

And whether this was real or a dream into which I'd awakened, I knew I had to go inside. The doors were closed, but there, partially concealed by a barren climbing rose, a window stood open.

Once there would have been wooden pews, an altar, and a crucifix. But the chapel no longer served as a church, and it was not religion people came to find. It was art, and it was everywhere.

The stained glass remained. The thick windows on both sides of the church no doubt glowed with the sun. But the moon was not strong enough to penetrate, leaving the sanctuary draped in darkness. Fascinated, I reached for Dylan's BlackBerry and turned it into a flashlight.

I moved slowly, lifting the phone to painting after painting, some quiet and serene in soft swirls of colors. Others were bolder, angry. Others were playful, while others haunted. Still lifes and landscapes, plantations along the river, oaks dripping with moss and even an eerie white tiger crouched in the shadows of the swamp. There was a close-up of a large hand cradling a small one, and a child at its mother's breast. But none of me.

With every step the disappointment knotted tighter, until I turned to the last row, and saw the four empty spots.

And before I reached them, I knew.

The placards remained, bronze rectangles identical to those beneath every other portrait. There would be two names, that of the piece of art, and that of the artist.

I'm not sure how I didn't run to them. Then, as I lifted the phone, I wasn't sure how I would ever stop shaking.

Glory.
Ecstasy.
Rapture.
Eternal.

Each portrait had a different name, but the artist was the same.

Anonymous.

"No," I whispered, spinning around. Just . . . no. They couldn't be gone.

But even as the thought formed, the truth reverberated.

They were.

I ran, guided more by memory than light, until I reached the huge door to the lobby, where the other portrait of me hung. I yanked at the ancient handle, kicked it hard when it didn't budge.

That would have been a good time to leave.

But when I turned, I saw the dragonfly. And again, I followed.

I moved slowly, not wanting to scare it away, ignoring the hiss of the wind outside, the dead calm inside. On some level I was aware of the blast from an unseen heater, the way the air was almost too acrid to breathe, but none of that mattered, not when the dragonfly led me through a door I'd not noticed before, to where an old altar served as a worktable, and a sketchbook sat on top.

Mechanically, I reached for it, flipped it open, and saw. I was there, right there on the pages in front of me, not in bold dramatic oils as I'd been in the lobby, but in shades of charcoal. My eyes were wide, captured in that place between rapture and horror, my mouth open, contorted, but I could not tell if I breathed—or screamed. In the corner of the sketch, a dragonfly hovered, and vines tangled. At the bottom, one word.

"Again." Without thought, I flipped the pages, one after the other, but saw the same thing: me trapped beneath the surface.

Suddenly I knew I wasn't alone.

Dylan. But as quickly as his name formed, details began to register, all the little things I'd ignored before, like the intensifying heat inside the small room—and the crackling outside. And even as I spun for the door, I knew it would be closed.

Time fell away, and I was two years old again, in the small room with the rocking chair and the crib, and no way out.

"No, no, no," I whispered.

But the crackle became a roar and the heat an inferno, and as flames consumed and smoke poured in, I dropped to my knees and felt the burn sear my lungs.

There was no time for question or disbelief, only to get out. I clenched the BlackBerry as tightly as I could, but the faux flashlight was no match for the smoke. Crouching, I crawled toward the back of the room, using my hands when I found the wall. A window. That was all I needed.

I found only smooth panels of wood.

A thousand things ran through my mind, fear and shock and determination, horror, disbelief, questions and answers and dreams. Fantasies.

Reality.

They all tangled, preventing me from grabbing onto anything. There was only blind desperation, and suffocating reality.

The town slept. At some point, five minutes, maybe six, firemen would come. They would lift their hoses and attack the flames, but there would be no reason to check inside. Not in the middle of the night, in a building that should not have been occupied. It was old, wooden, a tinderbox. No one would risk their life to save a painting.

By the time Dylan realized I was gone . . .

Coughing, I made it to my feet and staggered forward, groping along the wall. I couldn't just sit down and wait to die. I couldn't—

"Trinity!"

Blindly I reached for him, even though I knew he was only in my mind. I grabbed at my shirt and dragged it over my nose, breathed greedily for the fraction of a second until smoke took over.

My eyes burned. My throat burned. Somehow I kept moving, even as something behind me exploded, and embers fell like rain. I knew better than to look back.

"Trinity!"

His voice was vague, far away, shouting from that place inside me, the place where the dreams came from, and to where I made them return. Or maybe it had nothing to do with him or a dream, but the fantasies of an oxygen-deprived brain.

And then I could see her, see her coming toward me from the trees in a gown of white, glowing, reaching for me.

"Mama."

Her hair was long, dark, and flowing. Her face was ashen, stricken.

"Mama," I said again, and then she was running so fast, screaming.

"No!" she shouted. "No!"

She was beautiful, her movements graceful. All I had to do was go to her and—

"Fight," she shouted. "Fight!"

But I was so tired of fighting, and my body was working against me. And all I wanted was to sink into her arms and let her take me.

"It's not time!" she said, but I knew that was just a mother's love talking, because even as sirens sounded, my lungs were shutting down, a sweet, gentle softness replacing the cutting edges, enveloping me.

And then the fire was licking closer, the heat fusing through me as I fell.

But I never reached the ground.

"I've got you." Suspended somewhere between here and there, between her world and mine, the words barely registered. *"I'm here—I'm always, always here."*

TWENTY-EIGHT

Dying is a lot like dreaming.

I'd heard that once, that when the body fails and conscious thought falters, the mind takes over, stripping away the fear and the pain, leaving only beauty and wonder, a few last, exquisitely gorgeous glimpses before it's all over. It's a chemical process, nothing more. Deprived of oxygen, the body turns to hallucination.

But as the words drifted through me, the fusion of dream and fantasy felt like so much more.

"I've missed you," I said, but like all the other times, it was more breath than voice. "So much." I was being lifted then, my body swept from the ground and cradled as heat blasted and flames danced. But none of it seemed real, none of it even mattered, not as we ran toward the darkness.

I'd always imagined light. I'd heard it compared to the end of a tunnel, a seductive pinprick, and that nothing would matter but reaching it. But I saw no light, not the bright brilliant glowing kind, just swirling reds and yellows and oranges slashing against the night. And the crackling, the hissing. They grew louder, surrounding us like sinister laughter.

But I wasn't scared. Not anymore. I wasn't scared, was barely even there. I wasn't out of my body, either, just suspended, lifted. Insulated.

I held on, held on so very, very tightly, didn't know how I'd ever let go. But not even that mattered. If my body gave out, I was being held, being held as tightly as I, in turn, held on, and it didn't matter if I let go, because he wouldn't.

He'd promised. So many times. He wouldn't.

And then, as the last few breaths were shredding through my chest, the flames fell away and the darkness turned pure, and before I realized what was happening, a breath of cool air enveloped me, and we were on the other side, running into the night as sirens screamed and new lights flashed. There was shouting and a new roar, but none of *that* mattered . . .

We ran toward the trees. It was all so familiar, even as it was new. And only then did I realize I'd buried my face against his throat. I pulled back as he slowed, made myself look.

"Easy," he said as he always did, and his eyes, they were so silver, glowing in that burnished way as if the fire that consumed the chapel was consuming him, too, consuming him from the inside out. But there was no pain there, no fear, just a fervor I'd never seen before, and it merged with the oxygen swirling through me.

"You're here," I whispered with what little voice I could find. It was raw and it scraped, but I didn't care, couldn't care about anything but the moment that was holding me. *"You're really here."*

"Always."

Conscious thought fell away as I lifted a hand to his face, my fingers feathering the warmth of his flesh. And when the illusion didn't crumble, when it strengthened instead, drawing me closer, promising me something I didn't understand but wanted so very, very badly, it was my face I lifted to the scrape of his whiskers, my eyes that closed.

"Always," I echoed. As my mouth found his I absorbed that first breath between us, that first kiss. It was slow and soft, achingly tender.

All I wanted was to touch him and feel him, to hold on and never let go.

"Everything's going to be okay," he murmured even though he didn't need to, because I already knew it, felt it with every beat of my heart.

The night held us. Arms around me, he lowered me to the grass and a new dream took over, not the dream of dying, but the dream of living.

"Trinity," he breathed as I pulled him closer. He'd come. Somehow he'd come. He'd known.

He always knew.

Behind us the fire blazed, but there in our own little world, a different fire healed. "Dylan—"

I froze, tried to understand. I had no conscious memory of sliding my hands beneath his shirt, of clinging to him in every way imaginable, but there was no denying the intimacy of our bodies, or the blind desperation that had exploded between us.

He pushed back from me, his body suspended over mine, but no longer touching.

I looked up at the dark hair sweeping against his cheekbone, shielding but not hiding the anguish in his eyes, and the ache in my heart deepened.

"This is so wrong . . ." It was such an odd time to start crying. But I did. Because it *was* wrong. So very, very wrong, on so very many levels. But even as the realization took hold, I didn't want to let go, and somewhere deep inside begged me to close my eyes and go back, let the dream take over once more.

"I'm with Chase now," I whispered—as much to myself as to Dylan.

Shadows shouldn't fall at night. It shouldn't even be possible, not with thick clouds of smoke obliterating the light of the moon. But I saw it, saw the shadow slip over him, and the beautiful silver of his eyes go flat.

"Then why isn't he with you?"

That was all he said, but it was enough. "Dylan—"

He stood and stepped back from me, his face twisted with something I didn't come close to understanding.

"Dylan," I said again, scrambling after him.

He caught me as the world tilted. "Just breathe."

I stood there as he held me, and tried. "I—" But the quick rush of oxygen obliterated my words, and I sagged forward, coughing.

"Don't try to talk."

I looked up at him standing against the fire consuming the church, and felt the loss slice in places I'd never felt before. His hand came up, as if to ease the hair from my face, but fell back before contact.

"You need to sit down," he said, easing me back to the grass. It was cool and damp, should have been refreshing. "I'm going to get you some help—"

I reached for him, again lifting a hand to his face, this time to slide that dark fall of hair from his eyes.

Wincing, he stepped away.

"Need a medic!" he shouted, as I absolutely refused to let another tear fall. And then he was backing away as I sat there, not looking away but not stopping, either, shouting until his voice registered over the insanity, and a figure ran from the parking area.

Everything switched to slow motion as the woman recalled me and dropped to her knees, lifting her hands to my face. "Oh, sweet girl—are you okay?"

I blinked short blond hair and kind brown eyes into focus. "I—I think so."

She leaned closer, sliding the hair from my face. "Oh, just look at you, you sweet thing." Glancing over her shoulder, she waved at a uniformed man running toward us.

Dylan was gone.

"Twice in one day," she said. "It's too much."

I didn't understand. "Twice in one day?"

Her eyes were so kind, but so incredibly sad. "I can't believe you were even able to get out of bed, not after the way you were this morning."

"W-what?"

"After accidents like that, it's usually a good day or two before you're able to get up and around."

I tried to swallow again. This time it didn't work. "Y-you . . . were there?"

Her smile was gentle. "*Mais petite chat,* you don't remember?"

I shook my head and sent the world spinning all over again.

"*Mais non,* me, I'm not surprised," she said. "You were pretty out of it when I got you cleaned up."

"You . . . cleaned me up?"

She smiled. "Someone had to, *cher.* You were like a drowned rat when Little Jim carried you in, all soaked to the bone and shaking, mumbling . . ."

Little Jim?

Dylan hadn't mentioned a word about anyone else. "W-who are you?" I asked, lifting a hand to finger my temple.

I would have sworn it didn't hurt anymore.

"Lena Mae," she said as if that explained everything. "Lena Mae Robichaud. I run the hotel. My husband Oscar is the sheriff." Then her eyes warmed, and the illusion of anonymity crumbled. "I've known Little Jim's daddy . . . *forever.*"

The paramedics gave me oxygen. While I sat they examined me, checking my heart and my lungs, making sure I had no burns, until finally they released me to the sheriff.

He questioned me. A lot. He wanted to know who I was and what I was doing in Belle Terre, why I'd been at the gallery in the middle of the night.

I was pretty sure he didn't like my answers.

By the time his wife brought me back to the hotel for a shower, the sun was about to rise.

And Dylan had never returned.

After mixing a pouch of cocoa powder with hot water, Lena Mae crossed to where I sat on a small old sofa. "Here, drink this."

I curled my hands around the mug, savoring the warmth—but when I brought the liquid to my mouth, I still tasted the aftermath of smoke.

I wanted to go to my room. I wanted to be alone. But Jim Four-cade's friend had insisted I come eat at her continental breakfast.

It was pretty obvious she'd been instructed not to leave me alone.

"You're exhausted," she said, piling apples and bananas and grapes onto a plate next to pastries. "As soon as Little Jim gets back, I want you back in that room—"

"He's not coming back."

She stopped and turned. "Of course he is," she said as the desk phone rang. "He asked me to keep an eye on you while he took care of something."

I put down the mug as she answered, looking away when she turned her back to speak in hushed tones.

Beyond the picture window, the sun was beginning to rise, and the town of Belle Terre was coming awake to the news that the his-toric church that had withstood two centuries, countless hurricanes, even the ultimate insult of desecration, was gone.

Just like Dylan.

I'm not sure how I knew, a feeling mostly, something raw inside me. I'd seen the way he looked at me and backed away—exactly like that night at Big Charity.

History, I knew. It repeated itself over and over again.

Until what? I wanted to scream. *Until what?*

"There's more, isn't there?" I asked when Lena Mae set the phone down next to a pitcher of orange juice. Perched up against the wall, news played from a New Orleans station, but the volume was too low to make out words.

"It's Philippe," she said. "He was found at his house."

"Found? Is he—"

She knotted her hands. "No—no. They're transporting him to New Orleans."

"But . . . how?"

"His house was ransacked. Looks like he walked in at the wrong time."

But I knew that wasn't true, just as I knew the fire had been neither random nor accidental. Someone had been there first. Someone had removed the portraits. Someone had—

The memory came with a blur of movement from the parking lot. The sketchbook . . .

I blinked and tried to remember. I'd had it in my hands when I'd spun around to find the door closed. I'd tucked it under my arm when I'd dropped to my knees and started to crawl. But after that . . .

The bell on the door jangled.

Absently I looked up—and—the rest of the thought fell away.

TWENTY-NINE

"Trinity!"

Before I could breathe, Chase was at my side and dropping to his knees in front of me, pulling me into his arms. "T," he muttered, running his hands along my back. *"You're okay."*

So much hit me at once. I was vaguely aware of sinking against him as Detective LaSalle strode into the lobby, of the way Lena Mae was looking at me like I was doing something very wrong, of the numbness spreading deeper.

"God." Chase pulled back to frame my face. "What happened?"

"There was a fire," I whispered, even though I was pretty sure he already knew that.

The blue of his eyes was so dark. "What were you doing—"

"Trinity," Detective LaSalle said, crossing to us. "Does this have anything to do with Grace?"

How like a cop to cut right to the chase. "How did you know? How are you even here?"

"Got a call after you were pulled from the fire," he said. "Told me I'd better come down and get you."

It was all so very anonymous.

Someday the spinning would stop, I told myself. Someday the

ride would end and I would climb off, stand firm on ground that did not rock, in a world that did not tilt, with trees that did not laugh, and a sun that did not strobe.

Until then, I rocked back, looking from LaSalle, to Chase. And my eyes filled. "Take me home," I whispered, diving back into his arms. "Please take me home."

I undid the locks. Chase opened the door. I walked inside the condo and deactivated the security system.

Chase closed the door behind us.

"Delphi?" I called, pretending everything was normal. "Kitty, kitty . . ."

"Trinity."

I stood with my back to him, staring dry-eyed through the window at the blanket of gray covering the city. The sun had risen, but thick clouds obscured the light.

An hour had passed since he and LaSalle ushered me inside the plain white sedan. He'd refused to let me drive, saying he would send someone for my car. I hadn't yet told him about the accident.

On the way home we'd covered the basics about the gallery and the portraits, the window I'd crawled through, the fire. But I'd held onto the details until Chase and I could be alone.

He was so not going to like the details.

"Are you sure you aren't hungry?" he asked, coming up behind me to put his hands on my shoulders and draw me back.

It took everything I had not to stiffen.

And that made me start crying all over again, silently. Inside.

This was Chase. *Chase.* He was the best part of my life. His touch shouldn't make me cry.

But that had been before my world went up in flames, and I'd cried out for someone else.

"I'm so tired," I whispered, wrapping my arms around myself. Of everything. Of the questions and the answers, the dreams. *The details.* And they just kept coming.

I didn't know how to make them stop.

"I didn't sleep at all last night," I murmured, fingering the leather curled around my wrist. It had survived, the accident, the fire . . . it had survived. It was still there.

He turned into me, brushing the softest of kisses against my temple—my temple that no longer hurt. "Then let's get you to bed."

I tensed.

He felt it. "Trinity—"

I cut off his words with two fingers to his mouth. "Hold me," I whispered. "Please." *And don't let go.*

He was tired, too. I could see it in his eyes. I could see everything else, too, the hurt and confusion from what he'd heard in Julian's room, the residue from our call last night . . . all the questions that still needed answers. But glittering darkest was the same need that burned through me, to push the world away, to step back from everything that wedged between us, and just . . . be.

Be us.

My eyes stung as he took my hand and led me to the sofa, easing me down against the funky, fringed pillows in pinks and purples and leopard prints. "The party," I whispered.

"You have all day to rest," he said, and while his voice was quiet, it was tight, too, contained. "Just close your eyes."

He sat next to me, brushing the hair back from my face. "It's okay to let go," he promised as lethargy thrummed and swirled, pulled. "I'm not going anywhere."

The edges of my vision grew fuzzy. Blinking, I glanced toward the velvet drapes and would have sworn they stirred. "Delphi . . ."

"I'll find her."

"But . . ." I tried to bring the edges into focus. There was something there, something I needed to see. *Feel.*

"Close your eyes," Chase murmured, and then he was there, stretching out next to me and easing me against him.

"I . . . can't . . ." But even as I fought, my body grew heavier, and my eyes slid closed.

Running. I was running so fast. And I didn't understand. Only a heartbeat before flames had licked around me, and I'd known there was no way out. I'd cried out, started to pray.

Now I ran through the cold fog, and I could see the stream of long dark hair ahead of me, see her *stumbling through tangled vines. She was afraid, so afraid. I could feel it—taste it. I had to get to her, fast, before—*

She was gone.

I lay there, trying to catch my breath. But I knew there wasn't time. My body told me that. There wasn't time to stop and breathe, wasn't time to wait, not when everything inside me knew. I had to reach her—

The light blinded. I blinked against the sting—and saw the silhouette against the window. He was tall, his legs long and his shoulders wide, his body deceptively lean, and when he turned and the hawkish eyes gleamed, the rush started all over again, deeper this time. *"Dylan."*

And I didn't understand. I didn't understand how he was there—and why Chase wasn't. Chase had been there when I fell asleep. He'd been holding me.

But now he was gone and Dylan was crossing to me—

"Welcome back, cricket."

The silly endearment punched through the fog and finally I saw, not dark hair, but silver. Not the son—but the father.

"Detective Fourcade," I murmured, struggling to sit. I glanced around, saw the big grandfather clock, the little hand between the two and the three.

The last time I'd looked, it hadn't yet been nine.

"Was wondering when you were going to join me," Dylan's father said. "I've got some po-boys if you're hungry—"

My mind blanked. "Where's Chase?" I stood. The room tilted. "What's going on? What are you doing here?"

His eyes warmed as he came to put a hand on my shoulder. "Chase is at the shop. He called and asked if I could come stay with you while he—"

"Worked my shift," I breathed. I'd forgotten. With all the craziness of the fire, I'd forgotten all about Fleurish!

But Chase had remembered.

"He didn't want you alone."

Hugging myself, I sat back down. "You know, don't you?" His eyes, so concentrated and worried, made that obvious. "About the fire."

"I do."

I swallowed. "And the portraits."

"Dylan told me."

Something inside me squeezed, but I didn't ask where he was—wouldn't *let* myself ask.

I felt more than saw him sit beside me. "And I think I have a few answers for you."

Through a tangle of hair, I looked up at him, at the deep lines time and pain had carved into his face, and knew he'd lived this before. With my mother. "About the portraits—or the guy who tried to kill me?"

"Maybe both." His mouth flattened. "According to the sheriff, those pictures were painted several years ago by a teenage girl who lived a few miles outside of town."

The girl I'd seen painting . . . "Where is she now? Can I talk to her?"

"I'm afraid that's not possible," Detective Fourcade said, so, so gently. "She drowned last year."

It was like getting punched in the gut. "But I saw her . . ." The second the words left my mouth, I realized my mistake. The people in my dreams, there was no rule that said they had to be alive. "But I don't understand—why would someone who died years ago paint pictures of me?" When I'd still been in Colorado. *"How?"*

He sucked in a sharp breath, let it out slowly. "She had precognition," he said quietly. "Just like you."

Everything flashed, and a whole new door opened. "She saw things before they happened, too?"

"And painted them."

I looked away, toward the sun slanting through the windows. "And she saw me," I murmured. The possibility—the implications—made it hard to breathe.

"Just like you saw Grace," Detective Fourcade confirmed. "And Jessica."

"But . . ." I struggled to put the pieces together. She'd known, this girl whom I'd never met, she'd known years ago that someday I would go to Belle Terre.

"She's the reason I was there," I said, trying to understand. As if I'd been summoned. "Because I saw her, *in my dream,* painting."

"And if you'd never gone," he said as I turned back toward him, "she would never have painted those pictures."

Even though she'd painted the pictures first. It was one of those chicken versus egg loops that defied logic—and made my brain hurt.

"We think of time as linear," he added. "It's easier that way. But it rarely is."

Part of me wanted to reject what he was telling me, and yet, how could I? I, of all people, knew it was possible to see things long before they happened.

"What was her name?" I asked.

"The girl's?"

"Yes."

He hesitated a long beat before answering. "Faith."

But the chill was immediate. "She must have known Grace," I murmured. "I saw envelopes in Grace's apartment with a return address of Belle Terre." Maybe that's why Grace showed me the image of Faith painting, but I still had no idea why.

"What about the guy in the gold car?" I'd seen Faith in my dream, and she'd seen me. That was between us, and Grace. The guy's presence didn't fit. "How did he know to be there?

Something flashed in Detective Fourcade's eyes. "I think he was hunting."

"Hunting?"

"Maybe he saw the envelopes, too—and went to see what else he could find."

My throat tightened, and the memory came slicing back, of the night we'd taken the Ouija board to Grace's, and the guy in the black boots had broken in.

"Maybe that's what you saw," Detective Fourcade went on, but his voice was different now, lower, darker, as if recounting something horrific.

Or seeing it for the first time.

"What you've been seeing all along."

"What do you mean, what I've been seeing all along?"

He looked down for a second, obviously considering, then lifted his eyes back to me. And this time, there was no silver, not even a trace. They were dead dark. "Him. Hunting."

I couldn't breathe, process—understand. "W-what?"

"You heard Grace," he said. "And you saw the buildings. So you assumed, you assumed she was the connection, that you were seeing what she wanted you to see."

I stilled, but the cold kept bleeding, faster and sharper and deeper. "But you don't think so?"

He looked at me as if I'd just asked him to confirm something horrible, like someone had died—or never even existed.

"What else have you seen?" he asked. "Any other dreams, anything strange that didn't fit, that maybe didn't seem to have anything to do with Grace?"

I thought back. "Running," I said. "Just now, when I woke up, and before. I was running."

"Someone was chasing you?"

"No, I . . ." Could feel it, feel it still, the dizzying rush of adrenaline, anticipation . . . "I was. I was running after someone, and all I could think was that I had to catch them, before it was too late." Before they got away.

His eyes flashed.

"Omigod," I whispered, stunned. "You think it's him, don't you?

You think I'm connected to *him*—that I'm seeing through his eyes, not Grace's."

Slowly, he nodded. "It happened to your mother."

I lifted a hand, saw that it shook, pressed it to my heart. "The guy who killed her?"

He looked away, but not before I saw the streak of pain, and sliver of memory.

"Do you think he knows? Do you think this guy knows I can see what he does?"

Horror. It was the only word to describe what I saw as his mouth flattened, and his eyes again met mine. "It's very possible."

"That's why he tried to kill me." Saying the words felt surreal. Even after I'd learned the truth about my mother's work with the police and the psychopath who'd murdered her and my father, even after I'd gotten involved with finding Jessica, and now Grace, I'd never imagined that what I saw could endanger me.

"I'm going to talk to LaSalle and Jackson." Standing, he reached for his phone. "But I don't want you alone, okay? Not even for a second. Stay with your boyfriend. At the party, tonight, stay in public, stay with crowds." From a plastic bag I hadn't noticed, he pulled out a small box. "Dylan said yours was destroyed."

Numbly I stood and stared at the new BlackBerry. Victoria would be here soon to do my hair and makeup. Chase would pick me up. We'd go to the party . . .

"You think he's going to come after me again?" I murmured.

Detective Fourcade crossed to take my arms in his hands. "I'm not going to let anyone hurt you, you hear me?" His voice was somewhere between wild—and deadly quiet. "I'll kill anyone who tries."

Everyone wore masks.

Some were simple, little more than felt or plastic strips of black or gold or silver, concealing only eyes. Others were more elaborate, garish, like tigers or wolves or peacocks, concealing everything. Some were beaded. Some had . . . feathers.

Standing at the back of the crowded courtyard, I fiddled with the pink-and-silver butterfly mask Victoria and I had picked to complement my glittery baby-doll dress. For herself she'd picked a jeweled creation resembling a crown.

Detective Fourcade's, shaped like a gold jester's hat, covered his entire face.

He'd escorted me to the party and turned me over to Chase, then relocated to the edge of the stage, where he could see everything.

"Omigod, look how awesome he looks," Victoria said, gesturing toward the two guys cutting through the crowd.

I didn't need to ask which one she meant.

Trey swaggered straight up to her, isolating her against a bead-draped tree.

"She's a mess," Chase murmured beside me.

I looked up at him and felt my heart kick really hard. His mask was black, like Zorro's, and from behind it, the blue of his eyes looked even more electric. "But you look awesome."

I stepped into him, and smiled. Victoria had spent over an hour on my hair, straightening it so that it fell like black silk against the spaghetti straps of my dress. Even though our faces were hidden, we'd experimented with glittery powders and a new plumping lipstick, an amazing blackest-black mascara. She'd even used eyeliner to create Cleopatra-like wings for both of us.

For *later,* she'd said. And though, in her tight, hot pink dress she'd glowed, the word made something inside me twist.

There always had to be a later. At least, if you believed in forever, there did. There was a now, and there was a later.

The key was knowing what belonged when.

This was the first time Chase and I had been alone in almost forty-eight hours. And during those hours, a lot had happened. Changed.

And I needed to tell him. I knew that.

I just didn't know if it should be now—or later.

Because I knew he wasn't going to like it.

"Mile High!" Deuce said, coming up behind me to wrap me in a quick tight hug. "Chase told me what happened—you okay?"

I felt my eyes warm. "I'm good."

He pulled back, and even though his half-black, half-white mask hid his face, I could tell he didn't believe me.

"You gotta watch out for the crazies," he said, drawing my hand up to brush a soft kiss along my knuckles, before walk-dancing off to retrieve his friend.

I watched until he vanished, leaving me staring at the twinkling lights strung from a pair of skeletal crepe myrtles.

Chase slid a hand around my waist. I could feel the warmth of his fingers, his palm, and for that one heartbeat, I closed my eyes, and wished. Wished for so much. Wished that things could be different, that none of this was happening, that we could go back . . .

But I wasn't sure to where. To Friday morning, before I'd headed to Belle Terre? To Thursday, before the dream regression? Or further, back to the point where it had all started—

"You can't keep pretending."

Robotically I turned to him in his costume of all black, a swanky silk shirt that looked like it belonged in the 1970s and skinny black jeans, his slightly parted lips, and blue, blue eyes—all that the mask revealed—and the sweep of dark brown hair against his forehead.

And something inside me shifted. "I watched the sunset last night," I said, lifting a hand to touch his chest—the chain around his neck, with dog tags and a fleur-de-lis. "I stood at the window and watched the colors fade, and then it was just dark." His flesh was warm, his pulse strong beneath my fingertips. "And I realized that even though I'd been watching I had no idea when the day ended and night took over."

Something about him changed, shifted, his shoulders going a little more rigid.

"But how is that even possible?" I asked, as much of myself as him. "When something major happens, it seems like there should be a moment, a turning point, when you can look back and isolate it, see that one decision, one breath, that changed everything."

But I couldn't see.

Chase's hand found mine and tugged. "Come on, let's get out of here. We can go somewhere quiet—"

Around us the party swirled, laughter and music and drinks, but none of it registered. "I think," I said, curling my fingers around his, "sometimes it's just so much bigger than us."

He tugged me again, urging me toward a cluster of festively decorated trees.

"Maybe someone we don't even know casts the die—" or lifts a paintbrush . . . "—and sets an entire chain of events into motion, and even though you had nothing to do with it, nothing at all, somehow it still touches you."

Changes you.

Chase slid the hair back from my shoulders, letting his hands settle there. But he didn't say anything.

"It's like that butterfly-effect thing," I said. We'd seen a documentary on it one night, the reality that a simple butterfly fluttering its wings in South America could alter wind currents enough to spin a tornado in Texas in an entirely different direction. One decision, one tiny pebble tossed in a pond, sent ripples in countless directions.

Drawing me closer, he fingered the dragonfly at my chest. "You worry too much, T. Nothing has happened that can't be undone."

I wanted to smile. I tried to. But something inside me kept pulling tighter.

"I think about last fall," I said, hesitating as a voodoo queen floated toward us. Her gown was black, flowing, with lace, and a necklace of bone. Her mask, black and intricate, covered her entire face, leaving only a ringlet to slip against her shoulder.

And she was really skinny . . .

My eyes widened as she closed in on Chase, and pretend-stabbed a needle into his heart.

"Still playing with fire, huh, Amber?"

After whispering to Chase, she swirled back to me, another needle in her hand. "No, Trin-Trin . . . that's what you do." All serious-like, she held out the needle.

I took it, and let it drop to the cobblestone.

For a long moment she just stared at me, long enough for me to see the hate in her eyes. When she finally turned, she grabbed onto Chase and spoke in an overly loud voice. "Be careful, *sha*. The night is young."

Then she . . . vanished.

"Omigod," I whispered, watching after her.

But Chase put his foot down on the needle and took my hand. "Last fall what?"

I turned back toward him as the speakers crackled, and thought about changing the subject.

But knew that I couldn't.

"I think about what would have happened if I'd walked away," I told him. "If I walked away instead of walking inside the house on Prytania." That was the moment, the turning point. "We would never have played truth or dare. Jessica would never have locked me in that closet—and Pitre would never have lured her back to teach her a lesson."

She would never have been abducted.

And Chase and I would never have come together to find her. Sometimes it was hard to know how things were supposed to be, and what was the aberration.

"You can't blame yourself, he said. LaSalle told Jessica's parents it looked like that guy had been watching her for weeks."

"I know, but—" My heart started to race. I stood there so completely still, but everything inside me accelerated, as if I was running, running fast.

"Trinity?"

Everything kept blurring, smearing, bleeding together until there was no color or light, just dripping darkness.

"T—" Chase said, and I could feel him, at least I thought I could, hands on my arms, curling tight.

But the screaming wouldn't stop. It grew louder and louder, until I spun around, searching—

Hunting.

The spinning slowed, and I saw her, saw the angel standing against the darkness, tall and crumbling, her arms lifted, a single black feather mask dangling from a wing.

"What's going on?" someone screamed, and then I blinked again, and it was Victoria closing in on me as Chase made me sit.

"Omigod, it's happening again," she whispered, going down on her knees. "You're so cold . . ."

I blinked her into focus, the fear and the confusion, just like the night we'd taken the Ouija board to Grace's apartment. "I'm . . . okay," I whispered.

But everywhere I looked masks mocked.

I stood, trying to make my way toward the stage, where Detective Fourcade watched.

But Trey and Deuce had started to play—how had I not realized that?

Chase reached for me. "Come on, Trinity—you need to sit."

It all blurred, the masks and the laughter, the music and the dancing and the drinks, swirling like a carousel. And even though I wanted off, I kept moving, looking—

"Something's not right," I murmured.

"What do you mean?" That was Chase. He still held me. "What's not right?"

The whispers came from all directions, swarming, making it impossible to discern one from the other. I spun around anyway and saw—

He stood beyond the far drink station, as motionless as the statues, tall, shoulders wide, face hidden by a smooth, round mask. A hooded black robe concealed everything else.

"He's here," I realized as three laughing women danced through my line of vision. I lunged toward him, stumbling but not caring, stopping only when the women moved on, and the corner stood empty.

Chase caught up with me. "Who's here?"

"I don't know." On the stage Deuce played the sax and Trey sang—but Detective Fourcade no longer stood.

Chase pulled me closer, steering me to a secluded bench and help-ing me sit, taking my hands.

And I knew later had come.

"Tell me what's going on," he said, and his voice was so quiet, so gentle, something inside me started to cry.

As if in slow motion, he lifted a hand to strip off his Zorro mask and let it fall to the ground. "This is me," he said. "There's no reason to be afraid."

I looked toward the angel with her uplifted arms.

"It's Belle Terre, isn't it? Last night."

The breeze blew colder.

"I wish I'd been there," he said. "If I'd driven down after we talked, none of this would have happened."

The butterfly effect, I thought again. It was natural to wonder, impossible to know. "Maybe," I acknowledged. "Or maybe you would have walked to the church with me. Maybe you'd have gotten hurt—trapped." Died.

I squeezed my eyes, opened them a breath later. Looking at him hurt.

"It killed me to see you this morning," he said raggedly. "To hear you cry for your mother."

I stilled. "W-what?"

"Your dream," he said. "After I brought you home, when we were on the sofa."

Another whisper of ice moved through me. Oh, God. *What had I said?*

"You said 'mama,'" he answered, as if I'd spoken. "You reached for her and started to cry, you told her how much you missed her."

All day I'd been holding on, living one moment to the next, not allowing myself to look too far forward, or even a nanosecond be-hind me. To not lose myself in leftover fear, or grieve things that had not yet come to pass.

Now I realized I'd only been hiding. Because the past was always there, and the future always came. It was that whole forever thing. There had to be a before, and an after.

Maybe Belle Terre was it, that one defining moment when everything changed. And I couldn't keep being vague, witholding details.

"I thought I saw her." My throat tried to hold onto the words. "When I realized I was trapped and couldn't get out, when the smoke got thick and I couldn't breathe . . ." Hours later, the acrid residue lingered. "I thought I saw her running toward me."

His hands squeezed mine. "You were scared. It makes sense you'd imagine—"

"I wasn't imagining." My absolute certainty surprised me. "She was there."

"Trinity—"

"But not to greet me, or take me. But to . . . warn me."

He pulled back. "Warn you?"

"Not to give up," I said, searching his eyes. "She told me to fight, that it wasn't my time."

Around us, the sound of Deuce's sax and Trey's singing fell away.

"But I went to her anyway," I whispered, and now it was me who was squeezing his hands. All I could think was if only I held on tight enough, it would be okay. "And that's how I got out."

The lines of his face tightened. "That's how you found the window?"

"No," I said, and I could feel it, even before I lifted the invisible knife, I could feel the horrible slow slice, straight down to my soul. "That's how I found Dylan."

THIRTY

There are moments you want to hold onto. They're the ones you return to over and over in your mind, and your heart. You replay them like a much-loved movie and lose yourself in them, let yourself linger, remember. Relive.

And then there are the moments you want to forget. They're usually the ones you never will. They sear into your life like scar tissue, bit by bit, excruciating detail by excruciating detail, and no matter how hard you try to erase or rewind or go back, to rewrite, it's one piece of history that never wavers. It's there, it's real, and it changes everything.

The party rolled on. Lights twinkled, the breeze swirled, alcohol flowed, Trey sang, and Deuce played. Victoria danced, a woman draped in Mardi Gras beads laughed, and a waiter stood in the shadows, texting. Everyone wore masks—everyone, except Chase. Worried about me, he'd stripped his off, so I could see him, really, really see him.

And I don't think I'll ever forget it, the way he looked at me, the horrible, blank confusion, as if he had no idea what I'd just said, or who I even was. As if his life had just gone absolutely blank.

"What?" was all he said.

Around me, the party faded. I knew what I had to say—hated what I had to say.

"He was there," I said, as I should have so much sooner. There were so many should haves, going back further than only the day before. But when you stood on a ledge, when there was nothing to break your fall, it was so hard to make yourself take that first step. "He's how I got out of the fire."

I don't know what I expected. Anger, I think. Jealousy. But Chase just stood there. I didn't even see breath move through him. "You were with Dylan?"

His voice was so horribly empty, like the dead calm of the wind in those few fragile moments before a storm broke.

"Not *with* him," I said, pressing into Chase as someone bumped me from behind. "Not like that. He was there, that's all."

"That's why you went without me," he murmured, and against mine, his hand went slack.

"No." I held on, held on for both of us. "No!" I said again. "I wanted you there—I asked you to come, remember? You said you couldn't."

He stiffened. "So you found someone who could."

"No." It was coming, the calm about to implode. I could see it in the hard lines of his body, the way his skin stretched across his face. "Chase, please." I grabbed for words. "That's not what happened. It was his father. He was worried about me—"

His hand fell away, and the blue of his eyes washed black. "He's who you missed."

The dead calm was really starting to frighten me. "W-what?"

"On the sofa," he said, and finally it all clicked, those sharp, incriminating pieces slicing together with horrifying perfection. "When you were sleeping," he said, and I totally thought I was going to throw up. Because I knew. I knew what was coming—what I'd said, done.

Remembered.

"I thought you were dreaming about your mother," he said. "But I saw the look on your face. I heard your voice. And the way you were clinging to me—

"It was him, wasn't it? You were holding him."

Oh, God. "Chase, please—" Desperately, I reached for him. "I hardly even know him."

He pulled his arm back.

My breath caught.

His breath ripped. "I was out of my mind," he said in a voice so bleached out I felt more than heard it. "When LaSalle called and told me about the fire, that you'd been trapped, the whole drive down there, wondering what I would find and beating myself up for not being there . . ."

I tried reaching for him again. "Chase—"

He caught me by the wrist, his hand closing around the leather bracelet and holding me at arm's distance. "And now I find out you were with another guy?"

The buzz grew louder, distorting everything, and then it was last fall again, in the house on Prytania, with the world blowing up around us—and Chase not able to hear a word I was saying.

"It wasn't like that. I had nothing to do with it. His father sent him to protect—"

"Then why didn't you tell me?"

"I am telling you!"

"Was he with you in the hotel, too?" he pressed. "Did you share a room? Did you—"

I just stared at him.

"I can see it in your eyes," he said. "Something happened."

I stepped back, devastated. I'd known he wouldn't like it. I'd known he would be upset. But even then, when I'd projected myself into this moment, when I'd made myself imagine every possible re-action, I'd never imagined it would cut so deep.

"I was scared this would happen," I whispered, stunned. Just like last fall. "That you wouldn't be able to look past the fact that Dylan was there, that nothing I said would matter."

"Have you been talking to him this whole time? Is that why you shouted his name at Horizons—"

"Stop it!" Jerkily, I lifted a hand to rip the mask from my face.

"Look at me," I said, trying not to break. "This is me—Trinity. You know me better than that."

The blue of his eyes went so, so dark—so lost. So gone. "Did he touch you?"

It was like being in some horrifying alternate universe where nothing played the way it was supposed to.

"How did you thank him? Was it *hot*—"

"*Omigod,*" I whispered, stepping back. Because in that moment, I was the one who no longer wanted to touch. "Are you *serious*?"

His mouth twisted. "It's a little late to ask me that," he ground out, turning with the words, turning so fast he bumped into a waiter.

And exactly like last fall—exactly like the night on the levee—he walked away.

I stared after him, didn't understand. Couldn't understand. How had that just happened?

"Chase!" I shouted, going after him. "Don't do this!"

He stopped abruptly, as if my words were rocks against his back. But he did not turn.

I went to him and laid my hands against his back, needed so badly to touch.

"Think about Pensacola," I said quietly, even as my heart cried. "I am."

His shoulders went stone hard.

"You can't keep walking away from me like this—don't you see how much that hurts?"

Still he did not turn. "You took the first step."

My breath caught—my breath *stabbed*. "No—"

He tore away, pushing around a group of men smoking cigars—and this time when I moved, it wasn't toward him.

Everywhere I turned, people pressed. I pushed through the laughter and the dancing, the masks in black and gold and silver, the demon and the jester, the whispers, the buzz that kept growing louder.

They didn't know, I told myself. They didn't watch.

I had to get out of there was all I could think. I had to get out of there before all those sharp, jagged pieces sliced to the bone. I needed to find Victoria—or Detective Fourcade. He would take me home—

I stopped abruptly, looking.

He was gone.

"No," I breathed, spinning so fast I never saw the man in the black robe until I ran straight into him. I felt the pain as I looked up, the quick sharp slice to my side.

Then I saw the eyes.

THIRTY-ONE

I knew those eyes, knew them despite the round mask that covered his face, the one in all white that made him look more dead than alive. I'd looked into them through the window of my car, and moments later on the bank, as he'd lifted a hypodermic needle to my arm.

"Oh, *God, no*—"

"'Fraid you're praying to the wrong guy," he snarled, yanking me against him.

I twisted—

"Don't fight," he warned, pressing something sharp against my waist. "Or she won't be the only one who pays the price."

I tried to yank back, plant my feet. "Detective Four—"

He pulled me into him, his big beefy arms pressing my face into his black robe as he dragged me toward the gate.

"It's already done, sweet thing," he said. "And you were too distracted to notice."

Everything blurred. I tried to wrench free, to run. But he was bigger, stronger, and the loud pulse of the music stole my cries. No one was paying attention. This was New Orleans and this was Mardi Gras and the party created a weird anonymity. Everyone danced and laughed, pressed and swayed. No one thought twice about how tightly he held me.

"Chase!" I tried, thrashing. But he didn't hear, wasn't there. "Help me—"

A sweaty hand slid over my mouth.

I bit down—hard.

Laughing, the guy from the gold car shoved me through the gate and threw me over his shoulder, into a fireman's carry. "Fight all you want," he grunted, running. "But I don't do loose ends."

Panic sliced deeper than the knife. I knew what would happen if he got me alone. LaSalle had drilled that into my head, the importance of staying in a public place, never straying into an alley . . .

But we *were* in an alley. And even if there'd been someone to hear me scream, the sound of Deuce's sax blaring from the speaker absorbed everything.

I pretended to relent, submit. I knew my options were limited, that I would get just one chance. It had to be perfect. With my legs dangling and my arms sandwiched between his body and mine, timing would be everything.

"Good girl," he panted, running. "You and me, we gonna have us some—"

I reared back and twisted, did as I'd been taught and closed in on his ear, bit down as hard as I could.

Howling, he recoiled, but I ground down harder, cringing when I felt cartilage give way between my teeth.

"Bitch!" He grabbed my hair, tried to shove me away.

Without warning I let go.

He staggered back. Momentum dropped me forward. I landed hard and rolled into myself, scrambled to my feet and started to run.

"You stupid little—" he started, but never got the chance to finish.

On a dead run Dylan rounded the corner and didn't stop, didn't slow, not until he plowed into him. I never saw the switchblade until it flashed between them.

"Dylan, no!" I shouted as a loud grunt of pain erupted.

The guy from the car stumbled back, his eyes huge and glassy.

Dylan went at him again, and again, and again, lunge-dancing with the knife, pressing his advantage as the car guy jerked deeper into the darkness. And then he turned and ran and Dylan was running, too.

Back to me.

"No! You have to go after—"

"You," he said, and then he was there, taking me into his arms and holding me against him. And something inside me let go, the tight grip on the fear and the horror, and all I could think about was losing myself there in that moment.

"*Oh, my God,*" I murmured, stunned. So close. I'd come so close to not getting away.

"I've got you," Dylan said, as he always did. Because . . . he did. He always did. He was always there, even when I didn't see him.

Even when I said I didn't want him.

"It's okay," he said. "*I promise it's okay.*"

I struggled back, needing to see his face. Unlike everyone else, he wore no mask, none other than the ferocity that stripped me bare.

"It was him." The pain wouldn't stop. Wincing, I pressed a hand to my side, stilling at the warm stickiness. "The guy from the car."

"He's not going to hurt you again. I swear to God he's not even going to look at you—"

I sagged.

Dylan caught me, his hand sliding to mine, as the silver of his eyes caught fire.

"He had a knife," I whispered as Dylan slid down along the brick wall, lowering me to the cool damp concrete and drawing me between his legs. His movements were gentle as he slid back the destroyed fabric of my dress to reveal the torn flesh at my side.

"I'm going to kill him. I swear to God, I'm going to—"

"Dylan, no—"

"I tried," he said, and I don't think I'd ever heard someone sound so tortured. "I couldn't get there in time," he said. "I tried—"

I looked up, finding that dark curtain of hair falling against his jaw, making the lines and angles look sharp enough to slice. "You were there?"

His eyes were narrow, concentrated. But instead of my face, they were on the movement of his fingers along the blood oozing from my side. "I've been there all day," he said quietly, as the strangest calm moved through me. "You didn't think I'd walk away now, did you?"

"But you were gone . . ."

He looked up, and his eyes met mine, and everything that had been momentarily frozen surged all over again. "Just because you can't see me, doesn't mean I'm not there."

It was a crazy time to start crying. But there on the ground against the wall in the cold dark alley, with his legs and arms around me, all I felt was the stream of warmth, and the salty flood to my eyes.

"This isn't over," he said, still so quiet, so ragged. "And I'm not going to walk away."

Tears slid down my cheeks. *"Like you did before,"* I whispered without thinking, and then his eyes were the ones with the sheen.

"I had to," he said, and though I didn't understand, I knew that he believed.

He drew me closer, wrapped me in the warm refuge of his body, and held on until there was no more cold, no more shaking, no more pain.

I don't know what made me look up, toward the front of the alley, where Chase stood with his mask in his hand, watching. Our eyes met, but tired and hurt and bleeding, I couldn't make myself move, couldn't make myself go to him or explain.

Without a word, he turned and walked away.

———

"Delphi has to be here somewhere," I said, emerging from Aunt Sara's bedroom. I'd showered and changed into sweats and a long-sleeve T-shirt, blown my hair dry and let Dylan tend to the knife wound. Finally it had quit bleeding.

At least on the outside. On the inside . . .

I swallowed against the memory, couldn't let myself go back to those last few moments with Chase. But I couldn't stop myself from looking at the leather wrapped around my wrist, and the word on top: HONEST.

I knew how hard it was for Chase to trust, but I thought he knew me better than that.

"I saw her yesterday before I left," I said, looking up.

Dylan turned from the big window, still wearing the black jeans and dark gray henley that had allowed him to blend in at the party. After talking with his father he'd cleaned up, too, but blood still stained his shirt.

"Cats like to hide," he said.

I'd checked Delphi's favorite spots, including the cabinets where she sometimes napped in my aunt's cast-iron skillet.

"She was a street cat," he said as I opened the coat closet for the hundredth time. "She knows how to take care of herself—"

I turned toward him, vaguely aware of the twinge in my side. "How do you know that?"

I would have said he went even more still, but that was impossible. I didn't know what it was about Dylan Fourcade and stillness, but even when he moved, he was so very, very contained. "You must have told me—"

"No, I didn't." It was phenomenal how hard my heart started to slam. But the pieces were all there, pieces I'd never seen before— never even really thought of, much less attempted to put together. And with them now, I made myself move toward him.

We'd been alone together before. I'd seen him in light and in dark, inside and out. He'd pulled me from the river and a fire, had tended me when I was hurt over and over again, physically, emotionally, but had refused to undress me, even when I was unconscious, opting for help from Lena Mae. He'd seen me running and screaming and cry-ing. He'd seen me hiding.

But this was the first time I'd seen him inside my condo, my world and on my terms. And something about the sight of him stand-ing beside the velvet curtains, with the curtain of his own hair in a sharp line against his cheekbone, while the silver of his eyes glowed hotter with each step I took, brought a focus that rocked me.

"It was you," I whispered, closing in on him. "You gave me Delphi."

He looked away, and I had my answer.

I stopped, and my throat knotted. I don't know how I'd never pieced that together. Six days after we found Jessica, I'd been alone in my room when the intercom buzzed. I'd answered, but no one had responded, so I'd glanced outside the window where Dylan now stood, and seen a plain brown box on the doorstep. Inside, I'd found Delphi, scared and emaciated, staring up at me.

I'd wondered who'd put her there, who'd brought her to me. Chase, Aunt Sara, and Detective LaSalle had all made my suspect list, but they'd denied any involvement. But I think I'd assumed it was one of them anyway. They were the ones who'd been there, helping me find solid ground after the insanity of Jessica's kidnapping.

I'd never thought about Dylan.

But that wasn't true. I *had* thought about Dylan. I'd wondered where he was and why he'd walked away, why he'd never followed up, called, texted, anything. Why he'd vanished without saying good-bye.

I'd wondered all of that, but I'd never connected him to the kitty from the wharf—the one only the two of us had seen.

Now I saw, and now I knew, and the knowledge did strange, strange things to the ebb and flow inside me.

"Why?" I asked.

Dylan didn't need clarification. "Because she needed a home," he said, looking back from the shimmer of lights below. "And you needed to give her one."

For one of the few times in my life, I was at a loss for words. But

I wasn't at a loss for emotion. It bubbled beneath the surface, and before I even realized I'd moved, I had a hand at my chest, my fingers around the smooth edges of the dragonfly.

"She's gone," I whispered. "I don't know how, but . . ."

He did away with the last of the distance between us, taking my shoulders in his hands. "No, she's not."

I wanted to believe him. "But I feel something," I said, opening myself to the disturbing vibration I'd been trying to write off as nerves. "I felt it the second I walked into the condo, this strange emptiness."

"You're not used to being here alone."

"It's more than that," I said. "It's . . . like this ringing in my ears, this hollowness." I'd sensed it that morning, when Chase had brought me back from Belle Terre. Bone tired, I'd attributed it to leftover shock. "I can just tell."

"When's your aunt coming home?"

My sigh was automatic. It was also bizarre. Aunt Sara had only been gone two days. And considering we'd been virtual strangers six months before, I hadn't expected to miss her. But I did. Maybe Dylan was right—maybe the emptiness had nothing to do with Delphi and everything to do with my aunt.

"Tomorrow morning," I said.

"Then you should get some sleep. I'll keep an eye out for Delphi."

Because he wasn't leaving. "Why are you doing this?" It was a question that had been bothering me.

His hands fell away. "My father—"

"Not your father," I said again, as the play of shadows across his face fascinated me.

There were so many questions, it was hard to collapse them into one. "You let me go," I said, my voice dropping quieter. "Last night, you knew I left the hotel room, didn't you? That's how you were at the church. You followed me, when it would have been so much easier to stop me."

It's what everyone else tried to do.

"Is that what you want?" We were the only ones there. No one could hear us. There was nothing to hide. Yet neither of us used full voice. "For me to stop you?"

"*No.*"

"It's not what I want, either." Lifting a hand, he smoothed the hair from my face, his fingers hesitating where, only the day before, there'd been pain. "You're not the one I need to stop."

Everything got a little fuzzy.

"And if I did, you'd keep right on trying," he added as his hand fell away. "And sometimes it only takes a second . . . ."

He didn't finish. He didn't need to. I knew.

It only took a second to lose everything.

The scream woke me.

Ripped from the darkest corners of sleep, I opened my eyes and listened, didn't trust myself to move, or even breathe.

Delphi crouched beside me, her ears flat back as the terror again cut into the night. "No—no!"

And with the voice came recognition.

I called out for her to come back, but she didn't, and then I was on my feet, running.

Darkness stole details, but I knew I couldn't stop, couldn't wait. There wasn't time. I had to find her—fast. *Now.*

The silence stopped me. It pulsed from all directions, muted and distorted, the perfect backdrop for . . . sound.

I heard her. I heard the chop of her breath. And she heard me.

Clumsily she took off like a frightened animal, and this time I knew where to follow.

And then I saw her, through the darkness, the shadows, standing statue still, nowhere left to go. Long dark hair cascaded over her shoulders, falling against the torn lavender of her little dress.

I stepped toward her—and saw the knife.

"I've been so patient," he said. I said.

We said.

Moonlight caught the serrated blade in its upward arc, and she screamed, twisting around—

"*Trinity!*"

I froze, the voice piercing in from behind me. And then someone was reaching for me, pulling. "Wake up!"

I hung there a cold, wordless moment, as the distorted edges came into focus, and I realized I was no longer standing amid tangled vines, but in my bed, and that Dylan was on the edge of the mattress, and that the first rays of morning spilled through the sheers at my window.

"Omigod." I tried to breathe, couldn't. I couldn't move, either, even as everything inside me kept running. *Screaming.*

"Tell me." His hands found mine, and held. "What were you seeing?"

But already the images were fading, draining. Looking away, I found my blown-glass dragonfly lying on its side next to my aunt's nun doll. The tip of the wing was broken.

"I-I woke up," I said, trying to understand. "I woke up right here with Delphi . . ." My heart slowed as I looked down at the mattress—and saw no sign of my cat.

When I looked back at Dylan, he silently shook his head.

Delphi was still gone.

"I-I heard someone screaming." Could still hear them, but quieter now, distant. Fading like the dream.

"Do you remember who?"

"No . . . I . . . It's not there anymore. I tried to follow her, knew I *had* to follow her. But everything was so dark, and I was running—"

The memory stabbed through me, not from the dream, but from Dylan's father. "Oh, my God—it was him, wasn't it?" The man who'd taken Grace. "I was seeing through his eyes." That's why I'd run so fast, wanted so badly. That's why I'd seen the knife—in my own hand. "He's hunting again."

His eyes went dark. "I want you to text your aunt." Standing, he retrieved the BlackBerry his father gave me from the nightstand. His movements were stiff, forced. "Ask her when she's going to be back."

I took the phone, didn't understand why I couldn't feel anything. "W-why?"

"Just do it. I'll be right back."

I watched him leave, then texted my aunt.

> Hey!

I knew I had to pretend. I knew I had to act like everything was normal.

> When will u b home?

Then I caught the green glow from the clock, and realized it wasn't even six-thirty in the morning. So much for being all casual and normal.

> Chase and I had a fight.

I sat and waited, hoping she would buy my reason for texting so early.

It was almost five minutes before she responded.

> Ah, cher. I'm so sorry. R U OK?

Relieved, I exhaled.

> I will b.

This time she replied more quickly.

> R U alone?

Mindlessly, my fingers fumbled across the keys.

No.

"Did you reach her?" Dylan asked from the doorway.

I looked up as he crossed to me, and felt a chill cut through me. "What is it?"

The lines of his face were tight, closed. Shadows ringed his eyes, making the whites look whiter—and the silver burn as he slid down beside me and took the phone, saying nothing as his fingers flew across the keys.

"What are you doing?" I asked, scrambling to see what he'd typed.

Should I take those new necklaces to the shop?

I blinked, didn't understand. "What necklaces—" But before I could finish, my aunt's response zipped in.

That would be gr8.

My heart started to pound, pound really, really hard—Aunt Sara and I had not talked about any necklaces.

Dylan never looked up.

K. Want me 2 string a few more?

The second he hit send, quiet fell between us. Questions burned my throat, but I held them there, didn't trust myself to give them voice.

Was terrified of the answer starting to form.

Then Aunt Sara responded, and the horrible, incessant drone became an all-out scream.

That'd be great, cher.

Everything stopped. It just . . . stopped.

"What necklaces?" I whispered, even as deep inside, I knew.

Dylan's eyes met mine, but before he even spoke, the answer sliced through me.

That was not my aunt.

THIRTY-TWO

He put down the phone. He took my hands. He held on tight. Normally, when he touched, there was warmth. Normally I could feel it heal.

This time, I felt absolutely nothing.

"You're scaring me," I whispered.

"Your aunt's friend, the one whose wedding she was going to. Do you know how to reach her?"

The sun was coming up. Light was bleaching out the room. But shadows edged closer. "Naomi? I . . ." I'd never had any reason to call her, and Aunt Sara didn't have a landline where the number might be stored. "I-I think there's a Christmas card list on my aunt's laptop."

Dylan's eyes remained so very, very steady. "Go check."

Five minutes later, Naomi's sleepy voice shredded the kernel of hope I'd been trying to hold onto.

"She texted me," she said, confused. "Said she'd come down with a stomach bug and couldn't get out of bed . . ."

My aunt's name. During the dream, when I'd been running, I'd cried out for her—and Dylan had heard. That's how he knew . . .

"She never boarded the plane," Detective LaSalle gritted out, throwing his phone across the room. "She never boarded the fucking plane!"

I'd called him the second I'd hung up with Naomi. He and Detective Jackson had arrived within minutes.

"I dropped her at the airport," he said, staring, but I had no idea what he saw. His eyes were too glassy, too drenched in darkness. Everything else was pale, even his mouth. "I walked her to security and kissed her good-bye."

And no one had seen her since. For two days. Fifty-one hours. Three thousand, sixty minutes. Over thirty thousand breaths . . .

And no one had realized she was missing.

"She texted me," I said sickly, but even as Dylan's eyes met mine and the detectives twisted toward me, we all knew the horrifying truth.

Whoever I'd been texting with, it had not been my aunt.

"I should have known," I said, wrenching from the sofa and shooting across the room, to the votives on the bar. But the second the words ripped from me, the truth bled through.

I had known.

I'd known it the second I walked back into the condo. I'd felt the emptiness. I'd been *told*.

But I'd been too consumed by what happened in Belle Terre to connect the dots.

"Jesus," LaSalle muttered, and I could tell it was all he could do not to put a fist through the wall. "I should have realized. The second she said she loved me."

I spun toward him. "What?"

"In a text Friday night, after the wedding. She said that she wished I was there, that she loved me."

My throat tightened—and his eyes went flat.

"That was the giveaway," he said, and I had to wonder if he realized his hand had slid to the gun at his side. "She never said that before."

I crossed to him without thinking, took him by the arm. "You have to find her! You have to find her before it's—" I froze as the memory scraped in, the knife lifted high . . .

"What?" Detective Jackson asked, taking over. His dreads and baggy plaid pants made him look all funked out, but his eyes were like lasers. "Before what?"

Blindly, I looked from him to his partner. "She was running. I think she tried to get away. He followed—"

The horror of it all circled around me, pulled tighter. "She was wearing the dress from the wedding."

"What else?" Detective Jackson stunned me by asking. He wasn't one to believe. "What other details?"

"I don't know! It was so dark. I—*oh, God,*" I cried, only vaguely aware of Dylan crossing to stand beside me. I don't think he touched, but wasn't sure, because I couldn't feel. *Anything.* "This is all my fault."

The transformation was fascinating, the steely-eyed cop pushing aside the worried man and taking charge. "Your fault? Why would you say that?" LaSalle the detective asked.

"Because he knows. He knows I can see him."

The two detectives exchanged a sharp look.

"The dreams—the things I see. They're from him, not Grace. And somehow he knows, and when he couldn't get me . . . he got her." And again I had to wonder, where was the beginning, where had it all started? Last weekend, when Grace had gone missing? Or had the seeds been there far longer, back years before, when the girl named Faith had first lifted a brush—and painted my face?

"It's like I'm being punished," I whispered sickly.

Something flashed in LaSalle's eyes, something obscene. "Or *played* with."

The buzz started all over again, low—incessant. "What do you mean?"

He lifted his hands and pressed them together, as if in prayer, and tapped them against his chin. I could see him pulling away, back, could see him drawing lines between the dots. "Have you ever seen a cat play with a mouse?"

Automatically I looked around for Delphi—

She'd known. So many times I'd pulled myself awake, only to find her crouching beside me, her unblinking eyes focused on something unseen, her ears flat.

And now she was gone.

"They don't kill them," Detective LaSalle said. "That's not the point."

Slowly I turned back toward him. "Because then they can't play anymore," I realized numbly. "Dead toys aren't fun."

And that's what I was.

A toy.

"No," LaSalle said. "They're not. And for him, that's what it's about—the fun, the challenge. He has no conscience, no sense of right or wrong. It's all about the game."

A sociopath, I knew. Just like the man who killed my parents.

Jackson grabbed the dreads behind his neck and held them there, revealing something dark and faraway in his eyes. "Until they get bored."

LaSalle frowned. "And a different kind of game begins."

They wanted me to wait. They wanted me to stay in the condo, sit there and hang out, answer the five thousands texts Victoria had sent since the party last night or play on Facebook, while some psycho had my aunt.

Games, I realized sickly. We all played them, whether we wanted to or not.

Thirty minutes after LaSalle and Jackson left, I dressed and put on my shoes, pretended to play along. I pretended to wait. I pretended to be calm. I pretended to sit quietly while Dylan made breakfast.

Except, he was playing a game of his own. He may have stood benignly at the stove, his shirtsleeves shoved up his arms and bacon frying in the skillet, but even when he didn't turn toward me, he watched.

Silently, we both waited.

The only way I was getting out of that condo was behind his back. I just needed him to turn it.

Somewhere between cracking eggs and pouring milk, his phone beeped, and my breath readied. But I did not let myself move, not until I saw his shoulders stiffen. Then a quick glance showed him turn from me—

There was only one door. The angle of the kitchen made it possible to reach it without being seen. And I had the key to the double cylinder dead bolt. All I had to do was put the door between us. If I could get into the hall and jam the key into the lock before Dylan caught me, he wouldn't be able to stop me.

"You're not the one I need to stop. And if I did, you'd keep trying. And sometimes it only takes a second . . ."

His words chased me through the foyer. I twisted the knob and pulled, lunged into the hall and yanked the door as I stabbed the key—

It wouldn't close.

I yanked harder, but the door pulled me back toward the inside of the condo. And then I saw his foot crammed through the opening. I let go and spun, started to run. The stairs—

He caught me in two steps. Like steel bands his arms closed around me, dragging me back to him. I twisted as hard as I could, swinging elbows and stomping on his bare foot.

He held firm.

And in that moment I hated him, even as the fight drained and reality set in, as I sagged against him and he gathered me close, sliding down the wall to hold me there in the exposed-brick hallway.

"It's going to be okay," he said, his face a whisper from mine. I could feel him, the movement of his mouth against my hair. "I promise it's going to be okay."

"You don't know that," I said. "You *can't* know that."

"We'll find her. Detective LaSalle—"

"No." I twisted to look at him, stilled when I realized how close he was. "You won't. You *can't*."

Dark hair fell against his face, not in a sharp line, but stringy. It stunned me how badly I wanted to smooth it.

"He won't let you," I whispered. "It has to be me."

"That's not going to happen."

"But it has to. Don't you see? It's me he wants . . . me he's playing with."

"I don't care who he wants—he's not getting anywhere near you."

"But—"

"What?" he asked before I could finish. "What do you think you're going to do that the police can't? Where are you going to go? Someone's already gone after you. What if they're watching? What if they do it again? What if you'd succeeded in locking me out—what then?"

Deep inside, it started, the shaking I'd been fighting from the moment Dylan had ripped me from the dream.

"It's not his game anymore," he said roughly. "And I swear to God he's not going to win."

"Then quit trying to stop me," I whispered. "*Help* me."

I never saw his hand move. I never saw a thing, not until his fingers slid against the length of my neck. "Then quit shutting me out."

My breath stumbled. The riff of my heart stabbed deeper, and it was all I could do not to close my eyes, and believe.

"I need to go back." I'd been so blind, so consumed by terror, so busy spinning to someone else's tune, I'd failed to see the obvious answer.

"To sleep. That's the only way I'll find her."

"Do you think you can?"

I *had* to. It was the only way.

"She tried to warn me," I said, pulling back. "Grace did. She must have known, too—she must have felt me or something, that's why she screamed that he was one step ahead, that he knows everything."

That he was dangerous.

Dylan pushed to his feet and held out a hand.

I took it, held on as he led me back inside. The warnings had been there all along, like a circle being drawn around me, first so very far away, closer with each grind of the marker.

I could see it now, the beginning. Chase's accident had been a distraction, something to throw me off track. And it had worked. I'd been so distracted I'd never realized when the next move was made. First Grace, then Delphi . . .

"He was here," I breathed as Dylan closed the door.

I handed him the key. "Delphi was here when I left for Belle Terre," I said. "If he has her—"

He turned the lock and looked back at me.

"They're right," I said sickly. "Detective LaSalle and your dad . . . It's all some sick twisted game."

"Come on." Taking my hand, Dylan led me to the big table my aunt called her baby. Once it had sat in a plantation home, custom-ordered from France. Now it dominated the far side of the condo.

Seeing it, the project my aunt had been working on, the antique cross charms and brass beads, the clear crystals scattered against mahogany, made my throat close up.

"I don't know the rules," I murmured, fingering a small brass cross. "How can I win if I don't even know the rules?"

Dylan came up behind me. "We make our own."

I twisted toward him, looked up, and finally, finally felt a whisper of warmth move through me. "Thank you."

There'd been so many big, explosive moments between us. Our paths didn't cross simply or quietly or casually. There was always something intense going on, a chase or a threat, an accident, a fire. Everything was always perched on a razor's edge, moments lit from the inside out.

But there'd been very little quiet. Very little slow and easy. Very little time to take stock and simply let the moment be.

But for that moment, for that brief suspension in time, it *was* quiet. And slow. And easy. And the moment just was. And despite everything, I smiled.

It only seemed fitting that his phone would buzz, and those

beautiful, fragile edges would crumble. He stepped back as he retrieved the BlackBerry, his finger sliding to view the text.

I knew the exact second he read the message. I saw it in his eyes, the shift from simmer to grim. And even had I not seen, there would have been no mistaking the way he stepped back.

"What?" I asked, tracking him.

He tapped something out and waited a heartbeat before another message arrived. Abruptly he turned away, hunching his shoulders like a shield.

It was obvious he didn't want me to see.

I moved without hesitation, hurrying up beside him and pressing into him, looking over his arm as he tried to twist the phone away.

I grabbed on and tugged, could tell there was some kind of picture on the screen.

But nothing prepared me for the sight of the pale, naked body strewn along the edge of the river.

THIRTY-THREE

I let go and staggered back, bringing a hand to my mouth as if that could prevent me from throwing up.

"Omigod," I whispered. "Omigod!"

Dylan came after me, reaching me in one quick step and taking me by the arms. "I didn't want you to see that—"

"It's him," I said, horrified. Processing. "It's him!"

The guy from the gold car.

"They found him half an hour ago." His voice was stripped bare. "LaSalle sent the picture for confirmation."

I tried to breathe. "What happened?"

"LaSalle didn't say much, just that he'd had his throat slit before he was thrown into the water."

My stomach twisted. The guy who'd tried to hurt me was dead. He'd been killed, murdered. Disposed of.

"I don't do loose ends," he'd said, but never realized he, too, had become one.

"LaSalle's checking surveillance cameras," Dylan said.

"He won't find anything." I had no doubt. "Whoever did this, they're smarter than that." And they were one step ahead, like Grace said. Whatever game we were playing, it had been laid out with phenomenal precision, and executed with sickening ease.

"I-I have to stop him," I said, backing away from Dylan.

"It has to be me," I said, and then I was running, down the hall and into my aunt's room, darting into her bathroom and slamming the door behind me. Hers had a lock. I twisted it.

"Trinity—"

I had to stop him. That's all I could think.

The clock was ticking. There was no time to wait or be patient, to stretch out in my bed and close my eyes, wait for magic to happen. Because that was impossible. It wasn't going to happen. There was no way I could close my eyes and let go, start to drift, not when my aunt's life lay on the line.

"Trinity?"

I hardly recognized the face staring back at me from the antique mirror.

"Trinity. Answer me."

My rules, I thought. *My rules.* Numbly, robotically, I opened the medicine cabinet and pulled out a small white bottle.

"Damn it, Trinity—"

I reached for a paper cup adorned with puppies and kittens, and filled it with water.

Someone wanted to play.

I could play, too, I thought, opening the bottle. And I knew where I had to start.

Dylan rattled the knob. "Open the door—"

I dumped the nighttime allergy medicine into my hand.

"Trinity—"

There was something in his voice, a rough edge as if he knew what I was going to do.

Shaking, I crammed the handful of pills into my mouth.

My throat rejected them.

"Don't do this—"

Water sloshed over the side as I dragged the cup to my mouth, and the door crashed open.

I darted toward the tub and tried to make myself swallow, but Dylan caught me and dragged me back, turning me in his arms as his eyes went wild.

"Ah, Christ," he said, and his voice was so raw I could literally feel it. *"No, no, no . . ."*

My eyes met his, and from one breath to the next, the numbness started to crumble. "I have to," I whispered. "Please, Dylan. I have to sleep. You have to let me—"

"Not like this," he said, lifting a hand to my face.

I should have fought him. I knew that. I should have fought him, should not have stood there like an errant child while, with a powerful swipe of his finger, he parted my lips and retrieved the pills.

"How many?" he asked. "How many did you swallow?"

I stared at his palm, counted six. "One, maybe two . . ."

His eyes got glassy. "God, what were you thinking? You have to be strong," he said. "Alert. You can't hurt yourself—"

"But it's not about me! It's about her, my aunt. Don't you understand? *He has her!* And she could die."

"He's not going to hurt her."

"You can't know that. You can't know what he's going to do."

"She's more valuable to him alive than dead."

I shook my head. "Maybe now," I said. "Maybe today. But what about tomorrow? What if he gets bored? She knows who he is—"

"You have to let LaSalle do his job."

"Like that's going to do any good. That's what my mother tried and—"

I broke off the second I realized what I was saying. But it was too late. His hands fell away and he stepped back, the unspoken truth, the memory, turning the silver of his eyes to black.

It was *his* father my mother had trusted.

His father who'd failed to save her.

"I'm sorry," I whispered, and then I was doing it again, reaching out to him.

He stiffened.

My hand fell away.

"I'm sorry," I said again. "I just . . ." It all tangled inside me, the fear and the terror, the sorrow and regret. "She's all I have," I whispered, lifting my eyes to his. *"She's all I have."*

In the hollow of his cheek, a muscle thumped. "No, she's not."

I'm not sure how I didn't lose it right there. "I was horrible to her," I said, remembering. "Before she left, we fought. I said terrible things."

"She knew you didn't mean them."

"She thought I was gone. She saw me stop breathing and—"

Dylan moved so fast I never saw him coming. "What do you mean you stopped breathing?"

"With Julian." I shoved at the memory before it could form. That was one place I didn't need to return. "When he tried to send me to the astral, to help me find Grace. I was okay, but Aunt Sara freaked. She said I'm all·she has." And in turn, I'd told her she wasn't my mother. "She said she loved me."

More relaxed now, more normal, Dylan slid the hair from my face.

It was odd how naked that made me feel.

"I didn't say it back." In that moment I would have given anything to run back and do things differently, live the moment all over again. To say the words that had been trapped inside me. "I didn't even let her finish."

"Why not?"

"Because it was the first time," I whispered. "It was the first time someone said those words to me, and I didn't know how to give them back."

With a finger beneath my chin, he tilted my face. "No," he said. "It wasn't."

"What?"

"It wasn't the first time someone said they loved you," he said quietly. "And it wasn't the last, either."

I looked away, down at the fluffy ivory rug by my aunt's bathtub, where a pair of fuzzy pink slippers sat. I had to, because I couldn't look at him one second longer, couldn't let him see inside me like that.

Couldn't let myself see inside of him.

"What about Chase?"

The question, the tightness of Dylan's voice, locked around me. The answer hurt. All Chase had to do was look at me, and my heart sang. He'd taught me so much, about benign things like New Orleans, but deeper things, too, like what it was to share your life with someone, to want and to dream, how your whole world could rise and fall on a smile.

And, I realized, rubbing my thumb along the leather still wrapped around my wrist, how easily a heart could break.

"Shouldn't you call him?"

I looked up, back into the burn of Dylan's eyes. His hair had again fallen into his face.

"Shouldn't he be here?" he asked.

He should. But Chase didn't know how to hear me, or to quiet the doubt inside him. Over twelve hours had passed with not one call, one text . . .

This time hurt five thousand times worse than the last.

"No," I managed. Little voice came. "That's what you do."

Something dark flashed in his eyes.

"Over and over and over again," I said through the fragile swell inside me. "You're here. You don't turn. You don't run. You don't judge. You're just . . . *here.*"

The bathroom was small. I had him against the wall. There was nowhere for him to go, no way for him to move without, first, moving me.

He didn't try.

"You were *there,* too," I stunned myself by admitting, and with the words, my eyes stung. "When I stopped breathing and Aunt Sara freaked, when I was in my dreams . . . You were with me."

His eyes blazed, but he just stood there, so totally and completely still.

"And I need to go back," I said, lifting my hand to his chest, where, through the soft gray cotton of his shirt, I could feel the beat of his heart, fast, erratic.

"Aunt Sara begged me not to, but I have to," I said as the fog cleared and his hand joined mine. I didn't need pills to find sleep. I needed Julian. "It's the only way."

"Here, drink this."

Standing beside the bed, Dylan intercepted the mug before I could take it. "She took some allergy medicine—"

"Not a problem," Julian said. He'd been running when we called. It had been over an hour before we reached him.

The second he'd heard about my aunt, he'd gone quiet.

"It's just an herbal tea," he said now. "To help her relax."

Before, I needed that help. Now, courtesy of the pills I'd foolishly popped, I could barely hold my eyes open.

"Try it without," Dylan said, propping a hip against the edge of the mattress. He hadn't said anything, hadn't tried to stop me, but I could tell he wasn't thrilled. "She's barely hanging on as it is."

I forced my eyes wider, didn't want him to know how right he was. For two hours I'd been fighting the pull. "Okay."

As usual Julian was dressed in black, his shoulder-length hair fastened behind his neck. His closed expression was impossible to read.

"Try to relax," he said, but that was impossible. Detective Jackson had called right before Julian arrived. The news had not been good. There was nothing. Absolutely not a single trace of my aunt beyond the time she'd walked through airport security. She'd never reached the gate. No one remembered seeing her. The security feeds showed nothing.

It was like looking for a ghost.

"Do you think it will work?" My voice was slurred, thick.

"We're going to try something different," Julian said. He'd suggested we project from the condo. He said that by surrounding myself with my aunt's energy, I'd have a better chance of connecting with her—and not slipping into my past. "I'll guide you. Tell me what you see, and I'll tell you what to do."

Numbly, I nodded.

"And no matter what happens, stay away from the Abyss."

I blinked as Dylan moved closer. "The Abyss?"

"The portal between dimensions—the tear you slipped through last time, when you found your past."

And so much more. "But what if—"

"The past isn't important right now," he said. "Only the future."

"I'm going with her," Dylan said.

My breath stopped.

"That's possible, right?" he asked.

Julian said nothing, but he must have nodded, because Dylan shifted beside me, sliding until the length of his leg pressed against mine. "Don't be afraid. You won't be alone."

My voice was little more than a scrape. "I don't understand . . ."

"Do you trust me?"

"Yes."

"Then give me your hand."

The moment locked around me. I looked at his palm, wide and square, and slowly placed mine against it.

"It's okay to let go," he said, curling his fingers around my hand. "I've got you."

With New Age music echoing and the allergy medicine thickening my blood, I settled against the pillows and let go.

"You're on an elevator," I heard Julian saying, but the faraway voice had no edges or texture.

"You're safe."

Something enveloped me, wrapping around, holding me tight.

"Just push a button, and let yourself go."

With amazing lightness, I shifted toward the buttons and feathered my hand along one, saw the yellow glow and felt the elevator start to move. Down. Down.

Down . . .

"You're going home. You're going back to where you came from . . ."

Down.

"I want you to count backward."

"Ten," I whispered, drawn by the warmth, even as my fingers loosened. "Nine . . ."

Down . . .

"Eight." Vaguely I realized Dylan was counting, too. "Seven—" His hold tightened, and the door slid open.

The glare is so bright it blinds.

I step forward: it's all the same, the empty street with weeds overtaking crumbling concrete, puddles and trash and—

A buzz sounds, like an insect by my ear.

"Tell me what you see."

Turning toward the voice, I see him standing there, right beside me, his hand still holding mine. "Dylan . . ."

"I'm here."

He is. He's there. Right there with me in the corners of my mind . . .

"The buildings, do they mean anything to you?" I ask breathlessly. "Have you seen them before?"

A breeze sweeps hair against his face. "I can't see them."

"W-what?" Frantically I twist around. "They're right there—"

"I know they are," he says, his voice there, but somehow far away. "But they're projections of your mind, not mine."

I didn't understand. "Is . . . is that what you are, too?"

He steps closer. "No, I'm as real as you are. But what I see is different, from my mind, not yours."

And he didn't like it. I can see that, can see that in the way he's looking at me, can feel it in the way his hand almost crushes mine.

What? What could he see, what could be that bad?

But before I can ask he's tugging me to follow him.

"Be my eyes," he says. "Tell me what you see."

Beyond him purple and pink stain the sky, darkening toward the horizon. But I know that's not what he means. I head toward an overturned urn, where something small protrudes from a nearby puddle.

"A . . . dolphin," I whisper, going down on a knee to touch.

"You see water?"

"No, a stuffed animal." Dirty and torn. "An eye's missing."

"What else?"

Clenching the forgotten toy, I glance down the length of the street. "I think it rained." *Just like in New Orleans a few days before.* "Everything's dirty and dreary, sad."

"Are the buildings there?"

"Yes." *I step toward them—and he follows.* "They're on both sides of the street." *Left over from that long-ago time and place, with porches and shutters, windows broken and smeared . . .*

"Hurry! You have to hurry!"

Jerkily I twist back toward Dylan. "She's here—I hear her!"

He looks beyond me, where the buildings stretch but he doesn't see. "Then go," *he commands softly.* "I'm right behind you."

"Hurry! He'll find you!"

I start to run. "Tell me where you are!"

"He has her!" *she shouts, but the swirl of the wind carries her voice from all directions.*

I stop, listen.

"He has us all—even you."

Across the street, I realize, from the peach building with green doors. "She's in the hotel," *I tell Dylan, and then I'm running again. We're running.* "Who?" *I ask, closing in.* "Just tell me who or where—"

"Inside." *But now the voice is behind me.*

I spin, see the lemony yellow building on the corner. "The emporium—"

"You have to get inside," *she cries, but the voice is behind me again. Beside me. All around me.*

And then there's nothing but the sweep of silence.

"Trinity, what's happening?"

"I don't know." *I twist around, searching from building to building, window to window, door to door. And see the footprints. They're black, glowing like melted coal.*

I know I have to follow them.

Dylan is a step behind. "Where are you going?"

"Inside," I whisper. "Please don't let go."

And he doesn't, he doesn't let go, he holds on tight, goes with me as I step toward the door flanked by two wide columns, white once, grimy ivory now, and reach for the glowing glass knob. "She's here."

THIRTY-FOUR

My aunt. *I feel her, the desperation of her heartbeat, the twist of love and terror.* "But I don't think she wants me to find her."

"Why not?"

"It's like she's holding her breath." *Like everything was holding its breath—my aunt, the building.* The wind. *There's nothing, absolutely nothing, just a stillness so deep it throbs with each beat of my heart.*

"Aunt Sara!" *I shout, lifting my fists to pound.*

They slip right through, the wood nothing but air.

"Trinity, no—"

I lunge forward, and everything starts to spin. Stumbling I throw myself to the door—and fall straight through.

Dylan catches me.

I hang there, in his arms. "Oh, my God—it's gone." *All of it, the door and the building, the stillness. My aunt. I can't feel any of it, only the whirring around me, louder, louder—*

Frantically I twist away. "Aunt Sara!"

"Trinity—what's happening?"

"I-I don't know," *I say, stumbling again, starting to run.* "There's nothing here."

"Yes," said a different voice. "There is."

I freeze. "Julian."

"Let go of the fear," he said. "And look again."

Dylan stands a few feet away, watching. Beyond him the sky fades. "Do it."

I don't know how, I want to say—scream. But instead I squeeze my eyes shut, and when I open them a heartbeat later, it's all there again, the rotting buildings and the empty street . . .

"Tell me what you see."

This time I don't hesitate. I look beyond the hotel and the emporium—and blink. "They're . . . dancing."

"Who is?"

"I don't know." But I see them, swirling. "Wait, no . . . She's laughing." No. Screaming.

"Is someone with you?"

"Yes. No. I . . ." Spinning, I squint against the blinding white of the afternoon sky, where I would swear . . . "It's a highway," I murmur, and finally the buzz makes sense, the constant drone. Not an insect. Not my imagination.

But cars.

Everything slows, stretches. "There's . . ." I blink, don't understand. "An alligator," I whisper. "And a pelican." Animated, playful—crumbling.

I feel more than hear Dylan's rough breath. "Look up—look away from the highway . . ."

His words fade. The buzz grows louder. Because there where I've never looked before, something huge and hulking lurks against the horizon.

"Trinity—"

"I don't understand," I whisper as shape takes form, and reality twists. "What's that doing here?"

And with the question, the realization, a soft sound comes from behind me, like paper being torn. I turn and see the glow, the opening a few feet away, the air itself torn wide open.

"Trinity—what's happening?"

The last time the slit had been smooth, perfect. But now the edges are *rough, jagged. Instead of pink, the reddish-orange hues of a sunset leak through.*

I move toward it, know I have to move toward it. That's why it's there. For me.

Dylan stops me. "What do you see?"

The glow calls to me . . .

I move fast, ripping myself from Dylan, from everything, toward the portal—

"Trinity, no!" he shouts, lunging for me.

I step into it.

He snags me by the arm.

I rip away, twist into the void . . .

Everything flashes, keeps flashing. I spin around, spin again, but the landscape stretches in all directions, parched, desolate, leaving only shadows to twist against the dying embers of a fire. There are no buildings, no trees—no Dylan.

"Where are you?" I scream. "Where are you?"

"Trinity! Get out of there!"

Everything keeps shifting, jerky, off-balance and out of focus, like images from a handheld video camera. I don't know which way to go. I make myself run anyway, know I have to find her before—

Through the fleeting flickers I see her, see her where I'd seen her before, standing with her back to me, matted hair falling against her shoulders, her dress, the beautiful one we'd picked out for Naomi's wedding, shredded.

"Aunt Sara!" Screaming, I lunge for her.

Lightning strobes, and she's gone.

"No, come back—"

"Trinity!" Dylan's voice, strong—ravaged. "What's happening?"

"I saw her! She's—" Another ripple cuts into the darkness, showing the girl across the street, walking fast, her long white-blond hair pulled into a low ponytail, her maxi dress tangling at her feet.

"Grace," I murmur, breaking toward her. She's out. She's escaped, trying to get away.

But darkness sweeps in, fast—violent—and when it recedes, the street is empty.

I spin around, spin again, keep spinning. "Grace!"

The hall stretches through the shadows, long, doors lining both sides, closed.

All but one.

"Trinity."

Dylan's voice. I know it is. And I want to hold on, want so badly to hold on. But the echo of recognition is louder—stronger. I move toward it, down the hall, to the room with the open door, where the glass knob glows.

Just like four months before.

And I know. Even before I look, I know who I'm going to see. "Jessica." She's there, on that disgusting mattress, her hair matted and eyes drenched with bone-deep fear as she scoots back. "No," she cries. "No! Don't hurt me!"

"Goddamn—she's in the Abyss."

The words, Julian's voice, barely register.

"Get her out!"

"Trinity—"

I turn and start to run, stumble down the hall—and scream.

"What?" Dylan's voice. Dylan's voice! From behind me. Inside me. "What's happening?" he demands.

"It's me . . ." I stare, stunned. "I see me."

"What do you mean you see you?"

"At the house on Prytania, the night Jessica locked me in the closet. I'm there—I'm afraid."

"Get her out," he shouted again. "Now!"

I heard him, felt the tugging, but ripped away, stumbling toward the stairs and vaulting into the darkness.

People are everywhere, laughing, drinking. Everything sparkles—glitters. And then a girl with long blond hair breaks away, her eyes dancing, her smile flirty, and blows a kiss to a guy in the crowd.

"Happy New Year!" she enthuses, and then she turns as if playing, daring, and darts away—

"No, come back!" I try to go after her, know I have to—

The smell blasts through me, sharp, pungent. I gag on it, start to cough, and then he's there, Dylan, leaning over me and holding me by the arms, his chest violent with breath, the silver of his eyes burning.

"Oh, God," I murmured, looking around. My aunt's room. I was in my aunt's room, with Dylan and Julian, Julian who held a small vial in his hand. "What just happened?"

Somewhere along the line hair had fallen from Julian's ponytail, now fell against his face. "You went through a portal."

I jerked up. "They were all there," I remembered, confused. "My aunt and Grace, Jessica and another girl." And me. I'd been there, too. I'd seen myself.

"I don't understand," I whispered as the skin stretched across Dylan's face, stretched so tight, emphasizing the sharp lines of his cheekbones.

"You slipped into the hunter's past," Julian said, "*his* memories."

And something inside me started to break.

"He fucking played us," Dylan said. His voice was unbearably flat. "He played us all."

I grabbed him, held on. "What do you mean—"

"It didn't end last fall," he said. "The man who took Jessica—and the others. He's been waiting all this time."

"To hunt again," I whispered sickly. Lines veered from dot to dot, creating a picture I'd never imagined. Someone *had* died at Big Charity, but someone else had lived, and whoever that someone was, they were hunting again, hunting in a circle around me, ever closer. "Oh, my God—"

"But the game is about to end," Dylan said—vowed. *Promised.* "Because you found her."

"W-what?"

"You saw a roller coaster, didn't you?" he said, and on a quick, sharp rush it all came back, all the disjointed images, the hulking curved structure against the horizon . . .

"I want you to stay where you are," Detective LaSalle instructed five minutes later. "I'm on it."

The second the line went dead, Dylan and I ran for his truck.

Waiting was not an option.

Within minutes we were tearing out the garage while he filled me in about the former Six Flags park on the outskirts of town, abandoned since Katrina. For weeks it had sat underwater, but even after the swamp receded, no one returned.

"Hurry!" I said as the New Orleans I knew gave way to a desolate stretch of eastbound Interstate, littered by vacant strip malls and restaurants. "You have to hurry."

"Ten minutes."

"That's too long!"

He swerved onto the shoulder, jerking around a minivan. Minutes later we zipped past an exit ramp angling down from the highway—straight into the murky water.

Once, before the storm, there would have been a road.

"You've been there before?" I asked. "You know where you're going?"

He swerved onto the shoulder again, gunning around slower cars. "I was just a kid when it opened." The speedometer pushed ninety. "My dad used to take me."

"And later?" I prompted.

"Dad didn't come with me then."

The park had sat month after month, waiting, forgotten, while the swamp closed in. There'd been controversy and legal battles, a few rides had been relocated to other parks, potential buyers had come forward with plans to reopen, but while lawyers did what lawyers did, the remains of the park first known as Jazzland waited.

"Not much longer," he said, and for the hundredth time, I twisted to scour the blinding white of the horizon to the south. It was late afternoon. The sun, glowing from behind thick clouds, had not yet begun to set.

"I don't understand," I said. "How could she be there? Don't the police—"

"They do," he said, not needing to hear my question. "When they see something out of the ordinary or a local calls. But like Big Charity, they can't be there all the time."

"But—" I started, but the sight of the wooden roller coaster twisting against the horizon stopped my words.

"*Omigod* . . . Aunt Sara." The shaking came on fast, a terrible vibration from somewhere deep. "Hurry!"

Dylan zoomed down the exit and veered onto the road leading to the park, as the speedometer inched toward one hundred.

The park came into focus, rides and buildings standing as silent placeholders for all the storm had taken, and that nothing could ever give back. At a distance they looked normal. But the closer we got, the more the scene warped, shifting from daydream to postapocalyptic. The Ferris wheel and roller coasters still stood, our speed emphasizing the stillness to them. And the trees and bushes, once carefully manicured, now grew wild. A chain fence surrounded the perimeter. A simple sign read CLOSED FOR STORM.

The parking lot sat empty.

"There's no one here," I said, as Dylan stopped beside the barricade. "LaSalle said—"

He yanked the keys from the ignition. "Text him," he said, reaching for the gun beneath the seat.

I stabbed out a message to Detective LaSalle. His response came almost immediately.

New Orleans East patrols combed area.
Nothing there.

I just stared. I read the words, but they didn't register, didn't come close to making sense.

"What'd he say?" Dylan asked, grabbing his BlackBerry from the cup holder between us.

Blankly I looked up at him.

He took the phone from my hands and glanced down, frowned.

"No. That can't be. She has to—" Twisting from him, I shoved

open the door and sprung into the cool afternoon breeze, started
to run.

"Trinity—"

I kept running, knew he would follow. Knew he had the gun.
Knew I couldn't rely on anyone else to find my aunt.

At the fence I didn't pause, didn't care about the edges slicing into
my hands. I scrambled to the top and jumped to the other side, came
down with a jolt against the cracked concrete.

Dylan was a heartbeat behind me.

"They're wrong," I said, trying to run as he reached for me. They'd
been careless, hadn't looked close enough. "They have to be!"

He caught me and turned me so that I had to look up to see him.
"I'll check," he said. "But I want you to wait—"

"Don't say it," I said, fighting to breathe. "Don't even think it."

"Trinity—"

"Because you can't make me," I said, and before I had the chance
to finish, I saw the light flicker through his eyes, the memory of
the words he'd given me the day before, when I'd asked him why
he didn't try to stop me.

Because I wasn't the one he was trying to stop.

Because he knew I would only keep trying.

And one time he might not be there.

And it only took a second . . .

And that left only the truth, no matter how much he hated it:
the safest place for me was with him.

On a rough breath his hand slid to mine, and, holding on, we ran
toward the windswept silence of the entrance.

It was all there, all waiting, the redbrick path and once-cheerful
yellow building with white trim, the green railing and empty turn-
stiles, the naked mannequin leaning against the edge of a darkened
ticket booth. Farther back, the green building that had once wel-
comed visitors, now with peeling paint and mud-smeared windows.

I slowed. "Oh, God."

It was almost impossible to process the desolation.

Dylan stopped and slid a hand to my hip. "You don't have to—"

"Yes, I do," I said, taking off toward the green building, where a white door hung open. "Maybe the cops are still here," I said, slipping inside. "Maybe they left their cars out of—"

For the second time in less than ten minutes, the park stole my words.

Nothing prepared me. Nothing could have. Dylan told me the park had been abandoned. He'd told me everyone walked away one day, and never walked back. Like the park was stuck in some bizarre time vacuum, preserved but crumbling, waiting but fading, like a terminally ill woman who got up every morning and put on her makeup and her jewelry, styled her hair, did everything she could to look the way she once had, but all you had to do was see her in the bright glare of the sun to know that it was all just . . . an illusion.

Furniture still sat, falling apart and rusted. Computers and printers and telephones waited for users that never returned. That never would. Trash cans overflowed. Paper littered every available surface, a horizontal smear along the rotting walls that, after my short time in the city, I knew represented the water line.

It looked to be at least four feet.

"Oh, my God," I whispered, gagging at a decapitated teddy bear trapped beneath a mud-caked computer monitor.

Dylan came up beside me. "It's all like this."

I spun toward him, felt my stomach twist at the sight of the white-board behind him, where the names of all the rides were still listed, awaiting assignment.

"Aunt Sara," I whispered, and without a word, we were moving again, making our way through the maze of boxes and abandoned electronics, and trying not to breathe.

Staggering, I made it across the room, where a door led to the inside of the park, where the sun still shone and a fan swirled in the cool breeze, concrete crumbled and weeds encroached . . . and the ghost town stretched before me, exactly as it had in my dreams.

"This is it," I murmured. "This is what I saw."

Lifting his gun, he stepped in front of me. "We'll take one at a time," he said, heading for the first building on our left.

I wanted to run. I wanted to shout for my aunt as loud as I could. But even raw and threadbare, I knew what a mistake that would be.

The element of surprise was our best weapon.

Against the sweep of the wind, we made our way inside what had once been a gift shop, Dylan hugging the mold-smeared walls as he led the way with me tucked in behind him. And again, the moment twisted, and time disintegrated.

Stuffed animals littered the floor. Many had been gutted. I had no doubt rats watched. "Aunt Sara!" I wanted to scream, but bit down against the automatic rise of bile.

"It's so still," I whispered.

Dylan edged deeper into the shadows. "Someone's been here."

I pressed against his back, staring over his shoulder at the fast-food bags at the base of the counter. The cash register had long since been busted open.

"It's fresh." He pointed to a half-eaten po-boy. "By nightfall that'll be gone."

Numbly I closed my eyes and called to them through my mind, to my aunt and to Grace, to Delphi. *"We're here,"* I said without words. *"Just hold on . . ."*

The temperature dropped as we made our way past the unseeing eyes of teddy bears, outside past a photo kiosk where family pictures were little more than smears of color, to the snack shop where fading signs advertised hot dogs and fries and popcorn, but tables and chairs lay on their sides.

"Why is this still here?" I whispered as we made our way into another building, where the only light came through slivers and cracks.

Dylan stopped.

"What is it?"

He used his phone to cast light into a far corner—and found another discarded mannequin. I saw the hair first, tangled, strewn out like mud-caked straw. The clothes were typical New Orleans, a long, gypsy-print maxi dress—

And then she moved.

THIRTY-FIVE

My breath stabbed against my throat.

"Omigod!" I whisper-screamed, because I knew, before I even crossed the room and dropped to my knees, I knew who lay crumpled in the corner.

"Grace!" I reached for her and turned her gently into me, felt everything inside me cringe at the sight of her eyes swollen shut.

"She's alive," Dylan said at my side, sliding the hair from her battered face. Dried blood caked her pale cheeks like garish costume makeup. Her lips were dry, busted. "Pulse steady," he said, easing his hand from her neck to her chest.

"*Grace,*" I tried, but only a rasp leaked through. "I'm here—we're here. Can you hear me?"

Her eyelids fluttered, but did not open. I wasn't sure they could.

"Oh, God," I said, looking up at Dylan. "Who would do this?"

His eyes, drenched with the same darkness that twisted through me, met mine. "It's good that she's alive."

Or was it? Was it good that she was alive? Was it good that she would have to live with . . . this? And immediately my thoughts turned to Jessica.

Sometimes survival could be its own hell.

"My aunt," I said, twisting around to the boxes and crates and debris behind me. "She's got to be here—"

Dylan swung around, gun first, eyes sharp.

I lunged after him. "What?"

"Someone's out there," he murmured, pushing to his feet and edging toward the front of the snack shop.

I scrambled after him. "We can't just leave her!"

He kept his gun in front of him. "We have to—for now. She's stable. She'll be okay."

I spun back to her, lying so broken and battered and still, and felt something inside me reach.

"We'll be back," I promised. "Just hold on."

Wordlessly, Dylan made his way to the window, using his free hand to wipe the grime.

I felt him stiffen in that one horrible, fractured heartbeat before the sound of my name ripped through the silence—and we both started to run.

Outside, the bleached-out glow of late afternoon blinded. From the forgotten lake in the center the wind rushed, pushing and distorting, laughing. But above the cruel soundtrack, the voice registered again.

"Trinity!"

Chase. "Omigod." Heart slamming, I sprinted past a Southern belle swirling by herself and a forgotten wheelchair on its side, a falling down gazebo, swings swaying with imaginary riders. "Chase!"

Dylan shot ahead of me, toward the roller coaster hulking against the blood-washed horizon.

Everything was twisting, spinning, as if I was on the broken-down carousel in front of me, and it wouldn't stop, just kept accelerating . . .

And then I saw him, emerging from the far side, Chase—with Delphi cradled in his arms.

I stopped hard, slamming into an invisible wall, and almost went to my knees.

He caught me before I could, his hand taking me by the arm and steadying me, as Delphi started to squirm.

"Omigod—omigod . . ." I didn't know what else to say. "What's going on? Where did you find her?"

And then Dylan was there, taking Delphi into his arms, leaving only me and Chase, and the wind whipping frantically around us.

I didn't understand. Didn't understand what I saw in his eyes—or felt crushing through me. "Chase," I whispered. His shirt—his favorite, the gray Affliction one I'd given him for Christmas—was torn, his jeans covered in mud. "What are you doing here?"

His bangs fell against the blue of his eyes, making them look bluer somehow. "I'm here because you are," he said, his hand sliding down my arm to close around the leather band still circling my wrist.

"I didn't take it off," I whispered. "I couldn't."

His eyes met mine. "I shouldn't have walked away last night," he said, as my throat locked up on me. "I was outside your condo all morning. Trying to figure out what to say. And then I saw you tearing out of the garage . . ."

With Dylan. "You followed us," I breathed, shoving at the hair slapping my face.

"What's going on?" he asked. "What are you doing here?"

And then I started to cry. So much. So much had happened in the space of less than a day. So much had . . . broken.

"My aunt," I managed, swallowing hard. "She's gone and the guy who took Jessica has her and he has Grace, too, but we found her and she's okay—"

"Wait, wait—the guy who took Jessica is dead—"

"No," I said, and then I was the one holding on, my hand finding his arm and squeezing so, so tight. "He's not. We were wrong. It's all some sick game. The wrong person died."

He dragged me closer. "What are you talking about?"

"I-I can see him," I said, looking around me, to where Dylan stood a few feet away with Delphi in his arms—and the gun in his hand. "I can see through his eyes—his dreams and his memories—and he did it," I said as Chase pulled me to him.

"He did it all," I said, holding on even as I kept looking—

looking, past the kids' play area with the twisting tube slides, past a rotting stage and huge carnival mask tilted on its side. *She was here.* "He took Jessica and those other girls and—"

My words died the second I saw the ice cream cone. It swirled up from the corner of the light blue building, with dark red letters along the top: BARBE'S ICE CREAM SHOP.

And everything inside me stopped. "Oh, my God," I whispered—or maybe I screamed. "This is it—this is what she was painting." And I could feel, I could feel Chase's fingers digging into me as I tried to pull away. "This is where I die."

He held on tighter, wouldn't let me go. "What are you talking about?"

The wind kept blowing, I knew that it did. I saw the flags flapping, and my own hair slapping my face. But I could feel nothing except the cold bleed of shock.

"The girl in my dream," I murmured, and then Dylan was there, too, Dylan and Chase, one on each side of me. Each holding on. "This is what she was painting—this ice cream shop." Two years before. Two years before, a girl I'd never met had painted a snapshot from my future . . .

Numbly I looked up and saw the hawk soaring against the crimson glow of late afternoon—and the mouse dangling from its claws. "Oh, God. I should never have said anything. I should have kept watching, then I would have seen . . ."

Chase stepped closer, blocking my view. "Seen what?"

And I could hear it in his deceptively quiet voice, the tight coil of horror. "Me," I whispered, dry-eyed now. Calm. Amazingly, horribly calm. "I would have seen me."

"You don't know that—"

"But I do," I said. "Because that's what she did. There were other pictures, pictures of me . . ." Dying.

"No." This time it was Dylan who spoke, Dylan's voice that broke. "You're not going to die here."

I swung toward him, oddly disconnected.

"But it does end," he vowed. "It stops here."

"You have to get out of here," Chase said as I whipped back toward him. "Before anything—"

"Not without my aunt—"

"I'll look." It was all there in his eyes, all that was unspoken between us, the apology and the regret, the fear. *The love.* "But you need to get out of here."

Stepping into him, I shook my head. "No, I can't . . ."

He looked beyond me, to Dylan. "Get her out of here," he said. "There's a warehouse by the employee entrance where I came in. There was a door open . . ."

I grabbed for him, tried to stop him.

"Stay with Dylan," he gritted out. "He has the gun."

The wind slowed, started to whisper. "Chase, no—"

He pulled me to him for a quick hard kiss, a kiss that promised all that I'd seen glowing in his eyes.

Twisting away, he took off toward the roller coaster.

I lunged for him—but Dylan caught me, held me. "Come on." His voice was as gentle as his hold. "He's right. We've got to get out of here." And then he was lifting Delphi toward me, and she was in my arms, and together we were running past the Mardi Gras Madness ride, with its forgotten cars empty and waiting in a line along the rusted track, darkness ready to swallow them, with beads scattered against cracked concrete, and a jester hanging upside down. Waiting.

Gift shops and cafes and restrooms, they were all there, just as they'd been before the storm. Waiting. Still.

And every one we passed, we searched. Broken glass crunched beneath our feet, graffiti swirled against the walls. We weren't the only ones who'd been there. That was clear. Trash lay strewn everywhere, abandoned like the gutted, water-sogged remains of stuffed animals.

"God, where is she?" I cried as we ran toward the triple loops of another roller coaster. "Aunt Sara has to be here—" I broke off and listened, grabbing the BlackBerry the second I heard another ring.

"Chase," I breathed as Dylan swung back toward me. "Omigod, where are you? Did you find her?"

The wind screamed around us, distorting everything. I turned away and held the phone tighter, Delphi squirming from my arms as I pressed a hand over my other ear. "Chase? Are you there?"

He was, I could tell that he was, but only distortion came through. "Chase, I can't hear what you're saying!"

"Trinity . . ."

"I'm here."

He still talked, but his voice was garbled—breathless. ". . . found her . . ."

I twisted back toward the direction of the ice cream shop. "Oh, my God—where?" My eyes locked onto Dylan's. "Where are you?"

". . . get out . . . mom . . ."

"What?" Already we were running. "Chase!"

But through the phone, I heard nothing, not even the static. "He found her!"

Dylan sprinted ahead of me, his gun held in front of him, looking every bit the cop that his father had been.

Then he stopped dead in his tracks. "What the—"

The harsh hues of late afternoon stole details, but I saw it the second he did, the shadow—the silhouette racing along a high curve of the wooden roller coaster.

"Oh, my God!" I cried, trying to see, understand. But then Dylan was running, shouting. "No! *No!* Get down—"

Time slowed. Maybe I heard the grinding moan first, the crack of wood splintering. Or maybe I saw the figure stiffen. Or maybe that all happened at the same time, the moment locking around detail, holding it for one cruel second, then releasing it to unfurl in horrifying speed.

One second he was there, perched along a high twist of the rotting wooden roller coaster.

Then the track collapsed, and he was gone.

The impact slammed through me, stealing my own breath. I ran, sprinting to keep up with Dylan, through the grotesque sweep of silence of the area that had once been cluttered with thrill seekers, toward the crumpled figure beside the rotting gate.

Dylan got there first. Gasping, I staggered beside him—and froze.

"Trinity—"

Vaguely I heard his voice. It was warped, distorted, through some hideous tunnel of time and space. But I couldn't look at him, couldn't answer, could only drop to my knees and try to breathe.

I'd been warned. I'd seen it time and time again. But I'd never realized . . .

"*Chase,*" I whispered, reaching for him and turning his face toward me, seeing the trickle of blood from his mouth—his nose. "*Oh, God . . . Chase.*"

Dylan kneeled beside me.

Everything shook as I ran my hands along Chase's body, sliding my fingers to his throat. "Come on," I prayed, pressing harder. "Come on!"

"Trinity, he's—"

"Don't!" I screamed. "Don't say it!"

Wordlessly, Dylan joined his hand with mine, shifting my fingers a fraction of an inch, where the faintest flutter . . .

"Yes," I sobbed, leaning over him and bringing my mouth to his. "Yes, yes, yes."

Cradling him, I ran my hands through his sweaty hair, kissing the familiar curves of his face, the blood at his mouth, just as I'd done the week before, when I'd found him by the canal. I'd thought that was the end.

I'd thought that was the end!

"You're okay," I promised. "We're going to get you to the hospital." Like last weekend. They would run tests, maybe hold him for observation. His parents would be there . . .

Behind me, I heard Dylan making the call.

"*And you're going to be okay.*" With one hand I found his, laced our fingers and squeezed.

"*Trin . . .*"

My heart kicked hard. "Chase?" I eased back. "That's it, come on, I'm here . . ."

His eyes, dull, glassy, met mine. ". . . get out . . ."

"No," I said, fighting tears. "Not without you."

I saw his mouth work, wished I had water to offer. "Y–your aunt . . ."

Slowly things started to click, memory overlapping the horror of seeing him fall. "You said you found her—where is she?"

"Get . . . LaSalle . . ."

Dizzy, I swung back toward Dylan. "She has to be close," I cried, not wanting to think about the agony I saw in his eyes. "You have to find her!"

The relentless breeze sent the long dark hair cutting into his face. "Trinity, I'm not going to leave you—"

"You have to," I said, crying again, harder this time. "*Please.* You have to find her . . ."

I could tell he didn't want to go. But I also knew that he realized I was right. "Call me," he gritted out. "If you hear anything, if a shadow so much as falls the wrong way—"

"I will," I promised, swallowing back tears. "I promise."

Still, I could tell he didn't want to move.

"Hurry," I said, blinking against the hot salty sting. *"Please."*

Finally he moved, not back toward the center of the park, but toward me. Eyes hot on mine, he reached down and held out his switchblade. "Take this."

Wordlessly, I did.

He turned then, and ran.

Blinking, I watched him vanish behind the Mardi Gras Madness ride, then twisted back toward Chase. "Help's coming. Just hang on."

Blood leaked from his mouth. *"Uhav . . ."* he mumbled, but above the roar of my own blood, I could hardly understand.

"Sh–h–h." I leaned closer, my mouth a breath from his. "Don't try to talk."

Crammed between us, I felt his hand move and pulled back,

saw him fumbling with his pocket. "No, no," I said. "Save your energy."

His movements got jerkier as he grabbed my hand and dragged it toward him.

"What?" I asked.

"Take . . . it . . ."

Confused, not wanting him to exert himself, I slid my hand along the—

Gray Affliction shirt.

Just like in my dream.

"Take . . . it," he murmured the second my fingers slipped against the phone crammed in his waistband.

I did. "Dylan already called," I told him.

His eyes rolled back.

"Chase!"

Limply, his hand lifted to close around my hair and tug me toward him. "Never . . . shoulda . . . w-walked . . ."

My heart squeezed. "It's okay . . ." I said, sliding the long bangs from his forehead.

"Trinity—thank God."

On a hard slam I twisted around and tried not to start crying all over again. "Detective LaSalle—omigod, you came! They're here," I said. "They're all here!"

Eyes grim, he stepped closer. "Sara—"

"We haven't found her yet. But Grace is in one of the buildings up front—"

He glanced in that direction. "Where's Dylan? What the hell are you doing alone—"

"Looking for my aunt," I said. "I made him go, couldn't leave Chase. Where's the ambulance?"

His whole body went on alert, the cop in command of the man. "Come on," he said, reaching for me and closing a hand around my upper arm. "We've got to get you out—"

"No!" I shrieked, jerking back. "I'm not leaving him."

"Trinity, you have to."

"No," I cried again as he forcibly dragged me to my feet. "I can't just—"

"You're a sitting target," he pointed out, positioning his body between me and the rotting buildings of the park. "If you want to see your aunt alive . . ."

I swayed, lunging back toward Chase.

His eyes, dull, unfocused, shifted to mine, pleading.

"No," I whispered.

Blood caked his mouth. *"La . . . Salle . . ."*

"Come on," the detective barked, and, crying, I knew I had no choice.

Dead toys couldn't win.

Blinking against my tears, I staggered in front of LaSalle, back toward the front of the park. "We have to find Dylan—"

"There's not time," LaSalle said, checking over his shoulder. "He knows what he's doing."

And so did I. Maybe LaSalle didn't think it was important, but if Dylan went back to the roller coaster and found me gone, he would think the worst. He would go nuts—

I'd left my BlackBerry by Chase, but his iPhone was still in my hand. I drew it close so LaSalle wouldn't try to stop me, and fiddled with the button. I could text Dylan—

The camera came up.

I started to switch to phone mode, but saw the picture against the screen, of the back of one of the buildings, and a woman with long dark hair wearing a lavender dress, draped in a man's arms. The man was running . . .

My throat closed up. The buzz in my ears turned to a scream. Picking up my pace, I walked faster, back toward the collapsed carousel and Barbe's Ice Cream Shop, where large blue and red flags flapped violently around a tangle of tubular slides . . .

"My aunt," I cried. "We have to find—"

"If she's here we'll find her," LaSalle promised from behind me.

And everything inside me crystallized.

The man in the picture, the man with my aunt in his arms, the man running in the shadows, was the same man hustling me out of the park.

The horror of it all crashed in on me, like a fog lifting to brutal clarity, then fogging over once more. But even as my mind raced, I knew there was no time for that. I walked faster, knew I only had a little time. Shaking, pretending that I knew nothing, I flipped through more pictures, one after the other, all of LaSalle.

Chase had seen him. He'd seen LaSalle with my aunt. Maybe that's why he'd climbed on the roller coaster—to get a better view. To get pictures.

Evidence.

Numbly, I slid my finger along the bottom of the screen, pulling up the text message option. And when the message requested a recipient, I fumbled in MOM.

Chase's mom.

She would know. No matter what went down in the next few minutes, she would have the evidence. She would know who hurt her son.

"What are you doing?" LaSalle asked, closing in on me.

"Nothing," I said as I brought up phone mode and entered Dylan's number.

He would know, too. I couldn't talk to him—but whatever went down, he would hear.

Heart slamming, I slid Chase's phone into my waistband—and at the last second veered toward the play area.

"Trinity—no!" LaSalle shouted.

I kept running, knew I couldn't stop.

"Trinity, what the fuck are you doing?"

My rules, was all I could think. *My rules.* "Aunt Sara!" I shouted, buying time. "Aunt Sara!"

"Trinity—"

I could feel him gaining on me. Zigzagging, I darted past the blue rail fence toward the toddler airplane ride. "Aunt Sara, please—"

"Trinity, no!"

Red and blue flags slapped at me. "Dylan!"

It was a game, all a game. I had to keep pretending, painting an illusion of my own. If he suspected that I knew—

"This isn't the answer!" LaSalle shouted.

I darted through the tubular slides, emerging on the far side of the play area. "Dylan! Aunt Sara! Where are you?"

"You're making a mistake," LaSalle warned, and I could hear it, the veil of the cop crumbling away, the edge of desperation taking over. Whatever game he'd been playing, it had been leading to this, to here.

To getting me out of that park.

And I couldn't let it happen.

Blindly, I made my way toward the kiddie swings, dangling in a circle from rusted chains, an ornate hub in the center, where the operator had once stood. If I could get to the other side—

His hand came down on my shoulder.

I twisted.

My shirt ripped.

I darted away, shoving swings at him as I lunged around the hub. "No," I said, trying to catch my breath. "I'm not leaving here with you."

He stilled, the ice cold of his eyes finding mine as he slipped the gun from his holster, and lifted it toward me. "Yes, you are."

My throat burned. My blood roared. "Not without my aunt."

The look on his face chilled me to the bone. He'd always made me uncomfortable, the way he'd watched me, the questions he'd asked. But I'd attributed it to the cop in him.

The truth sickened me.

"Trinity, don't make this harder than it needs to be."

I slapped at the hair flying into my face. Dylan was there. Dylan was close. All I had to do was buy enough time.

"I can't," I said. "Not when I'm this close. Don't try to make me—"

His mouth was a sharp, narrow line. "It's for your own good."

"No, it's not."

His finger slid to the trigger. "Stop acting like a child."

I inched farther around the hub. If he made a move, I would, too, around and around . . .

"Now, Trinity."

That was so not going to happen.

I wanted to throw it all at him. I wanted to throw everything I knew, to smear him with it. Because it all made sense now, horrible sense, the exact moment our paths had crossed last fall and he'd started to play. I'd contacted him to help. And I'd trusted him, told him everything, about my dreams, what I saw.

And in doing so, I'd given him a new toy.

He threw it at me first. "You really think you're going to win?" he mocked. "The game's over, sweetheart. And I win."

"I don't know what you're talking about."

"Yes, you do. You know . . . everything."

Frantically I glanced through the swaying swings, searching for Dylan.

"Don't you think I can read you by now?" he asked as I stepped back, never looking away. "Don't you think I've been doing my homework all these months, watching . . . studying? That I know exactly what you're thinking . . . when I *want* you to think it?"

My throat convulsed.

"You really want to force my hand?" he asked, caressing the side of his gun. "Because it won't feel very good," he said, still so grotesquely mildly. "And at the end of the day, the result is going to be the same. My mouse is out of moves."

"No," I said, heart hammering. "I'm not." In the distance, sirens sounded. "I'm not stupid, either." It ended here. If I left with him, he would never let me live. "I'm not going to be your plaything until you get bored with me."

He smiled. "Trust me, it'll be a *long* time before that happens."

I wanted to throw up. It was so clear now, I didn't know how I'd missed it all along. LaSalle the cop, LaSalle the one in charge. He was always the one there, one step ahead, asking questions, collecting evidence . . . directing the investigation.

Setting up a fall guy.

It was the perfect illusion. Even when he'd made me uncomfortable, I'd never looked deeper than what I thought was the obvious.

"You're good," he said in that same chilling voice. "Even when you had no idea we were playing, you played your heart out. Every test . . . you passed."

Everything, I realized. He'd been part of everything. That circle I'd envisioned before, the one being drawn around me, thicker and darker and closer with every scratch of the marker. He was the one circling.

"The guy in the gold car worked for you," I breathed.

He made a clucking noise. "Not anymore."

The cold wind sent trash swirling in all directions. And the sirens were getting closer. All I needed was time.

LaSalle stilled, listening. Then he lashed with lightning speed. "Time's up," he said, and fired.

I darted around the hub, heard the sickening clang of the bullet against metal a few inches from my head. Breathless, I started to crawl as another bullet exploded against the dirt at my feet.

"Freeze!" someone shouted.

Detective Jackson I realized, but knew better than to look.

"Trinity!" That was Dylan.

Scrambling, I inched farther around the hub, listening . . .

"Gotcha."

I looked up, and Detective LaSalle stood with his feet shoulder-width apart, waiting.

THIRTY-SIX

"No!" I screamed, scrambling.

He charged after me.

"Trinity—no!"

"Dylan," I cried as LaSalle lifted his gun—and his eyes went dead dark as his body bowed toward me, as if pierced from behind.

I saw the red bloom against the baby blue of his shirt, turned and started to run. But he was on me before I could take two steps, tackling me from behind and driving me into one of the swings. It rushed out from beneath me, leaving me to go down hard. He fell with me, landing on top as my head slammed against something sharp and metal.

"No," I cried, twisting against the weight of his body. But his hands closed around my neck, and squeezed. I fought, tried to hang on, knew I had to hang on—

The edges of my vision blurred as Dylan and Detective Jackson shouted. There wasn't time. I had to—

The switchblade. I still had it.

Silver flashes . . .

With his fingers crushing my windpipe, I worked the knife,

lashed out with everything I had left and jabbed the blade into La-Salle's side.

Everything tilted. His eyes went wide as he let out a shout of pain. His hands went slack. He jerked back. I tried to roll, knew I had to roll, to get away . . .

But the fog wouldn't let go, and then I could see her, her long dark hair trailing behind her as she ran toward me. "Mama . . ." I whispered.

And everything went dark.

"I've got you . . . I've got you . . ."

"Oh, my God! Is she—"

"Breathing."

I could hear the voices, hear them drifting around me. But could latch onto none of them.

"She's bleeding—"

"It's stopping."

I struggled, tried to move, open my eyes.

"Easy," someone said, and finally sensation came, a blanket of warmth. I was being wrapped in it, could feel it closing around me so very, very tight.

"She's so pale . . ."

"She's in shock."

The roughened voice whispered through me, and again I shifted, reaching . . .

But then someone else was there, someone else was touching. The feel was different, softer. *"Sweet baby . . ."*

"Mama . . ." The word leaked out, and with it I made my eyes open.

The harsh glare of white stabbed like needles. I blinked against it, squinted, and saw the scraggly dark hair hanging down toward me.

"Easy," he murmured, as he always did, and then his hand was there, the rough pads of his fingers streaking against the side of my face, where only moments before there'd been the most excruciating softness.

"Dylan," I tried to whisper.

He cradled me closer, bringing his face close to mine. "Don't try to talk."

"Paramedics are here," someone else said, and with another blink I glanced up to find Dylan's father standing behind him. The lines of his face looked hard. In his hand, his gun glowed.

Adrenaline kicked against the grogginess. "LaSalle . . ." I managed.

"Can't hurt you," Dylan promised, and even though everything was fuzzy, I could see the hot glow of his eyes.

"Aunt Sara—"

"Safe," he said, feathering his thumb along my cheekbone.

"Chase . . ."

His hand stilled, and the bleed of cold returned. "Sh-h-h," he said quietly.

"But . . ." The words were there, right there, the questions, but the heaviness swept back, surging through my body and carrying me . . . "Chase," I managed as Dylan and his father lost form, and once again the shadows stole everything.

She was holding my hand. I could feel her even if I couldn't make my eyes open. I could feel the gentle strength of her hand around mine, holding on so very, very tight, and not letting go.

My body wouldn't work. Everything was heavy, leaden. But I made my fingers curl. I made my fingers . . . hold on.

I was aware. I was aware of the ambulance ride, the hospital. I knew the exact second she let go, and the exact moment she came back. Even in the darkness, I saw the light. Even in silence . . . I heard her voice. In stillness . . . the promise.

Time stretched, dragged, fell away. They medicated me. A sedative, I think, a soft veil separating me from my body. I could hear, but I could not move. I could only drift, soaking in snippets of conversation, but feeling nothing.

Detective LaSalle was dead. His partner had shot him, and he'd died fast. My aunt was safe. Dylan had found her in the warehouse, bound and shaken and in shock, but physically okay. She'd confirmed everything, that Detective LaSalle had abducted her from the airport, and that he'd been playing me, *playing us,* all this time.

Grace was conscious. Delphi was safe.

There was only one name no one mentioned.

"Chase," I whispered, fighting. Chase. Over and over again. In my heart—my mind. I screamed.

But no one heard.

Not for a long, long time. Until the sedative wore off, and the thickness of my tongue moved against the cottony dryness of my mouth. "Chase . . ."

"Trinity."

Her voice was soft, gentle—just like before. Dizzily I made my eyes open and saw the hair, long, dark, silky. "Mama . . ."

Then she looked up and her eyes met mine, and the fragile buffer of illusion shattered. "Aunt Sara."

She was wearing a hospital gown. Her hair was combed straight, her face scrubbed clean, pale. "Ah, *cher,*" she whispered, taking my hands.

My eyes flooded. "Are . . . you okay?" I managed. Then: "I'm sorry . . ."

"No—no! This is not your fault—I'm okay, *cher.* He didn't hurt me, that wasn't what he wanted."

But that wasn't true. I could see it in her shell-shocked eyes. Maybe LaSalle hadn't hurt her physically, but emotionally was a different story.

"I was so scared," I whispered. "I . . . All I could think was what if I never saw you again. What if I never got the chance to say . . . I love you?"

Tears spilled over her lashes. "I love you, too."

The words settled around me in a gentle caress. Looking away, I blinked, but Julian Delacroix still stood by the window, his arms crossed over his chest, watching us. His hair was loose. He wasn't wearing . . . black.

His eyes met mine, and the strangest sensation of strength shifted through me.

There were so many questions, but at that moment, only one mattered.

"Chase," I whispered, looking back toward my aunt—and the leather bracelet lying on the bedside table. "Where's Chase?"

Monitors beeped.

His little brother stood in front of his father, both at the far side of the bed. His mother sat beside him, tears running down her stricken face. Drew sat at the foot of the bed, his eyes blank, staring. His phone was clenched in his hand, but he wasn't texting.

Chase lay in the middle, the white sheet stretched up to his chest. His bloodstained T-shirt—the one I'd given him, the one I'd *seen* in my premonition—was gone, the soft blue of a hospital gown draping over his shoulders. His face was pale, relaxed, like he was sleeping, with his bangs swept back to reveal the fading bruise at his temple. An oxygen cannula ran to his nose.

I'd never seen him so motionless, not even when I'd found him lying in the rain by the side of the canal.

Aunt Sara had tried to prepare me. She'd used words like massive internal injuries and critical condition, bleeding, but somehow I'd expected to see him propped up in the bed when I came into the room, like last week in the ER . . .

"*Chase.*" My aunt pushed me closer. The nurses had refused to let me walk. Instead I slipped toward the edge of the wheelchair and reached through the cord of the pulse-ox monitor for his hand.

"Can he hear me?" I asked his father.

Richard Bonaventure nodded. "I think so."

"Here," Drew said, helping me from the chair to the edge of the hospital bed.

"I'm here," I whispered, wincing as I leaned over him and took his hand. Aunt Sara said I had a broken a rib. "I'm here."

The limp heaviness against my hand shredded me.

Say something! Do something! The words screamed through me, but I couldn't say them, knew they were wrong, not what he needed to hear.

"You saved my life," I whispered through the hot sting at my eyes. "You saved us all."

By going to search the warehouse. By having the presence of mind to take pictures—to call me. To get his phone into my hands so that I didn't leave with the monster masquerading as a cop . . .

"He can't hurt us again," I promised. "Not ever, ever again."

I felt it first, the faint movement against my palm. Then his mother gasped and I looked up and saw the flutter of his eyelids.

"Chase . . ." I said through my tears, leaning over him to bring my face to his. "We're all here."

The glassy blue of his eyes found mine. "Tr-r-r-in . . ."

"Sh-h-h," I murmured, and then my hand was there, too, slipping along the side of his face. Touch him, it was all I could think. I had to touch him. "We can talk later."

About so much. Not just what had happened with LaSalle, but before then, at the party. About . . . us. About trust and honesty and secrets, where we went from here. *Pensacola.*

Against my hand his fingers moved, sliding to curl around the leather band hugging my wrist. "You're a hero," I whispered. If he hadn't been there, LaSalle would have gotten away with everything. "You know that, don't you?"

"You . . . found her," he mumbled as his dad moved closer. I could feel him beside me, near one of the monitors.

I wasn't sure if Chase could actually see me, so I kept my face close to his, sliding the softest of kisses against his mouth. "She's safe, too," I assured him. "Aunt Sara—"

"N-no."

"Yes," I said as everything slowed. Vaguely I was aware of his dad's voice, urgent, talking to someone. But I couldn't make out words. "She's right here . . ."

His fingers loosened. "Not . . . your aunt."

I stilled.

"Your . . . mom . . ."

The coldness came fast, sweeping in from somewhere deep inside, and wiping away everything. I started to tell him no, but the word wouldn't come.

"So . . . beautiful," he murmured so quietly I could barely hear him above the monitors. "Just . . ."

I held on tight, held on for both of us. "Don't talk—"

The beeping slowed, and his father started to shout. And Aunt Sara was moving closer, her hands to my shoulder, curving, holding . . .

"Like . . ." Chase whispered, and his eyes met mine once again, with a warm glow, a promise, the echo of that same promise I'd seen from the very beginning, when I'd walked into homeroom all those months before, and he'd looked up, and smiled. I could see him again, see him that day, the strength and vitality . . .

"You," he said.

And then the light faded, and everything about him relaxed; all the pain, the anguish, the torment he'd tried so hard to hide from the world, slipped away.

Still, I held on, held on so very, very tight. And even as his eyes closed, the illusion formed all over again, the one that would burn in my heart forever, and he was the way he'd always been, *the way he'd always be*—strong, protective, invincible—living the only way he knew how, perched on a razor's edge.

"Think about this summer," he'd said only a week before, when I'd told him how scared I'd been after the car accident. *"Think about Pensacola . . ."*

"I'm there," I murmured against the stillness of his mouth. And then I was doing it, doing what I always did. What everyone did. I was rewriting the moment, word by word, breath by breath, long after everything else had fallen quiet. Because there behind closed eyes was Chase's world, where the sun always shone, turquoise waters waited, and there was no pain. Where the only dreams that came true involved winning football games, going to college, and living happily ever after. And with nothing more than his smile and my dreams, I could go back, *I could always go back,* and live it all again.

"Standing in the waves," I whispered, closing my eyes. "With you."

Epilogue

I lit the votives, one at a time.

Around me dusk fell in a silent, shimmering veil. Even the breeze whispered.

I knelt in front of the intricate iron fence for a long moment, watching the flames flicker. Then I reached for the daisies. With quiet reverence I divided the flowers between the two stone vases, giving each half of my water.

Lifting my hand to the stone marker, I stared at the names forever etched in my heart.

John Mark and Rachel Monsour
Beloved parents

My breath caught. "Hey," I said, tracing my fingers along the familiar letters. "You know why I'm here, don't you?"

Normally St. Louis Cemetery bustled with tourists and other visitors, but I'd seen almost no one since Aunt Sara and I arrived. Earlier, beneath the glare of a bright winter sun, she'd stood holding my hand while the priest read Scripture, bagpipes played, and balloons drifted out into the morning. Now she waited near the front gate, just as she had the first time she'd brought me here.

Throat tight, I looked down at the image of Madonna and Child on the prayer card in my hand.

"I know you were there," I murmured, lingering on my mother's name. "He told me he saw you."

I'd seen her, too, just like I had so many other big times in my life. Life, death, breath or not, she was there.

Soon I would go home. Soon I would slip into my bed and close my eyes, and see Chase again.

But not yet.

I kept playing things over and over in my mind, the way he'd run to me with Delphi in his arms, the way he'd held me, kissed me. The way he'd looked at me. And I couldn't help but think he'd known. When he sent me off with Dylan, it was like Chase knew we were standing on a cliff, and someone was going to fall.

And he'd chosen for it to be him. That was Chase. That's what he did, the way he lived. And he hadn't been afraid.

The breeze stirred, and shadows slipped closer. Somewhere behind me, a twig snapped.

Twisting around I searched, but found only row after row of beautiful, undisturbed crypts—and a single dragonfly with iridescent wings of green, fluttering near my shoulder.

I turned back to the weathered Celtic cross watching over my parents' grave.

Tears ran down my face. It was like the whole world glistened.

"Take care of him," I whispered, and there against the soft leather band circling my wrist, the dragonfly landed.

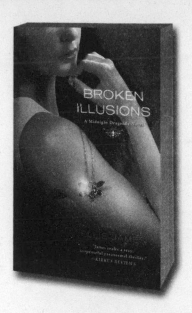

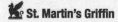